# IT'S
# COMPLICATED

*JULIA KENT*

ISBN-13: 978-1491265697

# CHAPTER ONE

"Where are the balls?" Josie shouted as she and Laura entered Jeddy's. The warlock waitress was missing, and the joint was empty, so it wasn't hiding behind some crowd of rowdy college students.

As she craned her head around to see if it had been moved, she was disappointed to find no trace of the cardboard monstrosity anywhere.

"Gone," Madge croaked, eyeing Laura's enormous belly. "You got triplets in there?" she asked, poking her tummy with a stylus. Laura wore a lovely pink cotton tent that used more fabric than a king-size duvet. Josie felt sorry for her these days, with cankles and sciatica and a belly that stretched so far she could use it as a sail after the birth.

It had been Laura's idea to come and eat lunch at Jeddy's, and against Josie's better judgment she'd said yes. The place held a few too many memories for her, but for Laura it was all about the food. And when a hungry, overdue pregnant woman suggests the place that serves her favorite comfort food, you don't argue.

"No, but I'll happily eat for three," Laura answered, making Madge's face crack into a grin. No, really—it cracked in half and she looked like a Muppet for a second. How a dried-up old prune like that could smile and make it look almost human was beyond Josie.

"You threw the warlock away?" she asked Madge as they chose their favorite booth and Madge slapped the menus down on the scarred tabletop.

"No. My granddaughter asked us to donate it to some fancy autism charity ball auction."

"Rich people want to buy a cardboard cutout that's been fondled thousands of times?" Josie asked as she slid into the booth. Laura turned sideways and tried to tuck her belly under the table. Nope. Stuck. Madge watched, head cocked, as she struggled to get in.

"How's that different from Paris Hilton?" Madge challenged, shaking her head as she observed Laura's pathetic attempt. Josie felt a pang of compassion and stood, offering Laura a hand to unwedge herself.

"Touché."

"You need a table," Madge said, moving the menus over to a four-top.

"I need a crowbar," Laura groaned. Josie smiled sympathetically and patted her hand. Two days overdue and Laura acted like the world was ending. The only part of her that seemed to function properly these days was her appetite.

"Let's get you started with some fried green tomatoes," Madge said, scribbling on her electronic tablet. "And you like the Peanut Butter Hulk Smash...." she mumbled, ignoring them.

"Coconut shrimp!" Josie interjected.

"With a side of Pitocin," Laura begged.

Settled at their table, the two women leaned toward each other, Laura struggling with her girth but finally managing to make it a foot or so as Josie whispered, "So, have you decided what to do?"

Laura nodded. "We want you to be the only one who knows."

Josie pulled back as if slapped. "What? Me? That's crazy. Why? Why *me*?"

Laura inhaled deeply and slowly through her nose, her hands sliding across the table, fingers splayed in an effort to control her breath. Josie respected that. She imagined that right now Laura's lungs were the size of quarters, shoved up into her collarbone by the baby.

"Because you're the person that all three of us trust."

"That's not a good reason to pick me," Josie protested. "I don't want to be the only person to know that kind of information."

Laura narrowed her eyes. "You're clearly the only person who should know. It's not exactly going to be my dead mom or Dylan's judgmental parents, right?"

Josie swallowed hard. Loathe as she was to admit it, Laura was making sense. This issue of paternity had been *her* issue. Laura had slept with two men and found herself pregnant under extraordinary circumstances, and now living with both men under even *more* extraordinary circumstances. Dylan and Mike had no desire to know which of them was the father, choosing instead to live with a kind of loving ambiguity that Josie absolutely did not understand, but had grudgingly come to respect.

Laura bought into it. That's what surprised Josie. If you were a baby's mom, wouldn't you want to know who the dad was? Lately, though, Laura, Dylan, and Mike had become this incredible threesome that exuded love and support and understanding.

Gag.

Josie wasn't about to try to put fissures in that, knowing full well that there was a way out—and it was through her.

"How do you want me to do this?" she asked Laura skeptically as Madge flew by and threw glasses of water on the table. Being the only person who would know who the baby's biological father was seemed like an outrageous responsibility to carry. Doing it for Laura was part of being a good friend, but that didn't mean she had to like it.

"We figure that the baby will be born, and we'll get the paternity tests done, and then only you will see the results. You can come in and put the father's name on the birth certificate and I'll never know as long as you cover that part when I sign. Neither will the guys."

Laura blinked rapidly and Josie could see that she was barely holding it together, knowing damn well that that was about the stupidest plan ever. *Of course* Laura would see the name on the birth certificate. She'd have to pull it out a million times over the course of the child's life for everything from getting a Social Security card to a passport to flying with her.

Treading carefully, Josie said as much in kinder words. "Laura, you'll have to see it at some point."

"Well…I'll…I'll just—"

Madge interrupted them with a plate of hot coconut shrimp and one of fried green tomatoes.

Laura scanned the table and looked at Madge with pleading eyes. "Where's the cake?"

Josie laughed and grabbed two coconut shrimp and put them on her little plate, careful to use the pads of her fingers. She'd just done her nails in a pink glitter in honor of the pending baby. If she didn't take her share, Laura would just plow through it and she'd never get any.

Madge shot Laura a derisive look and said, "It's coming. Cool your jets. You've got more than enough here." She looked at Laura's belly, looked back at Laura, looked at Josie and saw how Josie had cupped her hands around the little plate of her two coconut shrimp and said, "Ah, all right. I gotcha. Hang on, I'll get the cake out here. You need a side of ice cream with that?"

"I need two sides of ice cream with that," Laura snapped.

"I've had two kids myself and I know how bad it is when you hit the, what—493rd week?" Madge snorted. "But you don't have to bite my head off."

4

Josie tapped the table. Laura and Madge looked at her. "When you're pissin' Madge off, you know you've crossed the line."

Laura's eyes filled with tears. *Aw, shit,* Josie thought. "I'm sorry," Laura said, her lip trembling, wide, wet eyes looking at Madge like she'd just run over her cat. "It's just…you don't…it's just…" She flinched and grabbed her belly, bending over and taking a deep breath. "It's just hard."

"Is something wrong?" Josie asked.

"No." Laura's breath caught, a hitched gasp, and then smoothed out. "It's just these stupid Braxton Hicks contractions."

Madge waved her hand. "Early labor. Whatever. Call me when you've gone through twenty-one hours of labor alone 'cause your car's broken, your husband finally gets you to the hospital, and you end up giving birth in the lounge on top of some stranger's trench coat."

"That happened to you?" both women asked in unison.

"No. Just call me when it happens." Smirk.

Josie and Laura shared a WTF? look and then Laura dug in as if she'd just spent a year on Jenny Craig and this was her first off-plan meal. Josie had been right. Within minutes all the coconut shrimp were gone, Laura using her finger to scrape the last of the dipping sauce. Chugging down her water, she banged the glass on the tabletop like a Viking. Madge, as if reading her mind, zipped by with a pitcher, leaving it on the table for the two to share.

"I know it's not a perfect solution," Laura said, wiping her mouth, looking around the restaurant for Madge. Josie could almost hear the words "where's that cake?" coming out of Laura's brain. "But this way, the guys don't know, *I* don't know unless I choose to look at that part of the birth certificate, and yet the baby will be protected in case something happens to me because the real father—" She cringed at the words.

"*Biological* father," Josie helped.

"Yes, the *biological* father will be listed."

Taking a sip of water, Josie nodded slowly. It could work. She could see that. Or, at least, she could easily pretend that this would work. The hard part would be knowing and keeping her mouth shut. For—well, *ever*—she would have the answer to a secret that was at the fundamental core of Dylan and Mike's, and really Laura's, being. One that they wouldn't know, and one that could alter so much in their relationship if it were revealed.

She'd rather shit an eight-pound football than carry that around.

Almost.

Biting her lip, she decided to stuff her mouth with more food, and then looked down. She'd only eaten one coconut shrimp and now the other one was gone. "Hey," she said, tipping her head up and looking at Laura, who was now chewing suspiciously.

A guilty look crossed Laura's face. "Sorry."

Madge to the rescue with two pieces of cake. Josie wrapped her arm around hers and snarled at Laura. "Mine."

The three women laughed. "It's only yours if you eat it before I eat mine." Laura mugged and they began the chocolate fest.

"Not to bring up a touchy subject," Josie said through a mouthful of cake. *As if the baby's paternity hadn't been a heavy topic.* "But when are you going to finally have this kid?"

Laura glared at her. "You think that I'm hanging on to her for no good reason? She'll be born when she's born. Or when they make me give birth to her. Time's ticking right now, and Sherri says they can give me five more days. After that, it's going to be tough."

Sherri was Laura's certified nurse midwife. Josie admired the woman's approach. With a master's degree in nursing, she was sort of like an obstetrician and a midwife combined, except she couldn't perform surgery. If Laura needed a C-section she would have to use the obstetrician who supervised Sherri, or whoever was on duty that night.

Josie knew from enough years of working in hospitals that *that* was a crap shoot. Sometimes you got someone great, and sometimes you got a completely incompetent asshole. Most of the time, you got somebody in between, so she really hoped that Laura would have a smooth birth. The problem of too much fluid in the womb, the polyhydramnios diagnosis that Laura had gotten in her second trimester, had resolved enough that she could stay with the midwives, but she was still enough of a concern that Josie had some serious trepidations about the birth.

The medical issues were one thing. The other part made her scratch her head and wonder how this would work operationally. There were *two* dads, and while she was sure that the staff at the hospital was an enlightened group by and large, they probably didn't get too many situations where *two* men were in the room.

Rather than saying anything, because Laura was about as sensitive as any forty-week-and-two-day pregnant woman would be, she just nodded and said simply, "You've got my number programmed in your phone. You know where and how to find me, and I'll show up in my pajamas and barefoot if that's when this baby decides to be born."

Laura looked up from her plate, chocolate and peanut butter smeared at the corners of her mouth, her cheeks persistently pink and rosy, as they had been the entire last month of the pregnancy. "You will?" she asked.

"Of course I will. You know that," Josie answered. "And so will Dylan and Mike."

"They will, no matter what," Laura said, wiping her mouth with a napkin. "They live with me now. They have no choice."

About a month ago, the three had all moved into Mike's cabin. For the past two weeks, though, they'd been staying at Laura's place—her lease didn't run out for a bit.

Her place was closest to the hospital where Laura hoped to give birth. Josie had forgotten one day, absentmindedly dropping by for morning coffee, greeted at the door by a very wet Dylan wearing only a towel.

That was the end of her morning ritual with Laura. He'd invited her in, and Mike had poked his head around the kitchen to say "hi" and welcome her to join them for breakfast, but it had felt intrusive. As if she would be the outsider. Begging off had been easy. Finding a cup of coffee at a shop was simple.

Wiping the tears on the way to work and figuring out why she was so sensitive still plagued her.

"And so…how are things going living together?" Josie asked, a leer on her face, trying to scrub her own sad thoughts away.

"I'm not going to talk about my sex life anymore with you, Josie."

"I'm not asking about your sex life," she said. "I'm just asking how things are going." Truth be told, she *wasn't* asking about their sex life. *That* she knew more than enough about. What she wondered, though, was how you move in with two guys and live as a family unit. Laura had never lived with a guy before—at all—so this was an enormous step. Not quite marriage…but not *not* like marriage. Add in *two* guys and she figured there had to be a pretty significant adjustment phase.

"Okay," Laura said, shoveling another spoonful of peanut-butter sauce into her mouth. "The hardest part is that these two have been living together for ten years or longer, and they used to live with Jill, so they have all these ideas about how it works to live in this…" She put her hands up in the air in a gesture of helplessness. "This…whatever-you-call-it, and I *don't*. In some ways, I'm the odd person out in my own home and in my own…threesome."

Huh. Josie wasn't expecting to hear that. "What do you mean?"

After licking every drop of chocolate sauce off the rounded back of her spoon, Laura paused to explain. "Here's an example. It's first thing in the morning and I wake up to Dylan handing me a lovely decaf latte. Mike rolls over and snuggles and asks me how I'm feeling. They both put their hands on my belly and feel the baby kick, move around, or sing 'Ave Maria.' You know, because *our* daughter is already gifted." Laura shot her a big grin as she rolled her eyes playfully.

Josie felt sickly jealous. "And what's wrong with all that?" She struggled to keep the incredulous tone, the one that screamed, *Why are you complaining?* out of her voice.

*Jesus, woman. You have most of the coconut shrimp and two billionaires in your bed making you coffee. And your problem is…?* Biting her lower lip to avoid saying that aloud was leaving deep teeth marks in the pink flesh in her mouth.

"*That* I don't mind. But then maybe I want a shower, but Dylan's already in there, and so I have to wait. Meanwhile, Mike makes Dylan's eggs exactly how he likes them, and has the plate set up when Dylan's out of the shower. By the way, Dylan walks around naked most mornings, so—"

"Yeah, I noticed the morning I stopped by for coffee and got a bunch of eye candy instead."

Laughing, Laura stood slowly, rotund and awkward. "Gotta pee. I'll be right back." Her waddle would have been funny on almost any other day, but right now it made Josie nearly cry, knowing that this was one of the last days—if not *the* last—before everything changed.

Sunlight poured through the front window of Jeddy's, rays flashing across tabletops and chairs, the breakfast counter, and the rows upon rows of glasses ready to be filled for customers who hadn't come in yet.

Josie swallowed and took a deep breath, carefully cataloging her surroundings, taking a moment to be still, chuckling on the inside about how much that was like Mike. "Just be," he would say at times when she came over to their house and talked about her problems.

She knew he was right; moments like this confirmed it. As she took the time to look around, to breathe, to just *be*, she saw everything for what it was in a tiny flash of insight. Laura, walking away, ripe and ready, just waiting for the perfect moment for her baby to release itself from the tree that had given it life on the inside. That life would start on the outside soon—all too soon—if Josie and her intuition were right.

People moved on, didn't they? She certainly had. The little girl from Peters, Ohio, the daughter of the sainted, late town librarian and the local barfly had gotten out of her hometown as fast as she could, leaving everyone behind. Even Darla, her little cousin, who had also become fatherless in the same famous moment eighteen years ago.

*People move on.*

*Don't they?*

Laura's daughter would have two fathers. A pang of mourning hit Josie like a brick thrown from an overpass, smashing her consciousness in the face and shattering the atmosphere of the steady hum from the restaurant. The room closed in with a cold gasp that she had to breathe her way out of, using Mike's techniques, grateful now for the hours she'd spent in his presence, willing herself back to a surface-level calm.

"You okay?" Laura asked, returning to the table. She bent herself into a seated position that took the weight off her back, legs spread wide as she perched on the edge of her seat like a cello player.

Josie's heart pounded in her chest, but her mind came back, the shattered pieces assembling into a loose facsimile of what she'd been seconds ago. Nodding, she kept her head down and pretended to eat a sliver of something from her plate, the texture like Styrofoam peanuts.

She pondered the way Laura's hand grasped the fork as she ate her food with such joy and enjoyment, how Madge raced to and fro, not in a frantic way, but with purpose, with a drive that Josie admired. She wasn't generally the type to get sappy or reflective like this. It came as a surprise, like so many other things these past few months.

Staring at Laura, she felt her heart grow and a tiny part of her wanted to shave off just a little of what Laura had with Mike and Dylan, to hold it inside her chest, to turn to it when she was lonely or desperate.

The relationship that those three shared was something that Josie studied carefully. Everything from the nuanced looks between Dylan and Mike to Laura's plaintive gasps as she described how the three had worked these past few months to fit together as one. Laughter filled most of their conversations. It was awkward for Laura to be the new one in a three-way relationship, but as time passed, she had navigated it with increasing grace and ever-lessening insecurity. Josie felt her preconceptions, about everything from what daily life must be like to whether Dylan really was as much of an ass as she had initially thought, melt away as Laura's groundedness grew.

It turned out Dylan wasn't an ass at all.

Being wrong was not part of Josie's repertoire. Even that, though, was fading as she realized how much of the world she thought of in black and white terms. She was right, *they* were wrong. She was smart, *they* were idiots. She was emotionally evolved, *they* were assholes. You couldn't see the world as black and white so easily in a long-term threesome relationship, could you? She opened her mouth to ask Laura that question, pretty much knowing the answer. Black and white means that there are only two options—so when there's a third, that you absolutely have to include and respect, then how does that relationship math work?

"Where was I?" Laura asked. "Oh. Right. So the guys are on autopilot all the time. They've been together for more than ten years, and so this is all old hat to them. There's no room for my ideas. For me to imprint on the way everything flows."

Before Josie could even open her mouth to speak, Laura's eyes got wider than Josie had ever seen them, as if her eyeballs were about to pop out. The clanking of the fork against Laura's plate was all Josie could hear as she watched her friend's pale, creamy hand reach down below the table and grasp her abdomen, her head pitched down and an audible, long inhale coming through her nose.

"Braxton Hicks?" Madge muttered, eyebrow cocked up as she walked by.

Josie was starting to be on Madge's side, silently counting to herself as Laura started to breathe again on the exhale, in and out, for what Josie counted to be thirty-seven seconds. The nurse in her shifted to a different kind of math, not relationship math but *labor* math. How long were the contractions? How many minutes apart were they? How intense were they?

Laura's hands reached up for her face and smoothed her blonde waves away. Calm eyes peered back at Josie, though Laura's face was considerably flushed. "It's okay," she said—long inhale, long exhale. "Just a crazy Braxton Hicks contraction."

"Okay," Josie said simply. Who was she to argue with a pregnant woman? Nature would win. No need to poke the ripe lady.

Laura reached for the fork and started to stuff a piece of cake in her mouth, but seemed to think better of it. Instead, she looked at Josie and said, "So, I have a business proposition for you."

Whoa. Big topic shift. As her shoulders relaxed, Josie realized how relieved she was to change the conversation. More talk about the cozy world the threesome created threatened Josie's tenuous stability right now.

"No. I won't host a Mary Kay party for you," Josie joked.

"No, not that. But, hey! You know, my mom did really well with them."

"Yeah, I know. The pink Cadillac kind of tipped

everybody off."

Laura's face went from an amused, flushed look to one of nostalgic sadness. Josie had only met Laura's mom once, before she'd passed away a few years ago, a freak asthma attack that turned deadly. Obviously, she would never meet the baby—and Laura's dad had taken off years ago. They'd bonded over being fatherless when they had met in college. It was a club no one wanted to be in.

It wasn't a surprise to Josie that Laura, feeling alone in the world, had been so happy to find a whole instant family in Mike and Dylan.

"Laura, you realize 'a business proposition' makes it sound like you want to rope me into some MLM scheme."

"MFM, actually." Laura coughed.

"Wha?"

Laura put her fork down, leaning in, an intense stare practically pinning Josie in place. "I think, financially, we're a little beyond that. MLM, I mean."

"Well," Josie answered. "Mike and Dylan are. You…"

Insecurity poured out of Laura in waves stronger than any contraction. "You know, just because the guys told me to quit my job and just take care of the baby and that they would support me, doesn't mean—"

Josie held a palm up. She could see that Laura was on the verge of tears over this and had really struggled already, pride almost overriding their offer. "Laura—Laura, I'm just joking," she assured her. "I know the drill, and if I were in your shoes I'd have quit in a heartbeat too. Trust me, anything to get out of the daily grind."

"Anything?"

"Anything," Josie confirmed. "Do you have any idea what it's like working on a research trial for Alzheimer's? Talking to old people every day"—she corrected herself—"that's fine. The problem is that I'm dealing with people who are deteriorating. So every time I see them for a new appointment, most of them, first of all, don't remember me, and, second of all, they're worsening. It's pretty depressing to work a job where all of the people I see and serve are getting worse."

Laura furrowed her brow. "You went into geriatric nursing, Josie," she said slowly, as if talking to a child. "Didn't you expect that to be the case?"

Leave it to Laura to state the obvious. "Sure," Josie protested. "But Alzheimer's is a different animal. It's one thing to work with some ninety-year-old woman who forgets things once in a while but is otherwise sharp and has a body that's failing her. You try seeing a sixty-two-year-old or a seventy-three-year-old with kids and grandkids, who points to his wife of thirty or forty years and says, 'Can you tip the cab driver?'"

"Ouch."

"Yeah. Day in and day out. Not nearly as hard, though, as having Dylan bring you coffee in bed and Mike not attune to your shower desires." *Meow.* Where did that come from?

A patient, controlled look clouded Laura's features. She took two deep breaths and smiled sweetly. "You really want me to start talking about the shower desires Mike *does* meet? Because I have some stories that—"

"Stop!" Josie shrieked, fingers in ears. "I deserved that. Just stop," she begged.

"Go into another kind of nursing." Laura tapped her belly. "Labor and delivery."

Josie had an answer for that, but before she could open her mouth and spit it out, Laura leaned over again, grabbing her belly and doing the deep inhale. By Josie's guess, that was about seven minutes. Slowly, Laura worked her way through the contraction—about the same amount of time as before, thirty-eight seconds.

In her phone, Josie had programmed Mike's number, Dylan's number, the labor and delivery numbers for all the hospitals in the area, and even a handful of personal cell phone numbers for the OBs she knew in at least a casual way.

Without violating any confidentiality, Josie had called the doctors about a month before, explaining the basics of Laura's situation. Depending on which professional she talked to, the polyhydramnios made the delivery moderate or high risk, but Laura was determined to have a natural birth.

Now was probably a really terrible time to explain to Laura that she would make a *horrible* labor and delivery nurse. During her rotation of clinicals as a nursing student she'd actually dropped a baby once—fortunately, only three or four inches before catching it again. And the experience had chilled her so deeply that she had no desire whatsoever to do it professionally. Be there with her friend through the whole thing, from start to finish, as another body in the room there to support the mom? No problem. Have an actual professional role with responsibilities? No way.

Laura took a deep breath, drank about half of a glass of water, and gave Josie a giant smile. "Oh, well, maybe I'm just a little dehydrated."

*Or maybe you're just about to have a baby,* Josie thought, but smiled back with the same fake look. "Okay," she said.

She was saying that a lot lately. It was about all she could say because what she really wanted to say was, "Jesus fucking Christ, Laura, get in the goddamn car and let me take you to the hospital right now." But she wouldn't. She would be Nice Josie and keep her mouth shut.

"This business proposition," Laura said. "As you know, Mike and Dylan are filthy stinking rich."

"I kind of noticed, and most of Boston knows that too, now that there was the news report."

"Yeah." Laura just shook her head. "Hell of a way for me to find out, right?"

Josie softened. It was hard to realize it had only been a couple of months ago. "Right." When Laura had met Dylan and Mike they'd kept the fact that each had inherited more than a billion dollars from their late lover,

Jill, from Laura. She'd found out from a local newscast. Not the most romantic way to begin a relationship. Shortly after, she'd discovered she was pregnant. The reunion had been rocky. So far, so good, though, and the three had carved out a most unusual, though thriving, relationship.

Something about Laura's demeanor put Josie on alert. It was the silences, the pauses, that were getting to her, not the actual words in between. The crafty part of her brain started to feel suspicious. She'd had a feeling that this conversation was coming, but she hadn't expected it to be so soon.

"Mike and Dylan have given me...some..."—Laura stumbled over her words—"leeway in spending some money."

"You mean they give you an allowance," Josie said bluntly.

Laura pursed her lips. "Yeah." As if in retribution, she leaned over and speared the last fried green tomato and shoved it indelicately in her mouth.

"Why fight it?" Josie said, waving her arms in an expansive gesture. "You're with two billionaires. They make more money every year off the interest of that trust fund than most baseball players or football stars. Just go with it, Laura."

About seventeen different emotions flashed across Laura's face. Fortunately, for now, none of them was pain. A furtive glance showed Laura's belly higher and tighter. That was good. As long as it didn't suddenly drop lower, this was still fine. Avoiding a mad run for towels and shoelaces to boil in the back here at Jeddy's was her short-term goal. Although, if the baby was born here maybe they could name her Jeddy. Or Madge.

Or Coconut Shrimp.

Josie stifled a giggle and tried to look serious as Laura was saying something to her.

"And so I figure all you'd need is an office, very little advertising money, and maybe an assistant, a computer system with software—"

"*Whoa, whoa, whoa!*" Josie shook her head as if in a fog. "What are you talking about?"

Madge interrupted them. "Anything else?" She tore the bill off a pad, which Josie found puzzling. They used a computerized system for everything, and yet Madge still wrote out all the bills by hand. Slapping the paper down on the Formica, she said, "You need something, you flag me down." Madge started to run away, stopped herself, turned around like a robot, and marched back. Squatting down slightly, Madge put a hand on Laura's shoulder and caught her eyes. "It's going to be okay, hon. You're going to do a great job."

Laura's eyebrows raised high, and her bright green eyes watered, seeming to thank Madge without words. Josie felt tears fill her own eyes, the compassionate gesture catching everyone off guard. Satisfied that her words had helped, Madge's impossibly clay-like face cracked into a semblance of a grin.

She stood up and said, "Besides, everybody forgets the pain of shitting out a ten-pound turkey."

"Bring me a hot fudge sundae. NOW!" Laura gasped.

Madge cackled as she typed the order into her little device and ran to the kitchen.

Josie just rolled her eyes. "What is up with that woman?"

Laura waved her hand. "Eh, forget about it. I don't want to talk about her. I don't want to talk about shitting an eight-pound turkey." Laura frowned. "Does it really feel that way?"

Josie pointed to herself. "How the hell would I know? I've never had a baby."

"I still think it's barbaric," Laura said through gritted teeth.

*Oh boy, here we go,* Josie thought. For the past month Laura had ranted about how *barbaric* birth was, and how unfair it was that biology had designed women's bodies this way. Why couldn't there be a better way? And on and on and *on*. Even Mike—calm, peaceful, mellow Mike—was getting tired of the rant. It was born (*pun intended*) of fear. They all knew that. None of them had ever given birth, and two out of the three of them weren't even *capable* of it.

Josie could just watch and observe and cringe on the inside as she imagined what Laura was about to go through. She knew all the arguments that the suffering was worth the baby, but the pain, the loss of control, and the sheer horror of just *imagining* the pain, had consumed Laura recently. The three of them might be there to support her, but they really couldn't offer anything but a few clucks of sympathy and what they hoped were helpful factoids.

"I don't want to talk about that," Laura said, shaking her head, her voice clipped and no-nonsense. "I want to talk about this business idea."

"You want me to go in on a business with you?"

Laura snorted. "I don't exactly need capital funding for a business project, Josie." Madge delivered the ice cream sundae and Laura absentmindedly took a bite. "I want you to *run* the business," Laura said, her voice low and serious suddenly.

"What business?" Josie asked.

Laura cocked her head and took a deep inhale, her upper body lifting higher as the rest of her stayed in place, like she was two parts of one being. "The business I was just describing." She tried to lean forward and whispered, "I can't be any more discreet because I can't reach forward more."

"Why do you have to be discreet?" Josie hissed back.

"Because the idea is for a dating company that…you know…" Laura motioned as if it were a secret or something to hide.

Josie mimicked Laura. "You know *what*?"

"A threesome dating service," Laura whispered.

"What?" Josie screeched. She reached across the table

and grabbed Laura's sundae. "Gimme that. I need it more than you do right now." Plunging the spoon in, she shoved a big gob of vanilla ice cream covered in hot fudge and salted caramel sauce into her shocked mouth. She enjoyed the rich, yummy goodness long enough to let Laura's words sink in. Through a muffled mouth she said, "Are you out of your mind? You want me to run a business like that?"

And just then Laura bent her head down and took a deep inhale, and Josie knew exactly what the rest of her day was going to be like.

This one, by Josie's calculations, was five minutes from the last one and forty-five seconds long. She knew that if she suggested to Laura that they go the hospital right now Laura would freeze, get angry, and rip her tongue out. Not necessarily in that order. It was time to be covert and to betray her best friend.

Josie stood and nodded toward the bathroom. "I'll be back in a minute."

Laura smiled, a shaky grin that Josie hoped was a sign that somewhere on the inside she was facing reality and realizing that this baby was coming. Maybe not right now, but soon.

The bathroom was exactly the same as it had been the last time she'd been here, and probably the way it'd been ten years ago. No doors, shower curtains the only sense of privacy. No big deal to her because she didn't need to use the toilet; she needed to use her smartphone. Dialing Mike, she hoped she'd get through to *him* because he'd be much easier than Dylan.

Luck was on her side.

"Hello?" his deep baritone answered.

"Hey, Mike, it's Josie."

"*Oooooh*," he said, the word long and slow. "This isn't a call to invite us over for dinner now, is it?" he said, a spark of merriment in his voice.

Of the threesome, Mike had taken Laura's pregnancy

most in stride, viewing it as an opportunity to work on patience, love, calmness, and some sort of awareness thing that he was always going on about. He and Dylan had gone with Laura to an eight-week birthing course that focused on hypnosis. Mike had been a thousand percent into it, while Dylan cracked jokes the entire time, asking the instructor where exactly in the parking lot Laura could sign up for the epidural.

"No, I'm not calling to ask you if you want to watch the next game or come over for a Super Bowl party." She could feel the smile in her voice coming through as if it matched his, met it in the middle, and danced with it. "I think it's time. I can't be sure, but the contractions are coming about five…six minutes apart and probably—well, the last one lasted forty-five seconds."

He gasped. "That close?"

"Yep. She's claiming they're Braxton Hicks contractions and is guzzling water as if it were going out of style. But…I-I mean, I've never had a baby." Josie stumbled over her words, trying to explain her feelings about this. She could be wrong, and this could be yet another example of false labor, but something about the way Laura was handling these was different. She tried to explain as succinctly as possible. "Bottom line: you and your hyperactive Speedy Gonzalez partner will be ready for me to call you to meet me and Laura at the hospital sometime today."

"Today? You know, you don't have to spend the whole day with her," Mike said, his voice so neutral Josie had a hard time reading it on the phone. If they were face to face she could see the way the skin around his eyes wrinkled, the emotion in his irises and pupils, whether his hands were tight in fists or loose and free around his hips. Did he mean he didn't want her to spend that time with Laura? Did he mean that he was grateful that she would spend that time with Laura? All of this reading of intentions and emotions was making her tired, and she wasn't even part of the threesome.

She was, however, a fourth wheel most of the time—and maybe that was why she read intent and emotion into so many things. She was a foreigner in the country of Mike, Dylan, and Laura; culture shock, perhaps, had set in recently along with a healthy dose of jealousy. That was getting tiring, too.

"Mike, I *want* to spend time with her. This is important for me too, you know? And I think you guys will be there for the birth and she'll need you two hundred percent."

He chuckled. "And *we'll* need you there, too."

Her heart swelled at being acknowledged, at being wanted—*needed*—in the moment that represented the great bridging over for her best friend from "just Laura" to "Laura the mommy."

"Thank you," was all she could think to say.

"No, thank *you*," he said, and sighed. "I guess I need to go let Dylan know, don't I?"

"Yes."

"You know he's going to go and buy another eight-foot bunny."

"Yes," she said. The baby's room was already filled with toys Dylan had been buying for the past few months, or that his parents had sent. The whole family had an apparent fondness for oversized African animals.

There was a hesitation on Mike's end of the conversation. It was melancholic, uncertain, and she reached out to it. "Hey, Mike."

"Hmm?" As the conversation continued she could sense him pulling into himself, charging up for the biggest event of his adult life. Hers, too. Hell, everyone's.

"It's going to be okay."

"I know." The smile came back in his tone, an easy, warm baritone that made her feel safe and secure, shaking off her earlier shattering. "It's going to be *great*," he answered.

* * *

"It's going to be *horrible*," Laura moaned as Josie wandered back to the table to find the sundae glass empty and Laura tight-fisted, leaning forward in her seat.

"What's going to be horrible?" Josie asked.

"The birth!" Laura practically shouted.

*Aha.* Time for a walk.

She threw a few bills on the table to cover the check and grabbed Laura's elbow, helping her to stand. Josie peered at her, staring her down. Laura's face was more flushed, with a red that crept down into her neck and upper chest, the outer edges of her hairline starting to get wet with sweat. Trying desperately to keep the accusing tone out of her voice, Josie said, "You had another contraction while I was in the bathroom, didn't you?"

"I had a twinge."

"You had a *twinge*?"

"A surge."

"Twinge" and "surge" and "pressure" were the euphemisms that a lot of the people in the natural childbirth community had been using for contractions. It was a way to train the mind to think of the pain differently. "Searing, fibrous, ripping pain that makes you want to eat morphine-laden donuts and drop acid to avoid it" wouldn't make anyone want to have a baby, right?

So *surge* it was.

"All right. It wasn't a surge," Laura admitted. "It feels like somebody is reaching into my belly, and twisting it, wringing it like you would squeeze out a wet shirt."

"And how long did that last?"

Laura glared at her. "You're trying to figure this out, aren't you?"

"Yes." *Time to be blunt*, Josie thought.

"I'm not in labor," Laura said.

"And I'm not eighty-three," Madge said as she walked by.

Ambling out the front door, Josie kept Laura on track, one step at a time. "Let's just go for a walk. You've got plenty of water in you, plenty of food in you, and a walk will help you stretch out and just be—uh, *feel* more pleasant."

"Okay." Laura perked up. "We can talk about the business."

"The business," Josie said.

"Yes."

"The weirdo threesome matching business that you want me to run."

"You *were* listening," Laura said with relief.

"Oh, I was listening. That doesn't mean I *agree*." She said it lightly, though.

Her sarcasm meter had to be dialed down to zero as far as Laura was concerned. So many snappy comebacks, so many wisecracks that just pressed against her lips and teeth. She wanted to make bad, crude jokes about threesomes and dating services. About what was already happening and what was coming. But she couldn't. Her own coping strategies had to be put on a back burner for her friend.

Josie calculated out lead time. Mike would need a minimum of a half-hour to forty-five minutes to get into the city to reach the nearest hospital that they could choose in an emergency. This didn't seem to be an emergent situation, though—not yet. Laura's contractions were coming at a steady pace, at ever-decreasing intervals, and in ever-increasing duration. By the time it really *was* time, there would still be plenty of time for Mike and Dylan to get there.

Early May in the Boston area was a crap shoot. It could be seventy degrees and sunny, or thirty-five degrees, overcast with the lingering threat of very rare snow still in the air. A few years before, one winter had seemed to stretch into three, culminating in a Mother's Day sprinkling of snowflakes. This year, though, May had begun spring in earnest. The baby would be born in the perfect month for new beginnings.

\* \* \*

"Did you ever notice how blue the sky is, Josie?" Laura asked as they waddled along the city streets. Passersby shot Laura some very nervous looks, especially the moment her hands cradled the bottom of her enormous abdomen and she shouted, "Oh my God! Make it stop!"

If it weren't really happening it would have made a fabulous prank. *Why didn't we try this before?* Josie wondered. A pillow and a loose dress and they could have had some fun poking at worried passersby.

This, though, was all too real.

Crouched down in a near-fetal position, amazing even Josie with her dexterity and ability to limbo as low as she did, Laura defied gravity as she squatted, the contraction overwhelming her. A placid look and long, even breaths in and out attested to her hypnosis training, but Josie wondered: If it took this much effort to control one of the earlier, deeper surges, what would a tsunami feel like?

Trying to inject a little humor into the situation, Josie knelt down and sang the limbo song, which yielded only a prompt, ferocious glare from a thoroughly unamused Laura.

"I don't think I practiced my breathing well enough," Laura moaned, the sound of her voice shifting from a groan to a whimper as the contraction peaked.

"Just take a deep breath in," Josie intoned, breathing for her, providing an example. Laura followed and then breathed out—and soon the contraction subsided. Josie's mental math began a steady chatter of alert inside her head. Time to assume they were going in.

She knew that Laura knew this, that forty-five seconds to a minute, five minutes apart meant that you might want to consider heading to the hospital. She also knew, however, that if she suggested to Laura that they head off to the hospital, Laura would freak. And so, rather than poking the laboring bear, she decided that the most prudent action would be to play along with Laura's fantasy.

Walking with as much purpose and gusto as she could muster, Laura managed to get a few leg lengths away, her rounded ass enormous now and stretched by the baby, by the added fluid, by the pregnancy—and more than a few trips to Jeddy's. But Laura's time in the gym before the pregnancy showed; Josie still had to hustle to catch up.

"I think we can do a two-mile loop. What do you think, Josie?" Laura said, walking so fast that Josie almost burst into laughter at the level of delusion that her friend was in.

This baby was coming *now*, and if Laura wasn't ready, nature didn't give a shit. Josie sure as hell wasn't ready. The last thing she needed was to be reminded how far behind she was when it came to love, and relationships, and being a grown-up. Never one to dwell on the long term, she found a balance in life that involved picking a goal, focusing singlemindedly until it was accomplished, and only figuring out how she felt about that goal afterward. Then squaring herself toward the next goal, and moving on from there.

It's how she had escaped her little town in middle-of-nowhere, Ohio, full of people who lived in trailers and who thought that a high school diploma was a sign of an elite education, a few, though, choosing college. What others thought of as their first two years of college had taken her four, going to classes part-time at the local branch of a smaller state university and then finally transferring to the school where she and Laura had met.

Being the poorest kid was something that she was accustomed to but ready to put behind her, so her first goal had been finishing college and getting a degree in something useful, something highly *employable*. Nursing had been it.

Her second goal had been to never, *ever* have to move

back to a place where Friday night fun meant boozing it up at the local VFW and a fancy dinner involved cloth napkins and a higher cut of prime rib, with bits of bacon in the green beans they served on the side.

It wasn't that she hated Ohio, or even her hometown of Peters. It wasn't that she was ashamed of it, even. It felt more like being born into her community, where having your first baby by seventeen was something that didn't raise eyebrows and having three before the age of twenty-one was all too common, had been some colossal cosmic accident.

Her entire goal in life for the first twenty-four years had been to right that giant wrong. She had focused on the fact that having children too young meant that she would have to *stay*. Now, having spent the last thirteen or more years of her life trying desperately *not* to get pregnant meant that thinking about doing it on purpose gave her massive pause.

Her best friend was about to have a baby; colleagues in their late twenties and early thirties were finally setting aside their own birth control and changing patterns that were more than a decade old. It made her feel as if she were missing some sort of alert that every woman but her could hear.

*Beep beep beep—time to have a baby!*

Josie didn't like change unless *she* initiated the change. While she had control over her own body, right now she was watching her best friend lose complete control of hers, managed and manipulated by a tiny little being within who wielded power like a sociopath in an amnesia ward.

"Two miles it is," she said as brightly as possible, trying to point them in the direction of the nearest hospital.

"You think I'm crazy."

"No, I don't," Josie said, plastering on another fake smile.

This one, apparently, was a little too fake because Laura could see through it and she frowned. She stopped, forcing

Josie to come to a screeching halt. Laura planted two angry hands on two very lush hips and then lifted one finger and pointed it right at Josie's nose.

"You have no idea what I'm going through right now, so wipe the fake smile off your face and give me a real one."

Josie's face muscles twitched and tinged, and did all sorts of weird things that they'd never done before as she tried simultaneously not to scowl, frown, laugh, or sputter. Whatever mask came out was enough to make Laura burst into uncontrollable giggles and then whoop in a loud, strangled, weird respiratory sound that made her double over again.

Three minutes.

Three minutes this time. As Laura struggled to let her muscles go loose and to release the tension through her breath, Josie counted the seconds, hitting thirty, then forty, then fifty. If she didn't do something to convince Laura to get to the hospital, whatever thin thread of control Laura hoped for in planning her birth, in having it at the hospital she wanted, with the *midwife* she wanted, with Mike and Dylan and Josie at her side, was about to evaporate. The baby would be delivered here, outside one of the ubiquitous cell phone stores littering this part of the city. And then Josie's own inner loss of control would begin its lonely process.

"Laura."

"Yes?" she gasped.

"I think it's time." Infusing that statement with as much empathy as possible, Josie felt her voice crack, could hear the change in her tone, and hoped Laura could feel all of the things that words failed to say. A pale hand reached for Josie's and grasped it, fingernails digging hard into her palm. Josie needed her own breath to control the transfer of pain.

"I know. I know," Laura said simply. "I just needed to *pretend* it's not about to happen." Tears started to pour down Laura's cheeks and dot the fabric of her knees as she rested in a crouched position, her bloodshot eyes so bright and green they made Josie think of Caribbean waters reflecting white clouds and the air of possibility.

"Baby's coming," Laura said simply.

"Yes, honey, she's coming," Josie said.

"What have I done?" Laura asked. "Nine and a half months ago I sat in my apartment making you the nine thousandth pot of coffee *ever* and you made me go on this dating site—"

"I didn't *make* you."

"You made me. Don't try to pretend you didn't make me."

"Okay," Josie said, humbled. "I did."

"You made me write this stupid want ad to go whore myself out."

"You didn't whore yourself out."

"Hey—I'm the one having the baby, I get to pick what I say. Quit interrupting." Josie couldn't argue with that. "To whore myself out and then I go and find Dylan and…and then it turns out that Dylan and Mike were partners looking for a woman to share their life with…and…"

*That whole secret billionaire thing,* Josie thought.

Laura stopped talking as yet another wave hit her, and Josie felt the kinetics of the contraction kick into her through the strength of Laura's fingers, her fingertips pressing their tension into Josie's wrist and hand. Josie could even sense the layers of her uterus cramping and clamping and pulling, the fibers all acting in whatever strange pattern the body needed to weave in order to push this baby out into the world. If Laura had teleported Josie's mind into her body she couldn't have transferred that feeling any better.

Closing her eyes, Josie saw a red, blooming mist behind her lids, like the audio that Laura sometimes listened to, training the brain to perceive pain in a different way with hypnosis. Josie thought that was a big load of shit, and yet, somehow in this moment of intensity, this pinpoint of biological destiny, that was where her brain went—to that stupid, insipid, ridiculous image of a misty cloud blooming. Maybe, though, just maybe, it was her own internal pain receptors panicking and not some new-agey bullshit...because *damn*, did Laura know how to destroy her hand or what?

"We're going to get you back to my car," Josie said.

"Where's your car?" Laura cried.

"It's back near Jeddy's."

"That far?"

"It's a block, Laura."

"We only made it a *block*?"

"Yeah, hon, we did."

"No, I was walking...was...no."

"It was a *long* block," Josie reassured her as they slowly, step by painstaking step, made their way back.

"Why does it feel like I have a bowling ball between my legs?" Laura said, widening her stance and walking like a toddler with a heavy load in a disposable diaper.

*Because you do,* Josie thought, *except it's coming out of your front door later on today.*

Laura came to a grinding halt and gaped openly at Josie. *Oh, shit,* she thought, *did I say that aloud?*

"I am not giving birth to a bowling ball," Laura said, her voice trembling. Two people walking past stopped and gawked at the two of them, then looked at Laura's belly. It was a couple, a man and a woman, and the woman's face changed to an expression of sympathy.

"Dear, I've been there. The bowling ball eventually comes out," she said, and pointed to the man next to her who looked young enough to be her son, a guy in his early twenties.

Horror dotted his face as he stared at Laura's crotch and mumbled, "I wouldn't know anything about that."

"But," Laura said, "it doesn't *really* feel like a bowling

ball?"

The woman and Josie exchanged a glance, and Laura began to wail like a small child. "But that's not true!" she shouted.

"No, of course not," said the stranger.

*Oh boy,* Josie thought, *this is going to be a long birth.*

# CHAPTER TWO

Dr. Alex Derjian watched the scene unfold with a certain level of mischievous pleasure that he hadn't been able to access in years. He'd done a double-take when the crew walked in through the main emergency doors as he'd been charting, documenting the last hour or so of work on patients. A rotund and deeply pregnant, gorgeous blonde woman was flanked by an incredibly tall Nordic man and a smaller but more muscular Italian guy who looked like he could be on the cover of *GQ*. And then behind them a slim, tiny little buzzing dynamo he recognized instantly.

Josie. From the research trial his grandfather was in *Holy shit*, he thought. Of all the places to run into her.

The pregnant woman must be her friend…or her wife (*if so, his gaydar was broken*). He saw one of the certified nurse midwives, a serene and businesslike old hand at all things birthing, meeting up with them. Unless there were complications severe enough to warrant calling him in on a consult—he was one of two residents on call in OB/GYN-- he probably wouldn't have any contact with Josie or her…*whoever* the laboring woman was. The only time *that* midwife would call him in would be in a true surgical emergency.

Unlike some other obstetricians, he wasn't a slicer, preferring a medical approach as much as possible before resorting to surgery. It didn't earn him any favors and it hadn't landed him any top internships or residencies anywhere. Without the killer instinct to cut, he'd been told, he should have just been a midwife.

They said that as if it were a bad thing.

A deep smile crossed his face, dimpling either side of his mouth. A mixture of Finnish and Armenian blood coursed through his veins, making him not particularly *anything* anymore, though his Armenian last name won him some points in Watertown, a western suburb just outside the city lines where a cluster of Armenians all lived. If your name ended with I-A-N you were instantly assumed to be a local Armenian and treated as such, regardless of the truth. Josie's coloring was similar to his, dark brown hair and eyes, but otherwise there were no similarities. She was petite, and he was a solid foot taller. She would easily fit under his arm, an image that flickered past his mind's eye, brief and unsolicited.

*What is she doing here?* he wondered. Was she working as a nurse? Or with her friend? Or her wife? And who were the two guys with them? Deeply curious, Alex closed the chart and looked up, startled to find a pair of big, wide green eyes lasered right in on him. It was Lisa, one of the nurses who had a crush on him—one that was absolutely *unrequited.*

When he'd started here ten months ago she'd asked him out for coffee. It had gone about as well as a root canal performed by a sadist with Parkinson's. Since then, she'd stalked him as much as was professionally possible without losing her job. He'd struggled to find ways to be kind, finally resorting to completely ignoring her. Cruelty would be the next step, and he really didn't want to reach that point unless he had to.

Her eyes tracked Josie as the group loaded onto an elevator headed, he knew, for labor and delivery. "Do you know her?" Lisa asked. She was about the same size as Josie, but a good fifty pounds heavier. Like Josie's lovely pregnant...associate...Lisa had blonde, wavy hair and green eyes, though a completely different profile. Where the woman he'd just seen come in with Josie had a kind, open face, plump, sweet cheeks, and frightened but beautiful eyes, Lisa had a much more closed-off look, a pinched expression, and something to her features that spoke of scarcity, of life as a zero-sum game.

*That* had been the problem on their one and only date. All she wanted to do was complain about the coffee, the pastry, schedules at work, supervisors, her student loans, her cat—pretty much everything. Who the hell complains about their cat – and on a first date? Alex, who was sometimes working hundred-hour weeks, didn't want his precious free hours spent listening to *that*.

"As a matter of fact, I do know her," he said, absentmindedly. "I'm going to go and head up to labor and delivery and see if they need some help."

"But you have charting to do," Lisa said in a clipped tone, pointing to the seventeen or so charts stacked in front of him.

He waved his hand and broke eye contact, marching toward the elevator, decision made. "I'll deal with it later."

"But - but..." she sputtered as he walked away, the sound of her voice receding along with his tension.

For the past six months, he'd taken his grandpa Ed to the Alzheimer's research trial at the nondescript medical building in Boston where Josie was the nurse in charge of clinical data and interviews. Alex would wait for thirty minutes or so before Ed would emerge with a big grin on his face and some sort of a small reward like a gift certificate to a coffee shop or a new set of golf balls, and then they'd go out to lunch. Alex enjoyed the carved-out time away from the craziness of the hospital.

His mom had asked Alex to make that one promise, that once a month he'd take an hour out of his schedule and help out. And with rare exception he'd managed, happy to take some of the burden off his mom, his aunts, and his grandpa's girlfriend. It seemed like such a small gesture. The first time he'd taken Ed, he had been in the bathroom when Ed's name was called. The second month he'd missed because of a work commitment. But on month three he had gone and seen Josie for the first time and that had made him resolve to be there *every* month.

She probably wouldn't know him from Adam, because every time she came into the waiting room to call Grandpa Ed's name, she barely looked up from her paperwork. And she absolutely was not his type, had never been his type, would never *be* his type—and if you had put a gun to his head and told him he had to *say* she was his type, he probably would have to accept death. He went for luscious, curvy, brown-haired, Slavic-looking women with bright red lipstick and asses that went on forever. *That's* who he dated, that's who he bedded, and that's who he assumed he would eventually marry and have kids with.

Even her friend, the blonde pregnant woman, was more Alex's type than Josie. Staring at this skinny little pixie of a woman, he'd been dumbfounded to find every sensor in his body going mad. Four months ago he had seen her for the first time, and the sad part was that he had squandered every single opportunity to say something, *anything*, other than "hi" to her.

When she walked in the room wearing a lab coat and whatever clothes were on under that, it was as if her mere presence was enough—actually interacting with her was too exquisite. What a great lie he told himself—the bottom line was that he was too much of a pussy to actually come out and introduce himself, get to know her, ask her out and see if whatever triggered this animal instinct in him that made him clam up and be a stupid eighth-grade boy was real.

Life was hectic. It was easier to go to a bar, pick up some chick, take her home, bed her, date her for a few weeks, and then end it all amicably—or not—than it was to actually understand why Josie triggered that reaction in him.

Hot breath on his shoulder surprised him as he waited for the elevator. "You don't have to do this, you know?"

He turned, stunned out of his own thoughts to find himself staring down at Lisa, who looked up at him, her nose piggish and bulbous, nostrils flared as if she were pissed off about something. "Don't need to do what?" he said.

"Don't need to go up on labor and delivery. Collins is up there, so they don't need you right now." Collins was the other OB resident on shift tonight. Known as the Barber of Boston, he was ready to slice and dice at will, with a C-section rate that pushed forty percent. If Collins got to that case first, Alex knew the inevitable outcome.

"So he's up there," Alex said as derisively as he could. He turned away and stared at the silver doors, willing them to part so that he could get on the elevator.

Lisa took a step away. "It's about that woman, isn't it?"

Hardening his body, Alex steeled himself and said, "What I do is absolutely none of your business, Lisa. Go back to whatever work you have."

Sniffing, she turned away and flounced off, to the extent that someone with a stick up their ass could flounce. The elevator doors opened and as he took a step forward his mind processed, atom by atom, molecule by molecule, the fact that there before him, in the flesh and in full, stood Josie.

She stared at his chest and then looked him dead on and said, "Alex Derjian?"

"Yes?" he said, taking two steps onto the elevator and turning toward her. How did she know his name? He touched his chest, the spot where she'd just stared, and realized his name tag had it in block letters. His heart began to race and an impulse to reach out and touch any exposed flesh on her body permeated him, making him take a long, slow, deep breath to hold back. *What the hell is this?* he wondered, the elevator air starting to swim, the heat transmitting out of his skin and seeking to envelop hers.

"Sherri Newsome asked for you up on labor and delivery," she said in a neutral voice, clipped like a nurse coming to a doctor with a request.

"Oh. Oh," he said. "Is it about a patient?" he asked, hoping it was about her friend, the blonde.

"Yes. She needs a quick consult." Her eyes were full of fear and concern, but also something harder, the chocolate irises outlined by the whites of her eyes and almond-shaped sockets that framed everything and gave her a pixie-ish look.

She really was quite enchanting, almost Icelandic looking, like a softer version of the singer Björk. She had the body of a dancer but no height. If she was five feet tall he'd be surprised, and she made him feel like a moose of a man.

With a practiced turn she pressed the L&D floor button and the pneumatic hiss of the doors caught his attention, making him turn and look out to find Lisa glaring at them both, her face like stone as the doors closed. He turned back to Josie, stunned to be in her presence and relieved to be away from Lisa.

"Hi, I'm Alex." Reaching his hand out to shake her hand, he was giddy with the opportunity to have a social convention he could use to access her skin.

She reached back and shook his hand, eyes widening at the genesis of their touch that connected the two. His palm embraced hers, soft and hard at the same time, commanding and tender as if he had to wring as much as possible out of this gesture. He pumped her hand two times and then slowed.

"Josie," she said, quietly. "Hi." She broke eye contact, looking over his shoulder and then directing her attention back, the skin around her eyes warming and narrowing a bit, face breaking into a smile. "Josie Mendham. Nice to meet you."

"Nice to meet you, too," he said, maintaining contact for as long as possible. Knowing that he would look like a creeper if he didn't let go, he reluctantly withdrew his hand, the feeling of losing contact like having the wind knocked out of him.

\* \* \*

Either a fireball entered the elevator and exploded in her body or she had just met her equivalent of Laura's two soulmates in a single man. With one touch, Alex—just another resident, just another doctor in a hospital working a twenty-four-hour or forty-eight-hour shift, the kind of guy she'd met hundreds of over the years—had transformed everything. Transformed the air in the elevator, transformed the entire experience of bringing Laura in to L & D into…transformed something about Josie herself.

His touch had seismically split her in two, tectonic plates altering her emotional landscape. *How could one person do that?* she wondered as their eyes locked and he shook her hand slowly, the tactile sensation of his palm pressed against hers like some sort of a battery recharging every cell in her body, warming her, making parts of her throb with a frequency that she hoped he could feel with his tongue someday.

Or now. *Now* would work.

Very, *very* naughty thoughts flashed through her mind as they locked eyes. And then a second series of thoughts berated her, guilted her over thinking about anything but her poor best friend, who was about to have her vagina split open by a speeding eight-pound flesh ball, all the nibbly parts on display for a crew of eight or nine people, not including the dads and Josie.

This was a teaching hospital, after all, and the only way

the interns, residents and the nursing students going through clinicals could learn was to watch people like Laura, to make notes, to get the queasiness over with and to learn by doing.

Right now she'd like to learn some really nice hands-on sexual lessons, lessons involving his hands on her naked ass, his mouth on other parts, her body entwined with Mr. Alex Derjian here—*Dr.* Alex Derjian, she corrected herself. Ever since a very messy failed affair her first year of nursing—an entangled, sweeping disaster that involved two doctors at work—she'd had a pretty firm rule: no dating doctors. But rules were made to be broken, right?

Introductions complete, he pulled his hand away, leaving her drained and empty and full of self-doubt. Had she been alone in the feeling that had just jolted through her? She wasn't imagining it, though—he seemed to feel it too. Fidgety and a little ill at ease, Josie pretended to study the silver doors as the elevator hummed its way up to an even bigger, more chaotic mess that they both encountered as the doors wheezed open.

There stood Mike and Dylan and Sherri outside Laura's door, engaged in an angry whisper campaign with another nurse. The pained expression on Dylan's face was shifting more and more into anger, while Mike coiled with a tension diametrically opposite his normal state. Snippets of their conversation floated into Josie's awareness as they approached.

"But there's a limit…"

"I don't care about the limit…"

"Why can't we…?"

"Does it really matter?"

"Is there a reason why we can't…?"

"What's going on?" Alex said, his voice commanding and clear.

It made Josie stand up straight and listen intently—not that she had any choice. She could have listened to him read a Windows 7 installation guide and been in a state of bliss for hours on end. A melodic baritone, he didn't have the standard Boston accent that so many men had, and there was a lilt, something foreign, but not quite. He wasn't a Midwesterner, not a New Yorker, and nothing from the South came into his voice. The sound of his voice was more his own accent, as if he had honed it carefully himself, born of an internal core that made him something distinct and unique and well worthy of everyone's immediate attention.

As he spoke, her eyes combed over his body. Brown, shiny waves in hair that needed a cut, but looked perfect tousled the way it was. Dark brown eyes, similar to hers, but with little specks of orange in them. His face was wide, with high cheekbones but the sprinklings of early five o'clock shadow. She knew, too well, that shadow would end up quite thick by the end of his long shift, the kind of stubble that left a slight, rough, red rug burn on a woman's face after a perfect, intense kiss...or twenty.

Broad shoulders and a body that indicated that he worked out. His scrubs lay flat against his skin, not too tight, but not the baggy, shapeless look that so many men acquired as residency added some paunch to their under-exercised, over-carbed forms. This was a man who took care of himself. And as the conversation continued, she recognized that he was a man accustomed to finding solutions and having them carried out.

Sherri turned to him. "Thank you, Alex. I'm glad you're here. I need you to consult on Laura's polyhydramnios case," she said, pulling him aside. "But we also have another issue here that has nothing to do with you."

The nurse who stood next to them was arguing with Dylan and Mike, and Josie heard, "But there can't be two fathers in the room."

"But there *are* two fathers."

"No, there *can't* be two fathers. It's biologically impossible. Our rooms are small and we can only allow one support person and one father."

"I'm the support person," Josie said. "I'm also an RN. What's going on?"

The nurse gave her a grateful look, as if Josie were an instant ally in whatever argument she was having with the men. Josie didn't like the assumption because she had a feeling that this was going to be one of those moments where she got ripping pissed and lost her cool. Doing that in front of Alex was one hell of a first impression she didn't want to make.

"Did Lisa call you, too?" the nurse asked.

"Lisa?" Josie shook her head, confused. The sly look on the woman's face pinched off instantly, shifting from a conspirator's countenance to one of officiousness.

"Both of these men say that they're the father." The nurse was in her mid-sixties, no nonsense. She had extremely short gray hair, thick bifocals, and the body language of someone who didn't take crap, ever. And Josie could respect that. If she worked here for forty years she'd be an impenetrable fortress of rules, too.

"Haven't you heard of a kid having two dads?" They were quite a crowd in the hallway now— Mike, Dylan, Josie, and the nurse clustered together, Alex and Sherri just behind them. The OB and midwife, whispering, backed up a few paces.

"Is this a surrogacy case?" the nurse asked, arms crossing over her chest tighter. A loud scream poured into the hallway from a nearby room, followed by the muted sound of a man's soothing voice.

Dylan and Mike exchanged a glance, and Dylan said, "If it was, could we both be in there?"

"Well, that depends. Is it?" The nurse was so cynical and challenging that Josie wondered if there was something personal going on here. Maybe she was homophobic and assumed Dylan and Mike were gay? Overt discrimination was rare in the Boston area, but it did happen.

"No, it's not," he admitted reluctantly, shoulders

slumping in defeat. Honesty prevailed, Dylan's instinct to lie not strong enough, Josie noticed. Ironic considering he had no problem lying when it came to other things. *Maybe he really has reformed*, she thought.

The nurse pointed to Josie. "So, you're the support person."

"Yes."

"Who is the dad?"

"I am," both men said in unison.

Out of the corner of her eye Josie saw Alex do a double-take and then whisper something to Sherri, who whispered something back. Alex's jaw dropped. *Oh, boy*, she thought, *this is getting interesting*. Who was she kidding? This had been interesting about ten minutes ago—no, make that nine and a half months ago.

"Don't make me do eenie-meenie-minie-moe on you," the nurse said, pointing her finger at Dylan, and then at Mike.

"They're not exactly a binary-oriented crowd here," Josie tried to explain.

The nurse shot her a WTF? look. "What's that supposed to mean?"

"It's complicated," Dylan muttered.

*Understatement of the year*, Josie thought as she tried to check out the gorgeous doctor's reaction, all of her senses on fire as she realized how turned on she was by his mere presence. A keen sense of familiarity made her think she knew him from somewhere. But where?

Sherri and Alex wandered back. "Have we decided the whole 'who's allowed in the room' thing yet?" Sherri said, clearly exasperated.

"There is a written hospital policy about how many people can be in the room," the nurse said, clearly not for the first time. A quick glare at the nurse showed exactly how Sherri felt about that. "It is rarely enforced, but it is on the books."

"What's the policy?" Alex looked at the nurse, then

added, "I've been here for a while and the only support person policy I know of is that only one person can be in the operating room for a C-section."

"One support person, one father." The nurse clamped her lips together in disapproval, not touching Alex's leading comment. "And she"—the nurse pointed at Josie—"is the support person."

"Who's the father?" he asked.

*Silence.* Josie, Mike, and Dylan sighed.

Sherri said, "I'm going to go and be with the actual *patient* and do patient care here." She gave the nurse a withering look. "Meanwhile, let's make the decision that's best for the *patient*. If she wants all these people in there, why can't they be in there?"

"If we need to get a crash cart in there it's too many people."

Josie had a thought. "Wait a minute—"

Alex interrupted her, which caught her off guard—she wasn't used to being interrupted. Normally, *she* was the one who interrupted.

Again that deep voice, that melody in his vocal cords strumming something in her that made her sit and listen attentively. "One support person is allowed," he said to the nurse.

"Yes."

"And one father is allowed."

The nurse pursed her lips. "Well, yes, normally there only *is* one father."

"Okay, fair enough. One father. Anyone else allowed?"

"No."

"What about a doula?"

The nurse tilted her head left and right and said, "Well, yes, we have had cases where—"

Josie was about to open her mouth and offer to back out of being in the room for the sake of Dylan and Mike when Dylan jumped up and shouted. "I'm the doula!"

"*You're* the doula?" the nurse questioned, incredulous.

"I'm the doula." Dylan's emphatic words showed in his new stance, the slumped shoulders long gone, body tight and defensive, ready for action.

"You don't look like a doula."

Dylan preened a little, pumped up his chest and said, "I'm a licensed paramedic and I'm a doula. I've got a therapy ball at home and some patchouli oil in my car. I do energy work." He waved his hands in front of him like some sort of mystic, coming within inches of the nurse's head. "Your energy is very negative. Maybe you need to get a sage stick and smudge yourself."

Josie bit her lips trying not to laugh. The male doula story was about to make the nurse's gossip rounds for the next six months at this hospital, as if Dylan didn't have his own notoriety when it came to Boston. And, unfortunately, here it came.

The nurse took a really long, good look at Dylan and then pulled back, her face shocked. She pointed and said, "I know who you are. You're the billionaire bachelor."

Dylan shot her a smug, charming smile. "Yes, I am."

"Then why do you need to be a doula?" she said. "You don't need to work."

That caught him off guard. "That's right. That's right," he said, fumbling for words. "I am a doula because I love the work and I want to support women in their birthing options." Josie motioned her hand in a circular manner that indicated to keep going. "And besides, there's nothing that you can do about it. I'm the doula. You go in there and you ask Laura and she'll tell you that I'm the doula and—"

The nurse pointed to Mike. "That makes you the father?"

"I guess so," Mike said, looking at Dylan with a very, *very* skeptical expression.

Dylan stood up on tiptoes and whispered in Mike's ear, "This doesn't mean that I think you're the father."

"I know that," Mike whispered back.

"Okay, just clarifying."

"Jesus Christ, Dylan, can we cut this out?"

"As cute as your conversation is," Josie said, a fake smile plastered on her face yet again. She was getting tired of this. "Let's just call it done." She put a hand on the shoulder of the nurse and said, "Can we just cut the bull and let all three of us in? Because right now we've wasted the past five minutes arguing about this and our friend needs us."

"You're not the doula," the nurse whispered, now unsure. It was three—make that four, if you included Alex, who had turned out to be their savior—against one, and the nurse was losing badly now.

"Ask Laura. I *am* the doula, and my client needs me." He waved his hands in the air around her, then clasped them in a *namaste* gesture.

The nurse softened and said, "All right. I'll let it go *but*," she said, taking a step closer to Dylan and sticking a finger on his chest, poking twice, "you better be the best damn doula I've ever seen in this hospital."

"You're on," he said. "Wait until you see what I can do with a massage wand!"

* * *

Josie walked into Laura's hospital room and found a weeping, hormonal mess sitting on a large therapy ball, rocking her hips and sighing through occasional mumblings of "Nobody told me this would hurt so much" and "Why the hell didn't I get an epidural in the parking lot?"

As Mike and Dylan entered closely behind her she could sense their absolute feeling of panic, compassion, confusion, and expectation—with just the slightest hint of excitement coming through, thankfully. Laura was going to need every drop of support from the three of them that she could get to emerge from this birth as unscathed as possible.

"Unscathed" wasn't exactly the right word, Josie knew. Having every mucosal section of skin in the nether regions shredded like mozzarella cheese over a pizza wasn't quite her personal definition of *unscathed*—and she knew that for the next three days after the baby was born Laura's best friend wasn't going to be Josie, Mike, or Dylan.

It was going to be ice packs and Lidocaine gently placed over her crotch and those stretchy, mesh panties that were anything but sexy, but that became a woman's life line as she recovered postpartum.

All of that, though, Josie had to push out of her mind because right this moment she had one thing to think about—and that was getting Laura through this. *Dammit,* she thought. Make that two thoughts, because right behind Mike and Dylan she sensed another presence, a masculine, self-possessed, and *oh, so seductive* presence. One that somehow managed to push Thor and his sidekick aside about as readily as a lion bats an annoying mouse.

How could the hot OB do this to her, to the room, to the world? How did someone she had just met ten minutes ago suck all of the negativity out of her atmosphere and fill it with a keening, sultry desire that made everything else go away? Her poor friend was sitting here, perched on top of an oversized playground ball, her head down, her breathing labored, her back wrenched as her hips split to let her baby emerge.

And all Josie could think about was grabbing Alex and finding a quiet room and riding him like a bull. A good friend would have anything *but* sex on her mind right now.

Apparently, Josie was not a good friend.

She happened to be standing at the end of the bed, and Alex came over to her left and reached across her to grab the chart. Her eyes were drawn to the smattering of dark hair that peppered the skin of his outstretched arm, the taut muscles of his wrist, the way the bones all moved so fluidly. Of course, he had surgeon's hands, with long, slim fingers that grasped the metal chart as if he were a catcher in a baseball game receiving a ball. Flipping open the chart, his forearms flexed with movement, the sinew and bulging veins speaking to some sort of outside activity that made him athletic and active. Her mind wandered once more to the bedroom. Was he athletic and active there?

She closed her eyes and squinted, trying to drive the thought away as he was mere inches from her. The scent of something citrusy, spicy, and a bit musky all mingled to make her hum even more vibrantly, like a magnet drawn to iron shavings— except the magnet was her nether regions, a familiar warmth pooling in her belly, threatening to make her breathing as labored as Laura's. The muscles that were clamping inside Josie may have been in the same area as Laura's, but they were producing a noticeably different sensorial effect.

"Excuse me," Alex said, looking over with a flirtatious tone to his voice.

"By all means," she said. "You are the doctor."

His eyes narrowed slightly at that and he shot her a puzzled look. "But I'm not in charge here," he reminded her. "Sherri is."

*Could you be any more perfect?* she thought. A humble OB? Impossible. There was no such thing. She wanted to say that, to test him, to push him, see where his limits were, but this wasn't the time. At that exact moment Dylan walked over to Laura and began rubbing her back while Mike poured a glass of water.

"Laura, you okay?" Dylan asked, bending over her shoulder.

"Am I okay?" said a demon voice from deep inside Laura's core. "Am I okay? Do I *look* okay?" she asked.

Josie winced. Dylan was about to get it. "No, I just mean…"

For the first time since they'd arrived, Josie got a good look at Dylan. He was wearing a navy polo shirt, some torn jeans, flip-flops, and a baseball cap. Red Sox. Must be a game day.

"It's okay, Laura. It's all right, babe," Mike said, coming over with a glass of water, trying to soothe her and glaring at Dylan. Dylan looked back, shrugging, his palms up in the air in a *what did I do?* kind of motion.

"It's not okay!" Laura shouted. "Quit telling me it's okay! You!" She pointed at Dylan. "And you!"—now at Mike—"aren't the ones who are about to have this baby come out the hole where you put her in. If one more person in this room," she shouted, looking around, her eyes wild and angry, "tells me it's going to be okay, I'm going to order you out of here. I'm going to strap you down and I'm gonna load a bunch of Pitocin in your veins and I'm gonna make you feel how it feels to have your asshole clamp down for forty-five to sixty seconds every two to three minutes and then I'm gonna make you shit an eight- pound brick. *Are we clear?*"

"Yes, ma'am," the men said in unison. Josie almost said it too, and then bit her lower lip, afraid to piss off Laura any more.

Alex leaned down and Josie could feel his breath before he said a word, the heat tickling her earlobe, making her lose about ninety-nine percent of the thin thread of resolve that was left. "I'm going to assume," he said, his voice like a soft touch, "that she's not always like this."

"No," Josie answered, whispering, her mouth so close to his earlobe she wanted to stand on tiptoes and bite it. "Only when she's shitting an eight-pound brick."

He nodded somberly. "Most of my patients find the brick is worth it." His smile lit up his eyes as he studied her face. "You have kids?"

The question shocked her. It shouldn't have—she was getting to that age where it was becoming more common—but it still did. "Um, no. I kill house plants and the only reason my cat is still alive is because he's smarter than I am."

He chuckled. "Not everyone's ready at the same time, right?"

*What was that supposed to mean?* "And some of us aren't ready even when reality is staring us down the birth canal," she said, nodding at Laura.

"Her level of denial must be pretty extreme," he said.

"You don't know the least of it."

Dylan was attaching some sort of MP3 player to Laura's shirt as she batted away the earbuds. "I don't want to listen to that crap," she said, bursting into tears. "I just want someone to hold me." A loud, winding-down cry like a toddler's poured out of her as she melted into a puddle of tears, sniffling against Dylan's chest, his body twisted in an awkward pose. He looked at Mike and shook his head, eyes begging for help.

*What do I do?* he mouthed. Josie started laughing.

She turned back to find Alex going over Laura's chart, his frown deepening as he read further. She stood up on tiptoes, raised her eyebrows, and tried to get a look, but he was too tall and the chart was too far away. "Anything to be worried about?" she asked in a low hiss.

"Nothing so bad that we can't continue with the midwife," he said. "But this is one I'm going to have to watch very, very carefully." Snapping the chart shut, he kept a very neutral—almost too neutral—look on his face, his voice professional and moderate.

His hand brushed against hers as he lowered the chart, and she felt a zing of every form of energy in the universe coalesce into that point of contact. "Unfortunately, it looks like you're stuck with me for most of the night on this case." Avoiding eye contact, he looked at a spot above Laura's head. "If Sherri agrees," he added in a slightly deferential tone. Unreal. Doctors didn't *do* that—defer. To anyone.

"Unfortunately?" she asked, cocking an eyebrow. "What do you mean?"

He seemed to consider that, breathing in through his nose, taking his time to answer. When he did, one hundred percent of his attention was focused on her. She liked that very much. "The unfortunate part is that her case is high risk enough that she needs an OB consult for most of the night," he explained, a practical tone in his voice that made her think she had completely misread what she thought was a flirtatious signal, her stomach clenching and her heart hardening to save herself the social embarrassment of thinking that someone this hot and this interesting would have any interest in her.

"But," he said, his finger touching the inside of her elbow, making a slow, steady trail into the soft inner flesh and then writing tiny circles in the middle, a pretty obvious symbolic move on his part, "the fortunate part is that, given the amount of time I'm going to need to focus on the case, and the nineteen hours left on my shift, I think you and I are going to become very well acquainted."

"Me?" she squeaked. His fingers stopped and she nearly sobbed with the exit of his touch, her solar plexus, her abs, her *everything* all tight with anticipation and with some sort of paradigm shift in the universe that made everything about *him, him, him.*

"Yeah, Josie. You."

"I need to pee!" Laura shouted. Josie deflated on the spot. *Way to kill the mood,* she thought, and then clamped down on her brain, which was far better than clamping down with some of the other muscles in her body that were pulsating right now.

What in the ever-loving hell was she doing?

All her attention needed to be focused on Laura, not on Dr. Alex Derjian. Flashing him a smile, she got herself out of the situation, extracting her ego, her attention, and her sex drive from this diversion. Two out of three of those should be focused on Laura and the third—well, she had a box of electronic toys to handle that one. She didn't need another crazy romantic entanglement right now, and certainly not in the middle of Laura's birth.

She should be focused on her friend's vagina—not her own.

# CHAPTER THREE

This was a new low, even for Alex. Coming on to a patient's support person *during* the woman's labor? Alex had seen unscrupulous doctors hit on doulas before. Twice in his short career, he'd even seen the expectant *fathers* hitting on nurses or other women in the room while the poor, laboring mom writhed in pain and agony. At least he wasn't the baby daddy here. Although, he thought as he peered around the room, he still wasn't sure *who* the baby daddy was. Sherri had briefly explained that this was an unusual romantic entanglement between the laboring mom and the two men in the room.

Alex watched how tender they were with her, how the tall blonde seemed to focus her in meditation and to calm her down, bringing her out of the anger and into a more neutral, calm energy that allowed her to handle the waves of contractions far better than she had while upset and bitter. He admired what they were doing, capable of so much more than he saw in most traditional unions. Flashing back on some of the two hundred births he'd been part of or observed, he couldn't think of another situation where two men had been so eagerly devoted to one woman.

Not wanting to interrupt them, he took a quick look in the chart and saw nothing noted under "father's name." He was curious. How do you do this? How do three people act as one? And which one was the father? Sherri had said that they didn't want to know, and that seemed even more astonishing to him. If he helped to create a baby, damn right he'd want to know that he was the father.

This was different, he sensed, as he watched the two men help Laura stand and begin to take some slow steps. There was an interplay between them, an easiness between the men that spoke of a kind of connection he respected but couldn't fathom. Under their eager assistance, she blossomed a bit, even laughing as the tall blonde made a joke, and somehow she chuckled through a contraction, the motion making her belly tighten. Alex watched carefully, his practiced eye noting that she still hadn't dropped.

Between polyhydramnios and the fact that she was a first-time mother, he guessed it was going to be a long night. *That* fact he celebrated in his head, a great contradiction to most cases. In nearly every laboring case, he wanted it over quickly. Not to rush nature, but simply to bring closure to the family and to greet the new life that came into the world in his trained hands.

With Laura, he hoped, too, that she would find as little suffering as possible, and that he could help Sherri in whatever way to make sure that the birth was smooth, managing the risks as much as possible. More than anything, he hoped that it was a long, slow, steady birth that gave him plenty of time to talk to Josie.

Touching her like that had been a gamble. Her blushing response emboldened him, made his body react so swiftly he cursed the scrubs, which showed all too publicly what regular pants could hide. That simple touch ignited him and made him want her more. Pretending to read the chart, he mulled over the handful of seconds he'd touched her inner arm, how her breath had hitched, the way the pulse at her throat had been visible, picking up.

She stood behind Laura now, rubbing a lacrosse ball up and down the chain of muscles from her mid-back to her coccyx. Laura bent over slightly, supported by the brown-haired guy, groaning with ecstasy—and then her knees buckled as another contraction hit, and both men shifted to hold her up.

The contractions were coming closer together than he'd predicted, and he and Sherri exchanged a glance. She tapped her watch and shrugged. He nodded, put the chart back, and backed out of the room. If they needed an OB, Sherri would call him. And if the birth went on past 7 a.m., whichever CNM took over for Sherri would call whichever resident took over for him, short of an imminent birth at shift change.

Mentally settling in for a long night and a long labor, he began to plot in his mind how he could use these hours to the fullest, assuming no more big cases came in tonight. Could he get Josie to join him for coffee? Could he come in to offer to help? Could he make it plausible that he wanted to read a fetal monitor strip or assess surgical possibilities?

All of that took up the rational part of his brain. Meanwhile, the irrational part drummed a steady beat as he looked at Josie and studied her more carefully. Her attention was focused solely on Laura's back, giving him a moment to stand in the threshold and just take her in.

The fire in her eyes, the sarcastic retort she threw out to the brown-haired guy, the way she seemed to be able to touch Laura and whisper something in her ear that instantly made the laboring woman seem a little more at ease—it was all part of the allure of Josie. Beyond that, though, he just didn't know. How could he pinpoint it when he'd exchanged more words with her in the past fifteen minutes than he had in his life prior?

If he could explain it, he would. But he couldn't. Some primal attraction that went deeper than the surface, deeper than language, made him want her, made him want to possess her, to be the center of everything for her. He knew it was crazy. Alex had built an entire career on the known, on *facts*, on medicine and science and that which could be measured and tested, and then applied to the human condition to provide relief, remedies, and comfort.

He had decided to specialize in obstetrics after going to his first birth in medical school. All the mother's kinetic energy had focused, even through the epidural, and Alex was transfixed. The head had emerged, and then one shoulder, and then the slide and slipperiness of the baby had poured out of the mother's body, a new life in the deft hands of the doctor. That transition from the safety of the mother's body into the light of the world was a bridge that Alex wanted to walk for the rest of his life. Obstetrics it was for him.

The surgical side had come easily; he had rock-steady hands, no matter what. It had become a joke in med school that you could feed him fourteen cups of coffee, a considerable amount of sugar, and probably throw in a Red Bull or two, and his hands would be as calm and neutral as Switzerland. Yet, handed that gift by some outside force, he largely rejected it, choosing to find as many medical methods as possible to preserve vaginal births for his patients. He didn't care that he was largely ignored, or worse, belittled, for his old-fashioned views. Medicine, for Alex, wasn't about reputation, or climbing a ladder, or any of the other petty things that his classmates considered important.

Helping patients was the focus, and the rest—money, prestige, competition—didn't appeal to him. Those issues weren't part of his ethical calculus. So why, if he could so easily reject conventional ideas about his career, did he find it surprising that he would fall for a woman in such an unconventional way?

He turned around and walked back to the elevators, riding them down to the main desk where his other patients' charts waited for him like baby birds begging to be fed. His handwriting looked like regurgitated worm as he scrawled his way through note after note after note of earlier patients. He found himself on autopilot, thinking solely about Josie, scheming to find a way to get back up to the labor and delivery wing without being too obvious.

\* \* \*

Josie tried to imagine what the four of them looked like, wandering down the halls of the maternity wing. Laura straddled an invisible bowling ball and stepped as if she were walking on burning coals. Dylan looked like a deer caught in the headlights, eyes wide and frantic, his entire being trying to keep it together whenever Laura looked at him. Mike was Mike, calm and steady, but holding on to a bracelet filled with beads and mouthing words as they walked along. Every so often Josie could hear little bits and pieces of whatever prayer he was saying—*Om, Tara, Pad me*—and she guessed it was something Buddhist.

If Josie were about to have her daughter enter into the world she'd be praying too, but it wouldn't be quite as calm and peaceful. It would be more like, *Oh, dear God, make the fucking pain stop!*

Laura was pretty close to that, but the walk had made a huge difference. She sipped on a cup of cranberry juice as they strolled at a pace about as slow as a bill making its way through Congress. On their second lap around the nurses' desk, a slightly pudgy, brown-haired shift nurse with piggish eyes joked, "There goes Mario Andretti." The guys had laughed and Laura faked a polite smile, but Josie's heart sank. That was the last thing that any woman in this condition needed, the joke failing miserably for the one person who needed it to succeed.

Time and space had condensed into *this* hallway, and the *next* hallway, as they made a left turn, the one after that, past the bank of born babies that they could "ooh" and "ahh" at and that could hearten Laura, to give her more spirit. Any rift in *that* and Laura's support network wouldn't be enough. Ultimately, they all knew, this rested on Laura's ability to dig deep and find a core of love and strength within herself that would allow her to ride this out, to bring a new life into this world. No chant, no prayer, from anyone else could accomplish that. And when all of this was over and Laura held her brand-new daughter in her arms, Laura alone would be the bridge this little soul had traversed into being.

The rest of them? They were there to remove obstacles from Laura and the baby's path. But not to complete the journey.

Mike seemed to sense that the nurse's tossed-off joke had had a deeper layer to it, and pulled Josie aside. "Should we avoid the nurses' station?" he asked, intense eyes steady and stable. Josie could look into them for hours and find peace. *Note to self,* she thought, *when—uh, if—I do have a baby, ask Mike to be there.*

"Yeah," she said, wrinkling her nose. "I don't think that was helpful."

He nodded. Laura was wearing earbuds, her attention focused on the music as she shuffled along. She burst out into braying laughter suddenly, punching Dylan playfully in the shoulder.

"What?" he said, his face lighting up as if a heavy burden were suddenly lifted and he were joyful.

"*You* made the playlist."

"I did," he said, grinning ear to ear, the charming smile that made women want to take their pants off and burn them now teasing Laura as she was about to give birth to *their* child. Josie kept reminding herself. Their. *Their, their, their.* Not his—theirs.

"Really? 'I'm Too Sexy' by Right Said Fred?"

"I thought it was a good one." He started to sing the song and they all laughed.

"He also thought 'Fat Bottomed Girls' by Queen was a good one, but I talked him out of it," Mike whispered in Josie's ear.

"Dead. He'd be a dead man if he did that," she whispered back.

"Twice dead. Laura would kill him and find a way to kill him again," he said, chuckling low. "His karma would be ruined for multiple lifetimes."

"He really thought that was a good song for an overdue pregnant woman in labor?"

"He said he loves fat-bottomed girls and never considered it an insult." Mike shrugged. Dylan started shooting them the hairy eyeball and Josie ignored him.

"That's because he has the social graces of a nine-year-old boy with a box of fireworks and three espressos in him."

"All this dance music on the playlist is fabulous, and the beats help me to get out of my head. Thank you, honey," she said, reaching out to touch Dylan's arm. "But I'm not doing that kind of dance." Her face crumpled, voice shaking. "I'm barely holding it together, because when I do dance, it's going to be the dance of being split in two so that a new life can emerge," Laura said seriously. Mike and Dylan wrapped her in a cocoon of their arms, and Josie felt marginal, like a moon orbiting them.

Laura's face was tired, and Josie knew that her reserves were running low already. This was like mile ten of a marathon, though. It was one thing to be this tired at mile twenty, but this early? It didn't bode well for what was coming. Love could be enough for a hell of a lot of things, and if love were the measure of how Laura would fare tonight, she'd be fine. Biology, though, could overpower love when it came to birth.

\* \* \*

Alex happened to be at the nurse's desk, charting away,

documenting the case where he'd sniped The Claw, taking away his ability to perform a C-section simply by reading the fetal monitor strip with the consultation of a nurse with thirty years of experience under her belt. With a little help from some augmentation drugs, the mom had crowned, and the baby had come out nice and slick, like a little seal pouring forth into the world, big, wide eyes open. The baby was safe in the NICU now, being monitored; if Alex had any sense of predicting the future, he'd say that the baby would be fine in about two days. Probably just some junk in its lungs causing minor respiratory issues.

So many of his med school colleagues had gone into obstetrics with a giant burden of fear yoked around their necks. Fear that a baby would be harmed, fear that a mother would crash, fear that a baby would be injured or die. Fear seemed to drive them and from the outside looking in, and they allowed themselves to make so many consequential decisions based on something that hadn't happened yet.

Alex made his decisions on data and, he admitted, on hunches—but when he listened to his gut there wasn't a third partner there screaming like a giant fire alarm that went on and on forever, and no flame ever appeared. He ruled over his psyche with a steady, reasonable mind that applied a calculus of optimism. For him, the baseline was *of course everything will be fine* and it was only data that shook that deep core of faith that would make him act.

When the alarm in Laura's room went off, he leapt and shot down the hall, barely hearing the clattering of the chart that he'd just been writing in as it slipped off the counter and banged against a chair. His feet pounded into the linoleum floor as he pushed his body as hard as possible—because that code meant that something was wrong and with a patient with her profile he could walk into damn near *anything*.

The flames of fear licked at his ankles right now; he had the briefest of appreciations for what his med school comrades had gone through. Fighting it back as his heart pounded in his chest, as his arms pumped him forward, climbing up four flights of stairs as fast as possible with no time for the elevator, all he could think was *get to the baby, get to the baby, get to the baby, get to the baby.* It became a chant, in his head as his brow began to pound, as his hamstrings began to scream and he burst through the doors just as Sherri came down the hall, wide-eyed and pointing.

Sherri, Alex, a nurse, and two hospital staff he couldn't identify slammed through the door to Laura's room. Sherri plowed through the suite to the bathroom door, finding it locked. His head swinging wildly, eyes darting around the room, Alex saw Josie resting in a chair, her head snapping up as the group crashed into the room.

"Where is she?" he shouted.

"What? What? What?" Josie said, sitting up, her eyes alarmed. "What are you talking about?"

And then, *slam!* The bathroom door unlocked. Alex charged in right behind Sherri, who was standing at a dead halt, staring at the scene that unfolded before them all.

A man's hairy asshole pointed squarely at the door, nearly at waist level to them all. To the left Alex saw Laura, completely naked now, sitting on the toilet bearing down, her face tipped up in flushed horror.

The owner of the brown starfish winking at them as he bent down to finish turning the jacuzzi water off appeared to be Dylan—who froze with his hand on the faucet.

*What fresh hell was this?*

Alex had seen plenty of strange things in his years on hospital rotations, and had walked in on some exceptionally sexual situations that ranged from the commonplace to the perverted, but going at it while a woman was dilated to six centimeters or so, in a hospital room bathroom, was a new kind of low.

As Sherri turned to him and bit her lower lip, covering her mouth with her palm, Alex took charge and asked, "Laura, are you okay?"

Her face was slack and frozen as Dylan turned around and stood, his naked form laid out in tight, muscled detail for Alex and the four women—*No, make that five*, he thought as he caught Josie out of the corner of his eye—standing behind the two nurses in the back on tiptoes, her head bouncing as she tried to see what was going on.

*If she needs to see any man naked, it should be me.*

Dylan said, "She's fine. What the hell is this?"

Alex raised his eyebrows and shot Dylan a look of marvel. "*You* tell *us* what this is," he said. "Someone in this room pulled the emergency cord."

Laura looked down at her right hand, which was pressed into the handicapped bar next to the toilet seat, her pinky finger wrapped in the small, thin white string attached to the wall. "Oh my God," she choked out. "I must have…I was trying to go and I was pushing up to stand and, oh…" She looked at Dylan with abject horror. "Oh, honey, I'm *so* sorry."

"Why are you naked?" Josie screeched.

"Because I feel better that way," Laura answered.

Alex felt the rising bubble of laughter in him, barely held back until Dylan, his toned firefighter body on full display, planted his hands righteously on his hips and asked Josie in incredulous tones, "Are you talking to *me*?"

Josie looked straight at his penis, and then back at his eyes and said, "You're the only one who really shouldn't be naked, Dylan."

"I was helping her get into the jacuzzi," he explained.

"And you needed to be naked to do that?" she asked.

Alex was struck by the sarcastic tone she used. There was clearly some sort of relationship between the two that relied on poking each other for amusement. He didn't have time, though, to think about their banter.

His eyes focused back on Laura. Sherri had moved and was checking her pulse, repositioning the baby monitor to catch the fetal tones which—*aha*, there they were, nice and strong. Good. Laura's face tightened and Alex watched her belly move down like an elevator slowly descending, the baby being pushed down to her pelvic floor. She breathed perfectly through the contraction, her body tense at first and then her shoulders slowly lowering to relax, her breath focused in what little bit of diaphragm control remained for someone so enormously pregnant. The belly breathing would help to keep the blood going to the womb muscles and would calm her—he hoped. Without her water popped, this was going to continue to be difficult for her but he wasn't in charge here—this was Sherri's gig.

"I think we need to leave them alone," Alex said quietly, stepping back, the gap between him and Josie now considerably smaller with Sherri in the bathroom ministering to Laura. He reached for Josie's forearm and she snatched it away.

"I want to know why Dylan was trying to fuck Laura in the middle of having a baby."

"I want to know why you *think* I was trying to fuck Laura in the middle of having a baby," Dylan said.

A low voice a few inches above and behind Alex said, "I'd like to know, what you're doing, too."

This was the other dad, what was his name? Mike? Mike—who stared at the display before him and he, too, looked at Dylan's naked form and shook his head. "There is a time and place for this and this is neither the time nor the place," Mike told Dylan.

"She wanted me to get in the jacuzzi tub with her!" Dylan protested. "We didn't pack a bathing suit. We didn't figure it would be a big deal."

"Yeah, yeah," Josie said. "I'm sure people here have heard that a million times."

"Actually, no," Alex and Sherri said in unison.

Laura's contraction was over and she stood, completely naked and utterly oblivious to her nude form, which Alex found charming. So many mothers added to the difficulty and the pain of the labor by being self-conscious. Of all the times in your life when you should be able to do whatever you want, isn't labor and delivery one of them?

"Out," she said calmly, pointing to Alex and the two nurses. She pointed to Josie, Dylan, Mike, and Sherri. "You can stay. Everybody else, I don't give a rat's ass what you think about what's going on here. I am having a baby!" she shouted. "I want my fucking birthing tub!" And with that she waddled over to the tub and slowly lifted one leg to get in, Dylan supporting her as Mike scrambled into the room to help out.

Alex backed away, admiring her fortitude and wondering if she was always like this. He and Sherri exchanged a look and she just shrugged, waving him out. Crisis averted—back to charting.

* * *

Now that Dylan's brown starfish crisis was over, Josie found herself flagging, needing coffee. It was 4 a.m. And while Laura's body was blossoming nicely, now at about six centimeters, without broken waters this could take quite a bit longer. Dylan snoozed in a very uncomfortable-looking pose in a chair in the room while Mike curled around Laura, spooning her while pressing his hands deeply into the aching muscles of her back. Laura, desperate for sleep, was grabbing whatever Z*zzzz* she could get between rippling contractions.

Josie knew that breaking the waters would be the next suggestion Sherri would make, and that Laura would probably comply, but do so with hesitation. Exhaustion had set in, and that meant her mind wasn't as sharp as it normally would be. Add in raging hormones, abject terror, and the whispers of a new uptight nurse and you had one big mess.

Coffee. She needed coffee. She shook Dylan, who jumped up and shouted, "What? Push?" He was as dog tired as Josie.

She leaned down. "I'm getting coffee. Want some?"

He just shook his head and closed his eyes, curling himself into a barefooted ball on the wooden legs of the visitor's chair, head shoved against a pillow. The chair folded out into a little bed, but he'd rejected that option for reasons known only to him. She wasn't about to pry.

The elevator ride down was eerie, the sounds of groaning women in labor and beeping machines cut short as soon as the elevator doors shut. Downstairs, she found a 24/7 coffee shop and grabbed a horrible cup of java that would at least buy her a little alert time. On impulse she bought two. She'd find Alex and offer him one as a prize. Anyone who came face to face with Dylan's naked ass—no matter how strong and hot it was—needed a little something else strong and hot to get over it.

Finding Alex proved remarkably simple, for as she waited for the elevator doors she heard that steady baritone behind her. "Josie?"

She turned to find him standing there, holding two cups of coffee. Uncertainty clouded his features, and then his eyes twinkled with mirth. "You just got coffee," he said, pretending to toast her with the cup in his right hand. "I was coming up with this to give you."

Could he be even more perfect? Apparently. "And," she answered, gently knocking her own cup against his, "this is for you." Eyes locked, they smiled at each other, the coffee burning her hand as they just stared. Maybe that burning sensation wasn't only from the hot liquid in the cup in her hand. Hot fluids were pooling in other places, too.

"Great minds think alike and all that," he said, not breaking the look.

She knew he had a handful of hours left of his shift, and he looked tired, but there was an energy in him that she admired. Competence and decency emanated from him, even in the blue scrubs. His name tag was askew, hanging from his shirt pocket like an afterthought, and his messy hair made her want to see it in bed, sunlight streaming behind him, naked and sleepy next to her, covered in their scent.

If he could read minds she was in trouble.

She had a feeling she was in trouble no matter what, though, because as their look deepened she felt herself falling, unsure where or how far, but definitely falling into a state she'd never been in before, her body and mind ready to leap right into something that should be carefully thought out.

And the last thing she needed to do right now was tear any of her attention away from her best friend. Laura, trying to sleep, and about to experience the worst pain of her entire life. In the middle of all that, what was Josie doing?

Flirting.

*Bad friend. Bad, bad friend.*

"We have a coffee surplus. Want to go sit down and get wired and jittery together?" Alex asked.

"Get some Mountain Dew and NoDoz and we could cure cancer in two days."

"We could do great things with two uninterrupted days together," he said, nodding solemnly.

The elevator dinged and the doors opened. Alex gestured for her to get on first, and she fumbled to push the button for the right floor, hands full of coffee cups, but she made it.

"You can tell you're a nurse."

She snickered. "A real nurse would make out with you between floors." Her mouth wasn't supposed to blurt that out. It was a thought! *A thought!* The line between thinking and speaking eroded after 1 a.m.

"Is that an offer?"

"Do you want it to be?" *Stall. Buy time. Stop inhaling his scent. Stop watching his arms flex with those coffees.*

What was he doing? Alex bent down and set the coffees on the floor, then approached her, two steps into her personal space, making her breath so hard to manage she worried she'd faint from lack of oxygen. Autonomous body functions continued, to her surprise, including a decidedly distressing flood of blood to her nether regions, which engorged and flowed, making her wet for him. How could she get out of this with her dignity intact, without throwing herself all over him?

"I don't play games, Josie." His eyes bored into her and she gasped, confirming that her respiratory system really was functioning right now, thank goodness. His hands reached for the cups she held and he placed them on the floor, too. Alex touched her shoulders as the elevator crept up, slowly, the seconds feeling like minutes. "Games are for people who don't know what they want."

Alex showed her exactly what he wanted next, arms wrapping around her shoulders, one hand sliding against the throbbing skin of her neck, his soft palm caressing her pulse at the jawline, mouth bending to her, upper body curling down to take her with impossibly lush lips that met hers with a sense of welcoming that was almost unbearable in its simplicity and grace.

He didn't push. This wasn't a kiss of overriding passion, which she expected, but instead one of invitation, of orientation, even. Rather than saying "take your pants off"—a sentiment with which she was all too familiar—his kiss said "hello." Which was so *un*familiar it confused her. The former she knew all too well. And then it shifted, moving decidedly into pants territory.

As his lips explored her, her hands splayed against his shoulders, feet standing on tiptoes to embrace him better, the distant *ding!* of the elevator's ascent registered and interrupted their embrace as the doors began to open.

Feeling like an errant schoolgirl, Josie pressed her fingers to her lips as he pulled back, a smile creasing his face and making those damn eyes even more appealing. The look he gave her pierced her heart, as if he really cared for her and this wasn't just some strange attraction that came at the worst possible time—ever—in her life.

No one entered the elevator, thank God, and she nearly kicked over two of the coffees in her haste to pull away and make sure no one caught them. She watched him, effortlessly, dip to one knee on the floor like a man about to propose, except his hand held java instead of a diamond ring.

Likewise, she bent down to retrieve her coffees and looked to him for reassurance, for direction, to know what to do next. His fixed stare made her smile, the grin a reflex that came from a deeper look at the relaxed calm, the knowing joy in him that he somehow transmitted to her.

*That* look she knew, but not personally. A touch of it was in the way Mike smiled when he talked about Laura.

What next? She followed him off the elevator and stood there dumbly, the quiet hush of sleep at 4 a.m. and the occasional groans from women not on traditional timelines (babies in utero have a remarkable disdain for modern American temporal convention) were the only major sounds.

Even Laura seemed to still be asleep, the room's door closed, no sounds coming from behind it. What next?

Alex's hand, holding a cup of coffee, made a flailing, circular gesture toward her. Huh? Then she realized he wanted her to follow him. As she ambled behind, she got a good look at him. How could scrubs fit so well? Seriously? Muscled and full, his ass was like some kind of trophy for Best Ass Ever contests. Seeing it naked would be heavenly. Her mind flashed to the most recent naked ass she'd seen, and she wished for brain bleach. Who wanted to think about naked Dylan right now?

Not her.

A small door with a tiny nameplate next to it and a covered window was Alex's destination. Ah. Now she understood.

The dreaded On-Call Room.

Meant to be a place for overworked interns, residents, attendings, and nurses to catch up on sleep, on-call rooms were really little more than free-sex rooms. The amount of amorous, ugly bumping that went on in those tiny bunk beds ought to have triggered a Board of Health alert. If Alex was bringing her there, it meant only one thing.

And God, did she want that one, big thing she imagined was waiting for her under those scrub pants.

"Hold on," he said, setting both his cups on the floor and grabbing the two she held. Marching past her to a nurse's station, he set down the two spares. "Free for the first person who grabs them!" he announced quietly. "Just milk." Two nurses snatched them up and murmured their thanks to Alex's back as he strode with great, sensual purpose toward Josie, making her wish she'd worn something more sexually attractive than a hoodie and yoga pants. Who knew she'd meet a hot doctor at Laura's birth?

And who would have thought that she'd be standing in the threshold of an on-call room as her friend labored nearby? All moral ambiguity went out the window as he playfully wrapped his arms around her waist and dragged her into the room, kicking the door shut.

"It sounds so crazy," he said, his mouth against her neck, hands riding up her back and sinking into her hair, the scent of him making her want to lick his skin just to have it in her forever, "but I don't think you mind my being this forward." He pulled back, eyes suddenly serious. "And this isn't your average on-call romp."

"I'm not average *anything* in an on-call room."

That made him pause, making Josie regret the words instantly. Instead of disapproval, mirth shone in those deep brown eyes. "I'm not your first?"

Snort. "You're my first *today*." Ugh! Why did she do that? Say the most heinous thing possible that would make him walk away, turn from her, and not want to be with her? Here she was, stupid, sarcastic crap pouring forth in a highly intimate setting. An extremely attractive, sensual man wanted to get naked with her and—

She said what?

Ferocious with need, he moved like a panther to her, taking her with a kiss that spoke of want and desire and heady sexuality. His mouth was on her and his hands everywhere. Dr. Octopus might not be her first on-call room jaunt, but he damn well could be her last.

Wherever that thought came from, it seemed matched by him. Breathless, he pulled back, leaving her mouth cold with air and abandonment, and said, "This isn't just sex."

Of course it was just sex. Men didn't meet Josie and do this. Not even the casual sex part. She wasn't the pick-up girl type. Sure, she had her share of one-night stands and on-call room quickies, but she wasn't That Kind of Woman. Guys didn't fall for her at first sight; neither lust nor love drove men to her. She was an afterthought, or a friend with benefits. Not the hot chick you felt a connection to and just had to have.

Why, then, was Dr. Coffee doing this?

And telling her it was more than sex?

"Can it at least *be* sex?" With that, she pulled her hoodie up over her head in one fluid motion, then eagerly reached for his shirt, helping him to wiggle out, his broad, muscled chest on display, a nicely distributed smattering of dark hair covering his well-defined pecs. Her fingertips caressed the six-pack she'd hoped was under those scrubs, trailing down to the navel, where the hair thickened, and his sharp intake of breath told her that a few more inches and she'd pass the point of no return.

Who was she kidding? They'd passed that the second she made that comment about nurses and elevators.

And she was right.

Hot palms made their slow way up her back, practiced hands unclasping her thin wisp of a bra, freeing small, pert breasts from their nylon encasing. Endowment had never been a problem for her—if anything, her figure was boyish, though gaining twenty pounds along with Laura's sixty or so had given her new curves no man had yet explored. In his hands, her hips felt womanly. The bottoms of his palms cupped her flesh, thumbs brushing with intent to make her nipples stand at attention. Oh, he had her attention, all right. No need for more.

More, though, was what she wanted, her hands riding from his waist up to his shoulders, until she looked up into smoky eyes, darkened with need, his face serious and mature.

"I mean it," he said in a raspy voice infused with desire. "I don't understand why or how, but this isn't just about what we're doing right now, Josie. Not for me."

The world's best come-on line.

"You make me want to do naughty things," he said, and bent down, his body over hers, his lips next to her ear, the lines of his arms and legs pressed against hers. There was an animal instinct to him, something calm that assumed that what he wanted was what she wanted, too. *Yes, yes, yes,* she thought.

Then a different animal instinct pierced the air. A sound that only a mother in the final stages of labor could produce came around the corner from Laura's room. They each jerked their heads up at the sound, eyes popped wide, comically frozen for a heartbeat. Adrenaline, like a bucket of cold water, splashed over them, snapped them back to reality.

Instantly, she shoved her body into her clothes. Unencumbered by the twisty aggravation of putting on a bra, Alex finished dressing ahead of her, and sprinted out the door.

Josie bolted after him seconds later, running as fast as possible back to Laura's room, her view of Alex's strong body in motion driving her forward. He had reacted like her, moving into action and dropping their amorous involvement in a split second to attend to Laura. It made her feel more connected to him, even as her heart raced and she entered the room disheveled and in chaos on the inside.

And outside.

"So soon?" she asked Mike, whose eyes were the first she could catch. He had his hands up in a helpless gesture as Laura crouched in an impossible twisting of her limbs over the bed, pulling on Dylan's shoulders for support. The grunt that came from her tore Josie in two, just as she imagined Laura was being torn in two right now.

"The waters broke," Alex said. "When did—"

"They just popped them," Dylan explained, standing next to Laura now as Mike tried to catch her eyes and help her to breathe through the pain. She checked the machines, the heart rate, pulse oxygen, all of it from Josie's quick glance looking fine. "Sherri used that long hook thing, put a bunch of towels down, and a ton of fluid poured out."

Sherri calmly, steadily strode into the room, hands tucked neatly in her scrubs as if Laura were the only person in the tiny hospital setting. "It looks like we're ready to meet your daughter."

She and Alex exchanged a look and he backed away, hovering in the doorway, whispering, "Mind if I stay?"

Sherri shook her head imperceptibly and then winked at him and he winked back. *He just loves births,* Josie thought, *even when he isn't the one in charge.*

# CHAPTER FOUR

Josie noticed that Sherri had dispensed with formalities, not even bothering to cover Laura's lower half with a sheet as she palpated her belly. A nurse's assistant tried to cover Laura to give her some privacy, but Josie just shook her head slightly and then Laura shouted in the middle of the exam.

"Don't bother," she said, her voice labored, and then she arched her back to the extent that a pregnant woman in labor can arch anything and tipped her neck back in a strange, unnatural curve.

She watched as the midwife seemed to do mental measurements—and that's exactly what she was doing, Josie realized—to determine how far along everything was, and then a big grin spread across her face and she said the words that everyone in the room had been waiting for. "You are probably complete. The baby definitely dropped."

"Probably?" Dylan asked, eyes bulging. "Can't you do an exam?"

"I'd prefer not to now that the waters are broken. I can if we need to, but—"

A primal sound emerged from Laura. No amount of

mellow meditation and breathing techniques under Mike's tutelage could stop the baby that was barreling out of her birth canal now. A sound like an opera singer being stabbed to death in the middle of an aria poured out of Laura's mouth as she stood, legs wide like a sumo wrestler's. Her face turned a pinkish-purple Josie thought wasn't quite found in nature anywhere *but* childbirth.

"You are likely complete. Laura," she said, quietly, "and you can start pushing now."

"She beat you to it," Dylan muttered, holding Laura's upper arm to give her support.

"I want an epidural!" Laura said, panting after the contraction had subsided. Sherri casually crawled on the floor, under Laura, placing Chux pads beneath her to mop up the fluids, mixed with a tinge of blood, that were coming out in waves as the contraction bore down, then subsided.

Josie would have thought the midwife was watering a plant, not monitoring a patient, given her neutral, calm countenance.

"It's a little late for that, honey," Mike explained, standing behind Laura now, arms ready to slide under hers and catch her.

"But I don't—oh, not more!" She moaned, her head dipping down, breathing slowing as the contraction made her belly tighten, and Josie swore she could see the baby descend, Laura's naked belly on display for everyone now, her navel roiling as the womb tightened so fast and so hard it made Josie wince. The strangled soprano sound came forth again, Mike now holding Laura up, arms under her armpits as she let him support her.

"That's it. That's it," he soothed.

"I can't do this!"

"You *are* doing it," Josie interjected. "You are doing it, Laura." Laura shot her a look of exhausted resignation, a contradictory look. Nothing could save her from what was coming in these next few minutes, and she knew it, Josie knew it—everyone in the room knew it. Paralyzed and horrified, Josie realized her entire role right now distilled down to one, simple job: to usher Laura through the most barbaric pain ever, a pre-condition for meeting her baby daughter. That was it. She couldn't soothe her, or take any of the pain away, or crack jokes to help Laura relax. This was real life, stretching back to the dawn of man, this baby entering the world the same way countless humans had before them, and no amount of intervention could give Josie any power to alleviate Laura's suffering.

The room began to spin and Josie reached out, grabbing onto the arm of a chair. She had never been queasy in her life in a medical situation, but right now was different. This wasn't just some random medical situation, some kid who'd cut his head open, or some Alzheimer's patient who needed ambulatory care or a diaper change. This wasn't an emergency appendectomy or a gunshot wound; it was her best friend having a baby. As Laura bore down, her body folding in half, Dylan and Mike supporting her, a nurse and Sherri pulling on her knees, so that the baby's head could emerge, Josie began a slow descent into a faint.

Strong hands wrapped around her ribcage and guided her to a chair.

"It's okay," Alex murmured in her ear, his voice comforting and solid. "You're fine."

He settled her in place and gently pushed her head down between her knees. "I'll be right back," he said.

Footsteps—she heard them walking away and then quickly come back. A tiny little cup of water shoved in front of her eyes. "Here, drink this. Sip it."

"She okay?" Sherri shouted from across the room, though Josie realized it wasn't a shout, it was a whisper, all of her senses distorted right now.

She couldn't be doing this, falling apart in the one moment Laura needed her most. It was like some sort of cosmic joke, especially a *nurse* losing it in the most stereotypically obvious way possible. A delivery room faint? Come on. This wasn't *A Baby Story* or some stupid trope in a television show.

"You did a great job helping Mike and Dylan take care of themselves," Alex whispered, his hands on her shoulders, her head still dipped down, "but what about you? Have you eaten or had anything to drink other than coffee this entire time?"

*I tasted you,* she almost said. She stopped and thought for a moment, then shook her head slowly.

"Hang on," he said.

The footsteps faded and she heard Laura scream through gritted teeth, a low thrumming sound, guttural and visceral. She'd been to plenty of births, but *that* noise was like a song that came from the base of her spine.

Alex shoved a protein bar in her face.

She batted it away. "I can't eat that."

"Take a bite. Trust me. Your friend is right on the verge and you want to be over there with her, right?"

She looked up and warm, concerned eyes met hers. She closed her lids, embarrassed. "I can't believe I'm freaking out like this and *I'm a nurse.*"

"I'm a doctor and I've done it. It's okay—it's different when it's your friend."

"Really? You've freaked out when one of your friends gave birth?"

"No, I freaked out when my mom was in a car accident."

"Oh." Another shot of adrenaline poured through her, triggering deep memories of her own of parents in car accidents. Alarmed, she asked, "Did she make it?"

"Through the accident? Oh, yeah. She was injured but I panicked. No one wants to lose a parent that way, you know?"

*No shit,* she thought. *I don't recommend it.* But now was not the time to talk about her past.

"We can chit-chat or you can eat the protein bar and

get your ass over there. Which is it going to be?" he said.

The tone in his voice gave her no choice, and she was grateful. Right now options were her enemies.

The protein bar purported to be peanut butter flavored, but it tasted like a combination of wax, sugar, and something else she couldn't put her finger on. But she swallowed it, felt better, chugged the water, and stood. The room stayed in place, and as she scooted over to hold Laura's hand she turned back and mouthed, *Thank you.*

He just smiled without showing his teeth, crossed his arms over his chest and leaned against the door frame to watch.

She was just in time as Laura bent in half again, her face turning an impossible shade of purple, and Mike stooped down to look at the opening where his child's head began to emerge.

"Laura, you're *so* close," he said.

Dylan craned over Laura's shoulder—he was propping her up from behind and unable to see.

Josie saw a mirror, a rather large one on a stand in the corner, and caught Sherri's eye. "Can I get the mirror?" she said.

"Ask Laura," Sherri answered.

"Laura, do you want to see the baby?"

Laura pulled out of the pain and looked at her with emerald eyes that were glassy and exhausted and exhilarated all at once and said, "Yes, please," and then bent down, pushing with all of her might as Josie wheeled the mirror over and positioned it so that Dylan and Laura could watch.

The next twenty seconds went by in such a blur that Josie, years later, would try to remember the exact sequence of events but never quite construct it. A growling scream from Laura, the sound of something popping, and then a slick, slithery sound as Sherri held the baby's head and one shoulder and then told Laura to push. The sound of relieved laughter, silence, and a baby's cry all mingled together into a joyful noise that would pull Josie through times of difficulty in the future.

The baby was, indeed, a girl. She caught that from a quick glance and as Sherri handled the wet, slimy, squalling little creature and placed it directly on Laura's naked breasts, Josie looked over to see Alex wipe away a single tear from the corner of his eye and then step silently out of the room.

"Oh my God, she's perfect," Mike said, bending over. The baby wrapped four little fingers around his extended index finger and his tears crested over, one dropping on Laura's chest, the other on his shirt.

Dylan stared at the baby slack-jawed, eyes wide but not wet, and then reached over tentatively to stroke her head. The baby opened her mouth and what had been a little, mewling cry turned into quite a lusty sound, Sherri smiling and gently laying a warming blanket over the baby.

Laura stared at the creature on her in complete, shocked silence. Josie was with her—right with her, in fact, because she couldn't think of a single thing that she wanted to say right now, or could say, that would match the majesty of the moment. And then Laura said the one thing that made the tears come for every single person in the room.

"I did it," she said quietly. With one finger she stroked the baby's cheek and the baby looked up, eyes wide and calm, mouth closing, puckering, the cries gone, her face alert, following her mother's voice. "Welcome to the world," Laura laughed, all her pain seemingly gone, her face lit up with such rapturous joy that Josie thought it was a manifestation of the divine, right here in these seconds.

Mike and Dylan leaned in, both kissing the top of Laura's head simultaneously, and then Laura whispered, "Welcome to the world...baby Jillian."

# CHAPTER FIVE

Josie got ready to go back to the hospital to see Mike, Dylan, Laura, and baby Jillian as if it were prom night. Five different outfit changes, two different re-dos on her hair, and make-up for the first time in ages. Add in the fact that the second Dylan would take one look at her she'd get teased for the next six months about her appearance, and all this fuss proved one simple thing: she was a *complete* idiot.

Alex had just finished a twenty-four-hour shift and there was no way that she would run into him. What she had was one big crush on a doctor she'd almost given it up for in the on-call room while her best friend was writhing in pain in another room—pain that was the result of doing exactly what Josie and Alex had almost done.

*Almost* exactly. Josie—unlike Laura—would use a condom. Plus she was on the pill.

That was one certainty in Josie's very uncertain life. No babies—not now.

Not ever.

She'd decided that a long time ago, even though her mind flip-flopped along with her heart, especially yesterday when she'd held that tiny, mewling infant in her arms, cradled close, warm, and new, and innocent, and just wanting to be loved. Love she could give. It was the whole idea of stability and emotional care-taking and being a good role model that scared the ever-loving hell out of her.

Her fear that she could never rise to the occasion, could never be a good parent because she had not been parented well herself, was what made her freeze in place at the thought of being handed an infant and told, "Love this! Mother this! You're it!" One hundred percent in charge of this entire human being.

No way.

She was one hundred percent in charge of *herself* and she couldn't even manage to figure out what to wear to go see her best friend and her new baby. For that matter, most days she could barely make her socks match and remember to pay her bills on time. Being the sole caretaker of a new life was something so far out of her grasp that Laura was suddenly catapulted into a whole new category of person that made Josie feel smaller. It wasn't that Laura did that—it was Josie who did it to herself.

When her friends started having babies—not her friends back home, who spat them out at nineteen and twenty by accident and were little more than babies raising babies—no, it was when her *best* friend had an accidental pregnancy but turned it into a loving family, *that* was when Josie's world view was shaken to the core.

Josie was one of a handful of people from her graduating class who had actually gotten out of her little town in Ohio, and not a single one of the women she'd known who had babies young had ever left. That was one reason she was so extraordinarily paranoid about birth control. In her world, the fathers faded away and weren't part of the equation, and so it was with great incongruity that she watched the saga of Jillian's *two* dads unfold.

Why was Jillian's birth triggering so many of her past issues at the same time that she was grappling with some very right-now issues, all wrapped up in the tall, dark, and handsome Dr. Alex Derjian? Every inhale, every exhale made her think of him, how his hands were on her, his lips exploring her in the elevator, how hot just being with him in the on-call room felt, how far she would have gone if baby Jillian's emergence into the world hadn't interrupted them.

*Thanks, kid.*

She wasn't sure whether to think that in her usual sarcastic tone, or whether it was genuinely heartfelt. Giving herself to Alex so soon might have been an enormous mistake, and now she was relieved that they'd been interrupted by nature, the visceral reality of what happens when two (or three...) people have sex and biology marches in its unyielding path toward fulfilling its pre-programmed destiny. No birth control? Then you roll the dice and take your chances.

Time to go see Laura and her little chance.

* * *

Alex walked into the hospital feeling more uncomfortable than he'd felt the first day of his residency. He *never* set foot on hospital grounds unless it was his shift. He was not the type to hang out, trying to curry favor or get in extra face time so that it looked like he was more serious about his work. When he was on shift, he was one hundred percent there—in mind, body, and spirit—and when he wasn't on shift he stayed the hell away, because otherwise this job could completely consume his soul.

Walking into the hospital wearing jeans, a polo shirt, and sunglasses made him feel like a civilian. He headed in and, on autopilot, found his body directing him to the changing area where he would put on scrubs and turn into a doctor, morphing from a human being to someone who was supposed to be both humble and god-like; know everything but be flexible when a patient had an idea that he had never heard of; be proficient at paperwork and yet drop everything the second a medical emergency came up; have outstanding social skills and yet know when to keep his mouth shut; be gloriously ecstatic for a family when the birth of a healthy little baby came to fruition after a long labor—and be respectfully mournful when it didn't.

Doctors—and especially OBs—were expected to be omnipresent, omniscient in some ways, and to be everything for everyone. And for some cases, to stay as far away as possible so that nature could do its work.

Entering the elevator after backtracking a bit from the changing area, he pushed the button for the maternity ward and then realized that he was going to the postpartum wing, furiously pressing a different number as he shook his head. A bundle of nerves this morning, he found himself worried about what he was wearing, which was insanely stupid because he never worried about what he was wearing. He just put on clean clothes and went about his day.

He knew exactly why he was here on his day off and why he was so nervous. It was a little bundle of joy—but it wasn't Laura's baby. It was Josie and the taste of something far outside his expectations that he'd gotten yesterday with her—and not just the raunchy taste that he had thoroughly enjoyed, too—that made him want more. His life was so circumscribed—work, the occasional trip with his grandfather, and more work—that when a flash of something deeper, of a connection so intense that he overrode all professional instinct and nearly took her in the on-call room—when that came along and was handed to him in the form of fate, he needed to seize it.

As the elevator doors opened onto the postpartum wing, he walked up to the main desk, took his sunglasses off, and asked for Laura's room. Just as the nurse started to tell him, "I'm so sorry, sir, are you a member of the family?" and he realized that he wasn't even recognized up here without his scrubs on, Dylan walked past with a stuffed giraffe taller than either of them.

"Hey, doctor…" Dylan's features changed to embarrassed confusion as he pointed and then splayed out his palm in a gesture of desperation, trying to retrieve Alex's name. "Doctor…you were there last night…"

"Alex. Alex Derjian," he said, extending his hand.

Dylan shook it with great power, which Alex managed to match, the two practically arm-wrestling in front of the desk on the postpartum wing to prove their firm grips were manly enough. Mike, the other father (*what a strange phrase, and yet it rolled through Alex's mind as if it were normal*) was a few steps behind, holding a tasteful bouquet of Mylar balloons attached to a small bunch of flowers in a mug.

"Alex," Mike said, those placid eyes meeting his, filling with a calm that seemed to make all of the nervousness of the morning dissipate.

Dylan nudged Mike in the ribs. "You remember his name?"

"Of course I remember his name. How could I forget the name of the guy who almost delivered our baby?"

Dylan turned a slight shade of pink and looked away. "Yeah…good point." Then he perked up. "But at least I didn't almost faint at the birth like *some* people."

Dylan's eyes were focused on a point behind Alex and he turned to the right to see Josie standing there, hands on hips, one leg cocked higher than the other, a sour smirk on her face as she said, "Oh, yeah? Well, at least I didn't show my ass to—" She froze, turning and realizing that it was Alex standing right there.

*I wouldn't mind seeing your ass,* he thought, biting back the offer.

"Alex," she said, various parts of her tensing and relaxing at the same time, her body language changing.

Something was completely different about her this morning. As he took a good, long look, still drawing on that calm composure that Mike seemed to have infused in him, he almost laughed. It looked like she had gone through the same morning ritual that he had, though in feminine terms: hair done, makeup, and an outfit he imagined she never actually wore. If she had put that much concern into her appearance this morning, could it be that she had hoped that she would run into *him* as much as he had tried to manipulate running into *her*?

The only way to know would be to let the next few minutes unfold the way that he had planned them.

\* \* \*

Leave it to Dylan to make some kind of dig to make her look bad in front of Dr. Perfect.

"Alex. Hi," she barked, shocked and consumed with a tingling feeling of realization at just how close she was to him, as if having him in proximity to her like this sent some sort of electric jolt through her. Which, apparently, it did—and that made the connection between her thinking brain and her mouth shut down entirely at the same time that the floodgates between her heart and her nether regions opened with a giant, roaring tidal wave.

"Hi, Josie," he said, reaching out and down, touching her shoulder briefly. The slight gesture of welcome may as well have been a flamethrower lighting her entire body on fire.

The awkward silence between the four of them was broken—finally—when Mike pointed to Dylan's enormous stuffed giraffe and said, "Meet Jillian's bodyguard."

"What's wrong with it?" Dylan asked, shrugging. He looked exhausted but exhilarated all at once, and Josie looked down and realized that he was wearing two different shoes. The night must have been tough—she knew they had taken the last twenty-four hours in shifts.

"That thing definitely won't fit in a bassinet," she found herself saying, and Alex laughed, a polite, slightly over-done chuckle that made her realize that he was just as interested in her as she was in him. And just as nervous *about* that interest as she was.

Dammit.

That meant that her awkwardness and his awkwardness were on display for Mike and Dylan to absorb and to amuse themselves with.

As if he read her mind, Dylan, with a mirthful look in those eyes, turned all of his attention to her and said, "What are you and Alex up to?"

Alex's eyebrows shot up and he looked down at her, just over his shoulder, and it was his turn to put hands on hips and say, "What *are* we up to?"

A sinkhole needed to open up and swallow her. Instead, Sarcastic Josie kicked it. "We," she said, fanning the air between the two of them with a hand that ping ponged back and forth, "aren't up to anything. *I* am here to visit my best friend who just shat an eight-pound thing out of a hole that is not meant to have eight-pound things come out of it."

"Yes, it is," Alex argued. "That's exactly how nature intended it."

*Fuck.* He had her there.

"If that's how nature intended it, then we all know God was a man because no woman would do that to other women."

It was the best she could do, and she stormed off to Laura's room. Fortunately she knew the number and she walked in to find Laura there, sitting up, her legs under a thin hospital blanket. With baby Jillian in front of her, completely undressed and unwrapped from her little burrito blanket, diaper in place, Laura bent gently over with the baby's entire foot in her mouth.

"Umm…hi?" Josie said, waving slightly. "The hospital food isn't good here, I guess?"

Laura slipped the baby's foot out of her mouth and started laughing quietly. Then she clutched her abdomen and winced. Josie wondered why. There had been no C-section, so why would it hurt to laugh?

The baby was asleep and startled at the vibration of the bed and the sound of their voices. Laura quickly swaddled her back into the little wrap and pulled her close, nestling the baby's cheek against Laura's bare chest. Laura held a finger up to her lips and Josie nodded silently, creeping carefully over to the chair next to the bed and settling in as Jillian settled down, little even breaths indicating that she'd fallen back asleep.

"Has motherhood turned you into a cannibal?" she asked.

Laura shook her head. She looked almost as tired as Dylan, with her face puffed and swollen a bit, blood vessels all around the ring of her eye socket bright red and popped, a sprinkling of them on her cheeks as well. Her face, though, exuded joy. And it was contagious, for Josie started to feel it too, seeping in and replacing the awkwardness and the desire that she had just felt out in the hallway with Alex.

"I just...she's so beautiful, Josie," Laura said. "I had this impulse to see if her foot would fit in my mouth."

"That must be a motherhood thing."

"I guess so. I don't know. I'm only on day one of this and there's really no manual."

Josie made it a point to crane her body around Laura and Jillian to look at the stack of parenting books and infant care novels on her bedside, all provided by Dylan, Mike, and Dylan's parents. "I beg to differ—there are plenty of manuals."

Laura rolled her eyes and sniffed with a derisive look. "Those will tell me the basics but no one tells you that minute by minute, hour by hour, you have to make this up on your own. You have to wing it." She lowered her voice to a whisper and leaned in. "It's like...the breastfeeding...nobody really explains what it feels like when that baby latches on or how, no matter how many consultants come in and try to help you with lactation, it's on *you*."

This was not the conversation Josie had expected to have with her best friend today. What was she supposed to say back? She had nothing in common on this one, and so she defied her own natural state of talkativeness and just nodded. This was her future with Laura, wasn't it? Lots of nodding, lots of absolutely not understanding what Laura would be going through, and a growing divide as she watched her best friend focus her entire life on this child and on the family that she was building with Dylan and Mike.

She'd spent years—decades, really, almost two decades—since her father had died doing nothing but escaping instability and seeking a quiet, peaceful existence. A safe existence that gave her the time to think. And all that escaping and seeking had ended—disappeared, really—the moment the baby was born. Josie had reevaluated everything that she'd been doing as an adult, through the lens of watching other people, like her best friend, grow up.

It made her want to do anything *but*. It made her want to grab Alex and fuck him in the on-call room, made her want to go spend outrageous amounts of money that she didn't have. It made her want to go on a spur-of-the-moment trip to Paris because she could—and Laura couldn't. Josie could do all of those things, and now she couldn't do them the same way.

It felt as if her friend's choices had stripped her of assumptions and deep, deep down in an abyss inside her that had a bottom she hadn't touched yet, she knew that this was good.

But on the surface? It was chaotic and overwhelming and too much for her to handle right now.

"How are you feeling?" Her eyes were riveted to the baby, a pinkish-purple creature with swollen eyelids and little dots of baby acne all over her face. She didn't look like anyone until Laura pulled the tiny, thin cotton cap off her head and smoothed the little strands of wavy blonde hair.

Was Mike the father? This was going to drive Josie a little crazy until she knew. Though it really wasn't her business to know, Laura and the guys had made it her business, so now she was eager to learn the truth.

"The testing," Laura said quietly, "is already in progress. Her blood type's not conclusive, so we had to send it for DNA matching after all."

Josie nodded, flustered by how quickly this had all happened. "Oh....." Her voice trailed off. Nowadays, the lab didn't have to give up if the mathematics of Mom's blood type plus Possible-Dads' blood types turned up an inconclusive result. A simple prick of the guys' fingers, and the baby's, plus a bunch of paperwork, was all they needed. For a few hundred dollars out of pocket and about a week or three of waiting, Jillian's idyllic life of three parents, all showering her with adoration, could still be shattered.

Because it was one thing to imagine happily-ever-afters...once they really knew, for certain, that it was Mike or Dylan, what would that mean? How compassionate and understanding can one man be when he imagines himself to be a biological parent and then science brings all that to a screeching halt with DNA analysis? Does the science override the love?

And only Josie would know the true identity of the bio dad, anyway—unless the three changed their hive mind at a future time. Josie had been analyzing the baby's features to get clues to her paternity. Thick blonde hair? Must be Mike's. Blue-black eyes that darkened by the hour? Dylan's. Long, slim surgeon's fingers? Mike's. A little chin that jutted out like a fighter's? Dylan's. It was maddening. Deep in her thoughts as she stared at the baby in Laura's lap, a greater, meta-awareness that maybe no one else was doing this struck Josie between the eyes.

Maybe no one else was trying to figure this out.

Maybe it was just *her*.

A baby's beginning should be about the baby and not about the wondering. None of the three really seemed to care—it was a formality that Laura wanted out of the way. Respecting that was part and parcel of respecting Laura and the three of them.

Josie put her hand on Laura's and smiled, catching her tired green eyes. "It's okay, Laura. We will do whatever we need to do and make sure that all the paperwork is taken care of. You don't need to worry about that right now."

"The only problem," Laura said, "is that the nurses here told me I need to sign the birth certificate within ten days of Jillian's birth. So I don't know if the tests will be back in time for that."

Josie frowned. "You can amend a birth certificate later, right?"

"I think so," Laura whispered.

"Why don't you just pick one guy and then amend it later if it's wrong?"

Tears filled Laura's eyes and Josie felt guilty for upsetting her. Then Laura inhaled deeply and her face shifted to a more practical look. "You're right. You pick." She pulled a piece of paper from a sheath on the nightstand.

"What?"

"I'll sign this. I already filled most of it out." It was a birth certificate form. "And you just add the name of the father. I don't want to know who you pick. And then when the DNA tests come back, if it's wrong, we amend. If it's right, we leave it alone."

"Geez, you don't ask much from your best friend, do you?"

Laura nudged her. "C'mon. Do it for me?"

Josie bit her lower lip, grabbed the form, and just picked the first guy who came into her mind—other than Dr. Alex. Scribbling quickly, she folded the form and handed it to Laura, who put it in an envelope.

"Done," Laura said, a huge sigh escaping from her.

*Not quite*, thought Josie.

The grateful, tired smile that greeted her words was all Josie needed. Well, maybe not all. "May I?" she asked, reaching for the baby.

Laura smiled and leaned forward to hand Jillian to her. As she shifted, though, she winced, flinching with a wretched look on her face. The calm but tired look was replaced with a tight, pained expression, then a deep breath. Two deep breaths. Three. Ouch. Josie imagined that her nether regions must look like hamburger right now—really nasty hamburger—and knew that the ice packs and the Lidocaine spray were probably the only thing keeping Laura sane. That and baby Jillian.

Josie very carefully, tentatively, took the baby, gingerly wrapping herself around so that her whole tiny body was supported with the length of Josie's arms and both of Josie's hands. She felt so lightweight, like a kickball, one of those big ones at Toys 'R Us that you grab and expect to be heavier than they are. Not even eight pounds, little Jillian was a heavy soul, one born into an incredibly unique situation with a family structure that made Josie see it in a different light for the first time.

How would society view the child of two men and one woman? Getting people to understand that some kids had two mommies and some kids had two daddies was hard enough. How was little Jillian supposed to walk into preschool and announce that she had two daddies *and* a mommy? This kid was going to have to be tough, to know herself deeply, to stand up to the taunts, to neutralize ignorance. Jillian was up to the task—but was Josie?

A deep, steely protectiveness poured into Josie as the baby snurgled and then sighed, nestling against Josie's arm. Josie smiled and kissed her little head, breathing the baby smell deeply and smiling harder at its sweetness. All worries for the future could wait. Huffing this newborn reminded her that life was good, and this was already shaping up to be a fabulous day.

Seeing Alex had sent her body into overdrive, senses alight and primed for something. Would he really be interested in her today, or was yesterday just some sort of fluke? Dressed in casual clothes, he seemed to be here not as part of a shift, but for a personal reason.

Was *she* the personal reason? The kiss in the elevator, the near-sex in the on-call room, his steady support as she nearly fainted—did it really add up to more? Maybe she hadn't misread a damn thing. Maybe he was as attracted to her as she was to him and made a special trip on his day off not to check in on Jillian and Laura, but to check *her* out.

"Is that Dr. Alex's voice I heard out in the hallway?" Laura asked. As they both looked, the giant stuffed head of a giraffe walked into the room as if it were animated and stalking all newborn babies on the wing. After the head, the neck entered the room, then the body, and finally Dylan, as if the giraffe were in control, pulling him in. His grinning face was stretched from ear to ear with a level of excitement and love that was contagious.

Josie matched his grin and looked down at Jillian and said, "That's one of your crazy dads. He's the craziest one." As Mike came in, she went on. "The *other* daddy is calm and peaceful and placid on the outside, but he's kind of weird, too. You'll just have to deal with it. Your mama is unconventional, but in a different way, so...Jillian, the deck is really stacked against you. Good thing you have your Aunt Josie to keep you normal."

Jillian's three parents all snorted in unison, and Alex walked into the room just in time to overhear Dylan tease back, "If teabagging the set of balls from Jeddy's in front of an audience is normal, then—"

"*Shh,*" Laura said, noticing Alex. "Hi, Doctor...I forgot your last name," she said, reaching for a glass of water and chugging it, a sheepish look on her face.

"Alex. Alex Derjian," he said, reintroducing himself,

shaking Laura's hand. "You had quite a bit on your plate last night, Laura. It's no wonder you don't remember my name."

"Thanks," she replied, tipping her head at the baby, who now rested in Josie's arms, her little pink cheeks slack with sleep.

"Teabagging?" He cocked one eyebrow and looked at Josie. "It sounds like I interrupted a very interesting conversation."

Shooting daggers at Dylan, who just smirked, she said, "Not as interesting as Dylan's butt—"

"Hey!" Dylan snapped. "Man Code says we don't talk about that."

"Man Code says you don't show somebody your brown starfish, either," she retorted.

Alex and Mike managed to stay neutral, their faces impassive, but from the flare of their nostrils she could tell they were trying not to laugh.

"Show what?" Alex finally asked, playing dumb.

Dylan reached out to shake his hand once again. "That's my man."

Changing topics, Alex stared at the baby pointedly and reached toward Josie. "May I?"

Josie caught his eyes. He looked just as good this morning as he did yesterday. Clean shaven now, the same spicy but dark scent she'd noticed yesterday coming off of him again. His face was open and he really did just want to hold the baby—she knew that.

She also knew that he wanted a lot of other things, including her.

Hands outstretched, she saw in his face the expression of a man meant to have children one day, a man capable of the deep love Laura, Mike, and Dylan had for the baby in Josie's arms.

The tiny, helpless baby whose entire existence rested in Josie's arms. Arms that could drop her. Or– not that she ever would—harm her. There was an element of unreality to it. How newborns were so utterly dependent on the kindness of larger human beings for their simple survival. Paralysis set in as the idea infused her, making her muscles freeze, her mind lock up, her body seize.

"Josie?" he asked. His arms were outstretched in a different way now, a bit more alarmed, the muscles taut, his knees bent slightly as if bracing himself to act swiftly. "Your face is pale the way it was yesterday at the birth. Hand the baby back to Laura," he said quietly, a soothing tone that cut through her ever-increasing panic.

Instinct kicked in and Laura responded immediately to Alex's words, lowering her voice as Mike and Dylan slowly stepped closer to the bed. Nodding, Josie kept her eyes on Alex and, without breaking the gaze, turned her body to rotate the baby toward Laura, who took her. The relief of not having those not-quite-eight pounds in her arms, of *not* being the only person in the world who could control Jillian's destiny, made Josie sag with a sigh.

"Excuse me," she said quietly. "I'll be right back."

Patting Laura's knee, she made her way out of the room without another word, deeply humiliated and embarrassed for reasons she didn't understand.

Out in the hallway, the shakes came, violent tremors in her fingers, her wrists, and her arms. She tried to walk it off, her eyes surveying the layout, looking for the water fountain that she knew should be wedged between two bathrooms. There it was. Homing in on it, she walked robotically toward it, her body stiff with purpose and sorrow and embarrassment.

As she drank greedily from the fountain, her mind turned into a splintered fog. What was it about this baby that was making her lose her mind? It wasn't just jealousy. That played a small part, certainly—not jealousy of the baby itself, but of the shift in her friendship with Laura. Something more must be at play, though, to trigger this kind of response in her.

A deep, thin thread of resentment and resignation shot

through her. The answer was there; it was buried, though, so deeply that she had no desire to dig that crap up again. *It'll come when it comes*, a voice said in her mind, that damn voice that came out when she least expected.

Her own childhood smacked up against what was supposed to be a joyful day for her best friend. *Friends*. She needed to start including Mike and Dylan in that circle. They welcomed her—albeit with limits—and it was time that she welcomed them, too.

"Josie?" The voice behind her felt like an embrace, though he stood far enough away from her to give her some privacy and space. She wanted to turn around, throw her arms around him, and have his hand press against her back, the other buried in her hair as he soothed the confusion out of her. Arousal should have come next, from that image, but it didn't. A deeper, more intense desire to *talk* to him, to confide in someone what was going on inside her, came bursting forth instead. Social acceptability trumped all as she swallowed her emotions, everything that pressed at the base of her throat in a giant lump. She pretended she didn't hear him, taking an extra gulp of water to help her swallow ever so much.

"Josie?" he said a little louder, not backing off. Firmness in his words nearly made her jump. Alex wasn't going to let this go.

*Good. Don't back off*, she thought. *Keep trying. You're going to need the persistence.*

She opened her eyes, swallowed hard, and turned around, not even bothering to pretend.

"Alex," she said haltingly. "I just…I don't even know what that was." Tears pooled along the lower rims of her eyes and she breathed slowly through her nose, cursing her outfit, her eye makeup, her not-so-comfortable shoes, all the preening of womanhood she normally shunned.

"I do." The look in his eyes was one of evaluation and empathy and something else—a camaraderie that wasn't supposed to be there.

"You do?" she asked. "Then tell me, because I have no idea."

"You look like every new mom who realizes the responsibility they've just taken on."

"I'm not the new mom," she scoffed.

"You may not be the mother here, but you have a deep connection to Laura and…" He shrugged, one hand on his hip, the gesture casual. There was none of the stiltedness of new attraction to him. "Every new mom goes through it, and that sickly feeling when you realize that you are God to that infant is your humanity coming out."

"Then I have an awful lot of humanity," she whispered.

Saying that was an accident. The words had been in her mind, but poured out of her mouth only as a reflection of the exhaustion of the past couple of days.

"You do," he said, stepping forward, bridging the gap between them. One more step and her breath halted. Finally, four feet from her, he paused, waiting three beats. He took another step and then reached out, touching a lock of hair that had fallen in front of her face, brushing it aside.

"I can see that," he said. "Your deep humanity. I think that's why this seems so…" He pressed his lips together in a smile and shook his head slowly.

"Impossible?" she offered.

"Serendipitous," he ventured.

"You win." She gave him a half-smile. "I like your word better."

His hands started to stroke her shoulder and she could feel the sickly sense inside her drain out, as if his fingertips just smoothed it away.

"I think…" Alex said, taking one more step closer until he was hovering over her. Her body absorbed his heat, and she was aware of every pore of skin on his neck, every bit of stubble that had grown in the past couple hours. Her fingers itched to touch, but held back, for reasons she began to hate.

"I think," he repeated, "that your answer may be more accurate."

"I can admit when I'm wrong." *Where the hell did that come from?*

He broke the space between them, bending down and planting a soft kiss on her cheekbone. He whispered in her ear, "I enjoy an impossible challenge.."

"Josie?" Laura's voice caught her off guard. At the end of the hall, silhouetted by the light behind her, her best friend stood in the threshold of her postpartum room, the gown diaphanous, wearing those little paper slippers that no one liked. "What happened?" Laura called. "Are you sick?"

"She's fine," Alex answered for her, his arm sliding around her shoulders, the comfort both overriding the sexual tension from the day past and tapping into it in a very different way. He guided her back toward Laura's room. "A big case of nerves."

"Nerves?" said Laura. "Josie? About what?" Long blonde hair poured over Laura's shoulders, covering one bare breast, the nipple tucked inside a flap of cloth. Modest Laura, who wouldn't go to the dining halls in college in her pajamas or without freshly done hair, was standing in a hospital hallway with her boob hanging out. Josie laughed inside at the incongruity.

"About holding your baby," Alex answered.

"I wasn't nervous about holding the baby." Josie broke away from him. "That is ridiculous. I've held hundreds of babies."

He shook his head as they reached Laura. "Not the same—it's never the same when you hold one that means so much to you."

Tears filled Laura's eyes. "That's how I feel too—like I've just been handed this tiny thing and its very breath relies on me."

"That's because it does," said Mike, who joined the conversation in the hallway. "And on me," he added.

"And me," said a voice from behind as a giant giraffe head poked through the door.

A loud, lusty cry came from the bassinet in the room and Laura took off in a near-sprint, stopping after two steps and then gingerly finishing the trek to Jillian. Mike yawned, covering his mouth and apologizing in muffled tones through the sound. At 8:30 in the morning the yawn would have seemed out of place to anyone who didn't know just how sleep-deprived they all were.

"We're going to go home and get some real sleep as soon as the baby settles down," Mike said. "Laura can manage for a few hours, plus they'll take Jillian—" He stopped short as the name came out of him, brow furrowed in a pensive expression.

"It'll take some getting used to, won't it?" Dylan commented. His face mirrored Mike's.

"It's okay, though." Laura's voice was strong and focused. "Her name suits her."

Dylan took the crying baby from Laura and began singing softly, a song Josie didn't know. The baby quieted immediately and focused her cloudy, bluish-brown eyes right on him. Mugging for her, he made cooing sounds, keeping Jillian transfixed. Josie hoped her dad had been like that with her when she was a little bundle of new flesh and love like Jillian. The unexpected thought made it suddenly hard to breathe, and she wanted to crawl out of her own skin.

"I think I'll go soon, too," Josie said, giving Dylan a short salute. "You guys are carrying on totally fine." *Nothing's fine*, she thought, edging toward the door.

Dylan handed the baby off to Laura and turned to the stuffed animal he'd brought, animating the eight-foot giraffe. "Hear that? It's fine, Daddy Mike." The giraffe was the only thing in the room taller than Mike, forcing him to look up to it. Standing on tiptoes, Mike gave it a big smooch on the mouth.

"Daddy Mike? That's what you're calling each other?

Daddy Mike and Daddy Dylan?" Josie asked.

"What else are we supposed to call ourselves?"

"How about Billionaire One and Billionaire Two?" Josie smirked. Laura gave her a warning look, but clearly was amused. Alex stared at all four faces, bemused.

"There's an inside joke here that I'm not getting."

"There are a *lot* of inside jokes here that you're not getting, dude," Dylan replied.

"Yeah," Josie said, looking hard at Dylan. "It's—"

Laura, Dylan, and Mike, from behind, all shouted, "Complicated!"

Frowning, Alex looked around the room again, then zeroed in on Josie. "Since they're so complicated, how about you and I go do something *simple?*"

"That's awfully forward of you," she said, pulling her shoulders back, pretending to be coy.

"I meant let's go for a walk. That simple enough for you?"

"Oh." She couldn't think of anything else to say. Getting out of the hospital would go a long way toward helping her to figure out how the hell she could get back to some semblance of stable. "Okay." She and Alex waved and left the new family to settle the baby and say their own goodbyes.

# CHAPTER SIX

As they rode the elevators down to the main entrance, Josie's mind flipped through three thousand one hundred and twenty-two scenarios, most of them involving being pinned to the side of the elevator wall.

Damn *Grey's Anatomy* for putting these ideas in her head. Ever since that show had come on, every hospital had a running joke about doctors and nurses having sex in elevators—and here they were, completely alone, riding down four flights. The half-smirk on his face as they stared straight ahead made her wonder what Alex was thinking right now.

The nearest coffee shop was a good five blocks away, and Alex turned toward it, which told Josie that this was going to be no simple, short stroll around the hospital grounds, but more like a...date.

Date? The word seemed too formal, as if she were ascribing something to this interaction that gave it more meaning than it really had. He walked slowly, and she was grateful; his long legs could have taken strides that made her walk as quickly as an officious little child. He didn't seem bothered by having to walk slower. That relaxed, casual nature made him comfortable with whatever situation he found himself in. His outfit was pleasant and the way that his pants hung on his hips and cupped his ass was much more appealing to look at than even the flowering dogwoods that lined many of the homes they walked past.

From all appearances, Alex shared none of the melodrama she was experiencing in every cell of her body. Damn him. His face was open, tipped slightly up, as if soaking in the rays. A beautiful May day like this in the Boston area was not unheard of, but it was certainly rare. She was happy to be outside with a light breeze blowing through her hair, strolling with someone who represented a new beginning. Giving herself that one concession of hope allowed her shoulders to lower, her body willed to relax by her mind.

They walked pleasantly without any tension between them, despite the tension within her, for about half a block, when he turned to her and smiled down, asking, "Do you know this area?"

"Only from picking up shifts here. I know we're headed toward the center of town, where we'll find restaurants and coffee shops."

He nodded. "Yeah, I was thinking about going to the little one."

"Anyplace but Jeddy's," she said, and he laughed.

"You've been there?" he asked.

"Who hasn't been there?" she responded quickly.

He shrugged. "That's true. Heck, even my grandpa's been there."

"Really? That doesn't surprise me. I think that place has been around since before your grandfather's father."

"Well, I don't think he went there, because he was in Armenia. Lived there his whole life."

"You're one of the many Watertown Armenians."

"My name should have given it away," he answered.

"Anything that ends with -ian, right?" She laughed. "I come from Ohio, so I had to learn when I moved here.

Mendham isn't exactly unusual."

"No, I'd imagine it's not. English?"

She nodded. "I guess so, I don't know. Nobody from my family came from anywhere as far as I'm concerned. We don't exactly have in-depth genealogists running around in my branch of the family tree."

He paused and frowned—a look of curiosity, not of upset. "What do you mean?"

"I'm the first one…to get away," she said. "I was about to say I was the first one to go to college, but that's not true. My father had a master's degree. But even he never left central Ohio. My whole family is from there, and is still there. My mom's back home, and I go back every year, but mostly to visit my niece. Well, she's not really my niece—we're cousins—but she's so much younger that I…"

Why was she talking about this? She could feel her mouth moving, the words coming out. She was functional and cognitively grounded, in that the sentences had proper syntax, the words made sense, and yet they poured out of her mouth like something in a cartoon bubble, that went on, and on, and on.

"Oh, look," she said, cutting herself off, "there's the coffee shop." It was lame, but it got her to stop spewing nonsensical shit out of her mouth.

"What's your favorite drink?" he asked. "Wait"—he interrupted her before she could even answer—"let me guess."

She stopped, planted her hands on her hips. "Go ahead."

"You're a…latte kind of person."

She cocked her head, looked down, thinking about that for a moment. He was right. Should she tell him he was right, or should she make him sweat it out?

"C'mon, I'm right, aren't I?"

She looked up, surprised by the confidence in his voice. He really thought he knew her already. "You're right. Lattes. Boring. Occasionally, I'll have a triple if I need the extra caffeine, but…"

"Espresso doesn't have as much caffeine as you'd think," they said in unison.

This time she flinched, but in a completely different way. "You *know* that?" she asked.

"*You* know that?" he countered.

They both laughed.

"How about me? Guess my drink," he said, waving at his chest, as they slowly made their way into the threshold of the coffee shop.

"I know you like coffee with milk from our…interaction," she said slowly, "the other night."

"Interaction?" He smiled. "Is that the word you use for it? I have plenty of better words."

"I'll bet you do."

The barista looked at them expectantly. Josie could feel eyes on her. It was as if everyone else in the room were from a different planet. As all his attention was on her, completely focused, waiting for something that she knew she was capable of giving, but hadn't known that until this moment.

"Macchiato," she snapped.

He pulled his head back, a bit perplexed. "What?"

"Macchiato. You're a macchiato guy. Not that Starbucks crap, either."

The barista flashed a giant grin at her. This was an independent coffee house, built into what had probably once been a barber's shop. The long, narrow space was shabby chic, with painted chalkboard walls and a handwritten menu colorfully chalked up daily. The biggest investment in this space was in the espresso machine, which looked like something out of the Steampunk Exhibition at the Charles River Museum of Industry.

"You're right," he said quietly. "How'd you know?"

"You're *that* kind of guy," she said, leaning back against the counter, needing the support to say what she was about to say. "You can sense, and taste, and feel the subtleties of life. You don't need to cover up anything with a bunch of milk and a ton of sweetener to make something bitter go down. You savor what you seek, and you know something special when you find it." The end of her sentence came out husky and dark, like a gasp. This felt like sitting in a confessional, with Alex the priest on the other side of the screen. Except, *thank you, Jesus*, Alex was no priest.

"Macchiato, huh?" he said with a lopsided grin. "You're right." He shook his head slowly, looked at the barista. "A latte and a macchiato, please." The barista just jutted his chin up in acknowledgment and got to work on the giant, shiny espresso machine. "I do like to taste life exactly as it is," he said, gesturing to Josie to take a table. There weren't many, most of the spots taken by people using the coffee shop as a pseudo-office, but there were two, and he grabbed the most private.

She sat down, grateful to give her shaking legs a rest. Talking about herself, talking about anyone, in such true terms wasn't something she was used to. But she'd done it, she'd actually told him something deep about her soul and about how she saw him, and he was still here.

This wasn't like in the movies, where the scene ends on this dramatic, intense moment and then switches over to three days later, with the main female character engaging in chatty banter with her best friend, confessing what had happened. Josie couldn't skip to a charming reflection that perfectly encapsulated all of the heroine's foibles and her journey toward accepting that love conquers all.

Oh, no.

Instead, she found herself fumbling to know what to do with her hands, her hips, her knees and feet, and the millions of brain cells flying fast and furious inside her skull, trying to compose a sense of self by making it up as she went along, second by second in Alex's presence.

He leaned forward on the tabletop and invaded her space as much as she could handle. Deep breaths helped center her as she willed herself not to pull back. It would have been too easy to lean casually into the chair's back and pretend that it was her sarcastic facade that made her so casual, so blasé. It was the comfortable and the known, but…at some point in the past two days, the comfortable and the known had become claustrophobic and stifling.

Alex was a breath of fresh air, and the Josie that she was just starting to get a peek of when she was around him needed more oxygen—not more containment.

\* \* \*

If he could have hit a pause button, as if life were a DVR, he would have, just to freeze in time what Josie was saying to him, so that he could *process* it instead of *react* to it. He tried, with marginal success, to keep a straight face as she talked about him, but he felt as if he had cracked his own chest open and revealed the flesh of his beating heart to her in stark relief.

Such a small thing. It was no big revelation, that macchiatos were, in fact, his favorite coffee drink. The fact that she understood *why* was what made his pulse race, made his back straighten—and other body parts, too. He was hard at the thought that she could know him so well with so little time together.

As much as he would have enjoyed a pause button, just being *real* would have to be enough. He reached over and clasped her hand in his, the shock of the connection of their skin making his heart simultaneously race just a little more, and calm down on a deeper level.

She didn't pull away. In fact, she intertwined her fingers in his, a confirmation of what he had suspected was there, making each step toward connection with Josie seem more preordained. When he reached out she responded, so why was he so unsure? He wished again that he could halt time and buy himself some reflective processing. "Dr. Calm, Cool, and Collected," as one med school colleague had called him, didn't get flustered like this. The fact that she could trigger this kind of response in him *meant* something.

She relaxed at his touch, and just as he was about to open his mouth and ask her how she knew what she knew about him, the barista called out, "Alex!"

He jumped, their hands separated, and he motioned to her to wait, he would get the coffee. He came back to the table, careful to set everything down with unshaking hands. It wasn't that he was worried that he would spill, but rather that time seemed to move in nanoseconds, while his brain raced at the speed of love.

They each took a sip of their coffee, then he asked, openly, with that unshaken sense that whatever he said had to be enough, "This is unnerving you, isn't it?"

"Me?" She waved her hand dismissively and took another big sip of her coffee, her face bisected by the rim of the white coffee cup, like some sort of demented librarian looking over the edge of a book.

"Why did you come with me?" he asked, hoping that the question sounded like the warm inquiry that it was, and not an accusation or some sort of creepy, low self-esteem narcissism.

"Because I always go out for coffee with guys who've been traumatized by looking at Dylan's asshole."

*Ah*, he thought. She was *that* threatened. Good. That meant she felt it, too.

Her face got serious and she set the coffee cup down. She leaned forward, elbows on the table, giving him a look at her cleavage as her shirt fell a bit. His fingers itched to reach out and peel the shirt all the way off, gain access to the flesh that had been so tantalizingly close in the on-call room. Oh, how he wanted to get naked with her again, let her explore all the ways they could read each other's skin, the way that she was reading him now with observations and words.

"Let's go for a walk," she said. "How often do we get weather like this in May in New England?" She stood, the question not really a question. She seemed to want to walk and he was up for it.

"Hey, you never know. It could snow tomorrow."

"It could," she said, and two people sitting at tables nearby nodded in agreement, ruefully smiling and rolling their eyes.

It wouldn't snow today, though; she was right, it was a good day for a stroll. He had finished his coffee already, the shot with a little milk foam on top about the size of a kid's Dixie cup, so he pitched it as they walked outside, and then took her hand in his. The gesture, so fluid, felt right.

She looked up at him, and for the first time since he'd seen her today, gave him a dazzling, open look of joy. This was a face he could fall into every morning, waking up next to it. This was a smile he could spend the last six decades of his life admiring. This was a hand he could hold, warm and soft in his, and this was a woman he could know from every perspective, and still find more to know.

As they walked, the heady scent of trees in full bloom filled the air. Alex smelled crabapple trees, and various dogwoods, and other things he couldn't name. Pink and white petals dotted the scenery in all directions.

"How did you know how I felt," she asked, "when I was holding the baby today?"

"I told you"—he shrugged—"I've seen it before. It's completely different when you're holding one that's related to you."

"Yeah, but Jillian's not related to me."

"Of course she is. Family isn't just about blood, so you're related to her."

She swallowed hard and then smiled again, a grin that reached her eyes and wrinkled the skin above her apple-cheeks, the only part of her face that had spare flesh. They made her look like a teen, carefree and a little untamed.

He stopped, unable to resist—*unwilling* to resist, in fact. He slipped his arms around her waist, going in for a kiss that made him feel as if all of the time between their last kiss and this were just wasted hours. This seemed impossible, yet he wasn't about to let the impossible get in the way of the luscious feeling of their embrace. Alex had spent most of his life making the impossible happen, starting with going to med school despite being the child of an eighteen-year-old single mom. Finding the impossible, though, in the form of woman that had eluded him until now.

As she pressed against him, Alex's body responding to hers with a predictable urgency that made him wish they had two weeks alone in a bedroom. His eye caught a small walking path that led down to a creek, and he pulled away, stopping the kiss. Josie looked up, confused, the sun shining on her pale skin, showing freckles he hadn't noticed before around the edges of her eyes. She had the blush of arousal on her cheeks, and it filled him with a great strength. He grabbed her hand and pulled her toward the small path, wanting privacy, wanting to talk more alone, knowing soon she'd need to go back to the hospital.

Josie hadn't come here to see him—after all, she'd come to see the baby and Laura, right?

* * *

Josie wondered if Laura would want to kill her if she didn't get back to the hospital soon, or if her absence would go unnoticed. Given the overwhelming demands that an infant exerts on its parents, she suspected Laura would be quite fine with her spending time like this with Alex. All the same, she couldn't leave her friend hanging. Or was that just an excuse to avoid the fact that every second she spent with Alex made her want ten thousand more?

His hands were currently playing that dance of early touches, where he wasn't quite certain where the boundaries were, yet wanted to cross them anyhow. Alex's tongue parted her lips and the softness, the eager, all-consuming pleasure of being in his arms poured forth from her, making her wet and ready to finish what they'd started in the on-call room.

The yearning was something she could feel in him, too—and not just his hard erection grinding into her navel. She was on tiptoes and he was curled over her, their bodies touching, legs and arms and palms and mouths searching for every part to connect.

She made the first boundary-crossing move, caressing his ass as their kisses deepened. A groan of lust came out of him, vibrating in her mouth as he nipped her lip.

"You do more of that and I'll…" he said with a rasp, glancing around.

Stepping back, she took his hand, pulling him toward the base of a bridge. The concrete was pebbled with small stones and covered in a creeping ivy that had reached out over the years to a nearby tree, making a canopy no taller than she was. Perfect. Once ensconced under it, she pulled him to her roughly, yanking his shirt out of his waistband, needing to feel the heat of his skin against her palms.

"You'll what?" she challenged, hand grazing his rock-hard cock, loving the vibrant feel of it through his jeans. A shot of adrenaline ran through her, fired by sheer arousal and a desire to be taken right here in broad daylight, the risk (*thrill?*) of public discovery making the blood pound in her ears. Her fingers teased the outline of his erection just to see how far he would go.

"I'll do *this*," he growled, making her moan with delight as he pulled her up into his arms and pushed her against the wall, grinding into her and making her so glad she'd chosen to wear a skirt.

Alex seemed to have the same idea. One arm and the weight of his muscled torso held her up as they gasped and bit and laved their way through a kiss that, by all rights, was enough to make her come right now. Then his fingers reached under her skirt and found her panties, pushing aside the soft, cotton fabric to find her wet and soft. His touch made her hips buck against it, her mind in a frenzy at the combination of his arms around her, the scent of him, and what they were doing. Danger turned her on, and he was about to have sex with her in public.

Could he *get* any better?

Reaching between them, she struggled to unbutton and unzip him, yet persevered, her hand encasing him. Impressive. A bit daunting, even—he was *big*, and not just hard and throbbing. The man was *enormous*.

A shock of excitement added to her already oversexed mind and body as Alex peeled her panties right off, shoving them in his back pocket as she watched kayakers paddle past, the leaves that stretched over them barely enough cover. If someone knew to look here, they could see everything.

His mouth bruised hers as his fingertips stroked between her legs with a surgeon's precision—oh, those hands—and within a tiny number of strokes she was biting his shoulder, clutching his shoulders, pulling at his polo shirt and practically screaming as he kept the languid circles going, making her climax over and over, her sight filled with the green leaves, ears catching the traffic on the road above, the lap of paddles gliding through water, the dusky sound of Alex's breath against her ear.

"God, I want you," he murmured. She felt for his back pocket, half mad with the need to have him fill her, and found his wallet. Opening it, she felt by touch for what she needed, blinded by the wall of chest before her and the man's ceaseless fingers prying her pleasure from her, one stroke at a time.

*Aha!* Wallet condom. She knew it. He was too responsible not to have one, and as she tucked his wallet back in place and flashed the foil wrapper at him, he chuckled.

"I thought this was an inventive way to mug someone," he joked.

"Wait until you see what I do when I kidnap you," she replied, not joking. Pulling away, she heard a low groan of shock, then of appreciation, as she ripped the wrapper open, hands as precise as could be, and rolled the condom on. He shifted her, arms holding her easily as her wetness slid along his upper thigh, their bodies able to do this because of his strength and her dexterity.

She centered her hips over his rod and—without pretense—welcomed him in, his breath hitched and coming out in little grunts, her own matching his as she reveled in the heat of being filled completely by Alex. Dr. Perfect really was perfect—that he enjoyed this, would even consider it, had *initiated* it ballooned her heart as her body tingled and thrummed, his mouth on her neck and his hips sliding up against her pelvis, knees bent and holding her weight, making love to her slowly.

"Is this okay?" he whispered.

"Are you kidding me? This is amazing," she said, shuddering as her wet walls clamped down on him, a tightness in her belly emanating throughout her entire torso, pulsing into her ears.

"No, I mean, am I too much? I don't want to hurt you." He stopped moving, the stillness both exquisite and aching.

"I'm a big girl."

He nuzzled her neck, still not moving. Wrapping her legs fully around his hips, she made little thrusts of her own, her position too awkward to get the long, deep strokes he could give her. That meant he was in charge, her orgasm at his command. The sound of bikers riding not thirty feet away, on a path near the water, zinged her with the idea they might be caught.

"No, you're tiny, and I am—"

Shutting him up, she slammed her mouth against his, lips pulling his apart, tongue ravaging his mouth, until he began to rock against her, the heat between them building.

As quickly as she'd first kissed him, she tore her mouth

from his, lips raw and burning. Catching his eyes, which were unfocused and smoldering, she reached up to cup his face in hers, the hint of dark stubble scratching her palms. *I wonder what that would be like on my thighs?* she wondered, tightening at the thought, making him groan.

Eyes locked, she simply said, "Alex? Shut up and fuck me."

That was all it took, his mouth twisting into a delighted smirk, his body thrusting so hard into hers she gasped, his tongue licking her collarbone, one masterful hand pulling her shirt and cotton bra down so he could reveal the nipple, the sensation of cold air and then moist mouth on her nipple pebbling it as he drove into her, hard, ramming her as her hands tried to clutch any part of him that she could hold on to for the ride.

Their twin orgasms slammed out of nearly nowhere, and his cry of "Josie!" mixed with her hiss of his name, the feel of the concrete wall against her bare ass, his body pinning her to the wall with his enormity, pushing into her and riding her up, up, up as if she could crash through the canopy of leaves. Her body seized as he groaned and tightened, the sun shining between new spring foliage, her face tipped up to the sun as she received the full offering of luscious, forbidden sex from Dr. Perfect.

His breath came in little pants, his arms slack as he held up her weight, and then—voices.

"Is someone in there?" said a woman from above. Alex moved slowly inward, closer to the thickening of the ivy, crouching down and sliding out of her with a regretful look.

"Sorry," he said, turning away to slide off the condom. Josie snatched her panties from the loose jeans that hovered around his upper thighs, the edge of the white cotton poking out from the pocket. Out of the corner of her eye, as she scrambled into her underwear, she saw Alex deftly snap and zip up, then toss the condom in a nearby trash can, wiping his hands on the grass.

Ah, romance.

The flush of what they'd just done made her legs shake as she straightened her clothes and ran her hands quickly through her hair, her flesh still on fire and the waves of desire and crested need still pounding through her. Had that really just happened? Did Alex like outdoor sex, too? Her boyfriends had considered her a freak for even hinting at it, and now the guy she met at Laura's birth turned out not only to accept it, but apparently enjoy it?

Dr. Perfect, indeed.

Slinging his arm around her shoulders, he looked her up and down. "You ready? Laura and the guys must be wondering what happened to you."

Nodding, she said, "I'm glad we have a bit of a walk ahead of us. One look at me and Laura could guess."

His eyes surveyed her. "You look exactly the way I like." A slow, deep kiss at the edge of the leaf umbrella made her toes curl in, turning her wet again, and making her crave a bed, a good Thai take-out menu, and a limitless supply of Barrington Roasters coffee. And a week alone with him.

"Get a room!" a canoer shouted, laughing.

"Too late," she and Alex whispered in unison.

"This is getting creepy," she said as they began the walk uphill, Alex's arm around her.

"Then quit repeating everything I say."

"Then quit repeating everything I say," she joked.

"Wait." He stopped her, turning her to face him, and began stroking the skin of her neck.

"More?" she said, incredulous.

"No. We need to do a tick check."

"We *what?*"

"It's that time of year, and we were just under a thicket that could have them," he answered, serious. "Lyme disease is no joke. I'll do you and you do me."

"We just did each other."

"Ha ha." His hands roamed through the hair behind

her ears, along her collarbone, then under her shirt, lifting it up and brushing against her breasts.

"You know I'm a sure thing, Alex. You don't have to invent tick checks to touch my boobs."

He laughed. "C'mon. Check your legs."

He was serious. She ran her hands down her legs with a cursory touch, and then stroked his neckline. Slipping the yellow polo shirt up, she felt for ticks in the thick thatch of hair at his waistband, then reached down under, playfully, stroking the tip of him. "Hmmm, I might need to get a close view here to see if there are any ticks there."

He groaned and gripped her hand in his, hard. "You're killing me."

"I'm very good at tick removal there," she replied, batting her eyelashes in a gesture of innocence. "With my tongue."

The laugh that poured out of him was pure joy and lust combined, head thrown back and stomach tightening, nearly rippling with the vibration of his amusement.

"Are we done with the tick check, doctor?" she asked, pulling her hand away from his heat.

"You can resume it another time in my bed." *Whoosh!* Her senses exploded.

The walk back to the hospital made Josie feel like the coffee that they'd had had been multiplied by a factor of ten, which was roughly the number of orgasms she'd also just had. Alex held her hand, except this time it wasn't a tentative, beginning-of-a-relationship gesture, trying to feel out where the physical boundaries lay. It wasn't just an affectionate gesture, either, one designed to send out a beacon, a signal, to point the other in the right direction. This was the clasp of a lover who knows that he has the easy intimacy of reaching out to touch another at will, and she loved every bit of it.

There was a spring in their steps, a jauntiness, a full-on joy. It wasn't just that they'd had phenomenal, slightly exhibitionistic sex outdoors, with the air perfumed by a nature eager to burst forth in its own explosion of growth and renewal. It was that something drew them to each other and made their hands undress each other, made their bodies press against each other, made this communion a series of touches, caresses, reaches, and embraces.

Then more.

As they entered the hospital and headed to the elevators, they dropped each other's hands. Alex was now in professional territory, and Josie was perfectly capable of respecting that. Two elevators opened, and the waiting patrons piled into one, Josie following them until Alex grasped her around the waist and pulled her back, holding one index finger up to his lips. He shook his head, then glanced at the open, empty option. She widened her eyes and raised her eyebrows, and marched into the empty elevator. Alex, hot and heavy behind her.

*Again?* she wondered as the doors snapped shut, and she felt her body slammed against the elevator wall, knowing that the four flights up might damn well be just enough time for him to take her again. His lips weren't tender now, probing and claiming with an intensity that somehow managed to match what they'd just done by the river. His hands were everywhere, on her hips, up her leg, on her breast, wrapped behind her, searing the flesh on the back of her neck as his hardness pressed into her belly.

*Ding!* The elevator stopped with an abrupt jolt, a fitting kinesthetic trigger to make them pull back, to realize that there was, indeed, a society in orbit around them. Others used the machine for far more banal purposes.

Smoothing her hair, she tried to look as nonchalant as possible, nurses and doctors piling in from the first floor. Whatever lipstick she'd put on this morning had been long worn away.

A young woman about her own age, blonde and dour, looked up at Alex and said, "What are you doing here? You don't work today."

He gave her an irritated look. "I'm here to visit

someone."

"Is everything okay?" she asked, concern infusing her words.

"It's fine."

His clipped responses told Josie that something was off here. This wasn't the Alex she expected, and whoever this woman was, there was a past.

"Is it a family member?" the woman probed.

"Lisa"—he shook his head slightly—"it's none of your business."

His quiet, final sentence made the woman snap to attention and look forward, eyes unfocused, on the hazy stainless-steel wall where the doors bisected the side of the elevator. Her nostrils flared and her shoulders slumped forward. She was angry, and Josie wondered why. Not enough, though, to take the shine off of how she was feeling right now.

Just as Josie suspected, the second that she and Alex walked back into Laura's room, some sixth sense inside her best friend made her cock an eyebrow and give them a look of appraisal that made Josie blush. It seemed to put a little pink in Alex's cheeks, as well.

"So, what have you two been up to?" Laura said with a cagey tone. The baby was lying in Laura's arms, eyes wide, alert, and roaming, searching her mother's face and taking in the pinpoint of the world that Laura's features represented to her.

As if she had been doing this for decades, Laura shifted the baby from one arm to the other, and then reached under her hospital gown to unclasp her bra. Josie watched, transfixed, as her best friend held the baby's mouth, pulling it gently open, then squeezed her own breast, shoving it into little Jillian's perfect, rose-petal lips. And then the unmistakable sound of sucking and breathing through the nose. It was a steady beat that you could almost dance to. *Suck suck, inhale, suck suck, inhale, suck suck, inhale,* with little gulps in between. Funny little noises and tones coming from the baby's throat.

"Sweet relief," Laura groaned, and Josie shot her a look of confusion. "Do you have any idea what it's like when your boobs are filled with milk, and they're rock hard, and all you want to do is go down to the nursery and grab two random babies 'cause yours is sound asleep and won't latch on, and just get the milk out of there?"

"No, I can't say that I know what that's like," Josie answered.

Alex walked over to the bedside table and picked up the mauve plastic pitcher, pouring a glass of water and handing it to Laura. "Here, drink this. You'll need it."

"The last thing I need is more fluid in my body."

He smiled. "No, actually, that's the *first* thing you need. The only way you'll keep up your production is if you keep hydrating."

Josie watched the two of them, her head bobbing from one to the other. It was as if they spoke Mandarin Chinese. There was a language of parenting, of procreation, lactation, attachment, that she didn't speak. Laura was quickly becoming not just fluent in it, but accentless. Soon it would be as if it were her first language. Alex was like an immigrant into that world, living there long enough to understand every single word said to him, but occasionally having moments when a slightly misused idiom tripped him up.

To Josie, what they were saying sounded like gobbledygook, and again it alienated her in a way that pierced her even more than it had a few hours ago, to be on the fringes. Knowing that Alex was closer to Laura, and Mike and Dylan, in some ways, than even she was, took the wind out of her. Pushing aside those thoughts, she sat down on the edge of the bed. Her hand instinctively went to stroke the baby's head, until she realized it was attached to Laura, and that that was probably a boundary she ought not to cross.

"Where're Mike and Dylan?" she asked.

"They went out to get some food. I'm really jonesing for some sushi."

"And you know...*all that?*" Josie said, spinning her hand around in the general direction of Laura's crotch.

"Well, *all that*," Laura said, quietly mimicking Josie's gesture, "is the equivalent of putting my vagina in a juicer. Whoever invented crotch ice packs is my new best friend." She closed her eyes and sighed. "Sorry, Josie. You've been replaced."

"Oh, God!" Josie said, "Did you really have to go there? The words 'vagina' and 'juicer' should never be spoken together!"

Alex just laughed, a sound of understanding that took away Josie's sense of alienation.

"You'll be...*here*," Laura said, spinning her wrist over her pelvis, "someday. You'll understand."

"The only way any of these parts are getting anywhere near a juicer is when I cozy up to the bar and lean into it a little too hard to get my fifth pomegranate margarita."

Alex slid an easy arm around her shoulders and squeezed her upper arm, a playful, affectionate gesture that made Laura raise her eyebrows even higher. "I'm sure you will," he said, and then dropped his arm, walking over to the base of Laura's bed and grabbing the chart.

Laura mouthed *Oh my God* to Josie, and Josie mouthed back *I KNOW*, and crossed both sets of fingers.

Leaning over the baby, Laura hissed, barely audibly, "I can't believe you picked a guy up at my birth!"

Josie just shrugged.

Laura pointed to Josie's belly and whispered, "You're having one of these someday," pointing at Jillian, then at Alex, then her.

Josie glared back. "You take that back," she whispered.

Biting her lips to keep from giggling, Laura shook her head.

"Then I curse you with twins next time you're pregnant," Josie growled as menacingly as a girly whispervoice could manage.

"You bitch," Laura hissed back. She didn't argue, though, at the idea that she'd be pregnant again. Her mock outrage turned to amusement.

If Josie were Laura right now, with a baby sucking the life force out of her, drinking her milk, and with a cold pack attached to her pubes, she'd be threatening homicide on anyone who suggested that she might have another one. Maybe Laura was just high on painkillers. That had to be it; it was the only way to explain why she would ever want to go through this obscenely barbaric experience again.

\* \* \*

*What had he just done, and when could they do it again?* The taste of her was still in his mouth, her juices still on his hips and thighs, the feel of her pushing against him still in his flesh, and her name still echoing among the leftover groans trapped in his throat. He helped lead her back to the sidewalk and up from the little alcove, marveling that they'd just used to have wild, hot, nearly public sex.

And she *liked* it.

Women never indulged in this—ever—with him. Once, in college, he and a short-term girlfriend had been so drunk after a football game that they'd had a quickie under the bleachers, ten thousand stomping and roaring fans above them. The complete abandon and the risk of getting caught made the act incredibly explosive for him and setting every sense ablaze.

This? What he and Josie had just done without effort, without talking, without worry or fear or hesitation?

A thousand times better.

How had the perfect woman, sexually aware and aggressive enough for him, willing to have outdoor sex and with a brain that intrigued, have been so close yet so far away for half a year?

*Holy shit.*

His brain was on fire as they walked into Laura's room. Alex could tell that Laura was exhausted; he shifted into OB mode, a bit relieved to focus on something less overwhelming. The full rush of hormones, and pushing, and breastfeeding, and the recomposition of atoms and molecules inside her to make room for motherhood, was etched into her face. It was in the way her hands moved, how she cradled the baby's neck, the subtle shift of her hip as she adjusted to having the baby's weight outside her body now. Every new mother went through some degree of it, the biological reality of birth setting in.

Alex wondered how the two fathers would make the similar adjustment. It was different, he knew that. No nine and a half months of hormones coursing through their veins, only bystanders to the violence of birth. Still, men had to go through a change as well, beyond being protective of the new life that they had helped to create. He thought he could tell which fathers were going to be good pretty quickly, even though he'd been without a father for most of his life. His grandfather had filled in, and was a fabulous father figure, but that's all he had been…a figure. The empty part of him that wished he had a dad made his stomach tighten as Dylan and Mike came in on cue, looking like they'd be among the good ones.

Josie had taken the baby—with confidence, this time— to burp her when she pulled away from her mother's breast. Mike and Dylan both grinned expectantly at the baby, but kept a respectful distance from Josie, who now cradled Jillian in her arms, swinging her gently, keeping the baby content.

"Josie's not fainting this time," Dylan stage whispered.

"Where's my sushi?" Laura barked. "You can talk about anything you want, but not until I've had my sushi."

Mike handed her two containers of California roll. "Sushi." He sniffed. "That's not sushi."

"Yes, it is."

"That's California roll. Sashimi...now *that's* sushi," Dylan said.

"Actually," Mike interjected, "neither is."

It sounded like an old argument.

"I can finally eat sashimi again, can't I?" Laura answered, just remembering. "Hmmmm..." She bit her lower lip and stared with great longing at Mike's raw salmon.

"You wanna trade?" he offered, reluctantly.

She gave him a closed-mouth smile. "No, go ahead, it's fine, but next time, get me some."

The three parents dug into their meal with gusto.

Josie seemed to have forgotten that anyone else was in the room, so intent was she on studying and absorbing the baby's features. She was a natural. Alex found his mind wandering to a future, and caught a glimpse of the woman he could love holding their child. He'd always thought of it...fatherhood...one day, but now he had a face to attach to the imagined reality.

"You want one?" Dylan asked.

Shaking himself out of his reverie, Alex looked up to find Dylan holding out a tray of California roll. "No. Thanks. I'm...I'm good." As if on cue, his stomach rumbled.

Dylan cocked his head and said, "Hey man, we've got plenty."

"You're hungry?" Josie said, snapping out of her own little world. "You want to get dinner?"

*I want to get that tick check you promised*, he thought. "Dinner would be great, but first, give me a chance to hold her."

"Oh, come on, I just got her," Josie protested.

"And you'll get to hold her...for"—he paused and looked around the room—"forever. Or at least until she she's too wiggly and won't let anyone hold her anymore. Then you'll get to play with her—running around the playground, digging for worms, or doing whatever it is that kids do when they reach the point where they don't want to be held. This is my shot, though. Let me have a turn?"

"I'm twenty-nine and I'd like to still be held," Laura piped up.

"Ooooooooh," said Mike, coming over and giving her a big hug. Dylan piled on, too, keeping his hands extended out so that his fish-covered fingers didn't touch her.

"That's not what I meant," Laura said, but tears filled her eyes. "I wish my mom could be here," she said quietly. She swallowed hard, and the tears spilled over, running down her bright red cheeks.

"Your mom would have loved her," Josie said, handing the baby off to Alex, and then walking over to the bed to touch Laura's leg in assurance.

Alex hadn't meant to hit so many nerves, but apparently he'd said the wrong thing. "So, I think we should be going." The soft heft of the baby wrapped in the flannel blanket made a part of him go soft and paternal, time slowing down as he acknowledged the wonder of this little girl's new life. She smelled like freshness and perfection, and as he traced her cheek with one finger he found the sweetness almost too much. Almost. If he let himself, he could sit down with new babies and rock them to sleep all day. Sadly, that wasn't his job.

Besides, he had some unfinished business with Josie. "Let's give the Daddies a turn with their daughter," Alex suggested.

Plus, he wanted to get Josie out of here. To do what, he wasn't sure. He'd love to do more of what they had just done down by the river, but he thought he should hold off. Having this start out so hot, so fast, risked burning it out just as quickly.

As he watched her chat with Laura, and lean in for a hug, then a kiss on the cheek, he saw a warmth to her that she only showed to people she was close to. Even Dylan got a hug from her. When she stood on extreme tiptoes to give Giant Mike an embrace as well, Alex smiled involuntarily.

"Hold on," Mike said, peering at the top of her head. Fishing in her hair, Mike untangled a leaf and held it up to look.

"You're sprouting these days?" the man asked her, and Alex suppressed a laugh.

"No comment," she said, avoiding everyone's eyes.

"Alex?"

"I defer to Josie."

"Just repeat that phrase a thousand times for the rest of your life and you'll do fine with her," Dylan added.

Josie laughed and moved toward the doorway. Alex took her cue, handing the baby off to Laura. He reached over and rubbed Jillian's soft little head, and then looked Laura in the eyes. "Congratulations, again. You did it."

She smiled and closed her eyes, swallowing hard. "Thank you. I did, didn't I? My midwife called me a birth warrior."

He did a slow inhale and smiled, his cheeks hurting from so much grinning. "I think that's pretty apt."

"Thank *you*," she said.

"For what?"

Laura's eyes darted over to Josie, who was speaking animatedly with Dylan about knocking it off with his giraffe.

"Oh," Alex said. He looked away, a bit flustered. "*That.*"

"Yeah"—Laura pointed her finger covertly at Josie—"*that.* Take care of *that*," she said, winking.

He nodded and turned away, not sure what to say. As he walked to the doorway, Josie reached out, tentatively, for his hand. The public gesture, two feet away from Dylan, made him swell with hope. It made other things swell as well, and now that tight feeling plagued him. Already? Yes, he was ready again, already, and as they walked out the door and said their final goodbyes, he wondered what would happen next in the elevator.

# CHAPTER SEVEN

Josie pressed the elevator button and reached back for Alex's hand. Out of the corner of her eye she saw that blonde nurse again, who was glaring daggers at both of them. "What's up with that woman?" Josie asked.

He froze and looked out of the corner of his eye, not moving his face.

Now Josie wondered what was up with *him*, because that was just not a typical Alex move. *How would you know a typical Alex move, Josie?* she thought. It wasn't as if she knew enough about him to be able to make a judgment call like that.

"That is Lisa," he said, a tone of regret and resignation coming out in a raspy voice, a hushed attempt at privacy. "I'll tell you more in the elevator."

The blonde woman charted furiously, her hand jerking across the page as her eyes flitted between Josie and Alex and whatever medical document she was working on. A red flush crept over the pale skin on her neck, and into her jawline and cheeks.

A creepy feeling spread through Josie's gut. Whatever this was about, it didn't feel good. She didn't like holding Alex's hand and not feeling good. It was so contradictory that it triggered a sense of panic in her. Not a full-blown panic attack, more a sense that she was nearing a precipice, and might have to struggle not to fall.

She decided to just head this one off right here. "Do I know you?" she asked in an even tone, turning to face her. The blonde ignored her and flipped the chart closed with a flick of the wrist, storming off.

A huge sigh of relief escaped from Alex, his chest lowering and his hand loosening around hers. The elevator dinged and the doors opened. No sexy ride right now; whatever that woman represented, it wasn't good juju.

As they stepped aboard and Alex pressed the lobby button, Josie said, "Okay. Spill."

He squared his shoulders and shook his head. "We went on one date. One. Coffee. She has this…thing about me."

"Coffee?" She punched him lightly on the bicep just as the elevator stopped at the next floor.

The doors opened and people poured in; he dropped his voice to answer, "Not the same *coffee* you and I had, my dear." The murmur in her ear sent a warm tingle between her shoulder blades as he straightened up, clasping his hands behind his back, pretending he hadn't just sent her into a topsy-turvy state.

Again.

By the time they left the crowd and reached the street outside the hospital, she was a bit more settled, and they resumed their conversation.

"She doesn't take the hint. I've never seen her behave like that, though." He frowned, then reached for Josie's hand, running his index finger down the lines on her palm. "Then again, I've never been seen at work with someone I'm…you know."

"No. I don't know." She wasn't going to give him an easy out. What did he think this was? If she was just an easy fuck to him, he had to say it. She wasn't going to. "Someone you're what? What's 'you know'?" People

121

rushed by all around them, but took no notice of their conversation. Speaking into cell phones, conversing into the thin air of Bluetooth, as if part of the Borg, heads bent over phones, texting—everyone's minds were on their little pieces of plastic and glass, not their surroundings.

He reached for her hips and pulled them to him, tight arms stronger than she remembered. As she looked up, his face blocked out the sun, the ends of his brown hair curling slightly from the slight humidity, his face relaxed and sly. "Do I have to define 'you know'?"

"Yes." The word hung between them like a dare.

A double dog dare.

Which he took. "Someone I'm dating." The back of his hand against her cheekbone, light and feathery, made the lump in her throat dissolve. Shielding her eyes with one hand, she looked up, feeling taller and bigger than ever.

"We're dating?"

"We are."

"Can we have more...*you know*."

"Your turn to define 'you know,' Josie." His voice held a laugh. Damn it. He knew exactly what she was asking, her heart beating as fast as he'd been thrusting into her an hour ago.

On tiptoes, she licked his neck and said quietly, "Danger sex."

"Is that what you call it?" One eyebrow cocked, his nostrils flared, jaw tightened, eyes narrowed. It wasn't an angry expression. This was the look of a man intrigued to find there was vocabulary for something he'd thought nameless.

"What do you call it?" Turning the tables back on him was a relief. Unbearably revealing, the conversation made her hot and ready as much as it made her want to crawl into a hole. *Hmmm.* Maybe they could have danger sex in a hole in the street. How heavy were manhole covers?

"I don't have a word for it."

"Liar." Crossing her arms, she went down to flat feet.

"'Fess up."

"Air fucking." Alex barked the phrase out as if it would somehow be better if he said it quickly.

"*Air fucking?* Is that like air guitar?" She pretended to strum an electric one, like Garth and Wayne from *Wayne's World*, until he grabbed her wrists, a pained expression on his face.

"Don't."

"Don't what?"

Closing his eyes, he sighed, hands still gripping her. "Don't make fun of something I never imagined a woman would actually want." A puff of air flew out of his mouth as if the secret, now out, needed to escape from him even faster.

She softened, feeling horrible now, "Oh, no. No, Alex, I wasn't making fun of you." She winced, looking down. "I'm mildly embarrassed, and because I have the social skills of a tree sloth on acid, I just make jokes. Bad ones."

A fierceness came over him and his eyes looked into her soul as if they were reading it. "You understand, though, don't you? You liked it. You wanted it. It fed something in you. That's how it is for me. Except I never imagined I'd find someone else who…"

"Yes." The intensity was almost too much to bear, and Josie felt something crack inside her, a tiny tendril of a new green shoot seeking sunlight.

"Good."

"Come over to my place for dinner," she ventured.

"Dinner?"

"Dinner and a movie."

"What's the movie?"

"It's called *My Bed*."

"I like that movie."

"You've seen it?"

"No. But I caught a great preview of it today."

"Maybe we could turn it into a drive-in viewing. You know, under the stars?" Something in him had cracked, too—the way he shifted and held his body was more intimate. She stretched up and kissed his lips lightly.

He blinked hard, then jumped a bit. Reaching into his pocket, he checked his phone. "A patient."

"It's your day off!" she protested.

"VBAC. She really wants to make this happen, and I promised I'd come in…" He raked his hair with one hand. "Damn it."

"I get it." Exhaustion she'd been ignoring asserted itself at the opportunity, reminding her that she really needed some rest, a shower, and to eat something. And she wanted to spend five hours on the phone with Laura, squeeing about Dr. Perfect. Dr. Air Fucking Perfect.

"What are you doing Tuesday?"

"I'm off."

"Then come…over."

He was five steps toward the front doors to the hospital when he ran back, grabbed her, and held her, a nice, comfortable kiss planted on her lips.

"I'll come. And so will you."

# Chapter Eight

In the handful of days since Jillian's birth, the only place that seemed to give Josie comfort was Jeddy's. And she resented it. The coffee was terrible, the companionship was awful. But the service was really great and, as much as Madge could be a sourpuss, at least she was Josie's sourpuss. So now, every morning around 6 a.m., she got a coffee and some kind of reasonable pastry breakfast and settled in a booth, wishing for the life that had unraveled over the past few days as Laura had moved on.

If Josie had said those words to Laura, "You've moved on," she would have heard a torrent of all the reasons why that wasn't true. Followed, probably, by lots of tears and an extra order of coconut shrimp or a hot fudge sundae. The protests, though, would come from Laura's understanding, deep down, that Josie was right. Laura had moved on, finding the true love—true loves?—that eluded Josie.

Sex had always been no problem for her, at least. Even before her recent encounters with Alex. Men found her appealing enough to proposition…but not worthy enough to stay. The few relationships she'd had that had lasted longer than one condom had been fraught with jealousy and anger and accusations of condescension on both parts, typically ending in a "fuck you" phone call. And then a regretful booty call a few days later.

And then—silence.

When Laura had first met Dylan and Mike and had learned about the threesome life that they embraced, Josie had told, for the first time ever, about her own threesome experience. It hadn't been intentional by any stretch, and it hadn't even been *good*. It had, however, triggered a sense of curiosity in her.

It had just been an option. She had taken advantage of the opportunity, lived the experience and woken up the next day alive, fine, and normal. Needing to pee, and eat, and shower, and wash her clothes, like any other day. With the minor additional need to decide what it had meant to violate a social norm and sleep with two men at once. Back then, in college, it had been a coup of sorts, some kind of quiet, dark mark as if she had joined an amoral club that no one knew existed and whose members all kept their mouths shut. If they were female.

A rumor had spread about what Josie had done with those two guys, but it had fizzled fast. She was this boyish, petite thing who had a motormouth; most people dismissed her as un-fuckable. The coup really was hers; her internal scorekeeper knew that un-fuckable Josie had managed to find two guys to sleep with her at the same time. Even the most attractive woman at their small college couldn't stake that claim. Not out in public, anyway. Being open about it would have brought her ruin. One hell of a Catch-22, right?

Two guys, though, right now...that wasn't what she wanted. What she wanted was one man, twice over...or to double her over. Alex filled her visual memory: the lines of his pecs, the narrow taper of his waist, the intensity in his eyes in the on-call room. How he had watched her with such steady power, her body on fire just from his look. Picking at the remnants of her croissant, Josie let herself revel in that memory for a few moments before sheepishly admitting a tinge of guilt. Laura had been just a few doors down, as desperate to push something out of her vagina as Josie had been eager to get something in hers.

She snapped back to reality when Madge zipped over, dumped a refill into her coffee mug, and moved on.

If Laura were more available right now, she would be sitting at this table right now, snarfing down a platter of fried green tomatoes, telling her so.

"That's bull," she would say, her finger pointed in Josie's face, happy to be on the giving end of angsty love life advice.

Laura wasn't here, though. All Josie had right now was her own imagination, her own inner divining rod, and it was saying guys like Alex don't want girls like her for the long haul—they want them for the quick and dirty. Josie could do quick and dirty. She could do quick and dirty *real* good.

But spending enough time with Laura, Mike, and Dylan, and now baby Jill, had changed something deep inside her. It made her see a possibility that turned all the other options into pale imitations of life and love. What if that possibility were out there somewhere for her?

Laura's voice popped into her mind. *What if Alex is that possibility?*

Josie took a sip of her coffee. It was hotter than she'd expected and burned a bit, shocking her. She drank some water to cool her mouth and then sat with the pain, knowing that she was sitting with a much more intense pain that no glass of water could alleviate.

*Just open up to this*, she thought. *Just do it.*

If she didn't give this a chance, a true *emotional* chance, she'd be left with a big, heaping hole of regret inside of her.

*But that's better than rejection*, another voice said.

She closed her eyes and listened to the cadence of that voice. Whose voice was it? Who was whispering these words that stopped her from acting on hope? It was the same voice that got her out of Peters.

The question was, who exactly was that?

If she were in a selfish frame of mind, which she was drifting into more and more lately, she would indulge in some deep self-pity over the fact that she and Laura had lost their morning coffee ritual.

What she'd got out of her ritual was companionship—someone to bounce ideas off of, a good, deep friend to share the boring details of her boring life and her boring job. Laura had a corporate job that was just interesting enough to keep her there and just boring enough to make it a bit dull. Until Laura had met Dylan and Mike, in fact, they'd both been boring. There had been equity between what Josie would tell and what Laura would tell, a mutual bitching session that in the end balanced them out.

Josie, though, had spent years trying to get herself into a stable economic situation, and boring was an *accomplishment*. Her life had been more interesting than anyone would wish, growing up. In addition to losing her dad, and putting up with her mom, she didn't have a smooth time of it at school, either.

"Smartmouth" had been the phrase that teachers had used the most with her. *Watch that smart mouth. You're a smartmouth.* And occasionally, along with fingers clenching her bicep, *cut it out, smartass*, hissed in her ear. That one was the angry English teacher, the furious phys ed teacher— pretty much whichever teacher had a temper and couldn't stand the fact that Josie did not defer to authority unless authority deferred back.

Socially, she did okay. Being a target for the teachers made her stand out, get noticed. Plenty of boys wanted to date her. Though "dating" was a loose term where she grew up. A date meant that maybe the guy paid the car fee at the drive-in and managed to drive you home after he got what he wanted. Or, once you were old enough for bars, on cheap beer night you might get treated to enough drinks to get you drunk—and then, again, a ride home if the guy got what he wanted.

She'd tired quickly of that scene and had hidden in books, her nose in a tome at the local library and later the university branch campus's meager stacks, hoping to read her way to a better life. It had worked. Nursing school had been her big ticket out of Nowheresville, Ohio. When she'd earned her associate's degree she'd qualified for a full ride at the small college in Boston, which, for whatever reason, had picked her out of a stack of Josies and made her a queen.

Once she'd transferred to the Boston area, she'd been able to breathe for the first time, a giant exhale of victory.

It was a big, giant *fuck you* to the rundown house she'd left, the trailer parks, the poverty, the misery of where she'd grown up. And most of all to all the people who had told her that her dreams had been foolish, that she had been overreaching or snobbish, or too full of herself. She'd had to struggle against it within herself—one part of her saying *give up*, another telling that part to fuck off. If she could have lifted a giant middle finger, tall enough to be seen the six hundred miles from Boston to northeast Ohio, she would have constructed it.

Instead, she faced a rather large structure of her own making that she needed to deal with—and that was nearly six figures in student loans. When you came from where Josie came from, people didn't have college funds, or grandparents who helped out, or even well-established scholarships. A local credit union had thrown $500 a year her way for four years, and she'd managed to get the full Pell Grant three out of five years. She'd spent four years chipping away at her associate's, and one of those years, her mom had never bothered to file her taxes. In the ensuing mess, Josie, still a dependent, had lost out on her Pell Grants. Community college and branch campus tuitions were low, but not *that* low.

It was so worth it, though. All worth it. Her graduation

day—their graduation day, hers and Laura's—had been such a triumph for her, in spite of her mom, Marlene, showing up looking and acting like an older, drunker, version of Daisy Duke. It hadn't been pretty. A day of massive pride for Josie had turned into unrelenting embarrassment. Rather than striking a chord of fury, though, the embarrassment had actually given way to gratitude. A deep, intense, sense of gratitude that she had made it, that these past six years doing everything possible to change who she was, to defy the trajectory that everyone had assumed she would follow, had paid off. She was not her mom.

If Laura had been there, she could have talked about all of that.

But Laura wasn't.

She'd moved on.

* * *

Inviting Alex over to her apartment for dinner was turning out to be a colossal mistake. First of all, she actually had to clean the place. Her apartment looked like early thrift shop, circa 1994, with a definite hippie tone to everything. She kept it *neat*, she just didn't keep it *clean*. She had spent most of the day dusting baseboards, pulling things off shelves and wiping under them, cleaning the crud out of the corners of the bathroom and making sure that everything that didn't really have a place appeared to have some kind of a place.

She opened the windows and aired the place out, and burned a little essential oil in an oil burner to fill the house with eucalyptus and lavender. It made her feel more alert, and calmer at the same time, excited to have a man over in her apartment for the first time in forever. Her cat, Dotty, was not a good helper, instead finding various sunny spots on the windowsills to curl up in.

She'd invited Alex for a 7:00 dinner. It was now 6:30.

She'd bought all of the groceries earlier that day, but now panic set in. What if he didn't like her cooking? What if this really was just about sex? What if she'd been too forward in making that joke about the movie? What if he didn't like her apartment? What if he was a serial killer and he was going to empty her freezer and put little chopped-up bits of Josie in there to snack on over the next month, and no one except Laura would ever know that she went missing, and all Alex would have to do is say, "Oh, I'm enjoying Josie thoroughly, don't worry," and Laura would think that was a sexual innuendo? *What if?*

As charming as all those thoughts were, Josie shoved all of those insecurities aside, and was grateful that she hadn't planned to cook any form of meat that looked like it might be human. Tonight, it was a simple pasta dish with an alfredo sauce, a rosemary focaccia, and a tossed salad, with something chocolate from a bakery for dessert. It was *great* first-date food.

Was this a first date? Second date? Was the coffee shop the first date? Was the on-call room the first date? Boy, if you counted all of those she was somewhere around her seventh or eighth date and she should have been putting out anal by now. Technically, though, she supposed that the coffee shop was date one, and that therefore, this was date two.

Phew, no anal yet. Time to put away the butt plug. Her bedside table was well equipped for what she assumed would be the real dessert. She had condoms, and lube, and a few toys, in case he turned out to be *that* adventurous.

Everything was set up in the kitchen, the salad was tossed, the bread was ready and sliced, cooling on the counter, and she had the pasta and the water and the salt all ready to assemble and boil once Alex arrived. The sauce was done, and so she found herself rearranging candles on her mantle, making sure that the remote control was next to the television, and shooing the cat off the bed.

Why was she was so nervous when this was a sure

thing? It was just a guy, and her, and a basic "come over to my house and let me make you dinner" kind of date. The kind that Laura had gone on when Dylan had cooked for her and Mike, and the three of them had solidified a lot of goodness and hope in their relationship.

Bingo! That's what made her so nervous. This was more than just a dinner date at her apartment, this was a trial for real life and real love. Alex wasn't just coming over for dinner and sex, he was coming over to give her companionship and depth, and to trade in that little back and forth, where you give a little piece of your integrity to someone else and see if you can trust them with it. That she looked forward to this scared and thrilled her all at once.

The test of a person comes when they're at their worst, that's when the soft underbelly of people gets revealed. Josie had learned that the hard way when her dad had died when she was eleven. She'd watched her entire world fall apart. Her mother had spent six weeks in the hospital, all the way up in Cleveland, recovering from a brain injury. And she'd come back different. When people get *hurt*, they come back different, Josie had learned. And Josie had gotten hurt, not injured, but hurt by that tragedy, and she had never been the same, either.

The doorbell rang, shaking her out of her reverie, and the cat ran to answer it, like a demented, furry butler.

\* \* \*

Alex stood on Josie's front porch and rang the bell. When she'd given him her address, he knew it sounded familiar, but he hadn't realized that he could walk here from his own apartment two blocks around the corner. They'd both picked East Cambridge for whatever reason, probably the cheaper rent, and he smiled to himself, realizing that the right person may very well have just been right under his nose.

The door opened and he found himself being evaluated by a *very fat* cat at his feet. It seemed to be unable to decide whether to rub up against him or to run away and hide, and as his eyes lifted to look at its owner, he realized that Josie had an expression on her face that said just about the same thing. They were both nervous. Was that how the whole night would be? The lazy casualness with which he carried himself most of the time disappeared around her.

Breaking the silence, she smiled and opened her door all the way, stepping back with an arm outstretched toward the hallway. "Please, please Alex, come in."

He'd walked through the door holding a bottle of wine. He hadn't been sure, red or white, and had made a last-minute guess at the wine store, going for rosé just to be safe.

Alex held up the bottle of wine, hand gripping it like an anchor. "I brought this, I hope it goes with dinner."

She took it out of his hands and her face softened, shoulders lowering, her body relaxing. "It's wine," she said.

"Yeah, you do *drink*…?" He leaned forward, arm outstretched, his face a mask, as it occurred to him for the first time that maybe she didn't consume wine. What if she were an alcoholic and in recovery, what if she abstained for other reasons? He should have called ahead, maybe bringing a tiramisu, or something chocolate would have been a better idea. Flowers weren't even safe nowadays. He'd gone on one date where he'd brought a bouquet that had daisies in it and the poor woman had ended up sucking down Benadryl and leaving early, her flower allergy triggered by what he had thought was a romantic gesture.

She laughed. "Of course I drink, are you kidding me? Do you know anyone in the medical profession who *doesn't* drink?"

He chuckled. "Fair enough."

Her turn to laugh. "The wine's lovely, thank you. I have no idea whether it matches this dinner, but I figure it's wine, so it matches everything." She walked down a long, narrow hallway, leading to a kitchen. She didn't seem to be in the middle of rushing around cooking, and yet he saw that a lovely meal had been prepared. A salad, some sort of bread, and pasta, about to be boiled. He liked it. Simple, to the point, no frills. Like Josie.

Just as she had on the day that they'd met at the hospital after the baby's birth, she looked like she put some effort into her appearance. He liked that, but she didn't need to. The way she'd looked when they'd met at the hospital *during* the birth had actually appealed to him more. Earthy, no makeup, no pretense, just very, very real. That didn't mean he didn't appreciate what she wore right now: a soft, heathered lilac v-neck top, coupled with some nicely tailored pants. She was barefoot, with a little toe ring wrapped around her second toe, a tiny opal set in silver. He couldn't remember a tattoo from that brief interlude down by the river the other day. Tonight, he hoped, he'd be able to explore every inch of her body and find out what sort of imprints were on it.

She set the bottle of wine down on the counter and turned to him, reaching her arms up for his neck. The embrace was a bit awkward as she planted a kiss on his cheek. He was surprised that she'd made the first move, and he stumbled, then reached around her, hands flat against her back, and pressed against her. From the way her muscles melted, he could tell that she was letting herself sink away from the anxiety and the nervousness. She inhaled deeply against his neck, and he wondered if she liked the cologne he'd chosen, a scent he'd worn since high school, something spicy and citrusy.

Her kitchen was tiny, but so was everyone else's in Cambridge. She didn't seem to cook much, he thought randomly; his mind was trying to catalog the room. He shut it off and turned on the animal inside, instead. He wanted to sink with her into a different state of being, letting his desire run untamed now as he pulled her back and settled in for a kiss.

The walk over here had been filled with questions about what exactly was going on between them. But as he bent down to take her mouth fully, and her fingers played with the curly edges of his hair as she slid against him, her body submitting to his, letting him use his lips and tongue and hands to re-introduce himself, what was between them most urgently was his rock-hard—

"Hi!" she gasped, coming up for air, touching foreheads. Grinning, her lips stretched in a feline smile, the kind a woman gives you right after a toe-curling session in bed.

Not *before*.

The night just got *way* more interesting. His hands held her hips against his thighs, and he assumed she could feel him, he wanted her to feel him, bending his knees enough to lean down and go for more of that luscious mouth. Maybe an appetizer in bed before dinner. And then dinner in bed. Then bed after dinner.

With a nightcap of sex on the baseball field across the street.

Shivers ran through her body as he held her, as if she could read his mind.

And then she did.

Pulling him by the hand to the kitchen counter, she offered him the bottle of wine to hold, then reached into a drawer for a bottle opener.

"Dinner doesn't have to be ready for a while. Let's enjoy a glass or three of wine." The sly smile tickled her lips and he found himself falling into her eyes, his body harder and needier than he'd been for any woman before. A light jazz sound tinkled through the air, his ears following the sound down the hallway. Her bedroom? What color was her bedspread? Her pillow? Her vibrator?

She had to have one. No one this sensual, this experimental, wouldn't.

Hell, she probably had devices he'd never heard of.

And then he realized she was eyeing him warily. Too

much silence, he suspected. Time to pay attention to the actual woman in front of him and stop ruminating on her battery-operated bedfellows.

"A glass of wine would be lovely," he said, taking the corkscrew from her.

"You live alone?" he asked, impressed. He knew what he paid in rent at his apartment, a two-bedroom he split with a roommate who was currently on the first week of six out of town on a fellowship. The solitude was refreshing. If she could afford to shoulder this place on her own, she was either an extreme introvert—which didn't make sense, given her personality—or she was doing well financially.

He suspected neither was quite right, though. Josie was complex. Complicated. Layered. Whatever her answer, he knew it wouldn't reveal all. He'd have to keep asking.

That was fine.

He would make the time.

"Yes," she said. "This is only a one-bedroom with a little den, and the owner lives on the third floor. He says he likes having a nurse as a tenant, and I've been here for years." He opened the wine, the pressure of the bottle against his crotch a bit unsettling as he used brute force to uncork it, narrowly missing a horrific groin splash.

Josie pulled two long-stemmed wine glasses from a noticeably minimalist cupboard. Two wine glasses. Two mugs. Two of everything but plates and bowls, and if his eyes cataloged it correctly, there were four each of those, all matching, all neatly stacked.

"I can't imagine living alone. I've been doing the roommate thing for so long," he ventured. Through new eyes he surveyed the kitchen. Nothing spare in there. She lived a sparse though comfortable life, the incongruity quite charming. Unlike his own rumpled, slightly disheveled place, where no one really paid attention to anything but eating, sleeping, and showering, she seemed to have put a lot of thought into her environment.

And, especially, into what she *didn't* put in it.

"I love it," she answered, shrugging. "Mmmm," she said through a sip. "Good wine."

"Good company," he answered, offering his glass for a toast. Something snapped inside, a sense of longing and crushing desire that made him want her even more. He wanted to spend days in her bed, ordering takeout Thai and answering the door in a towel, moving the coffeemaker to her bedside table so they could be sustained by caffeine and spicy peanut sauce. Licked off her navel.

*No. No, Alex. No!* He couldn't keep doing this—it really wasn't just about sex, even if the hollow in her throat as she lifted the glass to take a big swig made him nearly groan with the need to savor it with his tongue.

*Hold back, buddy. You'll scare her off if you make it all about sex.*

Their eyes locked and he saw something in her, a deeper calm that helped to ground him. For a woman who was so focused on movement and wit, she was remarkably subdued in her own home, casual and centered.

And she had let him in.

\* \* \*

*Oh my God, can he tell how nervous and screwed up I really am?* Josie wondered as their wine glasses connected, her hand frozen in space as she tried not to shatter.

Not the glass—herself.

On the outside, she worked very hard to be casual and free, but on the inside all she wanted was to pile into bed with him and be fucked mindless.

*No!* Sex couldn't be the focus here. Dinner was. Food, wine, talk, and just being together. The kiss they'd shared was a way to say "hello," not necessarily a preliminary to hot monkey sex. Whether they ended up in bed or not didn't matter.

Ah, hell. She could hear the snort in her head. Fooling herself was getting harder and harder.

And judging by what she could see of Alex's package, so was he.

Good thing she hadn't boiled the pasta yet. A part of her wanted tonight to be about getting to know each other, talking late into the night, curled up and cuddling in the living room. Or enjoying a nice summer stroll.

But...no.

Hot monkey sex it was.

His eyes raked over her body like a man determined, with a look of fire that licked at the edges of her skin, his heat unmistakable and impossible to avoid (not that she wanted to).

How could this feel so right, even through her nervousness? In the morning, she expected to see him in the kitchen at the table, shirtless and tousled, enjoying coffee with her and then, of course, enjoying *her* for breakfast. The coffee was merely a vehicle for extra energy and a second (third, fourth, fifth) wind. Plus the idea of a shirtless Alex relaxing in a sunbeam in her kitchen made her drool.

Drool was *good*.

Why try to fight it? She squared her shoulders unconsciously with the decision to go forth, and was keenly aware that the gesture pushed her breasts forward. Shifting to relax a bit only succeeded in loosening her hips, and the thought flashed through her mind of her legs wrapped around *his* hips. A flood of heat pooled between her legs and she sighed. The form-fitting cotton pants she'd chosen so carefully for the way they made her ass look now plagued her as she shifted slightly, body warming up and raring to go.

He took her sigh as an invitation to step closer.

Excellent.

What he had chosen to wear intrigued her, turning up the fire inside yet another level. A button-down oxford, somewhere between turquoise and light blue, with the top two buttons undone. A sprinkling of dark chest hair peeked out from the V at his throat. His leather belt was so distressed it might very well have been made from a dead cow dragged twenty miles through Arizona desert, but he'd looped it through very simple dark blue pants. His dark eyes watched her watching him.

The air between them held the scent of wine and a hungry tension. Neither seemed able to put anything to words, but gestures and expressions were also inadequate. The longer they stared, the more the energy seemed poised to crackle into actual sparks; even her fat cat, languidly sauntering past them, seemed to notice it, glancing their way and dashing inexplicably in a new direction. Cars rumbled past outside, and a sudden burst of field lights from across the street told her the Little League game was in session. Their glow added a surreal shine to Alex's eyes, fixed on hers as he finished the rest of his wine in one long gulp.

Copying him, she gulped the rest of her glass and held out the bottle, tipping the neck as if to say, *More?* He nodded, and her hand rotated slowly, his eyes burning into her as she poured his second glass. She flickered her gaze away only enough to ensure she didn't spill the wine, but missed only a blink or two of Möbius strip of reciprocal observation.

And then he asked, "Is Josie short for Josephine?"

Another preliminary to get out of the way. Names. "Yes. Josephine Elizabeth Mendham."

His smile lit up the room. And her heart. He bowed slightly, a joking move, and said, "Alexander Edward Derjian. At your service."

That name rang a bell, but before she could think twice, he closed the space between them and slipped an arm around her waist, his free hand first setting down his wine glass and then carefully prying hers from her own hand. His fingers so gentle and facile on the stem that she swooned. Surgeon's hands. Long fingers. Oh, what could those do to parts of her that cried out for heat and touch and more?

She was about to find out.

"Alex, I—" His fingers, achingly soft, landed on her lips, silencing her, and the arm around her waist tightened, the hand splayed against the middle of her back where her shoulder blades met.

"Let me speak first, Ms. Josephine Elizabeth Mendham." The roll of her full name off his tongue sent her knees into a weak state, thighs humming, and her breathing becoming a bit labored with lust. The very air between them felt changed, now thick with a new element, one of luscious, unqualified want.

His hair slid over his forehead, the brown waves out of place yet damn near perfect. His wide cheekbones and bright eyes competed for her attention with his fingers, which now played with her lower lip. Two fingers rolled out a peek of the wetness of her mouth as his touch trailed to her chin.

"I said the other day that this isn't just about sex," he continued.

"I know—" Now he pressed his middle three fingers against her mouth, harder. She moaned involuntarily, her hard swallow and slow, long inhale the only way to hold back from coming right there in his arms in full view of the damn cat, who had now decided to come back and study them like intriguing prey.

"I know you think you know." Alex pivoted and grabbed a kitchen chair with the hand that wasn't making love to her mouth, sitting down and pulling her into his lap. The push of his hardness under her ass made her center swell, her throat tighten with need, and her mouth seek his.

A smile tickled his lips as he stroked her hip, running one wide palm down her thigh. This was a man who enjoyed touching women, sending a thrill of damn near everything through her, as if what she had thought was an isolated, insular act—making love—was instead a blanket that covered her entire world.

Instead of separating and compartmentalizing—*This is sex time. This is lunch time. This is work time.*—he made it seem, in this split second, that it could all be integrated into *This is life*.

"I need to make *sure* you know, Josie. This is me telling you so. But first, I want to make love with you, because no matter how many times I tell myself this isn't only about sex, and that I don't want to scare you off by making you think I think it's only about sex, all I can think about is getting you stripped bare and using my hands and tongue and"—he shifted, making it obvious which other part of his body he wished to use—"to make you cry out my name like it's the only word left in your mind."

Josie had no words. She couldn't even try to speak.

"And then we'll work on the rest of the getting to know each other stuff, like your cat's name, and—"

Sweetly, with an exquisite motion that took time and broke it into little slivers of awareness, she rose up in his lap, wrapping her legs about his waist on the chair, the rasp of cloth against cloth a friction that set her entire body abuzz. With one finger, she traced a lazy path from his eyebrow down his face, the aroma of his cologne infusing her as she let all her senses come forth and accept this as it blossomed, time changing in the air between them.

The look of her skin against his, how his eyebrow raised with a questioning look, how his eyes told her more in an unspoken language than every word she'd heard in her lifetime could possibly have communicated.

The brush of her fingertips against his freshly shaven chin and the taste of his jawline as she leaned down to kiss it mingled with the sounds of kids and parents cheering across the street, blending with blues that poured out of the speakers in her bedroom. What had felt like a nervous rush since the second she'd met him in the hospital last week turned on a dime.

His strong, smooth hands now caressing the nape of her neck, his abs brushing against hers, their bodies seeking to fit into each other just right as their tongues found each other, a savored entwining that she deliberately drew out, as if to tell him in tender flesh that this *now* was not measured in seconds or minutes or hours.

It had its own timeline.

"Cats," she said slowly against his mouth. "I have two. One hides nonstop, but the one you've met is Dotty."

"Dotty," he murmured.

"Yes. Dotty and Crackhead."

"Crackhead?" he sputtered, wiggling his hips almost enough that she could have dry humped him and walked away with one of the best orgasms ever. It was, however, in her best interests to stick around and go for the more mature climactic approach. The way he moved *juuuust* enough to set her right on top of his erection told her he was thinking the same thought. Her lust twin.

How convenient.

"Now that you know their names," she whispered against his mouth, "are we done with all the 'not sex' parts, and can we move to the 'sex parts'?"

"I like your sex parts," Alex sighed, sliding one hand up to cup her breast, the nipple responding to his touch.

Her hand found his erection easily, though it was blocked by clothing. "I'd like yours more if I could see them," she teased.

"At your service, Ms. Josephine." Nearly falling to the ground as he stood, Josie found herself the only customer at a private striptease as Alex unceremoniously unbuttoned his shirt, his fingers precise and efficient. As the shirt hung open at the chest, she realized she'd only caught glimpses of his nakedness in the handful of romps they'd had, illicit moments stolen in an on-call room, an outdoor trail, an elevator.

Time for the big unveiling.

*Big.*

* * *

Alex couldn't remember the last time he'd had this much *fun* getting naked for a woman. Toppling Josie out of his lap had been tough, but necessary, if it meant he could take the lead and show her what "sex parts" really meant.

*You want 'em? You got 'em.*

The cat—was that Dotty or Crackhead?—sniffed with pretentious condescension and headed for the living room.

Good. The only audience he wanted was Josie.

As he slid his shirt off and slung it over the back of a kitchen chair, she joined him, to his delight. She reached down with both hands and pulled her knit top off in one intensely erotic motion, throwing the light piece of cloth onto a little bench behind her. The silken lilac bra underneath was so feminine, so achingly delicate, that he wanted to take it off her with a savage grace. Holding himself back, he took her in with his eyes while she returned the favor.

They both seemed to like what they saw.

He nodded. "Go ahead."

She frowned, hands on hips now. "Go ahead what?"

"The bra." He stood before her, shirtless, filled with a thrumming that blocked out the rest of the world.

"What about the bra?" she asked, looking down at it.

"You need to take it off or I'll rip it off with my teeth."

"You can't!"

"I have very strong teeth."

She lowered her eyelashes as if thinking of a retort, but after a moment, her arms slowly reached behind her, for the clasp. And then, before his mind could process what she was doing, Josie spun and darted down the hall, screaming, "Only if you can catch me!"

God, she was fast.

Running, his legs constrained by all-too-tight pants, he

chased her. He reached the door of her bedroom as she was laughingly turning back to it, her elbows still winged out as she wiggled the hooks free. "I beat you," she was gleefully crowing, but before she quite finished the taunt, he caught her, caught the loose strap as it began its slide down her left shoulder, and pulled the bra from her grasp.

Her laugh cut out as she caught her breath; she panted a few quick breaths as their eyes locked again. He slid the bra off entirely and momentarily looked away for a place to toss it.

The bedroom was nicely decorated, homey, with rather large bedside tables and a multicolored silk scarf suspended from the ceiling, covering a light fixture. The last of the day's light poured in from the windows, but soon dusk would make it too dark. He planned to be here through the stillness of the summer night.

And into the bright light of the sun's wake-up rays.

Her gaze pulled his eyes back to her and he let the bra fall to the floor.

He said, "I will always catch you."

\* \* \*

*Why did he have to be so damn hot?* she wondered, standing next to her bed, stripped down to her panties and trying to play off how much he overwhelmed her. As if she routinely played tag with men with washboard abs and faces like models, routinely ending the game in her bedroom half naked.

Like that happened *every* Tuesday.

*Maybe it can*, a voice whispered in her head.

Roadhouse blues floated through the air, the smoky tones of scratched vinyl mixed with saxophone foreplay adding to the perfection in the room. Dusk settled the edges of the window's harsh daylight glare into a more modest tone, but still she felt illuminated and on display as Alex's eyes hungrily ate her up.

She returned the favor as he revealed himself, stripping down to boxer briefs, the fluid lines of his powerful thighs making her even wetter and more ready—as if that were possible. Naturally olive-toned skin peppered with curly hair where it ought to be, thickening right where she remembered. The boxer briefs clung to his upper thighs, ass, and manhood exactly the way they should, as if female appreciation were woven into the contours of the cloth, directing the fibers to hug his body exactly as Josie wished.

She really could have watched him all day.

He had other ideas.

*I will always catch you.* Did he really just say that? She shivered with arousal, gooseflesh taking over her exposed arms, chest, and breasts, her nipples tightening. Before she could continue her mind's inner chatter, Alex had crossed the room like a lion leading a pride, his nearly nude body pulling her onto her patchwork quilt that covered the bed. The comfort of worn cotton invited her to stay awhile, the hot press of his chest against hers a sensation she could bathe in forever.

His kiss was slow and seeking, with a barely restrained urgency that made her back arch, breasts pressing into his bare pecs. So much flesh touching. Quite different from their first rushed moments. The completeness of it made her skin tickle, and the heat that emanated from their entwined bodies seemed to pool between her legs. A shift of his hips and his hard cock pressed into that heat, the frustration of two thin swaths of cloth enough to make her gasp.

The song ended, and an Etta James croon came on, enough to make him smile through a kiss. Alex propped his head, elbow on the bed, and looked at her with delight, taking his sweet time to survey her body. Immodest, she reveled in it, flouting all the chick-magazine-y rules on how to behave in bed with a man.

"Behave" wasn't in her vocabulary right now.

"Obey", however…might be, depending on what Alex

had in mind…

He was exquisite, and her hands took the liberty of running over his chest, down to his waist, where a sharp inhale told her what he wanted. No rush, right? As he dipped his head to watch her hand memorize each pore, every skin cell, that led her to what she really wanted to touch, he gripped her wrist and forced her to pause, his knuckles pressing into the soft flesh of her belly, inches above where she really wanted *him* to touch.

"No rush," he said, letting go, then sliding his palm along her hip. The slow journey up the curve of her waist to the edge of her breast, then to her shoulder, was like a long lick up an ice cream cone in August. She was, like the ice cream cone, dripping.

And then he rolled her onto her back, eyes taking her in. "Beautiful," he whispered as his mouth took one budded nipple and rolled it between his tongue and lower lip, the ache for completion driving her to arch up into him, begging him wordlessly for more. His calves brushed against her thigh as he changed position and angled his mouth at a better degree, spare hand sliding not down, but up to her jawline.

This would be slow, wouldn't it? Could she make love at the speed of Alex? It was a physics formula that jumbled into a potpourri of letters and words as his lips brushed a line across the valley of her breasts to give equal attention to both, as if the symmetry mattered.

What was he thinking, taking all the time in the world to explore her, the newness of him as foreign and exotic to her as she must be to him? Was this really about "sex parts"? If so, this would be enough. The chase was over. She was firmly caught. An all-body hum began the slow build inside her as his mouth now turned south, blood rushing to her ears and the red, throbbing core between her legs.

Peeling her panties from her hips, he took the time to caress her legs as his nimble fingers dispensed with the thin wisp of cloth, throwing it somewhere in the general direction of her vanity. Now the symmetry was broken, for she was bare. Time to make things even again.

"Fair is fair," she murmured as her hands slipped under the waistband of his boxer briefs, sliding them down to his feet with a deftness that belied her normally clumsy nature. Both fully nude, they paused, taking each other in. Neither was self-conscious. The mutual appreciation made her laugh, a low, throaty sound that sounded far too bold and sophisticated even for her.

"You see something that makes you laugh?" he asked as he looked down at their naked, interwoven bodies.

*Really?* He made it so easy to wisecrack, to hide. Fifteen different sarcastic retorts fought against her lips. Taking the harder path, she just smiled and said, "I don't know why I'm laughing. It's just…"

"Joy," he said simply, brushing a lock of her hair off her cheek.

"Joy? What is this 'joy' of which you speak?" she joked. Except she wasn't joking. Joy? What was that? Who talked like this? Happiness—sure. Contentment—okay. Pleasure—no problem.

*Joy?*

"It's a feeling," he whispered, moving down to her navel, his tongue slowly tracing circles around her belly button, making joy pour out of her body in the form of muscle spasms that needed him inside her to grip against.

"Oh, I'm feeling," she gasped, fingers reaching for his hair, working hard to fight against the tidal wave that splashed against her V. The last of the daylight flirted with the horizon, little touches teasing the clouds. Cooler night air wafted in the windows, making the room perfect.

"I want you to feel joy, Josie. And this, too." Closing her eyes, she knew what came next, the unhurried movement of her legs sliding apart on the coverlet, how her ass filled his hands, his forearms under her, the rush of his warm mouth on her, the slowness speeding up so suddenly, the world cracking at the edges and turning from a sphere to a relief map, all laid out on her skin for Alex to explore.

*Joy? Oh, yes.* Heart swelling in tandem with her sex, she took in his shoulders, lifting up to meet the gift of his tongue. The way his hands had touched her earlier, every time, had told her he enjoyed women.

His tongue confirmed it. As he explored her body's joy and desire through his mouth, stroking and tuning her to a new frequency, she faced a layer of intensity that she'd never experienced before with a man. The accumulated moments before this one all a nuanced tapestry in her mind and flesh, the knowledge that Alex liked her, that he wanted her, that someone so steady and hot and focused and real could be in her bed right now, naked under her palms, laving and giving without pretense—knowing it was more erotic than his actual touch.

And then there was his body. Opening her eyes, she allowed herself to see what he was doing to her, to watch rippling muscles in his arms as he took care of her first. Panting, her breath coming in little gasps, she felt the wave push into and out of her at once, hips bucking, as if the *thought* of what this meant for her and Alex was enough to take her into orgasm.

More than this, though, she wanted him above her, in her, driving home the connection and surrounding her with his scent, his heat, his light, and the sound of his own pleasure when it mingled with hers.

Her hands clawed at the bedsheets, pulling them from the corners and twisting as her body twisted, too, Alex coming up to kiss her with such certainty, her taste on him and now in her own mouth, his mouth so soft, hands on her breasts. Suddenly aware of how little she had focused on him, she moved past her own pulsing pleasure and reached down to stroke him, finding him hard and ready.

Joy. Joy coursed through the veins that made him so casually authentic, and when the song on the radio changed, his low chuckle made her halt her hand, fingertips enjoying the sensation.

"Dirty Dozen Brass Band," he said, kissing the hollow of her neck.

Knowing the song—and delighted that he knew the band, because no one she knew ever did—she stroked him twice, then slid her hand along the tight ridges of muscle in his inner thigh.

"'Don't You Feel My Leg,'" he said.

"Song title, or command?"

"Song title, of course," he whispered, eyes closing as she wrapped her hand around him, fingers struggling to touch. The tuba's deep bass line felt jaunty and joking, a bit out of place for this moment, and yet it was fitting. Whatever came to them just did, as if life orchestrated what fate poured into the air. He stopped her, opening his eyes and pulling himself up over her, giving her access to all of him. My God. How beautiful he was.

"I want to be in you, Ms. Josephine," he said, as if he had to ask permission. Yet it wasn't a question, was it?

"And I want you in me, Dr. Perfect," she replied, rolling over to open the drawer where she stored the necessary precautions. As she turned, his hand caressed her ass, lips dipping down to kiss her on each buttock, making her laugh. This was intense and frolicking, all at once. The two, it seemed, were not mutually exclusive in Alex's bedroom world.

"Dr. Perfect?"

"McDreamy was taken."

The baritone laugh that came out of him, his face morphing from sexual intensity to pure delight, made her fall a little more into something she feared was as close to love as she was capable of feeling. Where was the awkwardness? The self-conscious mental ricocheting of thoughts and worries and suppositions?

She and he were two people entwined on her bed, about to make love, and as he took the condom from her and dispensed with the formalities quickly, she found a glee in her that had never been present during sex before. Instead of hiding her emotions, as she normally did, focused solely on the animal nature of the act, on surges and rushes and highs and explosions, Josie allowed Alex to bring her to a new kind of lovemaking. It was almost too easy.

Almost. Tears threatened to fill her eyes, drawn out by a groundswell of emotion that made her look at him—*really* look at him—and see a man she could spend her whole life with, love—

"You are so amazing," Alex said, interrupting her thoughts. *Thank God.*

"You are, too," she said, her body surprised when he rolled and pulled her on top of him. Oh, he liked it this way? Enjoying the power of having him spread out before her, her hands washed over his chest, up his neck, to his face, tracing his lips with fingers that tried to memorize him. Adjusting her hips, she ached to have him in her. He made her feel tiny and delicate, but also on display as his hands roamed up her belly, over the edge of her ribcage, then cupped both breasts.

"This," he said, hands now on her hips, guiding her, "is amazing, too." And then all she needed to do was a small lift with one thigh, a knee placed on the bed just so, and the tip of him filled her, the pressure so inviting that he entered her slowly, the gasp of pleasure as their eyes met, the wordless communication and communion actually bringing those tears out.

Leaning together for a kiss, their bodies moved in rhythm, her deep core of heat growing, emanating out into her limbs while tightening at the center, her walls clamping down as Alex groaned, lips pressed against hers. At some point, the kiss became lost as each felt the climax form, something shared that could only be fueled by mutuality.

"Josie," he whispered through gritted teeth, just as she was about to say his name, too. Both felt it, and then he added, "Are you…?"

"Close?" she filled in for him. "God, yes."

That was all it took as Alex enveloped her hips with his strong, big hands, a conductor of the symphony's end, setting the rhythm and choosing strokes far more sensual than any she would have found on her own. One, two, three thrusts up and the orgasm slammed into her, grown large by an impossible sense of longing that played itself out in an embrace as she wrapped every spare section of skin against his body, holding on for dear life as stray strands of his hair caught in her mouth, ragged gasps her only words now, proving him right. She could think of nothing more than *Alex, Alex, Alex*, his name an infinite loop of pure joy, her body racked with wave after wave of *him*.

Whole body on fire, the heat receded slowly, her awareness of aching hips and a slightly raw feeling where he entered her reminders of the juxtaposition of their sizes. Alex was big, she was not, and whatever similarities they shared, in bed he was decidedly all *man*. He made her all *woman*.

A loud *crack* pierced the air, and then the crowd at the baseball field cheered, the sound bursting through the open window.

"Well, I knew I was good, but I've never had *that* kind of reaction before," Josie said, sitting up, her hand cradling Alex's face. Rich, brown eyes met hers with a kindness and depth that would have terrified her even a day ago.

"I would give you a standing ovation," he said.

"You just did," she said, squeezing a Kegel around him. Laughing, he slid out of her, then rolled her off him, spooning. So much warmth. The man's entire body was one big heating pad, and she wondered what this would feel like in the dead of winter, cozy in bed with Alex, no longer needing the cats to warm her feet.

That thought made her roll her eyes, the intrusion of cat-lady fears seeping into the afterglow. She and Laura had often mournfully joked about being alone in old age, surrounded by cats. Alex's steady breath filled her ear, the rasp of stubble against her neck, the slow, layered relaxation of her body against his banishing those fears. They were one right now, and then her stomach gurgled, a horridly intrusive sound that seemed louder than the crowd outside.

"We forgot to eat," he said, the rush of his breath against her ear a luxury she could become accustomed to making commonplace. As if on cue, his stomach growled as well, sending them both into giggles, their bodies shaking in bed, joy pouring forth in new ways.

The room had darkened enough that she reached forward to snap on the bedside table light. Still nude, their bodies were a series of legs and hips and arms, all mixed together like a bouquet of flowers. Peeling away, she searched the floor for her clothes, spotting each piece and cataloging. Whatever happened next was random, so she was uncertain. Get dressed? Slide under the covers? Hop in the shower? Boil the pasta?

Alex made a quiet exit from the room, his ass an inviting sight as he padded out into the hallway. Ah. The condom. How base and embarrassing it often was to have a guy deal with the aftermath of what had been hot and frenzied. Here it was just something to be done, like putting on shoes, or combing one's hair. By the time he returned she had located her panties and sat on the edge of the bed, feeling a bit unmoored.

Joy resumed as he stood before her, completely nude and utterly self-composed.

"I've never—" they said in unison, making Josie burst into laughter. Alex smiled and reached down for his underwear, slipping into them. Symmetry.

His face was solemn as he said, "You, too? You mean you were a virgin until just now?"

She snorted, a decidedly unfeminine sound. Again, fifty different wisecracks flooded her. As he leaned in for a kiss, she decided that saying nothing was the best course.

\* \* \*

As he leaned in for a kiss, she stayed silent. He took her solemn look as an invitation to continue being real with her. Their lips met and the kiss lit him on fire, made his legs tense, and yes, he was hard again. Josie seemed to trigger that condition twenty times an hour when he was around her. She shifted just enough that her breasts were soft and yielding against his chest, as he bent at the knees to press into her, to really kiss her in a way that he hoped would make her toes curl. Yet again their stomachs gurgled, like chirping birds desperate for a meal. He pulled back and she held three fingers up to his lips, mimicking his earlier gesture from a few hours ago. It seemed like a lifetime. Time had escaped him and for all he knew he was marking the minutes and the hours all wrong. She had that effect on him.

"Let's get dressed and let's eat."

"How about we eat and then get undressed," he said.

She laughed, reaching for her shirt and pulling it on, leaving the bra untouched.

*A good sign*, he thought, *of things to come*. By the time he'd pulled on his pants and his unbuttoned shirt, she was down the hall. He heard the sound of the refrigerator door opening, cupboards open and shut. As he reached her in the kitchen, she was in front of the stove, turning the stove up under the pot of water.

"More wine?" she asked, her hands slipping on the wine bottle, condensation having formed around it.

He'd brought it chilled, and now, based on the temperature as he took a sip of his poured wine, he could guess how long they'd been. Not long enough. Her nervousness began to rattle him. This was the awkward part, wasn't it? Perhaps he should have waited, but he couldn't, unhinged by her. Small talk seemed so trite, and yet it was a kind of social lubricant that made whatever needed to come next that much easier.

She took the lead. "So, what in the hell do we talk about after *that*?" she asked, nudging her head toward the door to the hallway to her room.

Disarmed, he burst out laughing and drank down half his glass of wine in one big gulp. "Is there a manual for this?" he asked.

"I've never seen one show up on my Kindle," she replied.

"Maybe there's an app that we don't know about." He reached for her, grateful for her bluntness, and his eyes recognized in hers the same searching that he was feeling. They looked at each other for a good, long minute, neither flinching, or wincing, or breaking eye contact, just letting it deepen. Their bodies relaxing layer by layer, their souls really seeing each other.

"Can we just agree that this is what it is, and it will unfold however it unfolds?" he asked. Her face clouded and he realized that she was taking it wrong; the words so noncommittal, the kind of thing assholes say...*Can we just take this step by step?*

He tried to explain what he *really* meant, which was, "Josie, what I mean is that this is one of the most extraordinary experiences that I've ever had with a woman. Not *this*," he said, his hand pointing vaguely toward her bedroom, "*this*." He squeezed her hips, pulling her tight against him, enjoying the feel of her hands against his bare back, sliding up under his open shirt. "This. Whatever you and I have, every second we're together, is new territory for me."

Her eyes went wide and her expression seemed to flip through her entire repertoire of emotions. She finally settled on a relaxed, open look, that he knew intuitively was not part of her standard operating procedure for relating to men. "I don't do this, Alex," she said quietly. "I don't have relationships with men. I have flings, I have casual friends-with-benefits-type things. I sleep around...did." She held up one hand. "Did. *Slept* around. That should be past tense, shouldn't it, when it's been years? I date. I see 'guys,'" she said, using quotation marks with her fingers to indicate some sort of self-conscious irony that he didn't quite grasp. "What you're proposing is that I show you who I really am, layer by layer, through wherever this takes me."

"Yes," he said simply. She got it; she knew exactly what he felt.

Her face became more serious, if that was possible, and she said, "Wouldn't it be easier to just ask me for a threesome?" Pause. "Joking!"

He pulled back and laughed at his own surprise and at her words.

"You're asking for a hell of a lot from someone like me," she continued.

"Someone like you?" he asked.

"I don't *do* emotional openness," she explained, "I do sex, I do fun, I do sarcasm, I do..."

"Your nails?"

"Yeah, my nails," she said. "You like them?"

"Cute." Her fingernails looked like lilac bushes, sprigs that matched the color of her shirt. "Then maybe it's time you tried something new," he said, pulling her close again. The struggle remained evident on her face; she wanted him and not just his body, he could tell. But something held her back.

"You said that we needed to take this moment by moment and let it unfold, right?" she asked, stepping out of the embrace.

Turning away from her, he closed his eyes, not sure what to say. "Yes," he said again, careful not to overwhelm her with more. Her hands shook as she stirred the boiling water, pouring the pasta in bit by bit. He was absolutely terrifying her, wasn't he? It dawned on him that whatever he felt for her, she seemed to feel it, too.

*When had this gotten so complicated?* he wondered, staring at her arms as her elbow bent to stir the pasta, her face obscured by rising steam.. The conversation had gone deep and a bit dark, suddenly, as if he were pressuring her for something rather than offering.

"I don't want more from you than you...want to give."

She smiled, an indecipherably bitter grin. "You were about to say 'capable of,' weren't you?"

"No, actually," he said, stopping the arm that stirred the pot and turning her toward him, "that wasn't the word in mind."

"What was, then?" she asked. On the surface, she was closed off, but he sensed that underneath she was fighting against whatever demons she had inside. He wanted to see those demons, expose them to the light, to his want, his acceptance, and—he couldn't believe he was thinking the word *love*, but yes, love, so that the demons could be vanquished. Getting her to drop that shield was his only hope.

Inhaling slowly, she closed her eyes, took a deep breath, and breathed out her mouth. The way her body moved, fluid and graceful as she made herself relax, made him appreciate her even more: the lines of her arms in motion, or her forearm in his hand, of how her neck sloped just right into her earlobe, the way the skin around her eyes told him twenty-seven different things in one look. And yet...she was not completely relaxing. Her muscles were still tense, a bit awkward, as if they weren't certain which Josie they were supposed to be.

"When did this get complicated?" she asked, as if reading his mind.

"It's always complicated." He shrugged.

"Don't say that," she growled through gritted teeth.

He stepped back, a bit surprised by her ferocious retort. "Okay," he said slowly, "then I won't say that it's always complicated. Do you want me to say that it's never complicated?"

"I don't know what I want you to say."

The words were the most earnest thing that had come out of her mouth in the week that he had known her, and it gave him hope. His stomach chose to speak for him in that moment, growling, almost matching her tone a moment ago.

"The perfect response," she said, resuming her cooking.

"You know how it goes, the way to a man's heart and all that…"

"I thought the way to a man's heart was through his groin?"

"Then you've got me already."

"Good, 'cause I'm a lousy cook."

"I doubt you're lousy at anything."

"Oh, trust me, Alex, once you get to know me you'll learn that I'm lousy at lots of things." She pulled the stock pot off the stove and drained the boiling water, clouds of steam covering her face and making her hair curl up at the ends. Her cheeks were pink and her face glistened from the moisture. The cloth of her cotton v-neck clung to the tops of her breasts, her nipples hard and tight. Without a bra her form showed better through the clothing, and he wished that they were in bed again. Already, already he was hard, dammit, his pants a miserable prison for his arousal. "What can I do to help?" he asked.

"Help me show you how lousy I am?" she said, a grin on her face. She poured the pasta into a large serving bowl and stuck a claw into it. Was there some official name for those utensils? He and his mother just called it the pasta claw.

"You could put the salad on the table," she said.

He did what he was asked, enjoying the domestic routineness of it, until finally the food was on the table, the dishes were set, and they sat down to eat, each covered in the other's musk, each starving. The meal itself was quite quiet, neither of them particularly interested in talking anymore.

"This is good," he said.

"You're just saying that because you think you have to."

"I don't say anything that I don't mean. It's good. Thank you. You've made a lovely meal."

She looked at him as if he had four heads. "You know, we already had sex, Alex, you don't need to butter me up. I'm kind of a sure thing."

"If you came over to my place for dinner, trust me, this would be a luxurious meal."

"What would you serve if you invited me over for dinner?" she asked.

"Takeout pizza, Thai."

"In bed?" She looked down at the bowl of pasta and grabbed a bit of salad, putting it on her plate. "That might taste better."

"The only thing that would taste better is you," he said without acrimony, and she smiled, reaching across the table for his hand.

"Thank you." She closed her eyes again and sighed deeply. "I'm sorry, I just have no framework for how to behave with someone like you."

Now he was hitting paydirt. "What do you mean?"

"I like you, Alex. I just don't know what men like you are like."

"The only way out is through," he said, squeezing her hand.

* * *

And just like that, Josie's ridiculously self-defeating forcefield melted away. The food that had felt like lumps of nothing in her mouth resumed its flavor, the oregano and basil bursting forth as she swallowed and drank a few mouthfuls of wine. Music lilted through the air, the low tones of a perfectly played bass lifting her heart. Alex's smile seemed less an indictment of her emotional stuntedness and more an invitation to a future.

Letting go meant *feeling*.

Surefooted and smart, he sensed it, leaning closer, filling his mouth with more wine and resting in place, letting the enormity of it all sink in. Together, they just sat there at her kitchen table as headlights flashed strobe lights on the wall, car engines turning on, rear lights blinking as the game ended across the street and people made their way back to their normally scheduled lives, the fun of the diversion over.

The diversion, for Josie, had been her shell.

Time for real life to kick in.

"Do you watch *The IT Crowd?*" she asked.

Alex's eyes narrowed; she knew he knew this was a test. "No."

"Want to?"

"Now?" His voice rose with the question, a bit incredulous.

"Now," she stated definitively. "All of the men I date have to pass the *IT Crowd* test."

"Or else what?"

"Or else…" Damn it. He'd caught her. "I don't know."

"How did the other guys do?"

"You're the first."

"What about *Downton Abbey?*"

"You watch it?" she squealed.

"No. Just asking. I don't watch anything, Josie. I work hundred-hour weeks."

So many responses. As the air pivoted, she realized she could use this as a lever to get out. *You don't have time for me,* she could say. *You've overworked. You'll move when your residency is over and leave the city. You will find someone better and leave me.*

Why even try, then?

Holding back from self-sabotage, she said, "We have time now!"

"We have lots of things we could do with our time."

"*IT Crowd* or *Downton Abbey* are good non-sex parts of a relationship."

One eyebrow rose on his face. "Is this a relationship?"

Caught. "It's a...*something*."

"I'm in a something with you?"

"Yes. Don't push your luck."

"What's the next step in a *something*? An *everything*?"

*Oh God, yes,* she thought. "A *maybe*."

"Ooooh, I can't wait for a *maybe*. Followed by a *possibly*?"

"No, after a *maybe* comes *anal*."

He slapped a palm against his forehead. "Only Ms. Josephine Elizabeth Mendham would talk about anal and *Downton Abbey* in the same conversation."

She gave him the stink eye. "You really *haven't* seen the show, apparently."

Sighing, he stood, refilled their wine glasses, took her hand, and walked her toward the television in the living room. Both carried their wine in their spare hands. "No, I haven't but now I have to. *Downton Abbey* it is."

"And *IT Crowd* next time," she blurted out.

"To next time," he said, holding his wine out for a toast.

"'Next time' is code for sex, isn't it?"

"Yes."

"Good."

# CHAPTER NINE

Some strange man's rather muscular thigh trapped her to the bed, her arms swimming to reach shore. A ringing in her ears pierced her fuzzy consciousness and she realized it was her phone ringing, and Alex, naked, was sound asleep, half on top of her.

The phone slipped out of her hands twice until she finally pressed the glass and shoved it in the general direction of her ear.

"'Lo?"

"I'm living with a squid who eats my body fluids!"

Laura. What time was it? She pulled the phone away from her ear and squinted. 8:22 a.m. "I don't want to hear about your sex life with Dylan," Josie hissed.

"I was talking about Jillian!"

Josie cleared her throat and said nothing.

"Besides, there is no sex life for me with anyone. You ever try to have sex with a screaming time bomb in the house that shits up its back at any moment?"

"No, but I did see an ad like that on the Craigslist personal section once."

A slow turn from the large, manly body next to her gave her eye candy to last for months. "Who is it?" he mumbled. "Did my phone go off? Is there an emergency at the hospital?"

"Who's there!" Laura shrieked into the phone. "Where are you?"

Josie wiped her eyes and cleared her throat. "I'm at home." The less said the better, as Alex reached up to caress one bare breast. In the daylight, his body was even better than she'd imagined, all protective and big. He buried his head in her hip, cuddling in a way that sent shoots of heat through her.

"Who said 'hospital'?" Laura asked.

"I did," Alex replied, chuckling into Josie's belly.

"Oh my God, is Dr. Perfect in bed with you?"

Time to give up. "Yes."

Alex grabbed the phone and spoke into it. "No," he said, kissing her hipbone, then sliding away, his receding warmth nearly making her cry. His muscled ass wandered into the hallway and she heard a door shut.

"*SQUEEEEE!*" Laura's scream could be heard five houses down by the deaf, ancient labradoodle that wore a diaper when its owner took her for walks every morning. "You're sleeping with Alex?"

"I am something*ing* with Alex."

"What's *somethinging*?"

"We're making it up as we go along."

"You let him spend the night?"

Silence. This was not an easy conversation.

"Josie? You *never* let guys spend the night."

"He watched *Downton Abbey* with me last night. We fell asleep in front of Netflix after four episodes."

"Men don't watch *Downton Abbey* unless they're trying to get in your pants."

"Well, it worked."

Another *squeee* from Laura. "You never, *ever* let guys stay over," she repeated, her tone of utter marvel making Josie's stomach flutter.

"I know, but *he* doesn't know that, and you're yelling as

if I were your deaf great-grandma, so cut it out."

"Okay," Laura whispered with great affect, like someone on stage.

"Why are you calling?" A gurgle in the distance told her Alex was making coffee.

"To complain about my sex life. But yours is much more interesting. Do tell!"

"Tell what?" Josie asked dryly.

"Is he perfect in bed, too?"

"God, yes," Josie murmured into the phone, cupping her hand around it. "Even better than the other day by the river."

"What river?"

"Remember the leaf in my hair?"

"You had sex with him the day after I gave birth?"

"Yes," Josie hissed. More distant gurgling.

"You picked up a doctor at my birth and then fucked him by the river while I was humping ice packs like a bride on a Sybian at a bachelorette party?"

Long pause. "I really can't go with that analogy, Laura."

Alex sauntered back in, gloriously buff, carrying two mugs of coffee. He handed one to her.

Perfect. Dr. Fucking Perfect. No man had ever brought her coffee in bed. Then again, no man ever had the chance to…

"He just brought me coffee in bed," she hissed into the phone.

"Did I interrupt sex?" Laura squealed.

"No, but you're about to," Alex said in a cheerfully loud voice.

"Byelauragottago," Josie said in a rush as she turned off the phone. Coffee, schmoffee.

If she needed a little something to wake her up…

Or something big.

"Want to shower?" he murmured in her ear as she took one last sip of her hot coffee, suddenly alert. Shower sex would be a first for her; her nipples tingled at the thought.

His hands caressed her belly, one sliding down already as the warmth of his arms around her, pulling her up, made the world melt away yet again.

A nagging thought crossed her mind, intruding. "I have to be at work by ten!" she gasped. Her phone said 8:30 a.m.

"We can have a quick shower." Yanking her arm, he bent his knees, exerting enough gentle force to make her lose her footing and crash into his wall of muscle.

"Wait! We need a—"

"Condom," he interrupted. She pulled out of his arms and circled the bed, opening the drawer and snatching one—fast. They ran to the bathroom. He'd beaten her by seconds and turned on the shower, the spray arcing over the curtain rod in places and making her shriek.

"You raised the nozzle!" she shouted.

"It was set at the height of a dachshund."

"Hey!" Standing on tiptoes, she tried to stare him down but was faced with his nipples instead. Playful and goofy, she reached out with her teeth and nipped one. Arms clinched around her and the sense of playfulness dissipated instantly, as if a switch flipped inside her that aroused every sense, making the feel of her bare skin against his hard legs, the push of his erection against her belly, and the lush movements of his hands on her ass turn her from a silly thing to a sultry woman.

Steam rose over their heads as the water heated in tandem with her blood, fire between them evident as his hands went everywhere—hers, too. Bodies tangled in a dance of strokes and sighs. Stepping into the shower, she bent over to set the condom on the edge of the tub and found him behind her, the push of his hardness against her thigh.

Oh, my. The shock of so much of him behind her, of the water pounding both their naked bodies, of his arms and hands and thighs and all of Alex pressed against her, slipping and sliding and taking her over made her flush and swell, eager for sex that would be fast and furious. Spinning around, she wrapped her limbs around his body and moaned as the parts matched up in just the right places.

Mouths hungry, the water hot and aimed right over her head, it pounded into his neck and sprayed around, he reached down to find her, one finger sliding in as she gasped, opening her eyes to find him wet and smoldering, as if that were possible.

One last, almost violent kiss and he turned her around, one hand grasping her breast and pinching her nipple so hard she nearly climaxed, and then the telltale sound of the wrapper tearing, a hand against the cleft of her ass, and his voice.

"Put your hands against the wall."

The order made her knees tingle, palms slapping against the white fiberglass wall. Splayed out, her hands bore witness to his arm wrapped around her waist, his hand roaming wherever it damn well pleased, his thighs sliding against hers as his other hand took his thick self and slowly centered the tip right where she wanted it most. Backing up, she helped him to enter her, the water's spray on her back now, thin rivers pouring over her breast, waterfalls cascading from her nipples.

Never a fan of sex where she couldn't be face to face, this was something completely different. Filled with an erotic uncertainty, she tingled and faltered, thrilled by his new dominance. The power of Alex's thrusts behind her, how one hand now rested on her shoulder, the other strumming her clit, made her lift one leg and brace herself against the tub edge, the new angle so exquisite she felt the rush of orgasm right then, her inner core muscles tightening with breakneck speed.

"Oh, God, Josie," he said behind her, the tension palpable in the wet air, his voice like gravel. And then— both tightened, hard, and she exploded into a million tiny fragments, slamming her backside against him, wanting to take in as much as possible, needing him to fill her and touch that thin line of flesh inside her that made everything whole and disintegrated everything, all at once.

Face down, she inhaled ragged breaths, the water pooling at her lips and dripping down, all senses focused on the muscle contractions that fueled a supernova of need and release. Slowly, Alex's deep thrusts receded, his hand on her red nub at a standstill, the sandpapery shift of his cheek against her shoulder blade a sign that both were done.

Sometimes it felt good to just be *fucked*. A quickie could reset her entire mood and make the world make sense. Bright eyed, she lowered her leg and he pulled out, taking the hint, as she leaned back against him, and the two stood, silent, in the downpour. Ear against his chest, she waited through each breath to hear the pounding go to normal, Alex peppering the top of her head with kisses.

Josie took a deep breath, exhaled, and said, through sputtering lips overcome with shower spray, "We should actually shower."

"I'll soap you up," he said, reaching for the bar.

"I'll end up against the wall again if you do that," she answered, dodging his hand as it traveled down between her legs.

"And the problem is…?"

Laughter poured out of them both, but, as if they were old hands at doing this, each split off to a separate section of the tiny shower and did a quick wash and shampoo, trading places under the spray to rinse off. Weak and completely wrung out, Josie climbed out and toweled off, enjoying the view as Alex did the same as he walked to the bedroom. He must have dispensed with the condom at some point, though she had no idea when. The man was a condom Houdini.

He returned to the bathroom dressed. She pouted. He shrugged and walked into the kitchen. The beep of a microwave was her soundtrack as she dressed, too, choosing a simple white button-down and khakis for work.

"I heated our coffees," he said as she waltzed into the kitchen. Coffee. *Ahhhh.* She used to say it was better than sex, but she couldn't say *that* anymore. Grateful, she sat across from him, playing footsie.

"You working today?" she asked.

"No. I need to catch up on sleep. My shift starts tonight. Twenty-four hours."

Awkwardness set in. Avoiding his eyes, she wondered what she could say next without sounding too needy. Part of her wanted to see him every day possible, to schedule their next date so that it was set in her mind, a firm joining that would allay her insecurities.

Another part wanted to fade out and avoid. Already at the brink of what she could handle emotionally, she felt fragile inside and ready to snap.

Living with both feelings was like an interminable sentence.

A quick check of the clock told her he needed to go— now. How could she ask him to leave? It felt rude. Wrong. Abrupt. And yet this was the longest she'd ever let a man spend in her apartment. He didn't know that, of course. Whatever was stirred up inside her would settle down eventually, she reminded herself.

The particles of chaos suspended in her every molecule right this moment, though, showed no signs of settling any time soon.

Alex stood, putting his mug in the sink. "You need to go, so walk me to the door and make love on the porch and I'll let you."

She stood, too. "I must have Stockholm Syndrome, because that sounds appealing."

"If anyone is the abductor here, it's you."

She snorted. "Right. Because someone who aims the shower nozzle at dachshund level could totally kidnap you." They reached the front door. Crackhead appeared out of nowhere, nuzzling Alex's legs.

Alex looked down at the cat. "Crackhead?"

Josie nodded.

"He? She?"

"It."

"It likes me." Tugging on her ass, he pulled her close.

"It's not the only one," she said against his neck as they embraced.

One last long, slow kiss from him and she nudged him out the door, needing the last few minutes to get ready and clear her head. While her body was back in alignment and utterly sated, her brain needed to refocus in the idea of work, that there was a life and a structure outside of her and Alex's genitals, tongues, hands, and mouths.

Unfortunately.

He turned the corner and she sighed, restraining an impulse to run to the window that paralleled the road he walked on now. Coffee. A quick blow dry and another giant mug of coffee would get her on her way to work, where what she faced was about as diametrically opposed to the past twelve hours as could be.

Relief and disappointment flooded her simultaneously as Alex's absence sank in. A quick march to the bathroom and she plugged in the hair dryer, snapping it on and furiously tousling her wet, brown mop of hair, the white noise of the machine helping to clear her thoughts. Inhaling deeply, she felt the air leave her body, as if it contained Alex and now he were being purged from her body.

No. Impossible. Her skin burned with his touch, her nether regions completely fulfilled with the last few hours of sex, and her hips carried her with a jaunty saunter that felt mature and primed, as if she were somehow more a woman now for having found a partner so fine. The Josie she had become in the past day had stumbled into a secret society; she as a full-fledged member of a group with a single requirement—being yourself.

He hadn't flinched, had he? Finishing up her hair and

dragging a comb through it, she let the relaxed waves frame her face. No makeup. She rarely wore it to work anyhow, so if she did today, people would tease.

Melting into the background of her ho-hum job was what she wanted most for this day.

Any more excitement and she would implode.

\* \* \*

Two days had gone by and she'd texted with Alex, who was finishing up a grueling twenty-four-hour shift. As her phone beeped, she hoped it was him.

Nope. The phone number showing on Josie's screen made her stomach drop into a hole in the floor. If she had balls they would have crawled up into her abdominal cavity and pressed against her throat.

It was her mother.

A phone call from Marlene meant only one thing. She wanted money. Money for her alcohol, money for her drugs, money for cigarettes, and money for her men. Josie had ignored the last two calls she'd had, abrupt and perfunctory voicemails Marlene always left when she was determined to get something. "Josie, it's your mom. Call me. *Click.*" She knew that Marlene would persist, though, so against her better judgment she pressed the answer button and said, "Hello?"

"Heeeeeey, it's my baby girl." The smoker's rasp rattled so deeply in Josie's ear she could almost smell and taste the cigarette smoke. Her mom and her Aunt Cathy had plenty of things that were different about each other, but on this one, they were united. Chimneys who filled their homes with the ever-present houseguest of nicotine residue.

"What's up, Mom?" Josie tried to keep it light. If she engaged in any possible way, this could get nasty.

"I was just thinkin' about you, and you didn't answer my voicemails."

"I was on shift, Mom."

"Oooooooh, okay."

From the tone in her mother's voice, Josie could tell she wasn't drunk or high. It was a rare moment of getting what was left of the real Marlene, one to one, and a thin tendril of hope allowed itself to unwind inside her. Maybe she'd get one good conversation, after all.

"I hope you're not overworking yourself. You know how hard that..." Marlene stumbled, and Josie could imagine her, cigarette in her right hand, waving it, as if the smoke could somehow coordinate to form the word that her stuttering brain couldn't find.

"Yeah, nursing can be hard, Mom," Josie helped.

"That's right." Marlene's voice became more confident. "That's right, nursing is hard, but I'm proud of my baby."

Josie's teeth felt like steel edges grinding against each other. "Thanks, Mom," was all she said. She wasn't going to fall for it and ask, "So what are you calling for?"

Josie knew her mother's monthly income. Between working a couple of pity shifts at the local bar, where Jerry let her work mostly to work off an ever-increasing bar tab, and survivor's benefits from her father's death, she knew that there was enough to at least pay the mortgage, cover utility bills and basic food.

There wasn't, though, enough to cover cigarettes, booze, and pills. When Josie had come home from college in her senior year she'd found the stash of Percocets, a hundred or more, in her mom's top drawer. She knew enough not to ask, and she knew enough to realize that her mother was probably going to multiple doctors to get that much. Traumatic brain injury, and neck and back muscles that were permanently twisted as she recovered from the accident, gave her the perfect excuse when it came to getting pain meds. Josie's problem was that teasing out how much of it was legitimate and how much of it was bullshit had driven her crazy for years.

"When you comin' home next, Josie?" Marlene asked, the question a formality; she knew damn well that Josie came home once a year, typically in August.

"Oh, you know, same time."

"You'll be here for a week?"

"Yep." She would spent most of that week with Darla, hanging out and chatting, and trying to convince the younger cousin to come back to Boston with her. This would be a different trip now, wouldn't it? Because Darla could be out here soon, if Josie took the job with Laura and asked to have Darla be her assistant. Darla had a natural acceptance of the surreal that made Josie think she'd be perfect for the very unconventional dating service Laura and her guys were proposing.

The rattlings of the implications of getting Darla to move out here made her teeth hurt even more. Marlene would ask the inevitable question, *If Darla can move in with you, then why can't I?* and that was a whole conversation that Josie didn't want to have.

"Mom, how are you doing?" Josie asked, giving her the entry that she needed.

"Ah, same old, same old here," Marlene said. "You know, I've been having a hard time with the house, though."

*Here it comes*, Josie thought.

Sometimes it was the car, sometimes it was her health, sometimes it was Darla and Cathy. When they were brought up it was easy to give Darla a call and say "My mom tells me your cat died," and Darla would say, "Oh, the fifth one this year?" and they'd laugh, because who else can you call when you need to talk about your crazy mom, and nobody else has a crazy mom. Aunt Cathy wasn't quite crazy, but she was depressed, and it meant that Josie and Darla could commiserate.

"What's up with the house, Mom?" she asked.

"Oh, the gutters, there's this problem with 'em, and they're rotting, and they're saying it's gonna cause all this roof damage and it could be thousands and thousands if we don't get it fixed now."

*Familiar.* Josie figured it had been about two years since she'd used that one. Back then it was the gutters were being ripped off the house by angry squirrels, and that she needed to have all of the leaves that had built up in there cleaned out, and that that was going to cost $600. Josie paused to see whether Marlene was recycling entire stories.

"What's wrong with the gutters?" she finally asked.

"Oh, it's these damn squirrels!"

Closing her eyes and rubbing her forehead, Josie hated to be right. "How much will it cost to fix, Mom?" she said, haltingly, mentally running through her own savings, wondering how much she could manage without putting herself in jeopardy.

"Not too bad, there's some guys in the neighborhood who say they can do it for four hundred."

"Four hundred."

"Well, maybe $300 if, you know, I flash 'em some tit and flirt with 'em a little bit." Marlene's throaty chuckle made Josie's own throat tighten, choking her on a ball of disgust and resentment, anger and embarrassment. And sorrow.

"I can get a check for you for three hundred, Mom, it's a little tight here."

"Oh, it's tight here, too, Josie. If you've got it tight then it must be a virgin asshole here," she cackled.

"No problem, Mom," she said, smiling. It was a sick grin, one that came from her out of a place of security of knowing that Marlene couldn't see it. Her phone flashed, some number she didn't recognize. "Hey, Mom, I gotta go, there's somebody on my other line, it might be work."

"Okay, hon, well, you take care and I'll just look out for the check."

"Yep, bye, Mom." *Click.* She flashed over. "Hello?"

"Josie," said a warm, deep voice.

Oh, how she needed this. It was as if he had read her mind and called to rescue her at the exact perfect moment. Gratitude flooded her, along with desire and need. "Alex," she said, "how great to hear your voice."

"That's the kind of welcome I like." The sound of him was filled with a smile, a happiness that infused her. "How are you doing?" he asked softly.

"I would be doing a lot better if I were with you," she said, the words coming out effortlessly. No anxiety, no nervousness, just a drained sort of honesty that she found very appealing within herself.

"I would love to be with you, too," he said quietly, a pensiveness to his words. "Do you want to go for a walk?" he asked.

"A real walk, or a *walk*?"

A boisterous laugh filled her phone, forcing her to pull it away from her ear a few inches. "I don't know…you tell me what I should say."

"How about we start with a walk and then see if later on we could go for *a walk*."

"I'd like that, Josie. I like you."

Seconds ticked by. Finally, she said, "I like you, too."

She could hear the smile in his words as he said, "Want to come over? We can have a glass of wine here and then go for a walk."

"We will never get to the actual walk part, Alex, if I come over."

"And that would be a problem because…?"

"Because you invited me for a walk!"

"Then I am uninviting you. There. You are not invited for a walk. Come over for a glass of wine instead. 34 Windsor. C'mon."

"You really do live close to me!" By her calculations, his apartment was about two blocks away.

"I know. If I squint and get a pair of u-bend binoculars and angle seven mirrors with SETI-like precision, I can see in your bedroom window."

Silly. She needed silly right now. Silly drove Marlene's acidity away. "And you know that because…?" she replied, yawning.

"You tired?" he asked, avoiding the question. The sound of ice cracking filled the phone, then water pouring. "I have a bed you could sleep on."

"If I am in your bed, sleep is the last thing we'd do."

"Yes, it is. The last thing after plenty of others."

Was this an invitation for sex and for an overnight? Could Dr. Perfect be calling in a booty call? Or had the relationship shifted, a casual approach to dating evolving into a more relaxed way of meeting up?

"On the count of three," she said.

"Oh, God, I have to chase you again, don't I?" he groaned. "Let me put on my shoes."

"On the count of three," she repeated, "let's run and see where we meet."

"You're not wearing panties, are you?"

"Yes, I am."

"I meant *only* panties."

"No. Why?"

"Because the last time you sprinted away from me, that's how you were dressed. Now—GO!" *Click.* He hadn't waited for her count of three!

Completely unnerved, she ran to the front door, grabbing her keys off a hook next to the door, sliding her feet into Crocs. Josie ran with about as much grace as a zombie in a 5K run. Only slower. Alex was practically at her doorstep by the time they met in the "middle."

"Half a block? That's the best you could do?" he asked, laughing. She wore a short camisole that was stretched taut against her middle. He patted it, palm flat against her ribs and belly, the gesture affectionate and thrilling. "You have a runner's body," he said, his face screwed up in a puzzled expression as she glared at him. "Don't you run?"

"Only when the ice cream truck passes by."

A big, slow grin spread across his face. One hand staying on her stomach, the other sliding around her waist, their torsos pulling together inch by inch as they stood on the sidewalk, a welcoming embrace slow enough to savor.

On tiptoes, her heels popped out of her Crocs and her calves elongated, all so she could bury her face in his shoulder and inhale. He smelled like soap and spice, and as he pulled back to kiss her, tension from her call with Marlene melted out of her fast.

This was a kiss between boyfriend and girlfriend, an assumption of access that seemed so natural, as if they'd been dating for months and *of course* they would greet each other so effortlessly with an embrace and a kiss. Gentle caresses of her waist and back twinned with a not-so-tender kiss, tongues dancing, increasing in urgency and desire.

"Get a room," an old man muttered, a rattling sound accompanying the jarring words. They pulled apart to find a homeless dude pushing a bent shopping cart, the metal frame overloaded with twenty or so overloaded bags filled with five-cent returnable cans. Sidestepping the cart, she and Alex wiped the kiss away, taking a deep breath as the guy passed.

"We should take his advice," Alex said, looping her arm through his, leading her away from her apartment.

"Do you always listen to homeless men?"

"Only when they give me sex toy tips," he deadpanned.

"Oh, dear," was all she could respond with. "You make going back to your place *so* appealing."

"I have wine. Netflix. A bed."

"Sex toys?"

"Uh…well…there's *me*."

"Even better," she answered, stopping to pull him in for another kiss. Smiling through the touch of their lips, she felt something soar inside, an energy that was all-pervasive.

"Why are you smiling?" he asked, running his hand through her hair, pushing it off her flushed face.

"Because I'm with you." A lump in her throat competed with her speedy pulse. She didn't say things like that to men. With Alex, though, it just spilled out.

"Then I hope to make you smile more." A kiss. A squeeze. And then—

"Home, sweet home. Welcome to the castle," he joked, gesturing at the front door of a building that was pretty close in age and architecture to hers. Same locked main door, same entryway with mailboxes, same hallway with apartment doors. Alex lived on the first floor, and as he unlocked his door and let her enter first, she burst out laughing.

Bikes. Three of them. And helmets, pant straps, and assorted other bike accessories. Of course he and his roommate were Cambridge bikers. Of course.

"What's so funny?" he asked.

"The bikes. It's so stereotypical."

"Of what?"

"The urban young doctor who is a fitness freak."

"Not!"

"You're fit," she said in an incriminating tone, running her hands along his washboard abs, trying and failing to find fat to pinch at his waist. She reached around for a squeeze of his ass. Solid muscle.

"Okay, so I'm fit. Doesn't make me a freak."

"I'll bet you compost, too. And in the backyard you have some cherry tomato plants, plus you use a solar charger for your phone, attached to the backpack you wear when you bike."

His jaw was on the floor.

"See! I was right!" she crowed.

"Wrong on all counts."

"What? But..."

"Although you just described my roommate to a T." With that, Alex laughed and marched ahead into the carved out living room corner that served as the kitchen. A partial wall formed a counter for two bar stools, leaving a full view of the cooking area. The place was decorated in shabby chic thrift shop furniture, like hers. A dining table from the '70s, a slim, steel gray IKEA bifold couch, a few halogen lamps, and posters from classic rock concerts ranging from Pink Floyd to The Doors.

Photographs of everyday locations in Cambridge peppered the walls, all black and white, with intriguing composition. Josie wandered around looking at them closely. A bike tire. The foot of John Harvard's statue. A crest on a building from Harvard University. An espresso cup on a laced-steel table top. "Who's the photographer?" she asked as Alex opened a bottle of something he pulled from the refrigerator.

"My roommate. John. He's out of town for a few more weeks on a fellowship."

"Medical?"

*Pop!* Alex used a manual corkscrew to open what she now discerned was a white wine—Chardonnay, from the looks of the label—and he poured a glass for each of them into very nice, if mismatched crystal wine goblets.

"Yes. He's a lab rat. Oncology."

"MD and Ph.D.?"

Alex nodded, sipping his wine. He seemed nervous, a bit rattled. Being on his turf was a change, and it gave her a touch of comfort to know that Dr. Perfect cared about what she thought.

"Nice," she said, holding the wine glass out after taking a sip.

He shrugged. "It's wine." The two shared a smile and Josie looked around. Dark wood baseboards and trim. Wide doorways. Tall ceilings. The heating bills were probably a nightmare in the winter, like hers, but it beat the tiny little modern apartment buildings with crazy-high rent, or the brick cubes that sardined people into cookie-cutter apartments.

"How long have you lived here?"

"About a year." His sentences were clipped. He was *really* nervous. What a change! Usually she was the nervous one on a date. Was this a date? He'd invited her over for a glass of wine, so she would count it as a date, even if she was dressed in a tank top and wore Crocs. Was he awkward because he wanted to hurry up to the sex part? If this was just a booty call, maybe she was reading his signals wrong. Indecision set in.

Awkwardness from one person was one thing; when both were being weird, it compounded the feeling by a factor of eight. Finally, he broke the silence.

"This feels really weird."

"Yes," she conceded. *But why?* she wondered.

Placing his glass of wine on an end table, he turned and put his hands on her shoulders. "I feel like a geeky eighth-grader because you do that to me, Josie. Like a stumbling teenager with his first crush. And now that I invited you over, and you're here, in my apartment—my *space*—I don't quite know what to do next."

Josie brought her glass of wine to her mouth and drank it down in two gulps. Alex's serious eyes remained on her the whole time. "You what?" she squeaked.

"I said that I like you when we were on the phone earlier."

She nodded.

"What I should have said is this." Bending his knees slightly, he made a heartfelt attempt to come eye to eye with Josie, but it didn't quite work, so he dragged her by one hand to the blue couch, pulling her in for an embrace. Curling her legs nimbly around his waist, her ass nestled into his lap, she studied him from an angle, heart thumping, wondering what the hell he was going to say next. The room was silent, with the faint hum of a fan in the background and the distant, slow whoosh of cars driving down the small street. Wine loosened her up, and whatever weirdness had descended between them earlier faded as he opened up about his own weirdness. It felt good to be weird *with* someone.

That was new.

She liked it.

"I haven't really dated a woman in a long time. Not like

this. And I realize," he said, his voice going low and hushed, "that it's been a very short time, but this isn't just…casual for me."

*Blink.*

"I'm really enjoying spending time with you. I don't get much free time. I have to be at work in twelve hours or so, and then I don't have another day off for three days. But whatever time I do have off, I want to spend with you."

"Why?" she blurted out. Even as the word passed over her tongue and between her lips, she regretted saying it, knowing it sounded so plaintive and disbelieving.

Those chocolate eyes turned pensive. "You don't realize how smart and funny and"—he growled a bit, squeezing her into him, one hand playful the other stroking her arm—"how sensual you are. You're the whole package, Josie. Let me in," he whispered, nuzzling her neck.

"Let you in?" The leer in her voice was evident.

"Not like *that*," he objected.

"Not *any* of that?" Deflecting was easier than directly saying what her heart was screaming. A stark boundary that she'd drawn around herself long ago, fortified against calls like the one she'd just had with Marlene, was rapidly disintegrating with each second she spent with Alex. She could almost feel it, fading away inside her. A diffuse sense of trust seeped in layer by layer as she inhaled him, let her fingertips trace his jaw line, smiled a musing little grin of acceptance.

"Well, *some* of that," he backpedaled.

Her smile spread to a full-on grin as she leaned into him and kissed, inhaling deeply, breathing him in, making him part of her.

"You're nervous," she murmured, their lips still together.

"Yes."

"You don't seem like you're the nervous type."

"I'm not." He shifted one hip and their bodies touched

in new places, his rock-hard shaft pushing up under her. A swell of need raced through her, forcing her to control her breathing. Just having sex would be easy.

Suddenly, Josie didn't want *easy*. Pulling off her clothes and fucking him right here on the couch, or on the floor, or in his bed—hell, the shower—would be easy. Staying for dinner and ordering Thai food in between sex sessions would be easy. Getting tipsy on wine and exploring each other's bodies would be easy.

Spending time together, getting to know one another, without using sex as a tool?

*Hard.*

"Let's go for a walk!" she announced, jumping off his lap and bouncing on her toes like a six-year-old eager to go to the park.

"A walk?" He moved slowly, as if dazed. And then she realized this really was hard. Or, at least, *he* was.

Stifling a snort, she walked quickly towards the door. "Yes—a walk. Remember? You invited me over for one."

"But I—"

Giving the guy a break, she called back, "Do whatever you need to do to go for a nice, long walk—the sunset will be gorgeous!"

Without a single clue of what she was doing, she marched out onto his porch and waited.

\* \* \*

The agony. His dick felt like one of those party balloons you blow up and twist into a dog. He had a fucking latex poodle in his pants. And a frog in his throat. His body was a zoo during a full moon, howling and frustrated.

A walk? After starting to pour his heart out and fumbling through it like a complete idiot, she wanted to take a walk? Calling her after a difficult shift at work had seemed so natural. Few births stayed with him for very long, but this one he couldn't shake. A mother who wanted a vaginal birth after a cesarean. Preserving her VBAC had been hard, but it had worked—insofar as she'd given birth vaginally. But the baby had had complications. The attending OB warned him there would be a review, and it hung over him like a storm cloud. If something had happened to that baby because his instincts and judgment had been wrong…

Coming home to his empty apartment, he'd picked up the phone on a whim and found himself dialing her number, as if on autopilot, as if this was what he did every day after a tough shift.

He turned to Josie.

No other woman had ever filled this role.

*Maybe no other woman ever will.* Whatever triggered *that* thought shocked him, made him stop cold as Josie hung out in front of his building, waiting impatiently.

Where in the hell did this huge case of nerves come from? And on his part. She was the nervous one, the person in this—*relationship?*—who deflected and held back. Not him.

And that was it.

Wedging the door to her heart open with a toe, he'd pried inside her by being the one to share first. Like stripping naked before sex, if he went first, she would follow. That was why this felt so unsure. Because he couldn't read her signals.

His signals? His were easy to read. Just look for the deflating poodle.

"Alex?" Josie called out.

*Shake it off. Shake it off.* A few deep breaths and he made his way outside. Thank God he was wearing jeans. Lycra running shorts would have made his erection stand out like a drunk Jets fan at a Pats game.

"You okay?" Josie asked, an impish smile twisting her lips.

"I am," he said, throwing an arm around her shoulders.

A walk? Fine. But on his terms. "So where are you from?" He'd held off on the standard "getting to know you" questions but now he was just going to go for it.

"Ohio."

"And your parents…?"

"My dad died years ago. My mom's still alive."

"Oh." He cringed. "Sorry."

"What? No. It's fine." Her voice was tense. "He died nearly eighteen years ago, so it's not like it's fresh."

Something in her voice said that was a lie, but he wasn't going to pry. "And your mom's back in Ohio?"

"Yep. What about you?"

"I don't have a dad, and my mom lives in Watertown."

"You're a medical marvel. Did they inject the Y chromosome into you using nanotechnology?"

He laughed. "That's why I'm an OB. So I can understand this whole reproductive thing." Explaining this was always hard. "My dad left before my mom even knew she was pregnant with me. I never met him."

"Oh." They were strolling toward the park as dusk settled in, the air cool enough to keep the mosquitoes at bay. No baseball games tonight, it appeared. A pink line in the horizon faded to nearly gray as the sun dropped out of the sky.

Thinking it through, he asked, "How old were you?"

"When my dad died?"

"Yes."

"Eleven." She wasn't giving him anything more than he asked. Still waters run deep. The way she sidestepped any additional information, and yet continued to answer what was asked directly, made him decide to push it.

"How did he die?" he asked gently, stopping and making eye contact. Her eyes were wide and yet guarded, the brown irises closed off, but the whites of her eyes seemed bigger, a contradiction of nonverbal signals.

"A car accident." The words slipped out of her mouth so simply, and yet he knew they were packed with hundreds of layers of meaning.

"I am so sorry. Were you—" He started to ask whether she was in the car but stopped, feeling like a jerk. Her chest rose and fell with shallow breaths and the hand he held in his trembled. The topic clearly upset her and he felt like an ass for bringing it up. And yet, it meant something special. If he could just understand her better...

"Was I in the car? No." For the first time in the conversation she added something he hadn't asked. "But my mom was. And my aunt and uncle."

"Your mom's still alive, you said."

"Yes. My dad and uncle died, but my mom and aunt lived."

"Oh, Josie." Emotion filled his voice as the impact of what her childhood must have been like hit him. "That's horrible. Were your mom and aunt okay?"

She snorted, shaking her head. "Define 'okay.'" The smirk that crossed her face was like a door slamming shut between them.

"I'm upsetting you."

"You're not doing anything. I just...I've never talked about this with a guy before. Ever."

His heart melted as it pounded against his ribs. Now he was getting somewhere. "If you don't want to talk, I understand."

"What about your mother?" she asked.

"She's a clinical psychologist. Alive. Forty-six."

Josie appeared to do the math. "And you're twenty-nine?"

"Eight."

"Oooo, I'm older than you."

"I like my women mature," he joked.

"Then find another woman, because 'mature' and 'Josie' definitely do not go together."

*I doubt that*, he thought, but said nothing, just smiling. The silence between them was comfortable. Warm. Tentative.

Josie broke it. "So she had you…"

"Had me two days after she graduated high school."

"And she earned a Ph.D.?" A low whistle of appreciation escaped her lips. "Smart woman."

"Determined woman. You have no idea," he added.

"No one wants to date a guy whose mother is an overachieving psychologist. You know that, right?" she teased.

"Before you decide that, what does *your* mom do?" he joked back.

The look on her face made him regret it. "She's…"

"You don't have to answer."

Squaring her shoulders, Josie seemed to struggle with how to answer. The pink straps of her tank top faded to light gray in the waning sunlight, the moon peeking out behind a cloud. Tipping her face up to meet his eyes, she seemed ethereal. Like a fairy, the edges of her brown hair glowing slightly, the shine of the low light on her eyes making them more aware than usual. "We're being open, right?"

"We're trying." *You're trying.* Alex was already open.

"She's a barfly."

"Oh." *What the hell do you say to that?*

"Not quite a Ph.D." The acerbic tone was back. "And my dad was a librarian." She said it defensively, as if it counterbalanced her mother's behavior.

"I'm not judging." And really, he wasn't. Whatever made Josie the woman she was—a nurse in a well-respected clinical trial—had been through grit and determination. Just like him. Just like his mom. Scratching the surface of Josie's shell took some time and hard work. Fortunately, he had both at his disposal, though plenty of the latter. The former depended on her.

"She wasn't always like this. The head injury in the accident…" Her voice trailed off. "You know, can we talk about something else?"

"Absolutely."

"How about air fucking?"

\* \* \*

Way to change the subject, right? The look on Alex's face made Josie laugh out loud, the sound and feeling so desperately needed after getting *that* deep with him. Never before had she talked to any man she'd dated about her past. Her niece, Darla? Of course. Laura? Sure. Those two, and...

No one.

Not true. There was the therapist she saw during the last two years of college. Her lifesaver.

Talking about her parents with Alex felt like having someone reach into her chest, through bone and sinew and muscle, and wrap their palm around her heart, squeezing it until all the blood dripped out. His reaction allowed the blood back in.

Restoring basic respiratory and circulatory functioning would take a while.

Danger sex could provide a shortcut.

He leaned in and put his lips right next to her earlobe, making her shiver. "Are you serious?"

"I never joke about air fucking."

He inhaled sharply. "Neither do I. Shall we go for a walk?" he asked, gesturing toward the park. Their path had taken them in parallel to it, a block from Josie's apartment, and they needed to cross the street. A thrill of heat flooded her. Changing the subject had been easy enough—mention sex to any guy and it was like that dog in the movie *Up*.

*Squirrel!*

Truth be told, she was struggling with the whole emotionally open thing and wanted to get back to her comfort zone. Except that wasn't possible; once she crossed over into the touchy-feely baggage-sharing phase, she couldn't stuff it all back in.

And that was okay, because Alex could stuff something

else in her.

Their pace didn't change, still a slow stroll, but the connection between them had altered from the moment she took the leap, and now the air between their bodies crackled with the forbidden. They crossed the street; Josie noted how few cars were out. By the time they reached the park's outer edge, she found herself scanning the area with danger sex in mind. The baseball lights weren't on. Sign #1 that this was meant to be.

Her eyes landed on a small garden on the far side of a building that typically blocked the view from her apartment. On the occasional walks she'd taken over the years, she'd registered it, but now, as they rounded the building, she realized it was perfect, made for what she and Alex were seeking. Sign #2. Add a trash can and a soft layer of moss and—

*Whoa.* Signs #3 and #4 screamed out to her, as if nature (or the Cambridge Parks and Recreation department) had read her mind.

What a wonderful world.

Were they really going to—

Thump. Alex pulled her down on the mossy ground, her nose filling sharply with the rich scent of oregano, the heat of his body against hers a pleasure she would never take for granted.

Wait—*oregano?*

"You smell like Italian food," he whispered, nuzzling her neck, one hand cupping a breast, his tongue licking right at the base of her earlobe, sending a full-body shiver through her.

"It's not me," she whispered back, fingering the ground cover. "It's this." Crushing some of the greenery between her fingers, she held them to his nose, his body pressing onto hers.

Alex inhaled deeply and said, "We'll have to try out all the herbs. Oregano today, tarragon tomorrow, and then we need to find a bed of lavender. And…"

186

His mouth crushed into hers, hands flying up her camisole, hot and fevered. The sidewalk was not five feet away, their bodies hidden by a small hedge and a bench, the chance of getting caught reasonably high. It made the blood pound between her legs, her breasts swell with excitement, and her mouth match his in intensity, the kiss transmitting a racy need to slam against him, to have his hands claim her, his hips hammering her, all under the open night sky as they took each other's bodies as nature intended.

With the stars as the audience.

Unlike the languid, luxurious night in her apartment a few days ago, this was fast and furious, her hands on his pants, unsnapping and unzipping, his fingers nimble with her shorts, pulling down, the cool night air smacking against skin that typically didn't touch outdoor breezes. His fingers slipped inside her, in and out, making her hips buck against them. Her Crocs flew off her feet, one settling under a hedge, the other next to the only park bench in the little garden.

Preliminaries be damned—she wanted him in her.

Now.

He didn't need to be told, fumbling in a back pocket for his wallet. A condom appeared out of nowhere.

"You planned for his?" she gasped, his fingers out of her now, her body aching to be filled by him.

"Yes," he chuckled, rolling it on as she laced her legs around his hips.

"God, I love y—" she blurted out as he entered her, the last word gurgling to a screeching halt in the back of her throat as he thrust nice and deep, filling her with everything she needed at once, her eyes taking in the shadows from the greenery about them, the handful of stars she could catch in the city sky, the blinking red light of a jet overhead...

Oh, no.

*No, no, no, no, no.*

She did not just say that.

She did not.

She did—

"I love this, too," he murmured in her ear, his arms on either side of her head, his face hidden by the inky darkness. A quick kiss, and then a hurried thrust as she quickened her own movements, the swollen need inside her clamping down as her orgasm rose up, stretching tall, elongating, ready to strike.

*An out.* "I love *this* so much," she answered, speaking slowly, as if that's what she'd intended to say all along. "So much."

Their kisses disintegrated into simple connections, heated presses against each other as her body went rigid, all her nerves in concert as she hissed, "Alex, I'm—" Colored clouds exploded behind her closed eyes as she groaned and pushed up into him, her inner core tightening so hard her diaphragm seemed to spasm, her slickness and his enormity working together to make some third wave between them. She bit his earlobe as he bent down to change the angle, her hands grasping his waist, pulling up against him as a moan caught in her throat, the urge to cry out muted by the need to be quiet, to avoid being caught.

Alex's body went tight, a growl in his throat as she bit him, his own climax evident in the way his hips stopped moving, how his thighs halted, their bodies trapped by their own heat and fire burning through and, now out, as they each finished. A dog barked, the sound too close for comfort, and the two of them scrambled apart. Alex turned away as he dressed, and Josie hiked up her shorts with one hand while the other combed bits of oregano out of her hair. Her body still humming from what they'd just done.

Maybe she really was starting to love him. The thought remained a thought, thank goodness, her mouth firmly closed. She could think it as much as she wanted, right? As long as she didn't say it.

Because who actually has danger sex and *likes* it?

Dr. Perfect. Of course.

As if nothing had just happened, Josie parked her ass on the bench in the little garden, whistling an off-key tune. Alex went around the corner to a water fountain, the sound of running water her clue. He came back and sat next to her, stretching an arm across the back of the bench, looking up at the night sky, whistling with her.

They burst into laughter.

A little corgi came around the corner, sniffing right where Josie and Alex had just had sex, the oregano apparently not enough scent to throw it off track.

"Oh. Hello!" A young guy, high school age, wearing a Red Sox cap and a matching Sox t-shirt, pulled on the dog's leash.

"Hi!" they said in unison.

"C'mon, Daisy. What's gotten into you?" he asked the dog as she bore down on the spot, sniffing furiously.

"Must be trying to claim her turf," Alex said in a *gee whiz* voice.

"G'night," the kid said, walking off, practically dragging poor Daisy down the street.

"That was close," Josie muttered.

"That was *fun*," Alex countered, kissing her.

*Bam!* The Klieg lights came on, bathing them in a flash of blinding light.

"What the hell?" Josie shouted.

Headlights began streaming in and parking in the small lot behind a community center, directly behind them. Adult voices. People on the baseball field.

"Holy shit," Alex said under his breath, adding a low whistle of shock.

"Danger sex, indeed," she whispered in his ear, giving his lobe a nip. "That was *really* close. Next time we should try this little garden off the library over in – "

"I know that one! With the giant Rose of Sharon bushes?" He stood, extending a hand to her. She took it

189

and the two scurried around the non-baseball-field side of the park, avoiding people. By the time they found their way across the street, they were in front of Josie's building, and Alex checked his phone. She was still stunned that he knew the exact library garden she was talking about. *Eerie.* How? She started to ask, but he spoke first.

"I have to be at work in the morning, but we can go back to my apartment and finish that wine…" He snuggled up to her, hips against her navel, arms around her shoulders. His embrace felt so inviting.

"You need your sleep."

"You sound like my mother," he said, smiling. "Who you should meet sometime," he added.

A huge lump formed in her throat. "Uh…" she drawled. "The clinical psychologist?"

He began to guide her down the street to his place. She stopped him. "I actually have to be at work in the morning, too, Alex. So…"

Uncertain, he stopped, studying her carefully. "I don't want you to think I just called you for sex."

"I'm offended."

"I was worried about that!" he exclaimed, running a hand through his hair.

She swatted at a mosquito on her shoulder. "I'm offended that you *wouldn't* call me for just sex."

"Huh?"

"I'm not good enough for a booty call?" *Joke with him. Catch him off center. Step away from the mother talk. Dear God, you told him you loved him during sex. Get the hell out of here, Josie.* The voice in her head was screaming at her.

"Ah. I get it." Smiling, he pulled her in for a toe-curling kiss. She could get used to this. Very used to this.

Too comfortable.

"I'll call you tomorrow?" he asked.

She nodded. As they parted, he made it halfway down the block and then ran back, an arm snaking around her waist and cinching her to him, the final kiss deep and exploring.

"It's not just sex."

"No. It's not," she replied.

*And that's the problem.*

# CHAPTER TEN

"Hey! Howzitgoin'?" Darla's voice boomed through her smartphone. Hitting "pause" on her movie, Josie curled up with Dotty in her lap, wondering what her niece was up to.

Niece. Cousin. Technically, they were cousins, but considering the seven-and-a-half-year age difference, and the fact that Josie had practically helped raise Darla after their dads died in the car accident, they just called each other "aunt" and "niece," finding it easier. There was no rhyme or reason to it—Darla had just started calling her Aunt Josie when she was four and they lived together while their moms recovered in separate hospitals, and it stuck.

"It's going. How about you?"

"*Booooooooring.* Everything is so *booooooring* here. Nothing fun ever happens. I'm about to drive home from my shift and it's *soooooooo* dull."

"I see nothing's changed back home."

Darla snorted. A cash register dinged in the muffled distance. "Nope. What about you?"

She thought about spilling her guts about Alex, but stopped herself. Her mom and Aunt Cathy always hoped

Josie would meet and marry a doctor, and then everything would be just perfect, as if she'd be rescued from her own life. For Marlene, she knew, a physician for a son-in-law meant money. Maybe access to pills. Ah, the delusions of a woman with the conscience of a cockroach and the narcissism of Kim Jong Il.

Her hesitation made Darla ask, "Josie? You got something to say?"

"No. Not really."

"'Not really' is different from 'no.'" Darla was fishing, and she was right—Josie wanted a friend to talk to, and Laura hadn't answered her texts or two voicemails yet. She was bursting.

"True."

"*Aaaannnnnnd....?*"

"Hypothetically..."

"Unicorns and fairies are hypothetical."

"So is my story, if I'm going to tell it."

"Fine."

"Hypothetically, imagine you're dating a guy who makes you feel like you can trust him. Like he doesn't judge you."

"Oh, look!" Darla shouted. "A unicorn with a fairy on its back, shitting gold coins!"

Sigh. "I know. Right? Impossible."

"Hey, if you found one of those guys, I wouldn't tell anyone. It's like having a winning lottery ticket. You cash it in all quiet-like and don't say a word. Just go off on a trip to Disney World and act like you're in the hospital for a bunion or something."

"You're comparing the guy I'm dating to a *bunion*?"

"You're dating? Josie, you never *date*! You make fun of men, grind into them with your body, and only spare them the black-widow treatment if they're lucky."

"Shut up."

"You're my idol. That wasn't a criticism."

"It's so touching how you support me emotionally,

Darla."

"I aim to please."

Josie laughed, the air now cleared of any desire to pour out her heart. "Why did you call? To bust my chops?"

"No." Darla's voice went quiet. "I just missed talking."

"You could come out and visit, you know." Every phone conversation ended like this. "I'll pay for the plane ticket."

"If you do that, Aunt Marlene will wonder why you didn't send *her* the money for one."

"So we'll find a way. What my mom thinks shouldn't stop you from visiting."

"You aren't the one who has to live around her and hear the non-stop bitching."

Bile rose in Josie's throat. Getting away from the enmeshed chaos of her mother had been nearly impossible, but she'd done it. That Marlene could somehow manipulate family dynamics so that Darla felt she couldn't even come to Cambridge for a visit made her temper explode and her heart crack in two at the same time.

How could she hope to have some sort of future with Alex when her past was such a burden? His clinical psychologist mother was from a different world. Her mom was a harpy in Lycra with a massive entitlement complex.

Marlene would probably hit on Alex if given the chance. The thought made Josie gag.

"Ewww, you sick? Or was your cat hacking up a hairball?" Darla asked.

"No, just thinking of something unpleasant."

"Like home?" Darla laughed; Josie joined her, though neither added much mirth to it.

The sound of wind filled the phone. "You outside?"

"Yeah. Gotta go get in the car and head home. I'll check in with you later in the week."

"Okay." Josie felt deprived. Empty. Full. Like an abyss of everything and nothing dragged at her from the belly.

As Darla got off the phone, Josie stared at her living room. A quick flash of Crackhead confirmed the cat was still alive. Dotty wasn't eating all the cat food, then.

She felt utterly alone and in need of a good talk. A quick check of her phone and—nope. No answer from Laura. Between her mother's dominion over everyone in Ohio, holding them captive through sheer craziness and narcissism, and Laura's new, baby-filled life, she felt like the only way to manage the churning newness of Alex was to hold it all back. Shut it down. Close up and stick to what she knew.

His comment, after their amazing oregano sex, about Josie meeting his mom, made her gut seize up and her lungs freeze. He was so normal. His mom was a clinical psychologist superwoman who had a baby as a teenager and raised him to be a doctor. They were normal people, not like her family. No dead father, no mom who tried to sleep with the band director at her college graduation. And the band director wasn't the only faculty member her mom had come on to.

Marlene's insatiable needs were legendary. Of all the parts of the brain to be injured and never recover, the worst was the sexual filter. It just…broke. Josie flashed back to the night before, with Alex, and how it felt to take risks. Not the outdoor sex, strangely.

The very internal risks she took with him. Wanted to take with him.

Wanted to take *for* him.

She'd been ignoring Alex, leaving his text messages unanswered, and the two voicemails hung out on her phone like dark, wet clouds waiting to unload their burdens.

Tears welled up, threatening to make her voice break and to rack her body with sobs. This was all too much. Too many feelings.

Alex threatened that because he was normal. Accepting. Loving? Could she dare use that word? And if so, was it a weapon or a talisman?

He lived in an emotional reality she couldn't fathom. What was it like to be raised by a mother who loved you so much and who struggled to reach her fullest potential—and to instill that in her child? Josie had gone to college in spite of Marlene. Not because of her. How many nights had she endured the grousing about wasted tuition money (*which Josie had earned and paid for herself*) and wasted gas in the car (*which Josie had paid for*) and how she'd never succeed?

Getting away had been so hard.

And yet she really hadn't escaped anything, had she? Marlene was all-pervasive, affecting Darla's travel here, influencing what her extended family felt they could and couldn't do, and infiltrating Josie's finances. And worse—living inside Josie, the voice of doubt and self-criticism and ragged pessimism.

How do you build a world with someone when you don't know what you are? How do you offer something to someone when you spend your life being *not that?* For the past decade she'd been so focused on the counterdependence of making sure she *wasn't* Marlene that it hadn't occurred to her that maybe she needed to zero in on what she *was.*

That gaping hole inside her couldn't be filled with Alex. It wasn't fair. He didn't have a hole like that, and she certainly couldn't ask him to fall into hers just because she was so damaged and incomplete.

Better to hide it.

Because letting him in meant he could plummet through the endless abyss.

And right now, she knew *exactly* what that felt like, and wouldn't wish it on anyone.

Not even Marlene.

\* \* \*

Meeting his mom for lunch had seemed like a great idea at the time when she'd offered it but now, with three days of complete silence from Josie, Alex was dreading the event. Meribeth Derjian was a force of nature. Pregnant at seventeen and *rotund* as she walked across the stage to accept her high school diploma, she had juggled single parenthood, college, and later, a master's and a Ph.D program throughout Alex's childhood.

She looked like Alex's older sister and even now, at forty-six, just eighteen years older than her son, most people assumed that she was a sibling and not a mother. The way that she treated him, however, was purely maternal. Her drive and good-natured calmness had infused in Alex an amalgam of her, his educational role models, and his grandfather.

Blessed with the same chocolate brown eyes and dark hair as Ed in his youth, Meribeth had inherited his grandmother's tininess. She looked like the average man could pick her up and snap her in two. At just over five feet tall, she was even smaller than Josie. Alex's height came from his biological father, whom he'd never met. Meribeth remained tight-lipped about him, though over the years as she'd moved into clinical psychology she'd shared more. Alex was the product of Meribeth's short-lived high school romance with a Harvard exchange student from Finland; he assumed that was where he got his height.

What his mom lacked in height and girth, however, she made up for in spirit. Never needing to know exactly when she was arriving, he could sense a change in the energy of the atmosphere in any social setting and know instantly that his mother was present. Today was no different.

As he sat in the Ethiopian restaurant in Cambridge, drinking water and sipping clove-flavored espresso, the sound of the door's bells had fooled him once or twice as other diners entered, and then *boom*. Like a genie in a puff of smoke, there was his mother.

The giant, tight hugs, the kisses on cheeks and the assurances that he looked ragged and exhausted and that she would start to call his boss to berate him for tiring out her poor child at the hospital were par for the course. Sitting down, she sighed deeply. Dressed in a light and airy peach combination of floating fabric and tight cotton knit, he didn't know quite what to make of her. The necklace around her throat was a series of chunky gemstones and twisted silver, her lips were painted a darker shade of peach from her clothes, and her eyes *glowed* when she narrowed them and stared at him intently. If he hadn't already known she was clairvoyant, he certainly would have realized it today.

She'd always possessed the uncanny ability to look at him and know what he was thinking, and he'd learned to just let her. Years ago he'd tried to fool her, thinking about baseball, or the *Watchmen*, or Mentos and Diet Coke experiments on YouTube—but none of it had dissuaded her from figuring out what was really going on inside him emotionally. Perhaps it really was a mother's intuition, but he suspected that she was part witch and that someday an invitation from Hogwarts would come for him.

At least, that's what he had hoped when he was a teenager. Alas, no invitation had arrived, and instead he'd gone off to UMass Med School. Which, while more expensive than Harry Potter's world, still taught him a means to fight evil. In a manner of speaking.

They knew the menu backwards and forwards and ordered Injera, the giant sourdough pancakes that came in a communal dish with various savory meals piled on top. From curried cabbage, carrots and potatoes, to some unidentified beef dish with a little bit of field greens, tomatoes, and feta in the middle, this was his favorite meal and his favorite restaurant. Meribeth tolerated it—she enjoyed the food well enough, but Thai was more her flavor.

As they waited for their food to be delivered, she

ordered a mango drink. And then, the formalities dispensed with, she leaned forward, elbows on the table, and said, "Who is she?"

"She?" Alex said, playing the game.

"Alex." Meribeth drew the word out. "Don't make me drag it out of you."

*Mom would like Josie*, he thought. They were both small and feisty, smart with sharp wits—but where Josie was closed off and behind a shield, Meribeth was all open and out there. She'd never held any secrets and she'd never really patronized Alex as a kid, choosing to err on the side of letting him explore the world and discover for himself where his own boundaries were. As he'd grown into adulthood he'd appreciated that more.

Josie was more the type to set up the boundaries and stay inside the lines until forced out of them. While Meribeth had never given him any lines, she'd just let him draw them himself. Except when it came to talking about his love life. Then she crossed *all* the lines.

The waitress delivered his mom's mango drink and she sipped as she stared at him expectantly. "There's a woman. She's different from the other ones—this isn't someone you just hop into the sack with—"

"Mom!"

"And you're not talking about her because… something is wrong."

"You should try out for a reality TV series, Mom. You could call it *My Mom, the Medium* or *Honey Mom Mom*. No"—he held up one finger—"how about *The Hover Mother*. You appear in a helicopter at moments where I'm trying to be my own man and—"

"I don't need a reality TV show. I just get to torture you—that's all the fulfillment that I require."

"She's not—"

"Does she have a name?"

"Josie." Even letting her name roll off his tongue filled him with a warm comfort. Unfortunately, it also came with a touch of concern. Not hearing back from her for days was making him nervous. His mom could smell it from miles away, her mother-sense as acute as Spiderman's spidey sense.

"Josie? Your grandfather's nurse in the research trial?"

"You're an encyclopedia." He stuffed a large amount of food in his mouth just to get a break from talking.

"No. I'm a woman. We remember details. Josie is a pretty old-fashioned name. It's not exactly common around here, where all the children are named Emma and Jacob. Or Caleb. Or MacKenzie."

"Don't forget Renesmee," he mumbled.

"What?"

"Never mind."

"She's an interesting choice for you," Meribeth continued between bites. "Not the shallow type you normally pick."

"Mom!" he barked, wiping his mouth with a napkin and sucking down half a glass of water. The curry was particularly spicy today, the sourdough pancake not cutting it. He reached for a handful of salad to cut the spice.

"Please. I'm not telling you anything you didn't know."

He shrugged in acquiescence. Point taken.

And then she added, "You don't know how to have a long-term relationship because I didn't model one for you."

Oh, boy. The never-ending dissection of Alex's relationship issues.

"I don't have long-term relationships because I haven't met anyone I like enough for that. Oh, and the hundred-hour weeks I work. And the babies born at odd hours. And—"

"And because I didn't bring a man into your life until you were in high school, so you missed out on that kind of relationship modeling during your formative years. You didn't see the emotional and sexual—"

"MOM!"

Meribeth pursed her lips and took a big bite of potato, pointedly ignoring the outburst. He knew he couldn't win; dissembling about his love life and the psychological underpinnings of it with a psychologist who was his mother was like trying to convince Rick Santorum to be the master of ceremonies at Pride Week. Not gonna happen.

"Do you like her?"

He shot her a look that said *duh.* "Yes."

"More than the others?"

A few seconds of hesitation was all she needed. Really, it was all he needed, too.

"A lot," he said.

"Finally!" she said loudly, golf-clapping for him. "And someone I've met, too! We need to have her over for dinner."

"We?"

"You do have a stepfather," she said drolly, picking out a spicy carrot and folding a ragged piece of pancake around it.

"Of course I do. Can he keep his pants on this time?" The last time—the only time—he'd brought a woman home, John had been in the living room sans pants.

"He was putting on a kilt for his bagpipes."

"Uh huh. Is that the euphemism your generation uses now? I don't need to know about your sex life, Mom," he teased.

She threw a piece of pancake at him.

"That's it. He's playing a nice Scottish piece for your Josie when she comes over for dinner next week."

*Your Josie. My Josie.* It had a nice ring to it. Nervous again, he checked his phone.

No texts. No calls.

No Josie.

\* \* \*

Ignoring Alex's texts was like listening to a Justin Bieber acceptance speech at the Billboard Music Awards.

Torture.

Once again, Laura was impossible to reach. Josie's calls to Darla were ignored. Who else was she supposed to talk to? Crackhead? As hours ticked by, and then two days, she started to think the cat was her only option.

How had it gotten this bad? When had her isolation become so complete? It wasn't like she didn't have work friends she went out with for drinks here and there. Small talk was easy and they laughed at each other's stories and jokes. But when she thought about it—really thought about it—not a single one of those people were someone she could turn to in the middle of the night in an emergency.

Only Laura and Darla.

Alex was the kind of man who could join that club. He was.

If you define yourself by what you're running away *from*, then how do you know when you've arrived at where you're going *to*? So many years of pulling herself away from a dysfunctional life, of establishing herself as a professional, as a financially stable young woman, had melded into one big concept of *not*. Josie was not her mother. Josie was not a sociopath. Josie was not incompetent. Josie was not the source of Marlene's problems.

Josie was *not*.

Then what was she? How do you live a centered life when you don't know where or what your center is? The thought looped through her mind a thousand times a day, the only anchor in her life. It weighed her down, pinning her in place, and as toxic as it was, at least it was there. Unlike Laura and Darla, who were absent at the most critical juncture of her life.

*Show up for your own life, Josie,* a voice said. *You don't need them. Do the right thing. Find your core on your own.*

And that was the problem with Alex. At the core, he was grounded and stable and knew himself deeply. What kind of doctor deferred to CNMs and patient wishes so fully? One who knew himself, who trusted his instincts, and who drew faith from an inner sense of truth.

What kind of man accepted her for who she was, quirks and all? Screeching brakes in her head made that thought come to a dead halt, because that was the fulcrum of her imbalanced soul. When Alex got to see the real her—the abyss inside that stretched on for eternity, the hole where Josie was supposed to be—he would change. Or leave.

Because that's what people do.

How could she develop any sense of grounded self when her mother was a whirlwind of splintered chaos, seeking to find her own center in Josie?

Worse—consistently and persistently destroying Josie's core because Marlene only felt better about herself when others around her were failing. She couldn't bear to watch someone else succeed, as if it were an implicit judgment against her. Narcissism at its finest, a character disorder not inborn but one created by a car crash that changed her brain. Insidious and disabling, it had made her mother wholly dependent on sarcasm and cruelty.

Josie maintained the former, but actively eschewed the latter.

For as painful as it was to shut him out, it was too dangerous to let Alex in.

Because when you say "I love you" to someone and mean it, what happens when they say it back—and there is no "you"? Who would he love if he said it?

Josie didn't know.

And that was the true torture.

\* \* \*

Josie was turning him into a stalker. Not really, but he

didn't need to go for a run nearly every day now. That his path *happened* to involve her street, and that running the loop around the park *happened* to take him past her building was sheer coincidence. Not creepy.

Right?

Her car was there every time, but that didn't mean anything. Taking the T was the norm around here. Pushing past her building slowly, he wished he had the balls to go up to her porch and ring her bell.

And what? Face rejection in person? He'd already been spurned electronically. Why add to it?

What had he done wrong? Sex in the park was astounding. Life altering. Phenomenal and passionate and exciting and…all of it. Josie was all of it.

Falling for her was killing him.

Work didn't help. A minor issue with a patient had snowballed, making his bosses frown and a few administrators schedule case reviews. Whatever it was, Alex didn't like it, and it made him uncharacteristically angry. Being questioned so that patient care was at its best? Absolutely fine. Having his judgment nitpicked and Monday-morning-quarterbacked and a whisper campaign of rumors and innuendo used to undermine him? Screw that. He hated how other respected residents had been rattled and shredded by similar hospital processes and he despised this part of his job.

As his legs pounded on the sidewalk, his heart rate steady, body pushing air in and out, legs stretching, he hit a flow state. Body occupied, his t-shirt soaking with sweat at the neck and underarms, he reveled in the fact that something worked right. No matter what, he could count on two things: his body and his mind. Both had served him well when he took care of them. Exercise regularly, eat reasonably well, and reduce stress. That took care of the body.

Harness and expand his insatiable curiosity—that took care of the mind.

The heart?

How do you keep that in shape?

As he rounded the corner, he saw Josie. The steady beat turned into a syncopated jazz set, his neck straining to watch her. Dressed in a red silk shirt and black pants, she looked like she was headed off to work. Strolling and taking time to look at the trees, her head bounced in rhythm to something. He guessed she wore earbuds and listened to music.

What kind of music? Did she have a favorite beyond the old blues she played in her bedroom? What was her favorite food? He knew she liked lattes. Italian food. And…that was it.

So many parts of her he hadn't met yet.

Patting his pocket, he found his phone. Checked for message. Nope. Voicemail? Yes.

Score!

It was his mother.

Damn it.

No woman had done this to him. Ever. Not the blowing-off part—that he'd experienced exactly twice. Neither time was fun, but he'd glossed over it quickly and rolled with the punches. There was always someone else to date. To sleep with. To have fun with.

He didn't want someone else right now.

He wanted Josie.

Pushing himself on her wasn't his style. If she didn't want him, he wouldn't—couldn't—be *that guy*. The one who weaseled his way in where he wasn't wanted. Finding a side street that took him away from her building, his last glimpse of her red-topped figure made him wince with indecision.

And resignation.

The bottom line was simple: she just didn't want him.

He could respect that.

For now.

But Alex wasn't the type to walk away without answers.

Checking his phone, he realized he had a plan staring him in the face. Today was his day off. He had one scheduled event.

And damn if he wasn't going.

# CHAPTER ELEVEN

Alex pulled into the parking spot in front of his grandfather's apartment building, turned off his trusty ten-year-old Honda Civic and rolled his tongue between his teeth and his cheek. Unlike the last few trips to take Grandpa to the Alzheimer's trial, this one he dreaded.

Never one to chase a woman to the point of ridicule, he had taken Josie's hint after phone messages and texts went unanswered. Her sudden Ice Queen behavior—especially after the heat between the two of them—made absolutely no sense. Sure, it had only been a week, but a week without her felt like a lifetime, and it was killing him.

Time to act. Not wait.

As he climbed out of the car, the door creaked, a reminder to put some WD-40 on there. He stopped and sized up Grandpa's apartment complex. It was small—only sixteen units—and income subsidized, which was a great help to Ed. Grandpa was the son of immigrants who had come to the Boston area seeking something better. Five years ago, when Grandma had died and Ed found himself alone at the end of a long line of bills for her care, the best solution had seemed to be an apartment in a complex with other senior citizens.

His Social Security check and meager savings allowed Grandpa to live a *comfortable* life; when Alex had his own finances under control, the six-figure student loans were tamed to a number that didn't make him gag every time he thought about it, he hoped to be able to help out Grandpa and his mom.

The building itself looked like just about any other building in Cambridge—brown paint, white trim, a long and narrow triple-decker, spanning far more of the backyard than you would expect. The front door bisected the entire building, splitting it down a long, narrow hallway with two front staircases at the entryway. Ed had scored a first-floor apartment, something that was hard to get. An old knee injury from fighting in Korea still plagued him occasionally, making everyone glad that he didn't have to battle stairs on top of his other obstacles.

It was Grandma's death that actually had made them all figure out just how mentally deteriorated Ed had become. What had been laughed off as his forgetfulness, while Grandma was still alive to compensate, had turned into whispered conversations between his mom and her sisters as they huddled around the kitchen table, looking at piles of bills that had gone unpaid, evaluating everything from the status of Ed's wardrobe to the spoiled cartons of milk sitting between cans of penny nails at his workbench.

Alex had been an intern then, too busy with his own world and sheltered by his mother and the aunts who wanted to keep him on the fast track to physician success. It wasn't until two years ago that anyone had bothered to bring him into the secret of Grandpa's Alzheimer's. Even then, it wasn't until he called Grandpa's property manager to get the front stairs fixed, citing ADA requirements with authority, that his mom and aunts had really realized he wasn't Little Alex, needing to be sheltered, anymore.

Med school had taught him one important skill that had absolutely nothing to do with medicine itself—be the squeaky wheel. If a patient could not advocate for himself, it fell on a family member to do it. And for most patients, that was at least sometimes the case. Most family members, though, weren't bold enough to ask for everything the patient needed. Grandpa's family was no different—until Alex took control.

Alex had no problem being bold—he'd gone immediately into medical databases, found advanced research trials, made phone calls, shamelessly used his credentials. Funny how the title "Doctor" in front of his name led to instant respect on the phone. He had totally manipulated whomever, whatever, however, any system needed, to get Ed into his current research trial. And also to find a primary care physician who would do something more than prescribe what had become a brown bag full of conflicting medications that actually added to Ed's addled state.

Seeing what everyone had thought was early-onset dementia partly reverse itself, little by little, as the med confusion had lifted, reinforced Alex's boldness and further emboldened him to step into the role as family patriarch. His aunts had all had girls—everyone had called him Little Alex, the youngest of the cousins, his mom's only child—so far. Only eighteen years older than himself, she was young enough to still manage another child if she wanted to.

The thought made him chuckle. Mom was forty-six, happily married to a man who had no interest in any more children. He'd been kind and pleasant when he'd entered Alex's life his senior year of high school but the two had little in common. They were cocktail party guests at best, competitors for his mom's attention at worst.

Ed's door was painted China red, with a little sign that said *Welcome*. Rapping three times on the door, Alex waited, knowing Ed, clean shaven, freshly showered, and dressed, was sitting with his hands folded in his lap at the kitchen table. All ready for what had become one of his favorite events. You would never know that Ed Derjian had Alzheimer's—but Alex did know, and that was why every month this trial became more and more important, as they hoped to unlock some kind of secret that would make them hang on to who Grandpa was.

The door opened slowly and Alex saw himself, about forty-six years in the future. Grandpa was about three inches shorter than Alex, with a full head of pure white hair. It was perfectly coiffed; a little bit of hair grease at the temples and around the ears to tame the little curls to smooth waves. Alex's own chocolate brown eyes peered back at him, buried behind layers of wrinkles around the eyelids.

Ed's practiced smile cracked into a wide natural grin upon seeing someone familiar. At the recommendation of one of the nurses, Alex wore the same outfit every time he came to pick Ed up. It had turned out to be an extraordinary tip. Now May was turning to summer, he was beginning to wish he hadn't chosen his merino wool burgundy sweater—but he'd find a way to deal with it.

"Alex!" Ed shouted, arms out, welcoming his grandson into a hug.

Alex accepted the old-world embrace happily, a kiss planted on his cheek, the feel of Ed's smooth skin loose and soft like a baby's arm. Sandalwood and lavender mixed in with a light peppermint scent greeted Alex along with Ed.

As they pulled apart, Ed said the same words he said every time. "Let me take a good look at you. Boy, have you grown! Where's your mother? Where is Meribeth?" he asked, looking behind Alex into the hallway as if genuinely expecting to find her.

"Grandpa, she doesn't pick you up for this appointment."

"Oh." His eyes clouded and Alex felt the bottom of his stomach drop. It was rare, but once in a while Ed could go into that place where only his daughters, in the flesh, could anchor him. Alex was one generation removed, just enough to make Ed hesitate.

The cloud lifted and Ed's smile widened even more. "Of course. It's just us boys. There aren't many of us, are there, Alex?"

"No, sir," he said, smiling.

"Just those lousy sons-in-law of mine and my delightful granddaughters. It's you and me Alex, all the way."

"That's right, Grandpa."

Ed shut the door, carefully sliding a key into the deadbolt, clicking it, turning it back and sliding it out, slipping the key on a thin string under his shirt. They had taught him to do this about three years ago and he took it as deeply serious as a big, overgrown latchkey kid. But no more lost keys, no more frantic phone calls from a neighbor who found him wandering.

As they walked back to the parking lot, Alex glanced at Ed's old car, forlorn and rusting out at the wheel wells. No matter how many times they explained to him that his license was expired, Ed would still try to get in the car. A handful of times he had managed to drive somewhere; the farthest he had gotten was from Watertown to Greenfield, a good hundred-mile jaunt that no one could really figure out. He must have just gotten on Route 2 and kept driving until he stopped at a Dunkin' Donuts. He had munched happily on about a half-dozen chocolate glazed before an employee had figured out that he was lost. It wasn't the first call from a kind Samaritan, but it was the last. Since then, Alex had disabled the car's engine and his mother, aunts, and uncles took turns about every third or fourth day, surreptitiously reconnecting the battery terminals and driving it around a bit. Just enough to keep it functional.

"My car is broken, you know," Ed said, pointing to the old gray clunker. "Damn engine—probably cost more to fix it than it's worth."

"Yeah, Grandpa, sorry about that." Alex diverted the conversation by blurting out, "So, I met a new girl."

"Your mother lets you date?"

Oh, boy. This was one of those days when Grandpa thought he was fourteen.

"Grandpa, I'm twenty-eight years old."

Ed frowned. "I guess that means you can drive then today, right?"

Ed reached Alex's car and he slapped the top of his green Honda.

"Yes, sir." The less said, the better.

They both climbed into the car. Alex started it up and they wended their way a handful of miles through the Cambridge streets, past coffee shops, Alex's favorite Eritrean restaurant, and finally Ed's favorite hang-out in Harvard Square—the chess tables.

When the study appointment was done, he would take Grandpa to his favorite diner for lunch and then over to Harvard Square for a few games of friendly chess. If Alex deviated from *that* routine he would never hear the end of it. Ed may float back to 1953 sometimes, and even as far back as the early 1940s, but there was one thing that he *knew* about 2013—and that was that he was going to get his piece of pie at the diner and he was going to play three or four rounds of well-matched chess.

"This girl," Ed asked, "she cute?" He held his hands out in front of his chest and mimicked a set of breasts, ogling his own creation.

Alex bit his lower lip and tried not to laugh. "She's… pretty, Grandpa. She's pretty."

"Did you… y'know?" Ed leaned over and nudged him with his elbow.

"Did we…?" *Oh, God,* he thought. *Please. Not this conversation.* It was easier to lie. "Uh, no."

"Not yet," Ed teased. "So, there's another date?"

"That's up to her."

As they made the left turn to go into the parking lot at the nondescript medical building where the research trial was held, Alex felt his body flush. It had been one thing in the abstract to decide that he was still going to bring Ed for their monthly routine, that he would catch her and leave her no choice but to face him. It was quite another to slide into the parking garage, press the button for the ticket, and move slowly through the dark concrete jungle.

\* \* \*

Josie did a double-take when Ed Derjian walked in to the room because there, standing behind him, was his two-generations-younger double. Taller, broader in the shoulder, and with a touch of something *different*, an ethnicity she couldn't put her finger on but a body she wanted to put all her fingers on.

Dammit!

Of all the people in her life to be Ed's grandson, how had she missed it? Somehow she had compartmentalized her life enough that work was work and everything else was everything else so Alex's last name hadn't rung a bell. Alexander Edward Derjian. She'd been blinded by lust. *He'd* blinded her with *his* lust. The easy familiarity in his eyes should have been a clue.

He knew her—or at least, knew *of* her when they met at Laura's birth. Or did he? Maybe he really hadn't recognized her and she was just making this all up in her mind as she looked him square in the eyes while Ed introduced them

"Oh, hey, Jackie. So, this is—"

"Josie, Grandpa. Her name is Josie," Alex whispered. It was a stage whisper with a quick little look of amusement that Alex intended only for her.

"Josie!" Ed said, slapping his forehead. "That's right. Josie. I knew that," he chided Alex. "Josie, let me introduce you to my *single*, eligible, bachelor grandson. He's a doctor," Ed added, waggling his eyebrows suggestively.

Josie couldn't help herself and laughed and extended her hand as if she had never met Dr. Alex Derjian before.

"Josie Mendham. Pleased to meet you," she said, her palm pressed against his, sending an electric current through her body that made her back stand at attention, her body filled with ice and heat, her breathing steady and slow in contrast to her heart, which sped up as if it were sprinting to the finish line of some race she didn't even know she was running.

"We've met before, Grandpa, actually," Alex said without relinquishing her hand, the steady pumping of their embraced palms slowing until Alex was just holding her hand for no reason other than she let him.

Their eyes locked and Ed crossed his arms over his chest and gave them a puzzled look. "Then why did Josie pretend she hadn't met you?"

She could feel the rush of blood to her cheeks and knew that she was blushing, but couldn't pull her eyes away. Finally, she did, tearing them as if fibers had been ripped in half by warring impulses. Ed's very amused, red-rimmed orbs met hers.

"Because I'm afraid I've been quite rude to your grandson," she said, filled suddenly with a perplexing shame. As if not answering a guy's calls and texts made her a disappointing child. It was funny how grandfatherly figures brought that out in her, as if she ceded authority to them simply because of their age. You would think that working on an Alzheimer's unit—and a research trial, no less—would disabuse her of that tendency. In fact it had strengthened it in her, leaving her helpless at times, feeling completely not up to the task of carrying the moral weight of being a good girl.

Alex was persistent, she had to give him that. It must have taken guts to come here in spite of her ignoring him.

Why?

Men played around with women like her—they didn't *chase* them. So, when Ed cleared his throat she realized she was in some sort of trance and then quickly lifted the clipboard lying limp in her hand and said, "Let's get on

214

with the appointment, shall we?"

Ed gestured gallantly to the small room where her short interview would take place. "Ladies first," he said, leaving Alex in the waiting room without a backward glance. Ed seemed relaxed and grounded today, really on his game—aside from forgetting her name, such a small lapse that it didn't trouble her. The handful of steps into the tiny interview room gave her just enough time to wonder about that level of comfort.

Routine was so important with Alzheimer's patients…if Ed were this fine and grounded, then coming here with Alex must be his routine. How long had Alex been bringing him? And how could she have missed such a fine man right in front of her face?

* * *

Alex felt like a drowning man holding on to her hand as he shook it, as if it were a life preserver or a last-minute attempt to pull him out of troubled waters. In reality it was neither. The expression on her face said that what had started out as a polite gesture—a farce, really—for Ed's benefit had turned into an acknowledgment of the attraction that he so keenly felt.

A million questions peppered his thoughts and nearly threatened to come out in a rush. Why had she ignored his phone calls? Why had she ignored his texts? What had he done to turn her off? What could he do to turn her back on? Did she remember him from these appointments? From the shocked look on her face he guessed not, which made him feel fairly pathetic. How could she be so memorable to him when she found him so easy to overlook?

Maybe he wasn't her type on the deeper level that he'd thought, and he was making more of this than there really was. Surface-level attractions could probably be as hot as their connection had been, and surface-level explanations were often enough.

He didn't *really* believe that, but some part of his bruised ego needed to think it through and at least contemplate it, because why else wasn't she jumping into his arms right now? What made her hesitate? Why would someone so interesting and quirky—and so passionate only a week ago!—be so measured in her reaction to him?

Measured—that was a hell of a euphemism he was coming up with, wasn't it? She wasn't measured. She was blowing him off. *She's just not that into you, Alex,* a voice said.

There was not enough in the waiting room to distract him from his thoughts, either. He was rather used to being at this sort of loose end. Few typical distractions engaged him—his interests were medicine, Grandpa, and quite a bit of philosophical contemplation over a macchiato as he tried to figure out what he was going to do with the rest of his life.

Med school had been the big goal, then internship, and now residency. He was solid in his knowledge that delivering babies and providing women's health care was exactly where he needed to be. It was a vocation and not just an occupation.

Outside of work, though, life was a giant hole, occupied occasionally with friends, a game of basketball that he picked up here and there. Could he fill that hole with something as satisfying as medicine? Could life away from work actually balance, complement, his work? Could finding *someone* be the same? Could you really find one person, like one career, with every element you needed in one package, an anchor for your sense of being, unswayed by drama or volatility? Was it possible to love someone and have them love you back, not 50/50 but 80/80?

Alex didn't know. He gave up entirely on the magazines in front of him and gave in to an *Angry Birds* app on his phone. His brain was exhausted. Flinging little red, round electronic renderings of real-life animals was easier than navel-gazing.

\* \* \*

"Josie, are you dating anyone?" Ed asked, reaching across the table and placing his hand on hers, the gesture grandfatherly and not at all a pass.

She decided to turn it into a joke anyhow. "Why, Ed? You looking for a girlfriend?"

Mirth filled his eyes and the boom of his laughter carried, she imagined, out into the hall. "Oh, no! Don't you dare even imply it," he said, laughing, his hands slapping the table. "I have a girlfriend, honey. I'm taken."

"Bummer!" she said, snapping her fingers in a gesture of frustration.

Ed just shook his head, those brown eyes filled with a kind of wisdom and focus that she didn't get to see very often in her patients. "My girlfriend and me, we've been together for two years, and Josie, honey, if she thought you were making a pass at me she'd come in here and rip your head off."

"Really?" Josie answered, slapping her palm against her chest. "You got yourself a sweet young thing who could beat me up?"

"I got myself a sweet *old* thing who's been around the block a few times and could take a whippersnapper like you down like snapping a twig."

Josie stood and Ed picked up on the body language, standing as well, understanding that the session was done. It was a small test, but one that she used for almost every appointment, along with a few other nonverbal social cues to see how aware her patients were. Ed was doing well— not as well as she had hoped, but reasonably well for a man his age and with his level of Alzheimer's advancement.

Her sense of empathy broadened, blossoming, carrying out to cover Alex. She didn't know which of Ed's daughters was Alex's mother, but all had come in here at various times with their dad, loving and supportive. The worst patients were the ones who were dumped off, left alone, the caretaker absent. Just a body in the driver's seat of the car waiting. Patient outcome or disease progression for those people wasn't nearly as positive as for those who had a strong family support network.

Ed would do fine compared to some of her other patients, but the whole family had a long road ahead of them. Thinking about this was depressing her, all of it floating through her mind in seconds, as she took Ed down to the prize closet.

Most patients *loved* the prize closet, especially those who'd grown up poor or who were currently poor. Even if they hadn't, or weren't, the prize closet seemed to be a nice little place where folks could indulge. She opened the slim door and there, before them, were three shelves. On the first shelf was a smattering of gift cards to local restaurants. The most popular had surprised her—a local coffee shop, not a chain, and after the fifth or sixth person in a row chose to take the $25 gift card as a "thank you" for the monthly meeting, she asked why.

"Every morning, before 9 a.m.," one of her patients explained, "seniors can get a dollar coffee. This will give me coffee for most of the month, and it's a real nice place. You get to sit there and just chat with people."

The next time the administrator went to order gifts for the prize closet, Josie had made a point to let them know about patient feedback and she found herself gently steering some of her older, lonelier patients to pick that, imagining a group of them sitting in this local coffee shop, sharing a cup of joe in the morning, finding the companionship they needed.

*That could be you,* she thought, the voice invasive and melancholy.

Pushing that thought aside, she returned her attention to the closet. The second row was covered with books.

Large-print books leaning more towards Nora Roberts and Tom Clancy than anything else, though some of the women *delighted* in the romance novels, clutching them to their chests and covering the book cover as if it were a clandestine gift.

The men tended to go for the third shelf, which had mostly sporting goods: golf balls, tennis balls, swim goggles, and kites—things designed to be played with a grandchild or to be enjoyed by the more active seniors.

Ed's hand went straight for the gift-card shelf and then stopped.

"Have you been to the coffee house?" she asked.

His hand was suspended in midair, shaking just a little. He didn't have an official diagnosis of Parkinson's, so she knew it was just the slightest of tremors that come with age. He put his hand back down, pursed his lips, and gave her a disapproving look. "If I'm going to get coffee I'm not going to get it there."

"Why not?" She had been thinking about gently suggesting that he take that to get out more, and enjoy conversation.

"I can get all of the coffee I want whenever I want. My girlfriend works at a restaurant," he said, nudging her in the ribs.

"Oh. That's a nice perk."

"No, honey, the sex is a nice perk. The coffee is just an extra."

If she'd been drinking something she would have done a classic spit take. Instead, she just choked, Ed grinning madly at her. "Okay, that's a little too much information, Ed, but uh... thank you for sharing."

"My pleasure," he said. "No pun intended."

"Okay, Ed, so let's stick to umm... finding your gift," she stammered, trying to extract herself from a very uncomfortable conversation. "How about this one?" She pointed to a card for an ice cream shop.

He snatched it up. "Oh, I love Christina's. Absolutely. I

can take my girlfriend there for a cone."

They walked back out to the waiting room, where Alex jumped up as if burned by their presence. "Josie," he said.

"Alex," she said, mocking him.

His mouth flatlined into an embarrassed frown. "How are things going?"

"We were just talking about our sex lives," Ed answered.

A couple of people sitting in the waiting room tittered.

"Really?" Alex's eyebrows shot up.

"Yes. Why don't you share, Alex? There's that new woman that you kissed recently. You were telling me all about her in the car ride over here."

Alex froze.

Josie turned slowly and looked at him, imitating what he'd just said a few moments ago, her own eyebrows shooting up to her hairline. "Really?"

"Grandpa, I think you're remembering that wrong," Alex said slowly, slipping his hand around the old man's shoulders. "Why don't we just get going now? It's time for—"

Ed interrupted him. "Josie, you done working yet?"

She reflexively looked at her wrist, checking the watch she hadn't worn for years. "Actually, I can take a break for an hour, or so…an early lunch. You offering, Ed?"

"I don't know, Josie, I've got a girlfriend. I can't really take you up on…asking me out." He waved his hand at her, as if saying "pshaw." "No, I'm just asking"—he glanced pointedly at Alex, and then at her—"if you'd like to go out for coffee and a bite to eat. There's a sweet thing I really adore over at Jeddy's."

Jeddy's. God, she couldn't get away from that place, could she? How did a hole-in-the wall diner like Jeddy's suddenly become the center of her social life? Alex had a look on his face like he was struggling to remain neutral, to seem as if he didn't care whether she said yes or no. The intensity of his eyes gave away what he was really feeling.

Ed's expectant look, so friendly and simple, was what broke her. Awkwardness be damned; she wasn't going to disappoint a very nice old man, who had just failed every part of the test that indicated any sort of halt in his disintegration through Alzheimer's. A pang of sadness shot through her—for Ed, for Alex, for his entire family—as she began to suspect that Ed was either on a rapid decline or, more likely, might be in the control group and not in the group that was receiving the experimental medicine.

"Sure, Ed," she said, reaching out to touch him tenderly on the shoulder, gazing firmly into his eyes, so he had her full attention. "I would love to enjoy a nice, sweet thing at Jeddy's."

They took two different cars, despite Ed's not-so-subtle attempt at getting her into Alex's old Honda, the kind of car you expected a six-figure-in-debt medical resident to be driving. Her own car was on par, a twelve-year-old Toyota Tercel that she held together with duct tape, gum, and a lot of atheistic praying.

Jeddy's was just a few miles away, and she scored an awesome parking spot, which made this ridiculous bit of Kabuki theater almost worth it. Finding a *good* parking spot was a form of sport in Cambridge and Boston, and she wanted a ribbon for getting one directly in front of the restaurant. A pang of guilt hit her as she watched Alex circling the block repeatedly, finally letting Ed out at the entrance to Jeddy's and then driving off, leaving her alone with the old man.

His warm, confident brown eyes were a bit clouded now, filled with a tentative fear, a look she had come to know all too well, professionally. He was confused, and in his confusion he reverted to the past. "Meribeth? Meribeth, what are we doing here?" he asked.

She remembered that one of his daughters was Meribeth. She wasn't sure whether it was Alex's mom or not, but right now it didn't matter. A split-second decision made her choose to ground him as much as possible in the truth, reserving the right to shift if needed.

"Ed." She touched him again, making that connection, smiling, exuding as much warmth and familiarity as possible. "Ed, you just came from the medical building where you go every month with Alex. Remember, you came to my office and I asked you some questions? I'm Josie, Josie Mendham." Maintaining eye contact, and speaking as simply as possible without condescension should do the trick. The fear dissipated, as if her words had marshaled an army that fought it back. Victory, she thought.

"Josie! Of course, I know you! How's my gal?" he said. This was a technique that some of the sharper patients used. He was covering, and she knew it. He didn't realize it…or did he?

She took a chance. "Ed, you don't have to pretend you know me, I want you to really know me. I'm the girl Alex…kissed."

His eyes shifted instantly, as if someone snapped their fingers, into complete focus. The man whiplashed back into himself, completely in the present. "Hot damn, I knew it! I knew you and Alex were a thing!"

"We're a *what?*" a deep voice said from behind her.

She closed her eyes and pressed her lips together in agony. This was not how helping Ed to ground himself was supposed to work. "Alex, you're here!" she said, acknowledging him because it would have been far worse had she shown her humiliation or acknowledged what Ed had just said. Looping her right arm through Ed's left, she marched him toward the entrance of Jeddy's, sidestepping, for now, Alex's expected question about why on earth Ed would have any idea that he and Josie were a thing.

The entrance to Jeddy's seemed bare without the warlock waitress who wore the pair of balls, but since it had been auctioned off at some autism event, it was probably now sitting in some millionaire's garage, gathering dust. At least the poor warlock waitress got a chance to retire. Madge, on the other hand, didn't. She marched right up to the group and then, to Josie's utter amazement, reached out for Alex, stood on tiptoes, and planted a loud smackeroo on his cheek. The kiss, intimate and friendly, and the kind a grandmother gives her grandson.

"You two know each other?" Josie asked, incredulous.

Ed walked over to Madge and slipped a sly arm around her waist, goosing her hip and laughing when Madge playfully slapped his hand. "You're the threesome girl, aren't you?" Madge said, pointing at Josie, narrowing her eyes.

Josie turned into a beet on the spot. A bright red, flaming beet. "What? No, I…what do you…?"

Alex and Ed looked at her with eyebrows practically up to the ceiling. "Threesome girl?" Alex asked, with a half-smile on his face.

"It's not what you…No, that's not what I…oh…" she stammered, completely flummoxed by Madge's comment.

"Yeah, she comes in here all the time," Madge said, "with this incredibly big, pregnant blonde, and the blonde is pregnant by one of two guys, but not in that Maury Povich kind of way, more in a…Mormon sister wives kind of way, except sister husbands, no…brother husbands." Madge waved her hand in a dismissive gesture. "Bah…now she's got me stammering trying to explain it. It's all…this quirky thing involving Thor and his little…model boyfriend."

"Mike and Dylan," Alex said.

Madge snapped her neck back in surprise. "You know them?"

"Yeah, I was just at Laura's birth."

"You delivered the baby?" Ed asked.

"No, but I assisted in the case."

"Maybe you'll get a fighting chance at some of those coconut shrimp now that she shat out the football,"

Madge laughed to Josie, a conspirator's smile on her face.

As the four of them stood there, ignoring the growing line behind them, Josie realized that suddenly she was something different to Madge. "How do you all...?" She cut off her own question. "Madge is the sweet thing that you like at Jeddy's, isn't she, Ed?"

His smile stretched so wide across his face, she thought it might meet at the base of his neck in the back. "Yes, ma'am, me and Madge have been together for a good long time, and she's my sweet thing."

"I thought you meant you had a favorite dessert here."

"I do," he said, with a lecherous smile.

Alex just shook his head and pretended not to be there.

Josie cackled. "We're quickly getting into 'too much information' territory here, Ed."

"When you're my age, you take whatever information you can get," he said.

"All right, all right." Madge batted his hand away. "I need to get you guys seated. Come on." She grabbed three menus, and Ed followed her, giving her a quick goose on the ass, making her giggle. The idea that Madge was capable of giggling threw Josie for a loop. As Madge showed them to their booth, Josie made it a point to sit across from the two men, claiming her space and needing to get as much distance as possible from both of them, to preserve whatever shred of dignity remained.

The first words out of Alex's mouth, as he sat across from her and locked eyes, were exactly what she expected. "Threesome. Care to explain?"

"You know what she meant," Josie retorted.

"No, I don't," Alex said skeptically. A smile struggled to stay inside as he grilled her, leaning forward, invading her space as much as possible in an effort to unsettle her. She knew it, and he knew it, and damn if he wasn't succeeding.

"She called me 'threesome girl' because I came in here *with* the threesome, not because I'm *part* of a threesome."

She looked down at the menu, knowing exactly what she was going to order, but needing to break eye contact. "I don't seem to be part of anything these days."

He frowned, genuine concern pouring into his features. His eyes warm again as he let go of the guardedness. It made her want to let go as well and talk to him openly, rather than play this stupid game that she knew was one-sided, all on her, trying to shut him out.

"You can be part of whatever you want to be part of," he stressed. His fingers started to tap the tabletop, and she knew that he was purposefully engaging his hands so that he didn't reach across and try to take hers. The gesture was touching.

That day in the elevator, their heated embrace while Laura was in labor, he had said to her something about games being what people who don't know what they want engage in. Damn, if he wasn't right. Playing this game was a reflection of her own internal turmoil, and she really didn't know what she wanted.

That was the problem. The longer she sat across from him, though, the more she wanted him. He was the real deal. Diving in with Alex would be a mature relationship, one that she knew involved giving it all. This wouldn't be a 50/50 or a 20/20, which was what she was more accustomed to. This would be a full on, 100% involvement, with each person giving their all. He'd mentioned having a family, and children, and she knew that she couldn't offer that. That's what had kept her away, the worry that he really was the whole package and that she just *wasn't*.

"Coconut shrimp and fried green tomatoes for you," Madge said to Josie without looking at her as she scribbled something in that little electronic device of hers. "Coconut cream pie and a cup of coffee for Ed...and Alex, I still haven't quite figured out what it is that you want."

"I know exactly what I want, Madge," he said, his eyes boring into Josie. "Unfortunately, it's not on the menu."

"I'm changing my order, Madge," Josie said flatly. "Give me whatever Ed's having."

"Don't you want the same thing Alex wants?" Madge said, those smoker's lips pursed like the puckered butthole of a cat.

*That's the problem!* her heart cried out, but her mouth, thankfully, didn't open and say those words. Josie chose this moment to ignore everyone, her wishes already stated, and took the coward's way out, standing and slipping past Madge to go and use the ladies' room.

* * *

Alex worried that maybe this had all been a mistake. Surprising Josie at work and bringing Ed in today had seemed like such a good idea at the time. Now, sitting across from her at the table filled him with so many conflicting emotions, he hardly knew which to act on. Teasing her about the threesome seemed to be a gentle ribbing that she could tolerate, but her speedy exit told him that he had crossed a line.

Grandpa seemed happy to be in a familiar place with his girlfriend nearby; her fast, sure motions around the rundown restaurant were reassuring, even to Alex. He liked Madge, they all did. She was a crotchety old curmudgeon, but she dearly loved Ed, and Alex, his mom, and his aunts were grateful for her stable, stalwart presence as Ed was in decline.

Alex reached out and tapped Madge on the elbow in one of her many trips past the table. She halted, like something out of a *Road Runner* cartoon, coming to a screeching halt and turning to him with a look of surprise.

"Yes, Alex?"

"Do you really know Josie?"

"She's been coming in here for a while."

"Hasn't half of Boston?" he asked.

"She's been coming in here for the better part of a year.

It started with the blonde, the pregnant one, and shortly after that, the two guys came in. They're the ones who made the warlock waitress, you know, back in the day."

"No way, Mike and Dylan were responsible for that?" he said in disbelief.

"They are indeed." She nodded somberly. "One of them stole the cardboard cutout from some video store and they came in here with their old girlfriend and they finagled a waitress's uniform out of me, and I don't even remember who the hell put the balls on there."

This was probably one of the longer conversations he'd ever had with Madge, who was already tapping her toe to get back into the kitchen and handle orders. She looked at the table in horror. "I completely forgot about your drinks!" she muttered under her breath.

Ed tapped her on the knee and said, "Don't worry about it, honey, we're good tippers, no matter what." The look of happiness on her face peeled back three decades—not enough to see the young girl she must have been at one time, but enough to see how much Ed's presence lightened her heart.

He wanted to put that kind of joy on Josie's face, just with his mere presence. The time they'd spent together a few weeks ago, everything from the birth of baby Jillian, to asking her to go on a walk, to their first time together at her place, it all had seemed seamless and ecstatic, electric and charged, with a strange combination of the new and the familiar. Call it fate, or kismet, or luck…whatever you called it, it had rolled out as if it were meant to be. Was the aberration Josie's cooling off, or was the aberration the connection that he had felt?

Coming to Ed's appointment, facing her head on, pushing her just a little to come to Jeddy's, to sit with him and Ed, had seemed like it was a way to crack the door open, to get his foot in there and wiggle it enough for her to accept him as an audience. To ask questions, to be heard, and maybe, just maybe, to go back to the slow unfurling of what had seemed like a linear development of a relationship.

She came back from the ladies' room with a chip prominently displayed on both shoulders. Her body edged into the booth with a non-verbal defensiveness that almost made him laugh at its rigidity. Somehow he had done this, and somehow he would undo this.

"Toffee mint cannoli?" he asked as she scooted into the booth.

"Excuse me?"

"Madge said they're experimenting with some new desserts."

Josie groaned. "I don't think I can handle more."

"What about coffee?" Madge barked, appearing suddenly with a carafe.

"Always room for coffee," Josie backpedaled.

Alex stopped Madge. "Not now. Thanks. We'll get a latte somewhere else."

"Latte," Madge huffed. "Well, excuuuuuuuse me for offering plain old brewed pig shit," she said, storming off.

Josie choked on her water. "She's always like that, isn't she?"

"Can you imagine being related to her?"

"Yes," Ed announced.

Josie raised her eyebrows and just looked at Alex, who humored Ed.

"Grandpa?"

"I want to marry her."

"You go for it, Ed," Josie said, cheering him on.

Alex gave her a death stare. They'd been over this with his grandpa plenty of times. If he married Madge, it would affect his housing subsidy and maybe future nursing home prospects. Madge was a nice woman, if a bit gruff with everyone but Ed, and she seemed firmly rooted in reality. The gesture was sweet, and he knew his grandpa did it out of a sense of love, but it was complicated.

"We can talk about it later, Grandpa," Alex said,

motioning to Madge to come to the table, pulling out his wallet.

"You think you're getting a check, Alex? Oh, please," Madge said, patting his cheek kindly.

"I'll pay the tip in bed," Ed added.

"Oh, God," Alex mumbled, standing quickly, desperate to get out of there. Josie snickered. Alex guessed she had no idea how badly Ed's filter had worn away this year. Then again, maybe she had. As much as it horrified him, Alex—or his mom, or aunts—should ask her whether Ed had been coming on to her. Fortunately, he always took "no" for an answer, and most of the young women he propositioned found it amusing, rather than threatening or creepy. But still...

And when he wasn't hitting on younger women, he openly discussed his sex life with Madge. Alex really, really didn't need another frank discussion about the kind of nipple clamps Madge liked.

*Really.*

"Josie, you ever heard of something called 'pegging'?" Ed asked as they walked toward the exit.

Madge had the decency to wince. "Ed, we don't talk about that," she whispered.

Hurrying his grandpa toward the door, Alex caught Josie biting her lips, clearly enjoying watching him squirm.

"I read Dan Savage's column, Ed, so yes," she replied as they walked outside, Alex's eyes taking a minute to adjust in the bright sunshine.

Ed nudged Alex. "Lucky young man."

And then Josie turned away, tears in her eyes from cry-laughing. Alex wanted to join her but he was too busy turning into a mortified puddle of flesh as his grandfather openly discussed pegging with the woman who had blown him off for the past week. The woman he'd chased down this morning, using his grandpa as desperate leverage.

Who was now talking about assfucking with a strap-on dildo.

So this was what his life had come to?

"I'll see you next month, Ed," she said, starting to walk off. "Bye, Alex," she added, like he was an afterthought. Headed toward her car, her back to them as she walked quickly, shoulders shaking from laughter, Josie faded out, and Alex felt a keen sense that somehow—at some unknown point—he'd just blown everything.

"Wait!" he shouted.

She halted.

"What about the latte?"

She froze, then turned slowly. "I'm too full."

"Too full for coffee?" The struggle to keep a begging tone out of his voice wasn't working, damn it. "Really?" he added in an incredulous tone, trying to sound jocular and not quite so needy.

Even Josie had to acknowledge her caffeine addiction. She took a deep breath and said, "Barrington Roasters on Congress. Tomorrow morning?" Her words leaked out like helium through a pinhole in a balloon, as if she were reluctant to let them go.

"When?"

"Seven?" He could do that. He *would* do that, even if he had to get coverage for two hours to make it.

"It's a date!" he shouted as she walked away.

"It's coffee!" she retorted.

Date. Coffee. Whatever.

It was a *plan*.

\* \* \*

The head of the research trial that Josie worked on was a lab rat, what they called a Mud-fud: an MD and a Ph.D. For him, practicing medicine was about studying human microbiology—not about touching human beings. Which was probably better for everyone all around given Gian Rossini's appearance...and mannerisms...and general tone.

He was more interested in glutamate receptors and how they functioned neurologically than in watching the love fade from the eyes of an Alzheimer's patient who could no longer recognize her husband of fifty-three years.

He was short, though like everyone, taller than Josie, about five-five. Squat, but not fat, more that barrel chested look of an Italian man who played a lot of soccer and ate his share of cannoli. Gian lived at home with his mother on Boston's North End, the Little Italy section of the city; she knew this only because he talked about his mother nonstop, adoring her and taking her to mass four nights a week and Sunday mornings.

He was in his early fifties, a bit of a recluse, and seemed quite content with his life. He had always puzzled her because she wondered how he could be happy the way he was...and yet, he was.

The problem with Gian had absolutely nothing to do with any of the issues that she'd just been thinking about. She had watched enough patients go through the trial now to notice a distinct difference. She had no way of knowing who was in the control group and who was receiving the new medication.

That was what a double blind study was. No one was supposed to know, and therefore the outcome of the trial could not be compromised. Josie was careful and ethical— and always would be—but that didn't mean that her very human instincts couldn't collect their own data, honed through careful observation skills.

Patients who had come in at roughly the same functional level were different. Some, like Ed, were definitely in decline, while others seemed to stand still— and when it came to Alzheimer's you begged whatever deity you believed in, for the patient to stand still. Some patients had deteriorated even worse than Ed had, losing a temporal sense. Lost in 1938, 1957, 1985, a few mistook grandchildren for children and one had taken to stripping naked every day and doing her gardening in the nude.

Their children, their grandchildren, their spouses, and girlfriends, and boyfriends, pulled Josie and the other nurse on the trial aside to talk about the real issues—not the twenty- to thirty-minute test that they gave every month, but daily life functioning. All she could do was refer them to support groups in the area. But as each week passed her teeth began to clench just a little more, her jaw aching, her occipital lobe tight and straining at her scalp muscles, causing tension headaches as she watched the growing disparity between about half of her patients and the other half, fading faster.

So she approached Gian with a sense of dread, not because she thought that what she was about to say was futile but because she knew how he felt. Well, actually "felt" was inaccurate—Gian didn't *feel* anything about science. He deduced, he hypothesized, he analyzed, he collected. Feeling? That wasn't Gian's style.

Lining up her facts, her observations, her data, and tying it all into an FDA regulation was her only chance of helping Ed.

The problem was that he was more stubborn than she was. It had to be some sort of hand of fate reaching down into her life and choking her, to make her boss as obstinate—no, rather *more* obstinate than she was. Once he got an idea in his head, especially one that was credible and backed up with facts and figures and data, there was little chance of changing his mind.

Gian's office was very much like hers, an eight-by-eight cell with fluorescent lights, a small counter, a desk, a chair or two, and reams and reams of unfiled paper. Most of what they did was crunched by the computer these days. Actual paperwork was typically stupid administrative crap from inside the research facility, regulatory nonsense that no one should have had to fill out.

"Hey, Gian?"

"What's up, Josie?" He pinched the bridge of his nose and smiled, a wan, weak attempt at friendliness.

"I just finished with some interviews and I'm noticing a pattern."

His face clamped down, as if an iron gate had been slammed shut. "A pattern? We don't like patterns in double blinds."

She had to tread carefully. "We do if they're positive."

He snorted. "How often does that happen?"

He had a point.

"There are some patients who are showing marked decline. Others are maintaining remarkably. It's pretty unmistakeable, and I—"

"You know how to report it." Gian could shut a person down faster than a prostitute who learns her trick is flat broke.

"I did report it. Last month. This month I'm seeing it too, especially with one patient."

"A sample size of one is not 'data.'"

"No, it's not. It's a human being." They'd been through this argument a thousand times before. Time to hit him with #1001.

He sighed. "I'll look into it."

"Thanks. If we have to break the trial—"

He reached for a Costco-sized jar of antacids. "Don't do this to me, Josie."

"*I'm* not doing it, Gian. The *data* is doing it." *Walk away and keep your mouth shut. Point made, Josie.* This might be the first of many difficult conversations that could lead to improvement for Ed and some other patients, so she needed to take it slow. Be diplomatic. Careful. Constrained.

Maybe she needed to buy her own jar of antacids bigger than her head. She might need it to make it through this maze.

Following that inner voice, she stepped away, holding her breath. She'd pass out, though, before he'd make any changes.

Easy part over, she went back to her desk and worried

a koosh ball to death with her left hand, sucking down her fourth coffee of the day. Was it worth calling Laura? Three sets of messages and texts had gone unanswered. This was getting ridiculous. She was ready to hop in the car and drive out to Mike's cabin, if for no other reason than to make sure her best friend was still alive and not being devoured by her cats.

Then again, Laura had Dylan, Mike, and the baby. If Josie needed to worry about anyone dying alone and becoming cat food, it was herself. Even Crackhead would come out of hiding for a piece of Josie's thigh.

Ever the optimist (*not really*), she grabbed her phone and punched Laura's number.

Miracle of miracles, her friend answered. "Hello?"

"*It's aliiiiiiiiiiiiive!*"

The baby screamed right into the phone.

"I didn't need that kind of proof!" Josie said, her ear ringing. She held the phone a few inches from her head. "Laura? You there?"

"Yeah. Colic. Jillian's been a horrible mess for days." A pang of guilt shot through Josie. Whoops. That explained the silence.

"I'm just glad to reach you," Josie admitted. "I'm sorry you're having a tough time with the baby."

*Burp!* A belch worthy of a trucker came through the phone. "Oh, thank God," Laura exclaimed.

"Was that you or the baby?"

"Ha ha. Now she's happy and on my shoulder. Whew."

"You measure your life in burps?"

"Yes. And milk letdown and naps and puke-covered shoulders and what color comes out of me today as the bleeding fades." Three weeks post-birth and she still bled? Josie made a pained face but said nothing.

"Nothing but glamor for you and your two billionaires."

Laura snorted. "I see nothing's changed with you, Josie. Or has it? How's Dr. Perfect?"

"Doctor who?"

"No. That's a television series."

Silence.

"Oh no," Laura groaned. "What have you done now?"

"I—"

"He was perfect for you!"

"Well…"

"You slept with him and then blew him off, didn't you? You always do this, Josie. Why?"

"I didn't call for a lecture."

"Too bad."

A rainbow-haired troll stared at Josie from across her crowded desk, its demented grin making it look like it was sneering at her stupidity. "You weren't exactly around to talk to about it, Laura."

"Don't use me as an excuse!" Laura huffed.

"Okay. Fine. I pulled away. He wanted me to meet his mother."

"Oh." Laura's anger drained fast, the syllable more contrite. That was more like it. "I see."

And this was why she missed Laura so much. Because Laura got it. Instantly. She didn't have to explain herself in depth, or fumble for the right words, or try to go down some analytical path to get to a conclusion. Shorthand between best friends was such a damn relief.

"Yeah."

"What's his mom like?"

"She's a clinical psychologist."

A sputtering sound came through the phone, like a spit take. Then laughter. "Oh, Josie, you've got to admit that's some awesome karma."

"I know, right? Can you imagine the moms meeting? Marlene could show her how to get a guy to buy her a top-shelf martini without having to give him a blowjob, and Alex's mom could use the DSM-V and a necklace of garlic to keep my mom at bay."

A sigh came through the phone. "But you know that's

not a good enough reason to throw away what could be the best relationship of your life."

*Yes, it is,* she thought. "Yes, it is," she blurted out.

"When are you going to separate yourself from your mom?"

Slap. "WHAT?"

"You are not your mother." Laura said the words slowly, with a resigned tone. "She treated you horribly after the accident. She lives with brain damage and has no real conscience. You were her scapegoat for years. That doesn't mean you get to hide behind all that and use it to keep yourself from real love, Josie."

"I'm not!"

"Yes, you are."

"But...no...it's that Alex just—" Damn. Laura was right.

"Do you like him?"

"Yes."

"The sex is good?"

Josie made an unintelligible sound of groaning delight.

"Is he kind and respectful?"

"Yes."

"Does he make you laugh?" Josie could hear the smile in Laura's voice as the trap began to work. She was caught.

Sigh. "Yes."

"Has he pursued you even as you try to blow him off?"

"How did you know?"

"I didn't. But now I like him even more."

"His grandfather is one of my Alzheimer's trial patients."

"No way! So did he know you when he saw you at the hospital at the birth?" Josie felt like someone had hit her between the eyes with a cannonball. Wait—what? *Had* Alex known who she was before?

"I never asked him that question," she answered slowly. A dawning insight opened up before her. Alex had brought Ed to his appointment and had known damn well who Josie was—must have known, in fact—the day she brought Laura to the hospital for Jillian's birth.

What did that mean?

"Maybe your hooking up wasn't a simple coincidence."

"I highly doubt he triggered your labor from afar, Laura," Josie replied dryly.

Laura laughed. "No, not that. Just…maybe you two clicked because Alex already knew who you were and was interested."

This was why she missed Laura so much. Putting all this together was beyond her ability these days. Laura's perspective gave her a better grasp of the messy pieces of her emotional chaos.

"I'm meeting him for coffee in the morning, so I'll ask him then."

"You're giving him a break?"

"I'm letting him buy me a latte."

Laura snorted. "You let me buy you lattes and you don't sleep with me."

"You have more than enough bed partners, Laura."

"Tell me about it. You try fitting four people in a bed."

"Four? You have a new guy?"

The two laughed, Josie relaxing for the first time in weeks. It felt so good to talk and reconnect. And then—

*Waaaa!* "Baby's up. Gotta go," Laura said over the wailing. "Let's talk soon!"

"Okay. I'll—"

*Click.*

She worried the troll doll's hair into Pippi Longstocking braids. So Alex may have remembered her from Ed's appointments.

*Hmmmm.* Coffee tomorrow morning was suddenly more interesting.

# CHAPTER TWELVE

With a headache the size of a doctor's ego, Alex's day couldn't have started off any worse. He'd come in to work at 5 a.m. to meet quickly with a small group of administrators and one lawyer. Funny how none of his fellow physicians were in the room. Medicine by litigation was a harsh reality these days. Every action had to be thought of in terms of a potential lawsuit.

By 6:15 the meeting was over and his headache had dissipated somewhat. So far, the baby in the case was doing fine, though still in the NICU. Being peppered with questions designed solely to test his professionalism and judgment hadn't been pleasant. He had run through the details of the birth in his own mind a thousand times over the past few days, questioning and playing Monday-morning quarterback. It was a judgment call.

The lawyers had made sour faces when he'd said as much.

More meetings would come.

More headaches, too.

"You look nice today," said a pinched voice. Alex was waiting for the elevator to take him downstairs, to catch a train and meet Josie at seven. The voice belonged to Lisa, who clutched a chart to her bosom and smiled.

"Thanks," he said, distracted. The vise grip on his eye sockets didn't help. He fidgeted with his tie, finally sliding it off. Wearing these stiff clothes—a starched oxford, dress slacks, grown-up shoes, and the tie–didn't help his headache. Anything other than casual clothes and scrubs made him feel like a phony.

"How's the case going?" she asked, moving closer, speaking in a conspirator's whisper. "I heard someone higher up has a bug up their ass about you."

"What?" He'd carefully shielded himself from office politics like this. The gleam in her eye was precisely why. Some people viewed this kind of social volleying as a game. Alex didn't play games.

Other than the games that involved chasing Josie in her panties...

"Rumor has it you were distracted. Didn't read the strip properly." Of course he had! The contractions were—oh, he'd gone over this in the endless loop in his mind.

"Rumor is *wrong*," he spat just as the doors opened. She followed him on, pushing a button for the second floor.

"It must suck to have your professional judgment questioned."

"You think?" Keeping the acid tone out of his voice just wasn't happening. Her eyes widened; he could see her expression, a silver blur, in the brushed stainless steel doors.

"Maybe you're just...busy." His toes nearly curled inside his shoes with the implications dripping from that word.

He snorted. "Which residents here aren't busy?"

"You have a new kind of busy in your life, Alex."

"Lisa, spit it out. I don't have time or energy for this kind of passive-aggressive garbage." Angry and frustrated, he let himself vent, turning her into an easy target. She didn't make it hard, but it wasn't fair to her. As soon as the words were out of his mouth he regretted them.

And yet it was the truth.

"You were...*busy* that night in the on-call room, Alex. One of the other shift nurses saw you in there with that Josie woman."

Lisa had him there. The birth had happened later that shift, shortly after Laura's baby had come.

"If three different attendings, two lawyers, and eight thousand hospital administrators can pore over those files and say I did everything correctly, Lisa, I'm not too worried about the titters of one shift nurse who claimed to see me taking a break in an on-call room," he snapped back, regret gone—*poof!*—replaced by outrage.

A wily smile graced her lips as the doors opened and she walked out. He jabbed the "Close" button and nearly punched the wall as the elevator made its way to ground level.

What the hell was wrong with him? Disappointment and humiliation poured over him like an acid bath. Years of striving to be the laid-back, low-key doctor who loved births and enjoyed supporting new lives as they emerged into the world could come to a painful reconsideration if this didn't go well.

And most of all, a baby lay in the NICU. Fortunately, there should be no long-term complications, but the breathing problems were serious enough to warrant further observation. Could he track the specific issues back to some choice he'd made during the birth? No. And neither could the lawyers.

But that didn't absolve him from the racking feeling of guilt and doubt that plagued him.

Comments from Lisa, casting aspersions on his attention level that night, didn't help.

Speaking of distractions, as he headed for the subway he realized he needed to discard as much of this as possible from his mind, purging the negativity. Seeing Josie for morning coffee meant getting a fresh start at something that should have gone very right, but somehow got derailed.

He didn't need to question his judgment in yet another arena of his life. What he needed was to get back to *living*. Not worrying or second-guessing. As the escalator took him down into the dark cave of the T line, Alex's grit and determination shored up. Josie could blow him off, but she'd have to do it to his face, and with a full awareness of what he felt for her.

Anything less would leave him looping endlessly through his own actions.

And he'd had plenty of that today. No more.

\* \* \*

*Tap tap tap.* Josie's foot bounced against the thick table leg like a jackhammer on Ritalin. Although she'd already had a two-shot espresso and now nursed a latte, it wasn't the caffeine that fueled her nervous movement. What a strange situation. Being pursued. Men didn't do that with her. They didn't keep trying. Once she decided to weed them out of her life they complied, a mutual agreement that it was over coinciding beautifully with the fact that it *was* over. Whatever purpose they'd served was over and she just moved on with her life. Done. The end. *Fin.*

Not Alex. Damn him! Ignoring him had been one of the hardest intentional acts of her life. The texts begged for a reply. His voicemails, with the warm, soothing tones of his voice, made her nearly cry—and nearly start dialing. An act of constant restraint kept her from responding, knowing she was being foolish. Her conversation with Laura yesterday confirmed that.

She was a fool.

Her heart stopped as she caught sight of him a few steps from the front door. Like those scenes in movies where everything suddenly shifts into slow motion, Josie eyed him from head to toe. The button-down oxford business shirt, crisp blue. The black dress pants, probably

241

from a suit. Wingtips that would fit in at any financial institution on State Street. Freshly cut hair and a clean-shaven face. A slightly worried look creasing his brow. Intense brown eyes that seemed impossibly deep.

His arm reached forward to open the door, the curve of his bicep tight against the cloth of his shirt. If the scene had a soundtrack it would be lurid and sensual, sultry and tantalizing.

What the fuck was wrong with her?

Why wasn't she with him?

Laura was right.

Laura was *sooooooooooooooooooo* right.

Every fiber of her being, nipple to clit to brain, strained for him. Their eyes locked. The expected friendly smile and wave didn't appear. Instead, his eyes narrowed, and he stopped a few steps inside the small coffee shop, hands planted on his hips. The shirt was unbuttoned at the top, a smattering of chest hair poking out. She licked her lips; he was smoking hot in dress clothes, such a departure from his casual look. He could be a CEO or a quant or a tech director. Or, he could be none of those and strip out of the striking outfit and be naked with her in her bed.

Or on the baseball field.

Heat poured into her core and she shifted, painfully aware of how sensitive she was, how her body ached for him.

And then his eyes stayed riveted to hers as he smiled, a grin so ferocious and predatory she felt the oxygen in the room disappear.

*Oh, fuck me now*, she nearly begged.

"Josie," he said simply.

"Alex," she rasped.

"You got coffee already," he said, clearly disappointed.

She shrugged. Words were gone. She could grunt in Morse code if forced.

Holding up one finger in a gesture designed to buy him a few moments, he entered the line. This gave her a great view of his ass for precious few seconds. Something about men in business dress had always made her pause and take notice. Maybe it was because so few men in her life had worn anything other than t-shirts and flannels. Perhaps it was the medical world, where scrubs and lab coats were de rigueur.

Or, perhaps, she was just really enamored of a grown-up, hot as *fuck* Alex standing there, just being.

Being *hot*.

What was Morse code for "I'll get the rope while you draw up the contract"?

Drink in hand, he took a seat next to her. Heat emanated from every inch of his body, his posture different today. More powerful. Tense.

Angry?

Not at her, though. She could feel it. There was relief and happiness and attraction. But something she couldn't put her finger on lingered beneath the surface. Animalistic and fierce, it seemed to have consumed Alex, though he did a good job of hiding it. A subtle shift, but she picked up on it. Finely honed skills in reading people, cultivated from years with an emotionally erratic mother, meant that she constantly scanned the emotional state of the person she was most invested in.

And that was Alex right now.

Whether he still liked it or not.

Having expected irritation or annoyance directed at her for blowing him off, this was a different animal (pun intended) altogether. His eyes were a bit wild and he carried himself with a more aggressive stance, eating the room as if it were his. The laid-back, grounded man she'd met at Laura's birth was still there, but with an edge.

She liked the edge.

"Thanks for meeting me," he said, toasting her with a white coffee cup. Laughing, she joined him. Both sipped in silence and she found herself grateful for his persistence. Mornings were the worst lately, the loneliness more acute.

Her own stupid—what? Pride? Fear?—had made her clam up and stop responding to him. Alex coming to the research trial with Ed was brilliant. And yet....

"You knew who I was when we first met at Laura's birth, didn't you?" she asked, bold and open.

His shocked look told her he wasn't expecting that. "Yes," he said simply. "I'd been taking Grandpa to his appointments for a few months and had..." His voice trailed off. Curling one fist, he leaned in, then relaxed his hand. "Had noticed you."

"Noticed me?"

"That's code for 'was too much of a wimp to ask you out.'" He drank half his coffee in one long swallow.

"So instead you nearly fucked me in the on-call room at my friend's birth?" Two women chatting next to them stopped, one leaning closer. He watched Josie take a dainty sip of her drink, her head tipped down, eyes looking up at him.

Alex began rubbing the bridge of his nose. "It's getting crowded in here," he declared, standing. He reached for her elbow and guided her up. "Let's go for a walk." No choice. It was an order.

She obeyed.

"Not a wimp move," she hissed. They both picked their cups up and drank greedily, downing more of their morning joe.

"What? Asking you to go for a walk?"

"And the sex in the on-call room." His hand reached out to the small of her back to guide her out the coffee shop's door. A tingle of excitement zipped through her as his palm warmed her. God, she'd missed him.

"There wasn't any sex in the on-call room."

"Only because someone else's vagina was 'Exit Only' at that moment. My 'Enter' sign was forty feet tall with rhinestones and blinking LED lights. And an eight-piece brass band. With tubas and everyth—"

The crush of Alex made her shoulders go flat against

the brick wall he pulled her next to, her arms up in the air, one holding a coffee she instinctively preserved, the other snaking through his hair as he kissed her with such ferocity her lips felt bruised. They'd dipped a few feet into a small alley around the corner from the firehouse museum, and as he raked her mouth with his tongue, all fire and need, she saw the bored morning walkers going about their business as if she weren't being ravaged a few feet away.

He smelled so good, and tasted like coffee and hope.

"Don't do that again," he growled, one hand on her waist, the other casually holding his coffee cup.

"Don't what?"

"Shut me out."

Swallowing hard, she tried to think of what to say.

"I mean it, Josie," Alex added, his eyes hard and soft all at once. The pulse at his jawline throbbed, his muscles tight. "I've had my eye on you for months, and it felt like fate the night you came in with Laura. It *was* fate. Everything from that moment made sense with you. All of it."

"Alex, I—"

He was breathing hard, the heat of his exhales pushing against her neck.

"I was so worried about coming on too strong. Maybe you faded back because I wasn't direct enough." One knee pressed between hers, his core pushing hard against her, their abdomens so close she could feel his heartbeat through a very obvious erection.

"I won't make that mistake twice," he added, punctuating the thought with a slower, unraveling kiss that made her stand on tiptoe to savor every bit of his mouth. Her hands loosened and she felt the coffee cup slide down, crashing to the ground, a light splash of liquid registering on her ankle, the taste of his soft tongue so exquisite she felt like she shifted into a new dimension. A vague, muted sound told her Alex dropped his coffee as well as his heat pushed into her, his lush skin sliding against her cheek, the sound of his breath like a dare.

Something between them began to buzz.

"Is that a vibrator in your pocket or are you just happy to see me?" she murmured against his mouth.

Pure delight poured out of him, the old Alex returning fast with his laughter as he broke contact with her, pulling back. Rummaging through his pocket, he found the offending phone. "Damn it. Work. Gotta go."

The march of people past them, to the left, was a blur of faceless bodies and feet, as if their heads weren't there. The alley seemed so detailed, in contrast, and every part of Alex's appearance, from the button on his collar that wasn't quite all the way through the button hole to the streak of her lipstick on his lips, seemed rich and coarse and solid. Real.

The hard, aggressive Alex was still here, but reduced by half. The man who stared back at her had a decisiveness that mixed with his openness and invited her in.

Invited himself in.

*Open the door, Josie. Say yes.* That was Laura's voice.

*Yes.* That was hers.

Josie's own voice replied. "When can I see you again?" she asked.

The worried look came back as he read something on his phone. Shoving it in his pocket, he shook his head slightly, as if banishing the thought. "Whenever you want." His hand slipped around her waist and he kissed her lightly on the lips.

A brief thought of Ed, of his decline, her conversation with Gian, hit her. Should she bring it up now? No. Not yet.

*Bzzz.*

"Damn." He kissed her cheek and began to walk away. "I really do have to go. Just text me. Promise?" Walking with purpose, he marched off.

"Promise," she whispered to no one.

*Promise.*

* * *

"Something's wrong with him," Josie began as she marched into the cabin Laura, Mike and Dylan shared. Then she did a double-take and made a low whistling sound.

"Holy shit."

"It's a little messy," Laura confessed.

"And my fingernails are a little over the top." She flashed her hands at Laura. They spelled I-heart-J-I-L-L-I-A-N-heart. The hearts were bright red, the nails pink and white.

The cabin looked like a baby bomb had exploded in it. Burp rags covered the back of every chair or couch. A hamper full of laundry was next to a spot on the couch with an end table littered with large, empty glasses and plates that held what appeared to have once been pizza. A few empty salad containers littered the area. Breast pads were stacked neatly next to the table.

And then there was the giant pile of laundry on the floor.

That moved.

"Jesus Christ!" Josie shouted, jumping back. A leg stuck out from under a pile of towels. The leg was attached to an underwear-covered ass and a naked chest.

Dylan was sound asleep in a pile of clothes in the middle of the room, snoring lightly. His arm curled under his head like a pillow.

Josie pointed. "What's that?"

"Dylan."

"Not who. What?"

"He's tired," Laura whined. "We all are. Mike's probably out there asleep in his Jeep."

Josie shot Laura a confused look. "His Jeep? Are you guys fighting?"

"No!" Laura wailed, pacing back and forth with the

baby in her arms. Cherubic and serene, she was so sweet looking. The rosy-pink skin and a smattering of baby acne on her nose reminded Josie of how tiny and new Jillian really was. A breathy snort came from the baby, whose mouth puckered and suckled in the air.

"Then why is he in his Jeep?"

"He pretends he's going for a run but every time he does that I look out there and he's asleep in the front seat."

"Um…why?"

Laura pointed at Dylan, who was now spooning with a nursing pillow and a beach towel. "Same reason as that. We're completely wiped."

Josie reached for the baby and Laura transferred her as if handing over a live grenade. "Don't wake her. I just got her to sleep." The handoff successful, Josie marveled at how lightweight the baby was. Wrapped in a pink fleece blanket and wearing a jumper with characters from an Eric Carle book, Jillian was a piece of perfection in a sub-ten-pound body.

"Thank you! Hang on," Laura said as she dashed out of the room. The distant sounds of a toilet flushing and running water were followed by Laura's reappearance. Josie wandered into the kitchen and searched for the coffeemaker. The countertop was covered with what looked like every dish in the house, two nursing bras, more burp cloths, and about nineteen coffee mugs, all containing anywhere from one to two inches of coffee.

But no coffeemaker.

Deciding to grab a cup of milk instead, she opened the refrigerator to find—

The coffeemaker.

What the hell? Jillian wiggled in her arms, making Josie freeze in place. How could someone so placid and sweet cause her three friends to fall apart like this? Something more must be going on. No one falls apart this fast from just having a little baby, right?

"Oh! You found it. Dylan said he couldn't remember where he put it this morning." Acting like it was no big deal that someone had shoved an entire ten-cup coffeemaker next to a bag of fennel in the fridge, Laura hauled it out, shoved a clean spot into the detritus on the counter, and plugged the machine in. Josie gingerly picked up trash from the counter and began throwing it away, trying to help.

"Don't you guys have a cleaning service?" Josie asked.

"Louisa's sick," Laura said. "Of all the weeks." With ruthless efficiency, Laura had coffee brewing in under ninety seconds, and turned to Josie, stretching her arms up in the air, giving Josie a front-and-center view of her right breast.

"Uh, Laura…." she said, pointing. The nursing shirt Laura wore had some sort of vertical slit, like crotchless undies, and as she lifted her arms to the ceiling it became evident Laura wasn't wearing a bra.

"Oh." Laura reached under the neckline of her shirt and did something that made a clicking sound. "My nursing bra was unclasped. Sorry for the peep show."

"I've seen worse."

"I know you have. You were at the birth."

They smiled at each other and Josie leaned down to huff the baby's head. How could she cause such chaos?

"And speaking of birth," Laura added, "how's Dr. Perfect?"

Carrying the smile a bit longer, Josie shrugged. "We had coffee. And a few hot kisses in the alley. I'm thinking about surprising him tonight with Thai and episode five of *Downton Abbey*."

Laura pretended to golf clap, miming it to avoid waking Jillian. "Well played. I know you're scared to death, but you're doing the right thing."

"Speaking of the right thing, I need to bounce something off you."

Laura made herself a cup of coffee and gestured for

Josie to go on.

"I already spoke with my boss about this, but I think Alex's grandpa isn't getting the meds in our research trial. I can't be sure, and I would never go into the records and look. It's a hunch."

"Did you say anything yet to Alex?"

"No. But I feel like I should."

"Of course you should! Wouldn't you want to know if you were Alex?"

"Yes."

"So what's the problem?"

Josie sighed. Jillian gurgled and smiled, a crooked grin that made Josie and Laura say "awwwwwww" in unison.

And then the unmistakeable sound of more gurgling, except this came from the diaper.

"Last time she made that sound she shat all the way up to her hair," Laura said, staying in her position across the kitchen, drinking her coffee.

A spreading warmth coated Josie's palm, the one that supported Jillian's ass. "C'mon. You can't say things like that and then just leave me holding her."

"Here," said a deep voice. They both turned to find Dylan standing there, rubbing his eyes. He wore blue boxer briefs, and Josie noted that they were just like Alex's while trying not to check out Dylan's bulge. Like she needed that image in her head.

She already knew too much about his body. Too, too much.

"Thank you for wearing underpants," she said as she handed the poopy baby over to one of her dads.

"You're in my house. You're lucky I'm wearing them," he grunted, turning away. "And save me some coffee!" he called back, cooing at the baby, who was now staring at him in absolute fascination as Laura and Josie watched his butt until he turned a corner and entered one of the back rooms.

"You're only allowed to stare because I say it's okay,"

Laura said, finishing her coffee. She looked at the counter and said, "Damn. This is really awful."

"I'll help. And his ass reminded me of Alex's, so I was just reminiscing."

"Why get nostalgic when you can go home and make new memories?" Laura opened the dishwasher and began loading coffee mugs.

"Because if I tell Alex about his grandpa, he might get...squirrelly. Families often don't want to hear the truth about decline, and Ed might be in a permanent downward spiral. It's...complicated."

Laura's sympathetic smile helped take the edge off her fear. "If you don't say anything you'll regret it. Maybe there's something people are missing. Alex is a doctor. He's not your average patient's family member."

"True."

Laura waved her hand at the mess. "Why am I cleaning? I have ten precious moments without Velcro Baby attached to me and I'm doing dishes? Ugh."

"I know. Let's go to a strip club and get a lap dance. Better use of our time."

Mike walked in the front door, stretching his calves as if he just finished a run. "Man, it's gorgeous outside."

"Yeah, the Jeep has the best weather ever!" Josie shot back.

A sheepish look on his face showed he knew he'd been busted. "I, uh..."

Laura walked over and gave him a kiss on the cheek. "It's okay, hon. We know you were sleeping in the Jeep. You've been doing it for the past week."

"You've been *what*?" Dylan bellowed, entering the room with Jillian on his shoulder.

"Subject change—are you going to work for the threesome dating service?" Mike asked Josie.

Three sets of eyes zeroed in on her.

"No pressure," she mumbled.

"No. Pressure," Laura insisted. "Pressure most

definitely there. Do it," she hissed. Dylan rocked in place, mercifully having thrown on some sweatpants. Mike stood over them all, eyes calm but exhausted.

"You're serious?" Josie asked, incredulous. "I thought Laura was just out of her mind with being 158 weeks pregnant!"

"We're serious," the three said together.

"Salary?"

Dylan named a figure. A damn *fine* figure.

"Benefits?"

"The guy who handles our HR issues at the ski resort can help with the new venture."

"My own parking spot?"

"Oooooooh, tough negotiator," Dylan joked. "How about a bowl of red-only M&Ms at your desk every morning and a Justin Bieber butt plug for each day of the week?"

"Why would I want a Justin Bieber butt plug?"

"If you're going to put that guy's face anywhere, it might as well be—"

*Waaaaaaaaaaaaaaa!* Jillian's cry pierced the air.

"I'm not deciding now, guys," Josie said as Dylan handed the baby to Laura, who reached under her shirt, latching Jillian on with an expert hand that belied her three weeks of motherhood.

"But you're considering it?" Laura asked hopefully.

No Gian. No Alzheimer's patients. No worrying about how to break bad data news to various researchers. More money. More flexibility. Working with Laura regularly.

What could be better?

"I am."

Laura bounced in place with excitement, unable to move because of the baby sucking milk out of her. Josie wondered what it felt like. Was it the same as getting a hickey? It couldn't be, right? You'd bruise all the time. She just stared.

"Hello? Earth to Josie?"

"What?"

"You said yes!"

"No, I didn't!" she huffed. "I said I'd think about it."

"Close enough."

Mike wandered in to the living room and took a good look at the chaos. "We need to clean this up."

"And by 'we' you mean you and Dylan," Laura piped up.

"Absolutely." He leaned over and kissed the top of Laura's head, then did the same with the now-happy Jillian, who opened her eyes wide and stared up at one of her dads.

"Come over to the dark side," Dylan called out from the kitchen, then joined the group with his own cup of coffee, plopping down on the laundry on the floor.

They were so happy. Exhausted and messy and overwhelmed—but happy.

Vulnerability didn't wear well on Josie but Laura and Mike and Dylan showed her that being vulnerable and willing to take emotional risks could be ... a different kind of strength. Being self-contained, Josie was independent, relied on no one; her strength was in her thick skin. She was proud of thinking through every contingency in any given situation, so she was prepared for disaster when—not if—it struck. But maybe the secret to being OK wasn't to close herself off and keep all the heartbreak at bay.

What if there were a different way to navigate life emotionally? Opening herself up to Alex felt like being flayed emotionally. Stripped of that thick skin.

Alex represented something more.

And Laura was offering something different.

Indecision ate away at her soul. Ed's deterioration was evident, and Alex had put his finger on something that Josie wished weren't true. His grandfather was in decline, and nothing anyone said would make a difference, the attempts at denial so obvious that even the people who tried to claim that Ed was fine couldn't do it with any sort of conviction. In contrast to Ed, other patients on the project, patients who had been at about Ed's level when they'd started, seemed to be doing so much better. It was as if the fog of Alzheimer's were lifting.

Too much knowledge tore Josie in half. She felt like Meredith Grey in an episode of that television show, *Grey's Anatomy*. In the exact same ridiculous situation where looking into the files to know whether Ed was in the control group or was actually getting the medication that was at the center of the research trial meant jeopardizing the integrity of the project and her job. Josie found herself frozen solid, fear permeating every cell of her body, her brain, and now, her heart. There was no way out.

If she didn't look up Ed's status on the research trial, and he wasn't receiving the medication, he could lose out on the benefits. If she did look up the information, then everyone who was benefiting could lose access to the experimental drug, and there was the tiny, insignificant little issue of violating every ethical and moral tenet of her profession.

Alex was a man of great integrity, of tremendous moral character, and it was part of what drew her to him. Violating that, even for the sake of a higher moral principle, would destroy his sense of respect for her.

Respect. She shook her head and laughed, so deep in her thoughts that her coffee cup went cold in her hand. Respect wasn't exactly something that she had become accustomed to in relationships, so the thought of losing it created a kind of pain inside her that had no outlet. She inhaled slowly and then let out the breath through her mouth, like a meditative sigh. Alex loved his grandfather dearly. Ed's daughters all loved him, too. There was a family culture of joyfulness, of love and compassion, and a sense that if you love someone enough, everything will be okay. Too bad Josie wasn't part of that family.

But she was part of this one.

Jumping up to make more coffee, Josie looked at Mike,

Laura and Dylan—of them, chatting happily, Laura leaning back against the couch, eyes closed, stroking Jillian's little head as she nursed.

For Josie, it was time for something more or something different. She didn't know what to call it, but as she'd said to Laura when she first started seeing Alex, she was *somethinging.*

That was a step in the right direction.

Because somethinging was better than nothinging.

* * *

The bags weighed her down as she walked from the Thai takeout place around the corner from their neighborhood, and the white plastic straps cut into her fingers, but Josie didn't much care. The scent of peanut sauce wafted up and made her mouth water. Or maybe it watered with thoughts of seeing Alex in a moment. Her stomach gurgled.

Fifty-fifty.

Both needs would soon be satisfied.

Cheerful and excited, she took a huge leap of faith in coming here. After walking past his building three times today, her day off, she had finally seen his car in the driveway. Dinnertime made for the perfect excuse to surprise him. What man could resist a woman bearing pad Thai and chicken satay?

And her heart. Oh—yes. That part. Laura had encouraged her to just jump in and see where things went with Alex.

Impulsivity wasn't exactly her trademark when it came to her emotions.

Alex, though, was different. Worth being different for.

Struggling with the bags, she set one down and rang his buzzer. Waited. No answer. Was it the kind with an intercom, or would he just—

"Josie?" Alex stood at the door, wet hair, a shirt on

255

backwards.

"Hi!" she said, chipper and overly friendly. Holding up the bags, she added, "You hungry?"

Confusion clouded his features. Had he been showering? Why else would his clothes be on backwards?

Oh.

*Oh.*

What if she'd misjudged everything and was horribly, painfully wrong? Maybe he'd just been fucking someone else in his apartment, and this was that bleak moment when she realized his interest was just a sham. A vortex of fear opened up before her, an abyss of nothingness, calling her name, beckoning.

And then he stepped forward and smiled. "I am, actually. Come on in." He planted a kiss on her cheek.

It was the best kiss *ever.*

Feeling stupid for doubting him, she walked into his apartment a bit dazed, haunted by the sudden horror that had enveloped her, so all-consuming at the thought of Alex with someone else.

"I hope you like Thai," she said, looking around the apartment. Something was off. Unlike her last visit here, the room was disheveled, as if no one had bothered to do anything for a week or two. Not filthy—just neglected. Items stood where they'd been casually thrown or abandoned. Beer bottles (good beer, she noted) dotted all the tables, along with cereal bowls, spoons adhered to the bottom by dried milk.

Alex caught her looking. "I've worked a crazy set of shifts this week, and, well…"

She waved her hand. "I wasn't judging."

He laughed, removing the food from the bags. "Yes, you were."

"Okay, I was. This is more what I expected to see the first time I came over," she admitted.

"Good. Because this is more the normal me. I cleaned before you came over last time." His sidelong glance made a part of her melt.

How intimate were they? The kiss in the alley yesterday, his leg pressing between hers, the way his mouth stole all the air and blew a desperate need into her rose to the surface.

"I'm sorry I didn't call," Josie said, stumbling over her words. "I just thought I'd pop in and—"

"I'm glad you didn't. I might have begged off." The aroma of spicy peanut sauce, lemongrass, and fish sauce filled the small kitchen, making Josie's stomach groan once more. And then her appetite faded completely as she digested his words.

What did *that* mean? Should she leave? Was this a bad time? He stood next to her, two feet away, and yet he might as well be on Mars. The red cotton t-shirt was on backwards, blue jeans shorts showing off powerful thighs, and his bare feet were planted firmly on the floor, his body casual and there. Yet a tension ran through every muscle, the lines of his veins straining against his skin, jaw tight and face immutable. A mask.

So much for coming here in a spirit of openness and renewal.

"Is this a bad time?" she asked, taking a step toward the door. Panic rushed into her, like a wave crashing over her on a beach, unexpected and choking, making it hard to breathe.

He seemed to sense her shift and immediately responded, closing the gap between them, arms around her like a rescuer. "No, no, not at all. In fact, I'm really glad you're here." A deep inhale from him against her neck made her feel welcome as his chest expanded, filling with her.

"I am so glad you're here," he repeated.

\* \* \*

Josie at his door. Bearing Thai food. If she was wearing

crotchless panties then she was *the one*, no doubt.

Why, then, was he being such an ass? If he didn't pull it together he'd ruin everything before they could get in a bite of Pad Thai. The second meeting at work today had been far, far worse than the initial one. The parents weren't suing, the baby was out of the NICU, and everything was fine, but Alex's judgment was being called into question and it was chipping away at his soul, sliver by chunk. Holding the line on unnecessary interventions and preserving the mother's wishes for a birth that made sense—within medically responsible boundaries—had never been easy.

Now it was downright grueling, and he didn't know how to explain to Josie that he was fighting for his soul right now at work.

Why burden her with any of this? None of the other women he'd dated had cared about his stressors. From pre-med undergrad days through med school, he'd kept his professional life separate from his personal experiences, finding most women completely uninterested in what he did. Shining eyes loved the fact that he was a doctor-in-training or, now, a true physician. But they were more enamored with the idea of dating (and, perhaps, marrying) a doctor than with the reality of being with a doctor.

Keeping that line intact would probably be the only way to save his relationship with Josie, already tenuous. He had no inclination to put any of his problems on her right now.

*Suck it up, dude*, he told himself. A deep breath, inhaling the scent of lavender and coffee that clung to Josie like a second skin, rejuvenated him. He pulled back from the embrace and kissed her softly.

"You read my mind."

"You were thinking about Thai?"

"I was thinking about you."

"Clearly you weren't thinking about your shirt." She snickered, breaking the embrace and dishing up some noodles. He looked down. Damn it. He'd been in the shower when she'd buzzed and his clothes were thrown on hastily.

Maybe they'd be yanked off just as hastily in the next few minutes. The thought should have excited him, but it only made him feel stunted. Inadequate. As if he'd failed her somehow by not being the centered man she expected him to be, by having his judgment questioned at work. Could it bleed into his personal life? Lately, the stress had.

What else should he question? You had to have at least a touch—even the tiniest taste—of a God complex to become a physician. Especially a surgeon. Alex's entire life had been built one one major premise: education and hard work will set you free. His compass was that simple, from watching his mother make her way through teen motherhood and poverty to a clinical psychologist's license and building her own practice through his own educational journey as the child of a poor teen mother.

For the first time in his life he wasn't being interrogated about his knowledge, or his skills, but rather how he assessed a situation and then acted.

And it sucked.

Sinking himself into Josie was what he needed most. Skin to skin, rolling in bed, making love until his last gasp was her name and all the stress and horror of his internal self-flagellation was gone. Drained. Depleted.

That was what he needed.

Thank God she'd appeared.

* * *

Josie reached out to touch Alex's elbow. Saying this was important—she wanted to get it out of the way so it wouldn't weigh on her this evening A fun evening of food, movies and sex—lots of sex—shouldn't be marred by her worry. He turned his shining eyes on her, focused completely on whatever she was about to say.

"I did the paperwork on your grandfather's most recent eval, and he's…he's definitely deteriorating," she said quietly.

Alex closed his eyes and nodded slowly, letting out a long exhale. "I'm not surprised," he said. "That matches what my mom and aunts have been telling me."

"Alex, I…I want to be careful here, because I don't want to cross any ethical lines…"

His face went hard, suddenly, like granite, a look she'd never seen on his face. "Then don't." The two words hung in the air, suspended by a tone of judgment.

"Then don't—what?" she countered, her voice taking on the same hard edge. Perhaps she shouldn't have brought it up. Their plates sat in front of them, ignored, and her stomach clenched.

"Don't do anything that would violate your professional ethics, or anyone else's."

"What would make you think I would do that?" she hissed back. This was not the conversation she had expected. What the hell had just happened?

"If you're going to try to tell me," he said, standing and leaning forward, eyes angry, "that you are at all tempted to find out whether my grandfather is in the control group or is receiving the medication, then we need to stop this conversation, right here, right now."

"Whoa, whoa, whoa," she protested, hands up, palms facing him, standing up herself. She nearly took a step backwards, simply to give herself distance from the near vitriol in his voice, his disdainful face, the puffed-out chest and the balled-up hands. "I wasn't implying that I would do anything like that," she said, her body mimicking his. If she could have stepped up on a stool and been face to face, eye to eye with him, she would have. As it was, she had to look up, craning her neck, and stand up, stand tall, as straight as possible to get her point across. A forcefield of fury buzzed between the two of them, seeming to come out of nowhere.

"You just said that you're worried that my grandfather's failing, and that he might…"

"He might *what?*"

"You were the one who was about to say it," he answered after a long pause.

"I was about to say that you might want to get a second opinion, or a third opinion, or a *whatever* opinion," she said, snarkily, "because Ed is falling apart, and I can't imagine that he's going to be safe living independently for much longer. Whether he's in the control group or not is not something that I'm privy to know, I'm just trying to tell you, as a friend—"

"*Friend?*"

The acid in his tone made her throat well up with salty tears. Her anger, still there, but now replaced with an ever-increasing layer of hurt.

"Is that what we are, Josie? Friends? 'Cause"—he leaned in, hot breath against her ear—"cause I don't fuck my friends by the side of the river. I don't invite my friends over, and make them dinner, and sleep with them. I don't let them fall asleep in my lap, and cuddle with them, and stroke their hair, and marvel at them. I don't know what kind of *friends* you have, but I don't do that with my *friends*." He pulled back.

Her brain raced, trying to process the implications of this conversation. "Fine, then." She lowered her shoulders, straightened up her neck, and looked him in the eye again. "I'm telling you, as someone who has just interacted with Ed on a professional *and* personal level, that for whatever reason, you and your mother and her sisters may want to consider getting more opinions on how you can slow down the deterioration that he's experiencing."

"And that's your professional opinion, *doctor?*" he said, a nasty sneer twisting his face.

Oh, no, he didn't.

"You went there? Really? You…*went* there?" she seethed. This was going to be about pulling rank? She was always going to be the cute little nurse, and he was always going to be the big, bad doctor? It was her turn to stick her finger in his face. "I may not be a doctor, and I may not have prescription powers, or have suffered through all the years of med school, internship, residency, and all the other shit that you guys go through, but I can tell you one thing. I can tell with reasonable accuracy, based solely on symptoms, which people are in the control group and which are not. I'm never going to cross a line that would jeopardize a multimillion-dollar National Institutes of Health-funded research project. This isn't *Grey's Anatomy*, and I'm not that Meredith chick."

He opened his mouth to say something, and she put her fingers over his lips. "You get one chance to pull that with me, Alex. Your chance is over, and you know what else? You had one chance with me"—her voice cracked as the tears that had formed in her throat struggled to take over—"and you just showed me who you really are and what you really think of me." She marched out the door of his apartment, eyes blinded by tears, and struggled to find her way down the street, to get as far away from him as possible.

\* \* \*

From the moment that Josie had talked about the medication group versus the control group, Alex's brain had been on fire. He'd been so careful his entire life, following every rule, never straying, being better than the best, having to over-prove himself, because he was, after all, a reject, right? A bastard.

His professional ethics dictated everything. His sense of honor, his sense of decency, drove everything in him. Violate that, and he might as well lay down and wait for death. As the words had come out of Josie's mouth, he knew what was coming next, he knew that she thought that she could override the research study's rules and help his grandfather, and that was when some circuit in his head just blew.

The conversation had gone very wrong, and as he watched her ass get smaller and smaller, as she marched out the back door, her legs pumping her forward as swiftly as possible to get the hell away from him, he deflated. The anger that had made him so righteously indignant, and had triggered all of those words that came out of his mouth, that had seemed to make sense at the time that he said them, was a flashpoint.

She was right, he had assumed, and when he made that crack about her being a doctor, it just...ugh. It was as if he were channeling "The Claw" or one of the other countless pompous asses at the hospital. It was like no matter how hard he tried to keep that kind of viewpoint out of his head, it somehow had seeped in by osmosis, through the process of so many years of med school, and internship, and residency.

He knew he could now go back to her and apologize a thousand times, but it was out there, it was said, and "good guy" Alex was now tarnished.

Self-aware enough to know that the mess at work had just spilled over into his personal life like a goddamned pot boiling over, he sat at the table, the abandoned food still smelling heavenly.

He wanted to punch something.

The yearning inside him that had drawn him to go to the appointment, to ask her out for coffee, still pulled at him. Her form faded as she marched down the street, as far away as quickly as possible from him, and something in him loosened. It was a sense of need. Not sexual need, an emotional need to bring her back, to apologize, to hold her, to have her arms snake around his waist, her cheek pressed against his chest, to go for long walks, to drink coffee, to make her dinner, to explore and have fun, and have not-fun. What would it be like to just do laundry together? To clean the house? To have a baby? To go on big trips? The banal, simple things that everyone took for granted.

Alex trusted science. Rigor, objectivity, measurement, re-measurement, trial and error, replication. All of those principles were absolutely critical for a drug's success. You couldn't do much of that with emotions. Could you measure them? Not really. Could you be objective? Hell no. Could you be rational at all times? If you could, he wondered how that would feel. He did a pretty good job of being mellow, but on the inside, he was just as wracked with indecision and confusion as everyone else, maybe to a lesser extent, but those feelings still ricocheted inside him.

Half stalking her at work when she hadn't replied to his many communication attempts, he hadn't been sure whether she wanted anything to do with him. Perhaps she was spurning him by not answering him, but now? Now he was certain he had managed to make her believe he was just a big asshole.

\* \* \*

Her phone rang. Great. She cringed and held her eyes half shut, like watching a horror movie scene you can't bear to handle full-on, as she looked at the phone number. Not Alex. Whew.

Why was that *whew* tinged with disappointment?

Darla. Her niece. Cousin. Whatever you call her. Her cousin who was seven years younger and who called her Aunt Josie because Josie had helped raise her. Josie picked up the phone.

"Darla, what the hell are you doing calling me?" That was one hell of a way to greet someone, but Josie knew this wasn't going to be good news. Someone had died, her mother was in jail, or Darla was pregnant. Or maybe it was buy-one-get-one-free day and two of those had happened.

"Oh, just slumming." Darla's tone was clear—Josie was being a jerk.

She softened and laughed. "You okay? You finally going to take me up on my offer to move out here?"

"Nope," Darla replied, the word clipped and clear. Hmmmm, Josie wondered. No mention of a death or jail. That must mean…

"That's not what I want to talk about." Here it came. A baby. Everyone around her was having a baby. Maybe Josie needed a baby so she'd be part of the "in" crowd.

"You talk about what you want to talk about, then." *Just get it out, Darla.*

"I need to talk about a man." Darla's accent had always amused Josie. You would think that they would both have the same post-Appalachia, not-quite-Yinzer Pittsburgh accent, but they didn't. Maybe because Josie's dad hadn't been from the area, or maybe because Darla was so bold in how she spoke, but Josie had ditched most of her central Ohioisms from her speech patterns, while it seemed Darla had absorbed them all and more.

"A man? How can you talk about a man? There aren't any *men* out there." The last guy back home Josie had dated was Davey Rockland, who had managed to fail out of the police academy because he couldn't keep track of how many bullets he'd shot from a clip. When you can't manage basic arithmetic up to fifteen or so, it's time to just go become roadkill.

"No kidding," Darla muttered, "but I actually managed to find one."

"So, who is this man you found?"

"I *literally* found him, Josie. He was naked, wearing nothing but a guitar on the side of the road."

*Huh?* Did Darla just actually say what she thought she said? The cat leapt onto the counter and headed toward the salad Josie was working on. One good shove later and she had an offended cat, tail up and puckered asshole sauntering away.

"What?" Josie barked, struggling to pin her phone between her cheek and shoulder while covering the food with plastic wrap to protect it from the feline menace.

"I'm not kidding." Darla's mantra. Even at three or four her stock phrase had been "I'm not kidding," one hand jauntily on her cocked hip, an insulted expression on her face.

"He was just standing there on I-76, wearing a guitar and a collar and sticking his thumb out, and so I stopped."

"Did you fuck him?" This sounded like the start of a good *Penthouse Forum* story.

"Wow, way to be blunt, Josie." She paused. Josie could imagine Darla biting the cuticle of her thumbnail, shoving her giant mane of blonde curls over her shoulder, buying time to decide how best to tell the truth. "Yeah, of course."

*Victory!* "How can I be blunt if I'm right?"

"You can be both."

"I often am, but don't accuse me of being too blunt when, in the end, the direct question I'm asking relates exactly to what you've actually done." Boy, that sounded wayyyyy too officious, even in Josie's head. She opened her mouth to say something to lighten the conversation when Darla spoke.

"I don't want to talk about *that*, either," Darla snapped.

"What do you want to talk about?" Where was this going? Was she pregnant or not? If she was, she would just blurt it out. Darla wasn't the type to keep *anything* to herself. Whatever was going on had to be complicated if it didn't pour out of her in the first few seconds.

"I want to talk about this man."

"What's his name?"

"Trevor."

"Trevor what?"

"Trevor Connor." Josie could hear the grin in Darla's voice. Trevor Connor. She knew that name.

"Trevor Connor...where have I heard that name? Why is that so familiar?" Josie asked. She knew it wasn't someone they'd grown up with. How was Darla dating someone whose name she knew?

"Wait a minute!" she practically screamed. "Trevor Connor? From Random Acts of Crazy?" A year ago one of the teenage granddaughters of one of Josie's patients had been blasting a song that Josie loved. One thing led to another and she'd downloaded "I Wasted My Only Answered Prayer" and sent it to Darla. The rest was history. Her niece had become a serious groupie for this tiny little local band, but Random Acts of Crazy was growing. Were they touring in Ohio already? If so, why *Peters*? Of all the places you could perform in Ohio...

"Yup."

"Darla." Calm seeped into her voice. It occurred to her that Darla might be calling her, high as a kite, and rambling on about something that wasn't real.

"Yeah?"

"Are you on something? Because you don't just conjure a naked man on the interstate, wearing nothing but a guitar, who happens to be the lead singer of your favorite band." Compassion filled her. This was not what Josie had expected, and her shift in focus went from her pending date to her far-flung niece. "Honey, do you need me to call someone?"

"I swear to God, Josie, I am not making this up." The tone in her voice was believable. If this were true, then how did Trevor Connor get to Peters? It was all too crazy.

And random.

"*Okayyy*," Josie said, skeptically. "And you fucked him?"

"Yup."

"Any good?" Wincing, Josie forced herself to ask the question. While Darla and she were adults now, there was still an ick factor in talking about sex.

"Hoo boy," Darla chirped.

"That good?" A flicker of her and Alex pressed up against the stone wall by the river sent shivers through her.

"Yup."

"So what's your problem?" *Please don't be pregnant.*

"My problem is that I don't know what my problem is and Trevor is about to leave any minute now and I'm going to pick up his friend Joe, who—"

"Joe? Joe as in Joe Ross, the bass player?"

"Yup."

"Quit saying 'yup.'" This one-word answer shit drive Josie nuts.

"Yes, ma'am. Is that better?"

"Actually, yes."

"Okay then, *ma'am.*"

"You're telling me that you're hanging out with the bass player and the lead singer of your favorite band in the middle of Peters?"

"Yup—yes, ma'am, I mean."

"You know they're from Boston, right?"

"Well, outside of Boston, some suburb named Sudborough."

Josie snorted. "More like Snob-borough."

"I picked up on that," Darla said. Josie could imagine the tongue roll, how Darla would mug, her eyebrows lifting in a goofy face. God, she missed her. Maybe this was the chance to get her out here. Finally. Aunt Cathy didn't need nearly as much help as Darla claimed she needed. Fear stopped Darla from even visiting Boston.

"Are they being assholes?" she said, coldly. "Because if you need me to—"

"What? What are you going to do, Josie? You're a hundred pounds soaking wet. You gonna go and raspberry them to death? Shake your finger in their faces extra hard?"

*Oh, great.* As if Josie weren't already teeming with insecurity. A wave of protectiveness rose up in her nonetheless, pushed through by a sense of indignation that these two metro-west Boston spoiled college boys might be hurting Darla.

"Fair enough," she said. What she wanted to say was

something devastatingly visceral, but this wasn't about her. It was about Darla. Her voice softened. "So, what's really going on?"

"Well, you knew I already had a fangirl crush on Trevor, so the problem is that now that I've spent most of the past twenty-four hours with him, I don't want to let him go."

*Aha.* An opening. "So don't."

"Don't what?"

"Don't let him get away. Come to Boston. Live with me here in Cambridge."

"You know I can't do that." *I know that's bullshit,* Josie thought. Deep breath, and then—

"Your mama's fine," she said, soothingly. "You can come out here. You can go on, Darla. You can move on."

"I don't wanna talk about that."

"Well, I do," Josie insisted. "And now you have a place to live, you have a guy—"

"Two guys." Darla's words hung in the air like a giant water balloon about to crash into Josie's face, Matrix-style.

"Two guys? You fucked them both?" Was this some trend Josie was missing out on? First Laura, and now Darla? Had *Cosmo* come out with an issue on threesomes?

"No... no," Darla said, stumbling. "Look, it's complicated."

"It's *always* complicated," Josie shot back. If she heard that phrase one more time...and now it was pouring out of her own mouth.

"No, actually, it's not. My life's pretty fuckin' simple, Josie. I go to my gas station job, I help Mama with her sugars and I try to find somebody to spend time with who doesn't think that *Killer Karaoke* is the height of American culture. Other than that, I don't have a complicated life and now, suddenly, in twenty-four hours it's become more twisted and more confusing than anything else in my entire life probably since I was four."

*Zing!* An arrow between the eyes couldn't have hurt—

or halted her—more. Forcing a deep breath, she inhaled until her belly filled, distending beyond her waistband, and then deflating, a forced relaxation that she felt in her bones. Good.

"I'm sorry," she said. "It sounds like whatever you're going through, it's pretty big."

"Yup…uh, yes, ma'am."

"How can I help?"

"Tell me what to do." Darla laughed, the sound wild and boisterous. "I don't want Trevor to leave—Joe's about to take him away. Uncle Mike's gonna fix his car."

"Joe's car is broken?"

"Yeah, he got here and then came into my little purple passion place—"

"Your purple *what?*" Was that code for drugs? Or some hotel nearby that rented by the hour? Or had something on her body gone purple with disease? Josie wished she could have been there more for Darla these past years. This call was clearly a cry for help.

"Oh, never mind." A long sigh told Josie Darla was as frustrated as she was. Whatever words were flying between the two of them didn't connect easily to what was going on beneath the surface.

"If you've got a place on your body that's turning purple from passion, Darla, then there are medications for that."

"It's not like that."

"*Ookaaayyy.*" Even the cat ran off this time, spooked by Josie's tone, her non-phone hand gesturing as if possessed. Josie's smart mouth was running dangerously close to ripping Darla a new one.

"I don't want Trevor to leave and Joe's an asshole but he's a really, really, *really* attractive asshole and I just…" A long sigh. "I guess it's all on me, isn't it?"

"Yes," Josie said. "It's all on you. I can't really help you. I'm here to listen, I'm here to give you whatever advice I can, and I'm here to caution you to please, please use condoms." *Please.*

Darla laughed, a belly sound that made Josie's shoulders drop instantly. "We did. No worries."

"Okay, good, because the last thing you need is to add a baby to this mix."

"I know. I know, Josie, I'm watching Jane go through it. Trust me, I do not wanna add a baby to anything right now."

"Good girl. I'm going to start clearing out my guest room just in case you wanted to, you know, visit. Or uproot your entire life and move in." A dawning sense of joy filled her at the thought. Rescuing Darla had been her mission years ago; leaving had been wretched. But now...

"Fat chance."

"Oh, I think the chance is better than you think, Darla," she said.

Shuffling sounds, and then: "I gotta go, Josie," Darla said. "Things are about to get even more complicated."

*More* complicated? What could be more complicated than two guys at once? Josie struggled to say the exact right thing, the one statement that would ricochet in Darla's mind and help her to make the perfect decision— which was, of course, to move to Boston.

"Just remember one thing, Darla," she said.

"What's that?"

"Whatever you do, it's your life—not anybody else's. You get to pick what happens next." *Click.* Darla was gone.

* * *

She knocked softly on the door. She wasn't nervous—a sense of determination drove her forward, knowing that this was the first of many, *many* arguments that she would be picking on this subject.

"Yes." Gian looked up. He was balding on top and wore glasses like something out of the 1950s, army-issue

271

thick black rims. His shirt had what looked like a tomato sauce stain on it and it occurred to her for a moment that he could have been Dylan's incredibly ugly older brother.

"Hey, Gian, I have a question."

"What's up?"

"I want to talk about the trial."

"Yes," he said. "Isn't that what we're here for?"

"I think it's time to break it."

"What?" He looked at her in shock and pulled his glasses off, rubbing the bridge of his nose, his brown eyes, one bloodshot from rubbing, the other quite white and normal looked back at her a bit bugged out. "Why would we break it?"

"I think for ethical reasons we need to. The trends I told you about are deepening." Barely holding it together, she found her brain taking over. *Quit quit quit quit quit*, it said, racing through what she'd already lost from the trial (*Alex*) and what she was being offered by Laura (*freedom*).

"Deepening," he said.

"And I'm documenting trends. It's becoming increasingly evident which patients are on the drug and which are on placebo."

He studied her carefully. He knew that she knew this stuff inside out. If it had been any other nurse, she knew, he'd have waved her away. "What makes you think that?" he challenged, propping his chin in his elbow, rubbing his upper lip absentmindedly.

She took a seat and pulled out a large folder. "I knew you'd ask that."

"Of course I'd ask that."

"That's right. I knew you'd ask, and so here's my data."

"Data. How refreshing—someone who works here who actually believes in the scientific process."

"I know, it's amazing, isn't it?"

After battling a political nightmare a few years ago where there was a near-corruption scandal involving bribes from a pharmaceutical company to help push a drug along,

Gian had been brought in. He had—if nothing else—a strict adherence to policy, squeaky clean, and in that respect, a bit like Alex. In the physical department? He was basically as much like Alex as the Gollum.

She opened the folder and handed it to him. "Look at the response rates; in memory, in reflex, short-term memory, long-term memory, all of these different fields. I keep seeing a growing divide. This folder is the group of people who perform well, or at least stay in place, and this is the group of people who don't. The metrics just keep showing that the same groups are getting more entrenched in their patterns—and the people who are getting worse are deteriorating at a very alarming rate."

He put his glasses back on and read over the documents carefully. Josie knew to occupy her mind—if it took forty-five minutes, Gian would sit there and take forty-five minutes. His meticulous nature, right here right now, was playing into exactly what she hoped. She wasn't setting herself up for disappointment, though. She was resigned to failure this first time, but, if nothing else, she'd plant a seed of doubt in Gian's mind and get him to at least think about it.

To her surprise, he snapped the folder shut and looked up within about ten minutes. "I see the trend—but we need more data."

"Are you kidding me?" she said. "That's not enough?"

"Nope. I'd say we need at least six months more."

"Six months! Some of these people don't have six months. Some of these families don't have six months."

"I'm not at all unaware of that."

"Oh, that's a lovely bureaucratic reply. 'We're sorry that your father is slipping into incontinence and doesn't remember his middle child but we're not unaware of that,'" she said with a snarky affect. Rage started to fill her, thinking about Ed and his confusion. How he was starting to confuse his daughters for each other and how he'd mistaken her, at one point, for one of them.

"I can't jeopardize the funding, Josie."

"Funding?"

"Funding."

She began to play angrily with the little Dungeons and Dragons figures and a set of magic dice that Gian had sprinkled across the front of his desk.

"Isn't there an ethics aspect to this for human trials, *Gian*," she said sharply, "that supersedes funding?" Her anger was coming out and as the tension in the back of her neck got worse it started to blind her, her eyes seeing everything through a lace curtain. Rage roiled up through her veins, spiriting into her fingertips, down her spine into her coccyx, and then dividing in two, running down her legs into her toes.

This was the range of options. If she hadn't had that conversation with Laura, Dylan, and Mike, if they hadn't offered her the opportunity to start this crazy business, if she didn't know *damn well* deep inside herself that she was right and that those people were in jeopardy by being forced to stay in the control group, then she wouldn't say what she was about to say.

"Look, you can snap at me," he said dispassionately. "It's not going to change anything."

"I know that." She stood and got right in his face, bending down, mustering as much intimidation as she could, which wasn't hard given her fury. She shoved her finger right in his face, making him flinch and pull back. "You get this straight Gian—I'm coming in to this office every fucking day until you convene a committee to look over what I've gathered. You know as well as I know that there's a point in any research trial with human beings where if it is a detriment to continue the trial when it's known, when it's *known* through data analysis, that the drug is so beneficial that it would be detrimental to keep it from the control group, that the research study can be broken. I am telling you—look at that data because I think it's time we do that."

"You're going to be in my *fucking* office every day if I don't do what you want?"

"I'm telling you I'm going to be in your office every fucking day."

"Then would you mind bringing me a Starbucks?" He smiled, the grin not reaching his eyes.

"Do you want it poured over your head or your crotch, Gian? Because then yes, I'll bring you a Starbucks."

"I'd like it in a cup." He turned away and began tapping on his computer. "I suppose now I need to make sure I wear one." He glanced nervously at his crotch. "If you're done, I'm going to write an email now."

"All right, Gian. See you tomorrow," she said, storming out.

It wasn't until she hit the stairwell that the shakes sank in. She'd left the folder on his desk, but she had five other copies back in her office, ready to deploy every day. There was one thing that her mom had told her over the years. "You are a persistent little shit, aren't you?" Marlene used to say. Josie had taken pride in it—it's what got her out of Peters, what got her through Daddy's death, and what got her to make the decision that—*yes*.

Yes.

If she was a persistent little shit then maybe she could persist in letting herself be in charge of her own life.

She slid her phone out of her pocket and dialed Laura's number.

Annoyingly real and torturously resonant, the pain of knowing that by trying to do the right thing she had only hurt so many others was the kind of stupidity she wished she could bang out of herself, one blow at the time, by flinging her body onto the jagged rocks at the bottom of a cliff.

While that might be satisfying to some of the people in her life, Josie knew that she would have to settle for self abuse of the mind, a never-ending stream of thoughts that dominated her twenty-four hours a day, seven days a week, an ongoing reminder of the failure of the heart.

*Wait a minute*, she told herself. Not fair! Some tiny shred of mercy flittered through her mind. The failure of the heart? That seemed harsh. She was a big girl, and could accept that she had screwed up. But flogging herself, and not loving herself enough to forgive, though, would hurt everyone, especially her. It was bad enough that so many people were in pain. She didn't need to add the complete annihilation of self-worth to the mess.

Dusting off her bruised ego, Josie took a deep breath. There were one million things she wanted to say to Alex, but instead she would have to focus on so many other things in her life.

Like quitting her job.

Laura had made a generous offer to her, to open and manage a very different kind of company. It was time to take the offer seriously.

Josie would do just that.

Picking up her smartphone, Josie dialed Laura's number. The phone rang four times before she heard Laura's voice, followed by the loud scream of a baby.

"Hello?" Laura's frantic voice answered. The sound of a baby's sharp cry pierced the air, and it ended quickly, with a muffled mewling that left Josie confused.

"Laura?"

"Yeah, Josie? Hang on, I'm just latching Jill on." Aha! That was what was going on. Josie paused for a few seconds to think about what Laura's life must be like right now. She had become so engrossed in her own new relationship that she hadn't given much thought to what Laura was going through with this new identity change. Plus, the physical changes must be overwhelming.

"Okay. Whew. She's on. What's up?"

"Is that offer still open?"

The grin on Laura's face could be heard through the phone. "Sure is! I was just looking into real estate, in fact."

"If I'm supposed to run the place, shouldn't I be the

one looking for the office?" she said in an over-the-top, officious tone.

"Yes, boss!" Laura sighed, the sound of relief clear. "Let's meet later today at Jeddy's. I'll bring Jillian and the guys and we can hash out the basics."

Indecision washed over her. This was too real, suddenly. "I haven't accepted. Just want to explore my options."

A groan from Laura. "Does that include exploring Alex, too?"

"I don't want to talk about him."

"Too bad. I do." Steel ran through her words. This was not the softer, insecure Laura. When had she become so demanding?

"You don't get to tell me what I can and can't talk about!" There wasn't any real conviction in Josie's voice.

"Yes, I can. I am attached at the nipple to an eight-pound vampire and sleep with two men who are walking zombies these days and who can't find two nights a week to bother with sex. It's your turn to dish about your sex life."

"Fine, I'll talk about air fucking *aaaaaall* you want."

"Air fucking?" Laura sputtered. "Is that like mime sex?"

Josie covered her face with her hands and dropped the phone; she was laughing *that* hard. Scrambling to retrieve the phone as Laura called out to her, she finally got it in hand, and with great, whooping gasps choked out, "It is exactly like mime sex."

"What fun is that if you can't scream when you come?" Laura said, an indignant tone in her voice.

Josie went blind with laughter.

"Meet us at four at Jeddy's tomorrow, Josie. You're crazy." Some mumbling came over the phone, and then a soft pout of disgust. "And the baby just shat all the way up her back and into her hair."

*Ewwww.* "That is quite an accomplishment," Josie said,

snorting. Her abs hurt from giggling.

"Gotta go! We'll talk about air fucking later!"

"I'm waiting with bated breath." *Click.*

\* \* \*

As if Darla were channeling her, the phone rang with her name on it.

The sounds coming from her phone were like alien communications, high pitched and screechy. "I can't believe I did this and they left!" was the best Josie could understand.

"Whoa! Darla. Slow down. What's wrong? Are you hurt?" Her voice went into that deadly calm she got during emergencies. Made her a damn fine nurse.

"Not physically."

"Who left?"

"Joe and Trevor."

"The guys from Random Acts of Crazy?"

No answer. What was going on?

"Darla? You there?" Her voice was firm again.

"Yes. And yes, the guys from the band."

"They went home?"

"Yep." Darla began to sob, wracking sounds that made Josie's heart hurt.

"What happened? Are you okay? What did they do?" Her voice trailed off, concern coming through loud and clear.

"They up and left me alone here at the truck-stop hotel," Darla bellowed.

"They wha—" As if chopped off with an ax, her voice just stopped cold. "They left you."

"They."

"*They?*"

"They—yes, *they.* It's a word, Josie. It means two or more people."

"MORE?" The pain in Josie's heart turned to a

thumping shock.

"No. Not more. Just *they* as in two guys."

"And you…?"

"*We.* Yes."

*Whoosh.* Josie pulled the phone away from her ear and let all the air in her lungs go out in one big stream of *holy shit.* Managing one man was hard enough—why were the two women closest to her suddenly handling *two*? Was there a message here?

A light bulb went on.

"Oh, honey," Josie said. "Do you want a job?"

"A job?"

"I've always told you that if you want to move out here you can, Darla. But you always said you needed a job along with a place to live. I'm changing jobs and can hire someone to work as my office assistant, and I'm offering it to you. The whole shebang—a place to stay and a job. What do you say?"

Josie held her breath. This was the first time Darla hadn't snapped a negative answer when begged to move out to Boston. Maybe, just maybe…

"And I know you'll claim you can't leave Aunt Cathy, but you know that's just a chickenshit excuse you've been using for years to avoid changing your life. You're too timid, Darla. You need to take more chances."

Too much silence. Darla must have been wavering, which meant there was a chance. Time to put on the thumbscrews. "Hint: The correct response is a breathy 'OMIGOD AUNT JOSIE YOU ARE THE BEST.'" She made a derisive snorting noise. "Not this silent, pensive crap."

"What's the catch?"

"No catch. Just start when you come out here, maybe in a week or two?"

"So what's the company?"

Umm… How was Josie supposed to explain?

"Josie?"

"It's not pole dancing."

"Well, thank goodness, because the only pole I dance on is—"

"Too much information, Darla Josephine. *TMI*."

"You're not really giving me enough details to leap and leave behind my entire life, you know."

Another snort. "I'm going to guess that right now you're either getting ready to go work at the gas station where the highlight of your day will be changing the urinal cake in the men's room, or you're trying to find a way to keep wiring the cable line from your neighbor so your mom can watch *Pawn Stars* again."

"When you put it that way," Darla said through gritted teeth, "it's kind of hard to say no. But you have to give me *something*. What does this company do?"

Buying time, Josie tried to think of how to say this. But then again, maybe not. If Darla was impulsive enough to jump into bed with two guys from her favorite band, surely she wouldn't care about working for a ménage dating service.

Right?

Finally, she said in a controlled, professional voice, "Let's just say you're a *perfect* match for the job."

"Okay, Aunt Josie," she said. "You got a deal. Give me a week or two and I'll be out there."

*Squeeee!* "Darla Jo, it's the best decision you've ever made."

"I've made some whoppers."

"Yes, you have, and this one's not one of them."

* * *

*This must be what adults feel like*, Josie thought as she walked in the front door of Jeddy's to find Madge waving a half-friendly "hello" and Laura, Dylan, Mike, and baby Jill already settled in a large booth, coffee cups in front of the adults with Jillian nestled in Laura's lap, attached to one breast discreetly.

The walk from the entrance to the booth where her friends had settled in felt transformative, like some sort of vision quest that took place through a ratty old diner with torn vinyl seats and scratched stainless steel grills. Each step felt like one more gravid foot closer to being expected to act in a more mature manner, to managing relationships with friends, with godchildren, with… what could she call Madge, exactly? Her not boyfriend's grandfather's girlfriend? There had to be a word for that, right? Whatever it was, she wasn't mature enough—yet—to figure it out.

The pity party she'd indulged in for the past month faded as she strode closer to the group. Instead of feeling alienated and like a fourth wheel—a fifth, now that she thought about it, with the baby here. A fleeting thought went through her mind like a ribbon unfurling: *These are my people. I belong here.*

And she did.

"Where's Alex?" Laura asked, her face hopeful and bright.

The scowl that Josie shot back made Laura's grin turn quickly into a frown, a melting of her features that made Josie feel a pang of guilt, as if she'd hurt Laura herself. "I don't want to talk about it."

Dylan muttered something unintelligible to Mike, and if looks could wither, she had just turned him into a desiccated raisin.

"I hope everything is okay," he said, and then, again, she had to feel something, a halting within herself where everything that she assumed had to be rolled back.

She squared her shoulders and reminded herself that no one here was judging her. "It's all, well… it's not good," she said, "but it's not bad. I just don't want to talk about him right now." *Not in front of your happy family*, she thought. "I do want to talk about the business."

"Yes," Mike said, swigging back the final bit of coffee

in his cup and banging it down on the tabletop just enough like Thor to make the corners of Josie's mouth pop up. "Let's talk about the business. How do you want to structure it?"

Josie and Laura exchanged a look. "I thought we'd figured that all out," Laura said.

"Maybe you two figured all that out," Dylan added, finishing his coffee off and looking around for Madge as if she held the only life preserver on the Titanic, "but Mike and I have no idea what you two are planning."

"You guys didn't talk about it?" she asked Laura.

"When we are able to talk to each other at home," she said, "it's never the three of us. Whichever one of us is in charge of the baby, the other two are out cold somewhere on the couch, in bed, on the toilet—"

"Hey! I was tired," Dylan interjected.

"You fell asleep on the toilet?"

"Don't judge."

"Fine." Josie held her hands up in a gesture of supplication. "Let's get back to business."

"Let's," Mike added.

Madge whipped past with a thermos of coffee, pouring Mike and Dylan's and then slamming the pitcher on the scratched tabletop, throwing down a little bowl of creamers and flashing past.

"She's my new girlfriend," Dylan said, emotion infusing his words as he cradled the cup of java as if it were a precious stone or his child, who was currently suckling off of Laura, the sounds of smacking hard for Josie to weed out as the baby latched on and off over and over again, making Laura wince.

"That doesn't hurt, does it?" Josie asked as she poured herself a cup of coffee from the pitcher and started to look at the menu.

"Of course it hurts." Laura glared at her. "Can you imagine having a baby's mouth on your nipple twelve hours a day?"

"Twelve hours a day?"

"That's what it feels like. You'd be all cracked and sore and peeling and—"

"Ah, God, I don't want to hear it!" Josie said. "Please, I'm about to eat."

"You're a nurse. If you don't have a cast iron stomach and can't hear a few details about breastfeeding, then—"

"I'm a research nurse now. I deal with old people."

"Not for long," Laura reminded her.

Josie bit her bottom lip, curling it in under her top teeth. Madge saved her from what she wanted to say, which was *Not in the way you think*, but instead she was forced to order as the old coot bore down on her, looming over, casting her shadow on Josie's seated form.

"What can I getcha? A hot doctor?"

Deflating, Josie said meekly, "I'll just have the fried green tomatoes and a tossed salad with Italian."

"What's going on with you and Alex?" Madge asked, suspiciously. "He's moping around, too."

Four sets of eyes lasered in on her, Dylan's eyebrows raised high, Mike calm and peaceful as always—either that or he was too tired to actually care.

"I would like the fried green tomatoes and a tossed salad with Italian dressing," Josie repeated, over-enunciating the words.

She was pissed.

These were her people, all right. These were her crazy people that she wanted to get away from.

"Okay, then," Madge answered, mimicking Josie's affect. "I. Will. Get. You. The. Wat. Er. And. The. Food. You—"

"Oh, God, cut it out!" Dylan snapped. "Just—just take the order."

Laura snapped back, "We're all curious. We all want to know what's going on with Alex. Doesn't kill you to be patient."

"Yes, it does. I want my food. I'm hungry."

Now it was Josie and Madge's turn to watch, because this was the first time she'd ever seen them snipe at each other like this. Trouble in paradise? Could it be?

"Well, maybe you wouldn't be so hungry if you had remembered to make lunch for everybody like you were supposed to," Laura said. Narrowing her eyes, she shifted the baby, who popped off and started to scream. "Oh, dammit," she whispered under her breath, fumbling with her shirt, looking around the room, her eyes filled with tears, and Josie felt everything melt away, filled with a sense of compassion for how hard this really must be for all of them.

Baby Jillian's wails filled their corner of the restaurant, drawing stares from fellow diners. "Omigod, people are staring. I don't want them to see me breastfeeding."

"Why not?" Mike asked. "It's the most natural thing in the world." His voice was reassuring but there was an irritability there.

Dylan went into protective mode, craning his head around the restaurant looking for a fight. He clearly didn't want to find one with Laura, so any passerby would do. "If anybody says anything I'll give them a piece of my mind," he mumbled, looking around like a Navy SEAL doing a reconnaissance mission. "You have every right to breastfeed, and it's beautiful and they can all just fuck off."

Madge just shook her head. "We didn't do that when I had my kids."

"Do what?"

"Breastfeed. Only the hippies did that."

"You weren't a hippie?"

She threw her head back and cackled. "Honey, I was more *Mad Men* than Woodstock."

She quickly took the rest of the orders and ran off to the kitchen. Laura shifted the baby out from under her nursing shirt and threw a burp rag on her shoulder, propping Jillian upright.

The back of her little head had a thin layer of that dark

blonde hair that had been so lush at birth. It had worn away like a balding old man in the spot where she lay against the sheets. Josie had seen that in newborns before and knew that the baby's hair would be back before her first birthday. Right now the bald spot was adorable and a reminder of how vulnerable and really, really tiny this baby was.

A belch like a sailor's poured forth from the baby. It was so loud that a group of college students—mostly guys but a couple of girls sprinkled in the eight top—cheered, giving baby Jill a round of applause.

That finally seemed to crack the tension at the table, Dylan and Mike shaking their heads and laughing as even Laura tittered just a bit. Dylan finished half of his second cup of coffee and then leaned in, his forearms resting and stretching out on the table across from Josie.

"How, exactly, do you plan to structure the business? Let's talk about the space."

Josie caught Laura's eyes. Laura nodded. Overwhelm was all too easy at this stage for the new parents. Hell, it was easy for Josie and all she had to do was take care of a cat.

"We need to get office space—nothing big, maybe a waiting area, two or three small offices and access to a bathroom and an elevator. It can be cheap and, frankly, it doesn't need to be in the hot part of town because this is a boutique firm."

Mike nodded. "I like that. How about personnel?"

"I'm only going to need me and one other person like an office assistant, somebody to do basic paperwork and filing and answer phones and respond to emails—customer-service-type stuff; anything that's overflow from what I can handle."

"You have someone in mind?" Dylan reached out to Laura. The baby had pulled away, deep in sleep, drunk off mother's milk. Her lips were relaxed and a perfect little red bow dropped open with a tiny little blister right at the little

V of her upper lip.

"What happened?" Josie said, turning away from all the business talk.

"Oh, that's just a nursing blister," Laura said quietly as she carefully, with Olympic-athlete-level precision, transferred Jillian over to Dylan with one hand and snapped her nursing bra shut with the other. Dylan slid his entire arm carefully under the blanketed form, froze momentarily as the baby snurgled and shifted, and then pulled her across. Laura let out a giant sigh of relief, leaned back and picked up her cold half-cup of coffee, drinking it as if it were the finest espresso at a Parisian coffee house.

Watching Laura take such luxury in the most commonplace of actions, finding it a pleasure to have seconds of not being responsible, physically attached to her child, made Josie marvel at the intricacies of this relationship that she hadn't understood.

Was her mom like that with her when she was a baby? What about her dad? Had Marlene and Jeff sat in the Ohio version of a diner like this with month-old Josie, Marlene breastfeeding—*wait, scratch that*. Her own thoughts invaded her own thoughts. Had she breastfed Josie? No scene, no imagined reality of her own infancy, would be complete without a picture of her mom with an inch-long ash hanging off a cigarette dangling over Josie's head, her little baby form in her mother's arms.

What she saw across the table from her and what she imagined her own infancy to have been were quite different. The similarity, though, was that there was a time in her life when she was so wanted and so precious and so vulnerable that her parents must have done the drudgery, have lived the endless marathon of seconds ticking by so slowly, of meeting every single need that she had that they could meet—her needs so simple yet so all-consuming.

And the idea that they loved her so much to do all of that made her appreciate all the more how changed her friends were.

"Who do you have in mind for an office assistant?"

"She could just take out an ad." Dylan turned and looked at Mike, answering the question before Josie could even open her mouth.

"Actually, I have someone in mind," Josie said.

Three sets of eyes looked at her quizzically.

"Already?"

Josie nodded. "My niece—well, she's not really my niece, she's my cousin, but we call her my niece."

Dylan started humming the song "Dueling Banjos". Josie reached across the booth and tapped him with the back of her hand on the arm, careful not to wake Jillian. He just grinned at her and laughed.

"It's not like that. She's my cousin by birth, our mothers are sisters, but I'm seven and a half years older and I've raised her—or, at least, been a major part of raising her since she was four—so we call each other aunt and niece. Anyhow, who cares about genealogy?" She looked pointedly at the baby. "Especially the three of you."

"She's got us there," Mike admitted.

"So, my niece, Darla—"

"Darla? You have a niece named Darla?" Dylan said. "What's her middle name? Sue?"

"No, it's Josephine."

"Darla Jo? Does she have an accent?"

Josie leaned back and crossed her arms, looking at Dylan pointedly. "What kind of accent do you think people from Ohio have?"

He pulled out the rankest, hickest redneck accent that it seemed he was capable of pulling out and proceeded to butcher it. "I don't know, y'all. How y'all doin'? Good, let's git on dow—"

"Oh my God, that is not how people from Ohio talk."

"How do they talk?" he asked.

"They talk like you and me, but without the flat Boston thing you do."

"I don't do a flat Boston thing," he protested. "It's not

like I pahk the cah in Havahd Yahd."

"You can't park a car in Harvard Yard."

"You know what I mean."

Laura nudged Dylan hard, almost waking the baby up, and then she cringed in horror, forgetting herself. "Shit! Shit, shit, shit," she muttered. "Just—just stop, you're going to wake up the baby," she hissed.

"All right. Fine. So, Darla Sue Billybob Jo Jennings—"

"How did you know her last name?"

"Her last name is *Jennings*?"

"Yes."

"I just…it's the hickest last na—"

"It is not a hick – "

"Cut that out." Mike stuck his hand out, finger pointed at Josie, and then at Dylan, and then at the baby. "If you two wake her up right now, I will lock you in a storage facility in one of those eight-by-ten rooms with no way out, a two-day supply of food, and you have to find a way to get along."

Laura put her hand up. "Can I go do that alone? Because I would totally take that deal right now."

Josie looked at her like she was crazy.

Laura looked back. "What? Two days alone, with food that's made for me already? Are you kidding me? That's like…that's like the equivalent of a week-long cruise to the mother of a newborn."

"Can we just get back to the business?" Mike asked.

"So, I've got Darla," Josie said. "She can be my office assistant."

"Does she have office skills?"

"No."

"Does she have *any* skills?" Dylan asked.

"She's worked at a gas station for the past six years."

"She's worked at a *gas station*."

"Which means she's dealt with customers, cash registers, and inventory."

"This isn't exactly that kind of business," Laura added.

"I'm not saying that you shouldn't hire her, she sounds fine, but—"

"Well, she does have one redeeming quality that is really, really vital to the company mission," Josie said, nodding slowly.

"And what's that?" Mike asked.

"She just had her first threesome with two guys."

Dylan sat up. "Really?"

He leaned forward, as did Mike and Laura, though Dylan was hampered by the baby in his lap. He carefully shifted Jillian, who made a little snoring sound that was so adorable that Josie wanted to hold her again.

Mike leaned forward and put his elbows on the table then pulled back, reached for the carafe of coffee, and filled his cup again. "Do tell."

"Well, Darla's twenty-two and there were these two guys in her favorite indie-rock band who somehow ended up in our dinky little town in Ohio, and it turns out all three of them discovered for the first time that this was what they wanted."

Mike and Dylan exchanged a look that seemed like ten years of history flowed between the two of them in an emotional exchange that left Josie breathless to watch—little tells in the way that their eyes moved, how their mouths smiled at each other, some sort of telepathic transfer of information and experience. Laura seemed to notice it, too, as she studied them.

"How did you guys figure this out?" Josie asked, venturing into territory she might otherwise have never wanted to know but had now become more crucial. It dawned on her that if she actually started this company, if this *really* went through, this was the kind of information that people would share with her over time or that she would need to elicit from them to provide the service—this very unique service—that the threesome sitting across the booth from her was proposing.

The look of affection that Mike gave Dylan was

absolutely adorable in a masculine and seductive kind of way. "Before I answer that question," he said, eyes on Dylan, "I think we need to ask Laura if it's all right to talk about this." He broke his gaze and looked around Dylan, a small shrug, eyes lifted, eyebrows up in an expression that asked the questions again.

"Of course," she said, nodding her head. "I can't imagine why it wouldn't be okay to talk about it in front of me or to tell Josie whatever you want," Laura said, finishing her coffee and reaching around Dylan who was besotted with his daughter, staring deeply into Jillian's face as if drunk on her pure existence. "I'm not threatened by the fact that you have a past. In fact, it's your past that makes everything that we have now as good as it is."

In that sentence, Josie realized why she felt like sitting at the big kids table seemed so mature and so adult-like—because it was. She was sitting with three very aware, very evolved adults—people who had more than a nanosecond filter between information and reaction, between emotional trigger and reaction. People who didn't judge automatically but instead evaluated experience and information and then made decisions about what to do next. People who valued love at the core of everything and yet respected folks who were different.

Watching Laura say "yes" to something that would threaten an awful lot of people in a similar situation, whether it was a monogamous male and female relationship, or a non-monogamous male/male relationship, or insert-the-pairing-or-the-multiple-relationship-of-your-choice, the unfettered desire to be respectful, to be loving and to apply compassion in all interactions was what she admired most about Dylan and Mike and Laura.

And, she grudgingly admitted to herself, Alex.

"Okay then, spill it," Josie said, looking at Mike then Dylan. "How did it work? What made you guys realize that"—she looked at Mike but gestured with her right hand to Dylan—"he completes you?"

Laura made a sour face, but Dylan laughed. He and Mike exchanged a look that Josie couldn't even hope to try to decipher, and then they both looked at her, brows furrowed as they tried to figure out what to say.

"You go first," Dylan said, looking at Mike with narrowed, laughing eyes.

"By all means, I defer to you," Mike said, pouring himself yet another cup of coffee.

The t-shirt Mike wore was a ragged mess at the neck, a faded band logo that she couldn't quite catch on the light blue fabric. His hands worried the mug handle, not in a nervous way, but in that distracted, tired way that one gets when too many nights of exhaustion kick in and the body just functions on autopilot. He looked at her with those crystal-clear blue eyes and tilted his head.

"You really should know this." He smiled, a small grin that showed no teeth. "I mean *really* should, shouldn't you? With this kind of business you'll get people like us." He nudged his elbow at Dylan. "You'll get people like Laura."

"What's that supposed to mean?" Laura piped up.

"Nothing. Nothing," he protested. "I don't mean that offensively. I mean people like Laura, women and men—I suppose—who don't realize that this is what they're looking for but find themselves drawn to it. Dylan and me, I think…" He fumbled for words, and Dylan picked up where Mike left off.

"We didn't *plan* it; it wasn't some overt thing. I knew I liked women and I knew I liked Mike. It wasn't like I went to college thinking oh, I'm going to go and find some guy who I'll partner with and then we'll go out and build this." He and Mike shared a chuckle, looking at each other. "God, we still don't have a vocabulary for it, do we?"

They shook their heads and Laura stretched, something in her neck popping as her muscles relaxed, the burden of the baby now carried by Dylan.

"You guys have been doing this for ten years and you

still don't have words for it?" Josie asked.

All three of them shook their heads "no" like a set of three trained monkeys, and it made Josie laugh.

"But when you were younger," she ventured, "what was the turning point? When did you realize 'Oh okay, this is the way my sexuality works'?"

"You sound like a therapist," Dylan said flatly.

She held up her hands in protest. "I didn't mean to. I really don't. It's just, like you said, there's no vocabulary for this and there's no real concept for it, and yet you guys make it work so beautifully. I'm going to have people coming to me basically saying how do I make *that* happen?" She pointed at the three of them. "And then they're going to ask me how do I make *that* happen?" Her finger extended at Jillian's head.

Dylan pulled his head back in surprise and then reached up and rubbed one eyebrow and then one eye, washing his face with his hands—it was both tension and tiredness that drove the movement.

Mike answered for him. "Nothing was deliberate. We were roommates in college and we got along really well and we realized that we got along so well, we liked to spend most of our time together, but there wasn't an attraction, it wasn't 'Oh, I'm gay and this guy is who I want.'"

"No, I firmly want women," Dylan said.

"Yeah, I get that. You've said it about nine thousand times."

"I've said it twice."

"Whatever."

Mike interrupted Josie and Dylan's sparring. "I think it was as much about being comfortable with each other in our friendship as it was about finding the right woman in Jill," Mike said, his voice contemplative and calm, a tingle of nostalgia coming through.

"She was so mellow." Dylan finished for him.

"Yeah," Mike said, nodding. "And it was so…"

"Easy," Dylan interjected.

Mike just nodded.

"How?" Laura asked, leaning back, running one hand through her hair to push it away from her face.

Just then, Madge arrived and delivered everyone's food with perfunctory efficiency. Laura and Mike dug in immediately, while Dylan did the one-handed parent eating thing, nearly dropping part of his salad, a giant cherry tomato falling off his fork and narrowly missing the baby's head.

No matter how hard he tried crumbs sprinkled down on her and Laura cocked one eyebrow, leaned down, and said, "Are you seasoning the baby again?"

"She'll taste better that way. Haven't you read Jonathan Swift?"

The whole table groaned. It was a really bad joke, but Josie had to hand it to them—anybody who could be this sleep deprived and still make jokes was doing all right.

"So, Dylan, you're the one who can't eat yet. You answer how, exactly, was it easy?"

"It was easy because Jill made it easy, just like Laura made it easy. We were these young pups. How old were we, Mike? I was nineteen, you were twenty?"

Mike nodded, his mouth full of food.

Dylan shifted the baby, just so, lifting her up onto his shoulder. She made a snurgly sound, and then nestled her little cheek deeper against the bare skin at the collar of Dylan's shirt. He closed his eyes and breathed in the scent of her little, perfect baby head. "We didn't have words for what we were going through, and when we met Jill, and we all got a little tipsy one night; the sex part just made sense. It was something that we didn't have a bunch of angst about…"

Mike swallowed and interrupted. "Actually, it was more that we had—we were worried"—he stumbled over his words—"we were worried about the fact that we weren't more upset at our own actions." Mike tapped his hand against the table as he said each word, as if thinking it through for the first time. He shoved an enormous coconut shrimp into his mouth, and gestured for Dylan to continue.

"There were all of these feelings that we were supposed to feel. I guess," Dylan added, "I was supposed to be jealous that Mike and Jill got along, and Mike was supposed to be jealous that Jill and I got along, and Jill was supposed to feel like she was perverted, or an aberration, or that she should be ashamed for wanting us both at the same time. We talked a lot…a lot, in our dorm room that first year about all of the things that people would assume about us if we were open, so we stayed closed off; we didn't tell anyone. People just thought that we were a group of three friends, and that Jill was just someone who liked to hang out with two guys."

Josie finished her last piece of fried green tomato, took a sip of ice cold water, and asked, "You never told anyone?

Mike snorted. "That's not quite true." He looked hard at Dylan.

"My parents know," Dylan said. His demeanor changed to one of discomfort, and Josie regretted the question.

"If I'm stepping over any boundaries here, just say so," she said, palms up in a gesture of supplication.

"No, it's not a problem," Laura interjected. "Dylan's mom and dad know, and they're mostly okay."

Mike snorted again.

Josie looked at him. "You don't think so."

He sighed, grabbed his glass of water, chugged it down, and then looked around for Madge, who, as if reading his mind, zipped by with a completely full extra pitcher, and then grabbed the coffee carafe, shook it a bit, and ran off, muttering to herself. Josie gave her two minutes to return with a full coffee pot.

"My parents are Catholic," Dylan said.

"Oh, boy," Josie answered, shaking her head.

"This…yeah, it was not well received, but back in

college I felt like it needed to...be open. That it was the world that was screwed up, that I was fine and I had my own standards, and that judgment be damned, I was going to be open about it—at least after that first year."

"How did your parents handle it?" she asked.

"About as well as you can imagine two cradle to—well, they're not dead yet, but when they die—grave, Catholics could be expected to hear that their son was in a relationship that was so odd, there wasn't even a coalition of people against it."

"Your parents did a good job of trying to create one at first," Mike muttered.

Dylan closed his eyes and shifted the baby to his other shoulder, stretching his sore arm out, and then yawning deeply. "Yeah, at first they did. It only took three years to wear them down, and the fact that they wouldn't let Mike come to any family events once they knew."

"Ouch," Josie commiserated.

Laura looked at her and nodded. "That's one reason why we didn't have a baby shower..." Her voice tapered off with a choked sound at the end, and Dylan took his free arm and wrapped it around her shoulders.

Josie did a facepalm. "You're right, we never did a baby shower. Was that my job? Was I supposed to do that and I just totally flaked on you?"

"No, no, no, no, no," Laura reassured her. "No, it wasn't something that was on our 'wanted' radar screen anyhow. It would have been very complicated."

"We should do something, though," Josie pointed out. "Maybe just a small party that celebrates her life. What you've done is just so amazing, and little Jill...little Jill," Josie repeated. She looked at Dylan and then at Mike. "In the rush of the birth and everything that happened, I never thought to ask, how do you feel about the name?"

Both men turned and looked at Laura, the deep love that was like a small fiber of energy that wafted out and connected the men with Laura.

"It shocked me," Dylan said.

"It thrilled me," Mike answered. "It's a fitting tribute to a really wonderful woman." Mike swallowed hard and Dylan seemed to be fighting back tears.

Laura smiled back. "It really was the only choice once I realized that if you could both love her that much, then I could honor her memory, and love her, too."

"Getting back to business." Josie poured herself a cup of coffee now, and began drinking it. It made her think of Alex, made her think about all of the ways that she was closing herself off, when what she should have been doing is opening herself up. Look at the three of them, across from her, happy, centered, relaxed and joyful. The confidence that all three of them had—that no matter what problems they faced from within or without, they would talk it through, and be reasonable, and use love as their guide—was what Josie wanted more than anything in the world.

Alex had seemed to offer the first steps in that journey for her, and yet she couldn't let herself sink deep enough within to be vulnerable enough to see what that looked like on a day-to-day basis. And now that chance was gone. What that did look like from the outside was the three very tired, very happy people across the table from her, with tangible proof of how much they loved each other. That eight-pound ball of proof, now nestled on Mike's shoulder, curled into a ball as she had lived inside Laura's womb, legs tucked up under, head turned to the side, lips resting against Mike's collarbone.

The business was about helping people to achieve what those three had. Was she deluding herself thinking that she could run such a business, when she couldn't even find one man that she could open up enough for? *Not quite,* a voice in her head chided her, *it's not that you can't find him, it's that you won't let him in. Don't pretend that that person or persons aren't out there for you. Alex is there, and you're pushing him away.*

"Yeah, the business," Laura said. She glanced over to see Jillian's state, and grinned a loving look at Mike, his arm wrapped up and around the baby's entire body. Curled up like a fiddlestick that was starting to unfurl. It was a beautiful picture, almost artistic, in the way his muscles rested in his self-assurance and confidence in holding his daughter. Laura turned her attention back to Josie. "What do you need?"

*What do I need*, she thought. *That's an open-ended question.* "I need the basics, the way that we talked about this before. An office, equipment, a couple people to help me run it, maybe only one—Darla might be enough."

"If she's going through what you're talking about," Mike said, using his left hand to awkwardly drink coffee while holding the baby with his right, "then she sounds resourceful. I'd start with one person and see where you can go."

"So basically you want me to create a dating service for people who want threesomes, and I'm trying to envision how on earth you advertise this thing. We'll have those Westboro Baptist Church fundies protesting outside our window in about three seconds flat."

"That'd be great publicity," Dylan said.

Josie glowered at him. "That is definitely not the way I want to start a new career."

"We can be subtle," Laura added. "I mean, I thought Ménage Match, Incorporated was a great name."

"Really subtle." Josie laughed. "I don't think that's quite right; we need something that's a little more sophisticated, something more…romantic, and not sexual." Josie went pensive, thinking it through. Here they were right in front of her, proof positive that this could work. How could she take Laura, Dylan, and Mike, and without revealing their identities, *use* them somehow, channel the goodness that they had found in each other. And then it hit her. She leaned across the table, and said quietly, "Good Things Come in Threes."

"Hell yeah they do!" Dylan said.

Mike's face went from interested to on fire, a giant grin spreading across his face, making those ice-blue eyes sparkle. "You just *nailed it*," he said. "Good Things Come in Threes. That's the company name."

"Now, we need to get down to brass tacks."

"Well, for funding, Laura can fund it however she likes," Mike said, looking uncomfortable suddenly.

"We consider this her thing," Dylan said, "we're just here to…"

"To disrupt the process," Josie choked.

"To give our input," he countered.

"Potato, potahto."

Dylan gave her a "fair enough" gesture, waving his hand and reaching, in the process, for the coffee carafe to fill his cup again.

"Do we advertise at all?" Mike wondered aloud. "What about word of mouth?"

"Do you know any other people in a situation like yours?" Josie asked, skeptically.

The three of them paused and thought about it. They all shook their heads. "No," they said in unison.

"Me neither," said Josie, "so how do we get started on this?"

"We could take out ads, you know, in the *Phoenix* or some of the other local newspapers that having dating site ads."

Josie mulled that one over. "Yeah, we could. It's kind of a unique service."

"Well, we need to make it clear, too," Laura added, "that this isn't just some…sexual hookup system."

"We'll get the creeps, though," Josie said.

"You'll have no problem dealing with them," Dylan ventured.

Josie smiled— that felt good, that he thought that of her. "Thank you," she said. "I appreciate that, Dylan."

He looked like he was about to say something else with

a snarky tone, and then pulled himself back. His eyes expressed surprise that she would give him that much credit.

Jillian woke up with a scream that made the fillings in the back of Josie's mouth shake. How could a baby go from sound asleep, curled up on Mike's neck, to screeching like a howling monkey? It startled Mike, who unwrapped his arm and began soothing her, patting her back carefully.

"Poor baby, give her to me," said Laura, reaching around Dylan to try to grab her.

Mike turned away just a little. "It's fine, I have to learn to be able to soothe her," he said, a tone of irritation in his voice.

Josie had a feeling that this was an argument they'd had on and off for the past few weeks. Dylan just sat between them, trying to relax and drink a cup of coffee at the same time. Nothing Mike did calmed the baby down, though. He stood and began pacing, four steps away, four steps back, four steps away, four steps back. The rhythm seemed to soothe Jillian, and then, *BUUUUUURP*. The biggest, juiciest, nastiest burp that Josie had ever heard came out of the baby, and then the inevitable spitup, all over Mike's clean collar.

"You forgot a burp rag, dude," Dylan said, reaching in the diaper bag to pull one out. He handed it to Mike. The baby whined a little bit at being wet, the front of her little onesie now soaked a couple of inches down. Mike traded the sour-milk-smelling infant to Dylan for the burp rag. "Thanks," they said in unison.

Laura just laughed, concern turning to relief.

"You're really living the life, aren't you?" Josie said.

"I am, I just wish that I could appreciate it a little more from the stance of having a little more sleep. Otherwise…" Laura leaned back and watched as Dylan took Jillian into the men's room to change her, and Mike patted at his shirt, uselessly, with the burp rag to clean himself up. "I am very, very grateful for what I have," Laura said softly. "How 'bout you?" Her eyes narrowed, and there was a look of real perception.

Josie knew she was being studied by the one person who knew her the best. Her niece Darla was a close second, and now that she knew she was coming here to live with her, Josie felt like a lot of her carefully constructed walls were starting to fall away, brick by brick. Alex, one of the many masonry workers, chipping away. "I'm well…no, I'm not okay. I was about to say 'I'm fine,' but we all know what bullshit that is."

"You and Alex still fighting?"

"Me and Alex aren't anything. He made a series of assumptions in the middle of a conversation that went from mild irritation to stalking off in…in anger." Josie deflated. She could feel the air pushing out of her as the memory took over. It had been two weeks, two weeks since they'd fought, and she hadn't heard a word from him.

"I'm sorry," Laura said, sliding one hand across the table, grabbing Josie's. It was the first time she'd had compassionate touch in more than two weeks, and it startled her how much her inner core needed that.

"Thank you," she said softly. "I'm sorry, too. I don't know what I did to break this and I don't know how to fix it."

"You could text him."

"I'm not texting him." Josie pulled her hand back. "I didn't do anything wrong."

"I know that, and you know that…" Laura said.

Mike sat next to Laura and watched the conversation in rapt attention. Josie realized he was there suddenly, dipped her chin down, and gave him a death stare. Laura joined her, and with four angry woman eyes on him, Mike did the smart thing without a word passing between the three of them, and got up and went to help Dylan with the baby.

Josie leaned forward and whispered, "The results came

in."

Laura went pale. "And?"

"We don't need to change the name."

Laura squinted at Josie. "You guessed right?"

Josie nodded.

"You have a hunch, don't you?"

"I did. And I was right."

Laura bit her lips, closed her eyes, and sighed. "Thank you."

"Any time. I know you'd help me if I need it."

"Alex is too nice to let get away."

"And here we go," Josie said dryly.

"I'm right! Sometimes I get to be right, you know."

"Well, if he's so nice," Josie hissed, "then why would he accuse me of making these gigantic ethics violations? I would *never* do that, *ever.*"

"I don't know," Laura said, "but look at what being stubborn got me. The guys missed out on the entire second trimester—hell, almost two thirds of my pregnancy—because I was a stupid, stupid idiot. I don't want to see you do that."

"I'm not pregnant."

Laura sighed, shook her head, and rubbed her eyes. "No, you're not pregnant, and no, it's not the same. You didn't sit there and watch yourself be humiliated on national tel—well, on local television, and find out the two guys that you're sleeping with were both billionaires. I was stubborn because they kept a secret from me, and it was wrong of both of…of all three of us. Ugh, I still don't have a vocabulary for the fact that there are three of us," she muttered, laughing to herself. "But the bottom line is that *I* let my pride get in the way. I let my insecurity, too, get in the way of the greatest love that I could *ever* hope to find, and *I* want *you* to learn from my mistake. I do not want to see you do this to yourself, Josie."

Leave it to Laura to say the one thing that could crack her fucking wall. "You know, I hate you," Josie said.

"I know. It's because I make sense."

"Now I hate you more, for saying that, because you're right," she said, slamming her hand against the tabletop, just as Mike and Dylan returned with a freshly changed baby.

"There's something I still don't understand," she said, her mind spinning, trying to find the right formula of words to make the equation balance as the guys settled down, the baby half asleep already. "How is it that you— what exactly…" She stumbled through her own thought process, trying to say it aloud.

Just then, Madge interrupted them. "Dessert?"

Laura groaned. "Oh, God."

"What?"

"I'm not pregnant anymore so I don't have an excuse." She patted her belly. She still looked pregnant—at least, Josie thought so, though she'd never say a word. Then again, it took a while for organs to shift and move, and some women held on to weight when it came to breastfeeding. It didn't detract from Laura's natural glow and she was slowly regaining that gait that she had, a self-possession and femininity that Josie could never emulate.

"How about we get two desserts and split them?" Dylan suggested, wolfing down the rest of his food.

"Oh, I like that idea! A gradual transition down." Laura perked up. "What should we get?"

"We have a nice caramel pistachio cheesecake today," Madge said. "And then there's the rhubarb maple cheesecake."

"It's cheesecake day?"

"No, we just happen to have some of these."

"Anything else?" Mike asked.

"Well there's a turmeric-infused candied pecan—"

"Stop there." Dylan held his hand up. "Is it cheesecake?"

"Yup."

"I vote for that as one of them. All in favor say 'aye.'"

Three "ayes" rang out into the air.

"How about two of those?"

Everyone nodded.

"Two slices of that."

"So, Josie, get back to what you were asking. I like watching you be awkward."

"Ha ha," she snapped back. The distraction had rattled her, so she just blurted it out. "How did you two guys know that it was okay to just be together without being together sexually?"

Mike choked on his coffee, Dylan reaching over to whack him in the back *hard*, repeatedly, as the guy coughed and rumbled.

"That's awfully direct."

"And having Alex walk in on your—"

"Okay, okay, I gotcha. I gotcha," Dylan said, holding his hand up. "I'll answer."

"Thanks," Mike croaked out, trying to recover.

"The problem with answering that question…" Dylan said, leaning back against the torn vinyl booth. "Most people don't have a framework for why I'm about to say what I'm about to say." His face changed and he became more serious, more introspective than Josie had ever seen in him.

He looked nervously at Mike and then even more nervously at Laura, and said in one long rush of breath, "I realized that what I wanted more than anything." He stopped. "No, not more, but *as much*, as much as I wanted Jill…I wanted to share her with Mike."

Mike blinked and cleared his throat, running a hand through overgrown blonde waves of hair that tickled the top of his collar. "That's probably what those two guys are going through, Josie—the ones with your niece. That dawning that comes when you realize that there's this ache inside you that *nothing*, nothing has stopped so you learn to live with it—it's just there, like a mole or a scar or an overbite and you try all sorts of things to make it go away.

You date different women, some people try dating other men—"

"Not me," Dylan said.

"It doesn't *matter*, Dylan," Mike said. "Everyone has that ache in them. It's not just that Dylan and me and Laura or people like us do—everyone does. But for me the moment that Jill and Dylan and I came together, I realized that I was missing something for the first time in my life. Not that I *had* something."

Mike's cool Zen demeanor shifted to a layer of excitement that made Josie lean forward in anticipation, his *joie de vivre* contagious. "I realized that I was missing that ache for the first time in my life. Do you know what it's like to go through most of your adolescence and early adulthood in pain and just dealing with it? And then, one day, it's gone. Just gone. *Gone.*" Slamming his palm against the tabletop just as Madge delivered the two pieces of cheesecake.

"This cheesecake's going to be gone in about five seconds. I suggest"—she pointed straight at Laura—"you not put a plate in front of her."

"Hey!" Laura couldn't finish her protest because Madge had left already.

"What about you, Dylan?" Josie asked as they each grabbed a fork and dug in.

The cheesecake was perfection, carafes of a turmeric maple sauce on the side and little cruets filled with candied pecans. The first bite of cheesecake and a candied pecan in her mouth at the same time made her want to stop the conversation instantly and do nothing but have a mouth orgasm.

"Ditto," Dylan said. "Whatever Mike said, that all applies to me."

"Ditto? You're talking about the most significant moment in your emotional journey through life and your answer is 'ditto'?"

"Yup."

"You have the depth of Justin Bieber."

"Ouch," Dylan said, holding his hand over his heart. "That hurt my feeling."

"You mean it hurt my feelings."

"No, my *feeling*. Remember, I'm shallow."

Everyone at the table groaned.

Josie snatched the piece of cheesecake out of his reach. "For that, you get less."

"That's fine. I'll just share with Laura."

"No you won't." Laura grabbed hers.

Mike looked around with a *what about me* expression on his face. "What happened to sharing?"

Josie shoveled a piece of mouth-watering goodness into her mouth and answered, "*You* guys might be into sharing but *I'm* not."

\* \* \*

"You've raised an incompetent asshole with a God complex. Aren't you proud?" Alex declared. Sipping jasmine tea, his stomach felt sour. The last time he'd eaten Thai food hadn't gone well.

Not well at all.

Sitting with his mother in a different restaurant across town didn't help dull the pain of the memory of his last moment with Josie in his apartment.

"I've done no such thing, Alex. I've raised a human being."

"All too human."

"Then I've done well." She smiled,, the kind of grin that made her dimples appear. His mother's face was unreadable, kind brown eyes so much like his trying to read him. This was the look she gave him when she was humoring him. He deserved it.

"I just…how could I have screwed everything up like this?" He'd been a complete ass. In retrospect, he could see it clearly. Affected by stress at work, he'd let it spill over into his love life, biting Josie's head off when all she'd tried to do was to help his family. To be fair, she had made it sound like she might be skirting ethical lines—no one in a double-blind study should know who was in the control group and who wasn't. Alex wouldn't know any more details, though, because he hadn't even tried to reach out. No calls. No texts. Other than going for an occasional run around the park across the street from her apartment, he hadn't gone near her.

"Alex, this isn't you. You don't have these sorts of neurotic insecurities. Where is this coming from?"

*Josie*, he thought.

"Hell if I know," he shrugged. "Between the tough case at work and screwing everything up with Josie, I feel like the person I've been all these years just got a personality transplant. I don't like questioning myself. It feels uncertain and chaotic."

"That's called growth."

"Then growing sucks."

Meribeth pulled back, brow creased with worry. "This is about Josie, isn't it?"

"And work. And Grandpa."

She waved her hand dismissively. "Everyone has missteps at work."

"But I—"

"Alex!" A harsh tone came through in his hissed name. "You're doing the grown-up equivalent of pouting when things don't go your way. It's really unappealing, especially on a twenty-eight-year-old professional."

Ouch.

Right or wrong, the comment hurt. Mostly because she was right.

"A baby landed in the NICU and my professional judgment was called into question, Mom. It's not like I'm moping because Josie wouldn't go to the homecoming dance with me."

"Separate the two. Which one hurts more?"

*Zing!*

"I don't know."

She reached across the table and felt his forehead. "Are you ill? Because my Alex doesn't say 'I don't know' when the answer is in front of his face. Heck, the answer could be doing a lap dance for as obvious as it is."

"Mom!"

"You're in love with Josie and you made a mistake." She took a long sip of tea.

"I'm not—"

"Oh, look at the pasties!"

"The metaphor is overdone. Point taken," he said through gritted teeth.

"I am going to guess you didn't share what's going on at work with her."

He set his tea cup down with a resigned sigh. "You know, in the 1500s that ability of yours led to dunkings. Who is my real dad? A warlock?"

Meribeth howled with laughter, turning heads. "That's the old Alex." His comment about his "real dad" shook her, though—her certainty in dealing with him as if he were a petulant schoolboy had drained out of her. Good.

"Josie grew up without a dad, too. At least, from the age of eleven on."

Meribeth frowned. "He took off?"

"Died. Car accident."

"Oh, how awful." In her trademark gesture, his mother put her splayed palm over her heart. "And her mother?"

He shook his head, picking up the tepid tea absentmindedly, forcing himself to drink it. "She didn't talk much about her. I get the impression it's not a good relationship."

"Two fatherless adults trying to navigate your first real relationship."

"Great, Mom. How high concept of you. You should pitch screenplays to Hollywood."

She laughed, putting her hands up like a director setting

a scene. "Hot ambitious doctor meets fatherless, ambitious nurse—"

"Hot, Mom?" He cocked an eyebrow and tried to suppress an embarrassed grimace.

"Where did you meet again?" Meribeth asked.

"At her friend's birth."

"As her friend crosses over into motherhood." Meribeth scowled. "At her *birth*? Why didn't I know this?"

"You never asked."

"You picked someone up at a *birth*?"

"I'm not proud of it."

"Her best friend's birth?"

"Yes."

"Your timing is…interesting. Most women would be in the room, supporting their friend."

"The dads were there to handle that."

"Did you just say 'dads'? As in plural?"

"Yes." *Oh, shit.* This was headed into territory he didn't want to have to explain. Then again, it took the heat off him, so maybe he should go with it. Too bad the restaurant didn't have a liquor license. He could use a beer or ten right now.

"Her best friend slept with two different men and they don't know who the biological father is?"

"It's…complicated, Mom."

"Sounds intriguing." She leaned forward and propped her chin in her hand. "And Josie's friends with this woman and the dads?"

"Yes."

"Anyone that open-minded is someone I should meet."

"It's a little late for that," he said, blowing a puff of air out, trying to relax his granite shoulders. "She's done with me. I made a horrible comment and questioned her professional ethics when she told me Grandpa needed a second opinion."

"She was right."

"I know." His aunt had received a call this week—the

trial was broken due to overwhelming evidence in favor of the drug. Josie had been right.

"We took Dad back in, but Josie's gone," Meribeth said.

"Gone?"

"They said she's no longer employed there."

Ice water ran through his body. Did that mean she quit? Was she fired? Had she crossed some ethical or legal lines?

"That's all they said?"

"Yes." Her turn to start with the one-word answers.

Rubbing his chin, he felt two days of stubble scratch against his palm. "And the new medication?"

"Dad will go on it soon. We just don't know." She shrugged.

"So Josie was right and I screwed everything up."

"Everything we do can be undone."

"Not this, Mom."

"*Everything*. If you want it bad enough." The look on her face was a blend of compassion and amusement, as if the eighteen years between them conferred some deep wisdom on her that he couldn't access. He wanted to believe it was true, but in recent years he'd come to see that she was just as human as he was, and that it was her compassion and deep devotion to him that mattered more than any perceived wisdom. Right now he just needed someone to listen. And he knew he could always turn to her because she was, after all, *Mom*.

When would he let another woman in like that?

"I do."

"That's what you say at a wedding."

He groaned.

"You left yourself wide open." She chuckled.

*No. I didn't. And that's the problem.*

\* \* \*

Darla's number appeared on her phone as it rang. "Hello?"

"Hey there, gettin' ready to move."

Darla's voice never failed to amuse Josie. After years of living in Boston, she was accused of having a Boston accent whenever she went home. Once in a while she would slip and call "Ant" Cathy "Ont" Cathy, which led to a ripple of giggles and laughs among the family. God forbid she say "rahther" and not "rather." A host of little things, including the word "wicked" being used as an adjective, had separated her from her beginnings. Good.

"So, I'm gettin' ready to come," Darla said, "and I have a few questions."

"What's that?" Josie said.

"How big is the bedroom that I'm gonna have?"

"I don't know…about ten by ten?" Josie was terrible with space and guesstimates.

"Wow, that's downright luxurious," Darla cracked.

"It's what you get in Cambridge, and it's probably bigger than your room back home."

"Fair enough. That's another question—I keep saying I'm moving to Boston, but I'm not…"

"No, you're moving to Cambridge."

"Cambridge is where Harvard is?"

"Yes."

"All the snotty people live there?" Darla asked.

"Not all of them, but plenty of them."

"And what do I need to bring with me?"

"We can get you a bed when you move here, Darla," Josie said. "I can buy it, it's not a problem."

"No, I've got some money saved up," Darla replied.

"You *do*?" Darla was notorious for spending whatever was in her pocket about as fast as she made it.

"Yes, I do."

The defensive tone set Josie's stomach on edge. This was the last thing she needed on a day like this, and it made her need an outlet. Darla could be the unwitting target. Laura couldn't anymore—she was off living house, not playing it, with Mike and Dylan and the baby.

"I got some money."

"You didn't do anything illegal…"

"I don't do anything illegal, Josie, you know that."

Josie thought for a moment. "It's the two guys, isn't it?"

Darla could never lie to her. Finally with a big sigh, she said, "*Yeeeees.*"

"They left you *money*?" Josie was a bit incredulous.

"It's a long story."

"You have a lot of long stories, Darla."

"Well, you're gonna get to hear 'em all now that I'll be be your roommate."

Josie laughed. "You're right. I'm sorry. I'm in a bad mood."

"Why?"

"Oh…stuff."

"Work stuff? Or dick stuff?"

"Dick stuff."

"You have a new man?"

Have. Have? *Do I have a new man?* she wondered. She had. Why did verb tense suddenly mean so much? "I have been dating someone."

"Is he a doctor?"

*Not this again*, she thought. "Yes, he happens to be a doctor."

"Same guy as before?"

"Yes."

"Hot damn! It's about time. You keep telling us that you'll never date a doctor because they suck."

"I've never said that doctors suck."

"Yes you have," Darla argued. "You've said it a million times—they all have God complexes, and they all have egos bigger than the state of Ohio. Josie, you've been saying that for years."

Darla was right. She had been saying that for years and

now she was caught in her own snare. "Yes, he's a doctor. No, he's not an ass. If anybody's the ass, it's me."

"Why are you the ass, Josie?"

"Because I'm stupid."

Darla laughed. "Anybody can be an ass when they're stupid. The question is are you being stupid and turning somebody away you really like?"

Josie had to think about that for a few minutes; it filled her brain with too much chaos and she realized that she didn't have to think about it, she could just defer and deflect. "Darla, I am not gonna talk about this right now," she said with a weary sigh, "so let's talk about you moving here. When are you coming?"

"Tomorrow."

"*Tomorrow!*" Josie shouted. "*Tomorrow?*" She walked into the spare bedroom and looked around. All of her extra junk was crammed in there. About half the floor was covered with boxes and a stray guitar from years ago, and some UMass-logoed stadium blanket a guy she had dated a few times had left. "Tomorrow?"

"It turns out Uncle Mike has a run and can get me as far as some city in Massachusetts called...Stur...bridge."

"Sturbridge, yeah."

"Yeah, well, Mike can get me there and I was hoping maybe you could come and get me? It looks pretty close on a map."

"Darla, Sturbridge is about...an hour and a half outside of Cambridge."

"Aw, damn it! Everything in New England on a map looks like it's close together."

Josie shook her head and wisely kept her mouth shut.

"Is there a bus I can take?"

"You could always hitchhike."

A loud snort came through the phone. "I've had enough of hitchhiking, trust me," she said.

Then Josie remembered, "Oh, that's right, the naked guy."

"And the other naked guy."

"They're both naked hitchhikers?"

"It's a long story," Darla rasped.

"Look, I'll find a way to get somebody to come to Sturbridge to pick you up. Won't you have a bunch of stuff that you need to put in a car? I mean, my car is pretty tiny."

"No," Darla said, "I decided to leave it all behind. All I need are some clothes, a couple of favorite books, my junky old computer, my phone. If I'm gonna start a whole new life and a whole new relationship, then why not start it clean? Why carry my baggage from my past around?" she said quietly.

If Darla had kicked her in the gut, she couldn't have knocked the wind out of Josie any harder. "That makes sense," she choked out. "So, tomorrow…"

"*Yeah, tomorrow!*"

Darla's excitement was just a little bit contagious, and it picked Josie's spirits up. "All right then, we'll see you tomorrow, and I'm so glad you made this leap."

"Me too," Darla said. "The only way to know whether something's gonna work out is to trust yourself, close your eyes, and just jump. Right?"

"Sure," Josie said, "if you say so."

They said their goodbyes and Josie hung up, elated and exhausted at the same time. Josie surveyed her place, this time looking at it through the eyes of a potential roommate.

Her apartment didn't really have a plan; it sort of reflected Josie in that sense. She had the first floor of a triple decker, right across the street from a giant park, but aside from her bedroom and her bathroom, the openness that had once been so appealing to her now became an issue. Darla would need privacy, and the only room that really made sense was this tiny—she wandered over to it…ten by ten would be a stretch—room that didn't even have a closet. Technically her apartment was allowed to be

313

called a "one bedroom" because the little room lacked the basic functions of a bedroom. On the other hand, she wasn't planning to charge Darla any rent for it.

Darla wouldn't complain, she knew that. The poor girl was used to living in a trailer in the middle of nowhere. Josie had grown up in a house. That had seemed to separate kids in their town—if you lived in a house you were somehow better than the kids who lived in the trailer park. Even though Josie didn't believe that, and had never treated Darla or any of her friends who lived in the trailer park any differently, there was a sense of pervasive shame about growing up in any kind of home that was falling apart.

Both of them had lived in dwellings that seemed to reflect their mothers' inner cores. For Aunt Cathy, the porch was perpetually falling apart, as if the entrance to her was so unnavigable that in order to reach her you had to get through the impossible and probably cut yourself and get hurt in the process. With Marlene's house, it was the other way around. The house was never in great shape when her dad had been alive, but he'd cut the lawn, they'd gardened a bit, and even if the house had peeling paint on the outside, on the inside her mom had worked really hard to make it homey and loving.

The first year after the accident, though, absolutely nothing had been done. Literally. Josie had turned eleven just before the accident, and on her twelfth birthday she wanted to invite some friends over and so had surveyed the place. Finding newspapers from the week after her dad had died shoved in a corner had given her a profound sense of just how neglected everything was, as if time had stood still. And as time, in fact, marched on, nothing got done ever again.

Marlene didn't have the gutters cleaned, didn't mow the lawn, didn't buy food, didn't even talk to Josie some days. She just lived in her own dysfunctional and sometimes florid world. Aunt Cathy had tried to explain to Josie that it wasn't that Marlene didn't love her, it was that the accident had changed her brain, made her selfish, made her focused on everything *but* love. The words had seemed harsh but she had known that they were true.

She began pulling her boxes of old books out of the room. Why was she keeping textbooks from ten years ago? It was easy now to get rid of them, something she couldn't have imagined doing six months ago. Back then they had represented her intelligence, as if the book were a physical manifestation of what her brain could do. That seemed so silly. Cleaning out the room made her face years of crap that she had been lugging around with her, and as she spent the next couple of hours sorting and decluttering, she found herself violently throwing object after object into the Goodwill boxes. A broken chess set...gone, an old phone that she'd intended to give to a domestic violence shelter...in the box, clothes that she hadn't worn in years and never would, but that represented some memory...gone.

Carrying the first box to her car that afternoon, the fresh air, the sun shining in a way that New England didn't get very often,  caught her off guard. A handful of clouds hung in the air like little cotton balls, evenly distributed across a vast sky.

The sun shone down, not harsh, but gentle. It reminded her of the day that she and Alex had gone to the river. Her body began to hum as she lifted the box and dumped it into her trunk, not bothering to close it as she marched back into the house. Five boxes later, her mind was still retracing the memory of Alex's hands on her ass, the power of his thighs lifting her up, how her back had scraped against that stone wall, the leaves pressing into her hair, the scent of him etched into her lungs, the hoarse cry that came from her throat as she came and came in his arms.

The room was nearly empty when she found it. An old box with a slightly chewed corner from some sort of creature that had nibbled at it back in the closet of her old house in Ohio. The box fell apart when she picked it up to move it and various items tumbled out. An old diary that she recognized from seventh grade, a corsage from some sort of awards banquet that she'd been to in high school, a trophy and…oh, God…her copy of *A Wrinkle In Time* by Madeleine L'Engle. That was her last gift from her father for her eleventh birthday.

He'd gotten it for her and taken her all the way up to Cleveland to go to the art museum, showing her the Cleveland Public Library and marveling at all of the newfangled computer systems that Peters just didn't have.

Her dad spent plenty of time with her talking about books, but this was different—it was like spending a day being a person with him, and not just a kid. When he had given her the *Wrinkle in Time* and talked excitedly about tesseracts and folding time and *IT*, the one mind that took everyone over until Meg and Calvin fought against it, she decided that she would read it the second she could. She'd been too tired that night, and had gone to sleep, the book set on her dresser. Three days later she'd been consumed with homework and hadn't gotten to it yet, and that night he'd died.

She cradled the book in her hands, turning it over, and then the tears came, mixing with a diffuse fury so great that her arms began to shake. She had never read the book. It represented everything that she hated about her life. It represented the death of her father, the metaphorical death of her mother, the complete 180 shift in her life, and her own self-abuse at the fact that she had not made reading the book and talking about it with her dad a priority, instead letting silly, childish things get in the way.

She'd been watching Darla that night, babysitting. They were at her house playing. Their parents were supposed to come home that night around eleven. When they didn't, Josie just thought that they were late. Morning had come, and still no parents. She'd walked next door to ask Mr. Topper, the neighbor, what to do. He was an old, retired man, a bit grumpy, but completely shocked and surprisingly compassionate when she explained that her parents hadn't come home.

Darla was happy munching Cap'n Crunch cereal and watching Saturday morning cartoons as Josie sat in Mr. Topper's kitchen, drinking an offered glass of orange juice in one of those tiny juice glasses that old people seemed to always have. He'd called the police station, and then very grimly set the phone down, a tortured look in his eyes that had disappeared rather quickly when he cleared his throat, and wouldn't make eye contact again.

"Someone's coming, Josephine. They'll be here soon to…figure all this out."

The rasp in his voice on his last word had made a hot ball of lead form in her stomach. She was smart enough to know that what Mr. Topper wasn't saying told her everything she needed to know. She didn't say anything, because what could she say?

"I have to get back to my little cousin," she had finally said, and now as an adult looking back, it was quite remarkable that he had let her, standing in the doorway and watching her make the trek back to her house, where she had walked past Darla, who was now openly fishing handfuls of cereal out of the box, picking out the red berries and eating them while throwing back the rest.

The years flashed past as she remembered how her room smelled, like the fabric softener her mother had used. The bed wasn't made, but the rest of the room was tidy, dusted even, back when Marlene did that sort of thing. She had picked up the *Wrinkle in Time* book and sat down on her bed, turning to the first page. She had started reading it, and made it to page eleven when the doorbell had rung. The appearance of the police hadn't surprised her, she hadn't expected the woman in the dress who told her that they were there to take her and Darla to go somewhere while they figured out what to do about their parents.

Darla had stood there, her mop of curls pouring down her shoulders. Wild and crazy, those giant green eyes like saucers. Her hand was all the way in the box, down to the elbow, and she was wearing Toy Story pajamas. "What's goin' on?" she'd asked, and the lady had nearly fallen apart.

"I need you to come with me, honey."

"Why do we need to go with you?" Josie had snapped, her finger marking the place where she had stopped reading in the book.

"We're trying to figure out what happened to your parents, and children can't be left alone when their parents are…"

The cop had cut her off with a hard look. Josie recognized him. Sometimes he came to the library where her dad worked. His last name was escaping her, but she knew that he had a daughter two years older than her in the school. Jane…Jane…something. And then, like an angel, the assistant librarian in town, Mrs. Humboldt, had swooped in. To this day, Josie didn't know whether Mr. Topper had called her, or whether she had heard the news, or whether, as Josie liked to imagine it in her eleven-year-old mind, by starting to read the book that her daddy had given her, she had somehow sent a cosmic message to the world.

That a fellow librarian needed to come to another librarian's child's rescue, and rescue she had.

Emphatic and officious, in a way that only a small-town librarian can be, she'd beaten the cops and the woman, who turned out to be a social worker, into submission. She had insisted with the ramrod-straight back of a woman quite accustomed to being listened to and obeyed that the girls were now in her custody, and that had been that.

As she sat in the room she was clearing for Darla, all of those memories flooded her, as if the book were transmitting them by some sort of pulped paper osmosis.

She hated this book. She hated herself. She hated her mother, and her uncle, who had made a terrible, terrible mistake and paid for it with his own life, and her father's life, and her mother's sanity. But most of all, she hated that she was such a coward, that she could not bring herself to read that fucking book, yet she carried it around with her, and always would.

Not being with Alex was the right thing. She was too damaged to be worthy of anyone, to be of any good to anyone other than Darla.

The phone rang, shaking her out of her angry reverie. Of all of the times for Marlene to choose to call, she picked this one. Ignoring it, she let her voicemail click in. She took the book and put it in the farthest corner of the back closet in her bedroom, where it needed to rest, hidden but omnipresent. And then, folding her heart in half like a tesseract, she finished the job with a coldness that filled her with a sense of relief.

* * *

Somehow, Darla had convinced one of the two guys she was with to come all the way out to Sturbridge, pick her up at some truck stop, and bring her into Cambridge. She'd accomplished all of this at one in the morning, though, and had failed to call Josie, so the quiet knock at the door in the middle of the night had made her grab a baseball bat and tiptoe to her own front door. The problem was that she was wearing a cami and underpants, and nothing else. So as she stood there, holding a baseball bat, half naked, when she pulled the curtain aside on the window of her front door, she nearly shoved the baseball bat into Darla's face.

"What the hell are you doing here at 1 a.m.?" she hissed. The taillights of a car moved back down to the main road.

"I got a ride."

"You got a ride at one in the morning?"

"It was the best time I could get here."

Josie undid the deadbolt, and the regular lock, and the chain lock, and let her in. "Jesus Christ, Darla, you scared the shit out of me."

"Apparently I scared the clothes off of you, too. Josie, what are you doing? Isn't this some sort of entryway where other people could see you?"

"Yeah, well, no one's looking at 1 a.m." She tiptoed back to her door, shivering. It may have been warm when she went to bed, but now it was cold. She welcomed Darla into her apartment, and then her little cousin gave her a giant hug. It was almost enough to warm her up. Where Josie was a stick, Darla was all curves and lushness. You would never guess that the two came from sisters. Marlene had been the skinny one, and Cathy had been the pinup girl—at least, that was what their moms always said. Although "pinup girl" wasn't quite right; she thought that came from her grandma. Darla wore a baby blue v-neck t-shirt, old jeans, and flip-flops, and carried just two suitcases.

Josie looked back. "That's it? That's all you brought?"

Darla shrugged. "That's all I need. Where's my room?"

"Come here. I don't even have a bed for you, so you're gonna have to crash on the couch."

"That's okay, I've slept on worse."

"Of course you have."

"Hey," Darla said indignantly.

Josie stared her down. "Is what I just said untrue?"

"No."

"Come here." Josie went in for a second hug, really giving her the time and the embrace that she needed. Darla was shivering just a bit, and Josie held on until both of them had stopped shaking. When she pulled back, Darla was noticeably more relaxed.

"This is a big city," she said. "Nothing like Cleveland or Pittsburgh."

"No, it's actually pretty small."

"Then it *seems* bigger," Darla added.

"That's what she said," Josie joked. The groan that came out of Darla made Josie realize that there was no hope that she was going back to bed. It was time to make some tea, sit down, and chat like sisters.

"Let's go have some tea and talk." Josie showed her into the kitchen. It seemed completely surreal to have Darla *here*, in her escapee life. When she went back to Ohio, it bothered her how easily she fell back into speech patterns and habits of thought that were more from her childhood. Including little things, like craving a cigarette whenever they went to Jerry's. She'd always had a cigarette with her beer until she moved to Boston, and decided that it wasn't worth the fight to try to find a bar that let you smoke. And it also was unsophisticated, if not a bit trashy, at least in Boston, to be a smoker. Everyone where she came from smoked—though Darla, she'd noticed, had never picked up the habit.

As she set the electric kettle going and pulled out about twenty boxes of teas, she heard Darla wandering through the rooms, and then...

"*Oh my god!*"

"What?" Josie said, trying not to shout and wake up the folks who lived above her.

"This is my room?"

"Yeah," Josie winced, "it's a bit small."

"It's *huge!*" Darla came tearing back into the room, her flip-flops making a smacking noise that Josie knew was going to bug her after two days of listening to that.

"It's bigger than my shed."

"Barely." Josie gestured to the boxes of tea and said, "Pick your poison." Josie had known Darla would go straight for the lemon, and she did. "Your shed?"

"I took that old shed out next to the trailer and turned it into my little place."

"You did?" Josie was intrigued. That thing had been

there since they were kids, and was probably home to more muskrats and raccoons than anything else.

"I cleaned it up real nice," Darla said, looking up at the tall ceilings. "Man, it's like something out of a movie in here."

Josie looked up. They were nine-foot ceilings with crown molding around the edges and large cracks through the plaster. It was an older building and she'd loved the charm, how it had been so different from anything she had grown up with in Ohio, and certainly a million miles away from her own home.

"This looks like something out of one of those old-fashioned ice cream shops you see on TV—like in a movie from the 1920s." Darla smiled, her eyes wild and her cheeks quite pink.

How she could be this alert at one in the morning blew Josie away. The kettle whistled, and Josie poured the cups of tea, joining Darla in her Lemon Enjoyment. As they sat at the table, Darla craned her neck around the corner of a wall and looked in the living room again.

"Cool. It looks like something you'd find at an apartment at Kent State."

"It's just thrift-shop finds. You know how well we have that drilled into us." The two shared a look that Josie could not exchange with any other human being on the planet.

Darla nodded and took a sip. "That's what my shed's all about."

"So, tell me about your guys."

"My guys." Peals of laughter poured out of Darla, and her chest shook as she giggled. "My guys. Yeah, I guess I have to think of them as *my guys*."

"My friend Laura thinks of hers as her guys."

Darla stopped cold, half dropping her mug of tea onto the table. "*You know someone else who has guys?*"

"I know someone else who has guys."

"*Holy shit!*" Darla's eyes widened, and she looked like

she was about to choke on something. "I'm not the only one?"

"You didn't invent threesomes, Darla."

"It sure as hell feels like we did, me and Joe and Trevor. I haven't said that aloud to anyone, Josie."

She could see the tension in Darla's chest relax, her body going from that excited, wired sense that you get when you travel long distances by car to a relaxed, easygoing countenance. "You can talk about it here," Josie said. "In fact, you'd better get pretty damn comfortable with it."

"With what?"

"With talking about threesomes."

Darla's face froze, brow furrowed in an expression of incredulity. The tip of her nose was pink and her ears turned red, as a flush crept up her neck and into her jaw. "Why?"

"Remember I told you that the job's with a dating service that my friend's starting?"

"Yeah." Darla's face went slack as she got the implication. She was never a dull girl. "Your friend with the guys is the one starting this?"

"Yes."

"And I'm perfect for the job because…" She left the sentence unfinished, forcing Josie to give her the closure she needed.

"Darla, I tried to talk about this with you on the phone, two different times, so don't give me that look."

"Well…I…but…" Darla stammered. "I would have let you tell me that little detail, Josie…if you had told me that little detail!"

"That makes no sense. You're being tautological."

"I'm being what?"

"You're talking in circles."

"Wait, out here they have a word for that?"

"Yeah, it's called 'Harvard.'"

"Hold on, hold on," Darla said, waving her hands in

the air. "I'm getting paid $40,000 a year to be an office worker in a dating service that caters to, and hooks up, and makes people have—"

"Threesomes."

"You are kidding me."

"Well, you were squealing on the phone, Darla. '$40,000! $40,000! Holy fucking shit, $40,000!' over and over again, and when I tried to give you the details it was like you were walking on coals and dancing after a touchdown all at once on the phone. It was as if I could feel that."

"Well, forty thousand fuckin' dollars a year is unbelievable, Josie."

"Not here."

"In Ohio it sure as hell is. I'm making federal minimum wage. Do you know the difference between $7.25 and $20?"

"Yeah, the difference is Ohio and Eastern Massachusetts." Josie took a sip of her tea. "But look, that's details."

"'Threesome dating service' is a pretty big fuckin' detail. I thought you were saying 'tree-hugger dating service.'"

"What?" Josie snapped, incredulous. "Why would I open one of those?"

"Like it's any weirder than the truth?"

Okay. Darla had her there. "Does it change your attitude about moving out here and working in the job?"

Darla stopped cold. "Oh, hell no!" she said, swinging her blonde bush of hair around over one shoulder. "It's just...man, I'm kinda glad I didn't know that detail."

"Why?"

"It would have been awfully hard to lie to Mama."

They both went silent at that one. Josie didn't have an answer.

"Anything else I don't know about?" Darla's eyebrows were raised so high they almost disappeared into her hairline. Figuring it was best to quit while she was ahead, Josie just shook her head.

"Good."

"Tree-hugger dating service?" Josie snickered.

"What? Trevor and Joe told me all about Boston and how crazy people are out here. How you walk cats on leashes and have doggy daycare. I mean—daycare centers for *dogs*, Josie."

"Lots of people have that."

"Then they're crazy. Babies and toddlers—sure. But what's next? Music classes and massages? French lessons for the puppies?"

"You joke, Darla, but…I think you're going to find Cambridge is like living on another planet."

"That's fine. As long as I can breathe the air, I'll find a way to fit in. For $40,000 a year I can do anything. Even a threesome dating service, apparently."

"And you think doggie daycare is weird?"

Darla laughed, a booming sound that filled the high ceilings. Josie had missed it. "Fair enough."

* * *

The first package for Darla arrived about three weeks after she moved in, and Josie just made sure to set it on the table right inside the apartment where she normally stashed the mail and assorted things, like her sunglasses.

Later that day Darla opened it and said, "Oh, huh…interesting." She pulled out a bright green mug, the same Kelly green you saw all over Boston around St. Patrick's Day or when the Celtics did well. It had the logo for a well-known fertilizer company on it. Darla fished around in the box and said, "That's odd."

"How random," Josie said.

Darla shrugged. "Free mug." She went into the kitchen.

Josie heard the water turn on and guessed she was washing it. Sure enough she was right, as she walked past she saw it sitting in the dish rack, already drying. It would stick out like a green thumb in the cabinet, next to Josie's white dishes. Being roommates meant having company, and it also meant questioning the omnipresent rules she'd developed in her head for her daily life, rules about things like matching dishes. She had to learn to unclench a little.

Later that week another package came addressed to Darla, so Josie left it in the same place and didn't think much of it.

The curious part about these seemingly-random packages, which began to appear with increasing frequency, was that there was no rhyme or reason to what arrived. Soon Darla was on a first-name basis with Luis, the formerly anonymous UPS guy. Josie had seen him before, maybe once a month. Darla's room, and then the kitchen were increasingly cluttered with key chains and mugs and anything else a brand name could be printed on. One box arrived with fifty romance novels, all of them historical romance of the type that Josie remembered Aunt Cathy reading voraciously when they were younger.

As Darla opened them, she burst out laughing. "This is one of Mama's favorite authors," she said, scrunching up her face.

They were in jammies, hanging out, watching *Downton Abbey*, which Josie had introduced Darla to. Both had become Edwardian fans in an instant, scandalized by the wealthy family's aristocratic pursuits.

"Your mom sent you fifty romance novels that you'll probably never read?"

Darla pursed her lips and thought about that for a minute. "Hold on," she said, walking over to the small table at the entrance of the apartment and grabbing her flip phone. She auto dialed, and then from a distance Josie could hear her Aunt Cathy's raspy voice. Listening only to Darla's side of the conversation, Josie was fascinated.

"Hey, Mama...Yeah, I'm good...Yep, still visiting my friends when I'm not working...Yep, yep, Trevor's still playin'…and Joe, too…I'm not gonna talk about that. Not gonna talk about that either." The shine in Darla's eyes faded with each comment. "Nope, not that either." She frowned. "How's Uncle Mike? I can change the subject if I want to. Yeah, speaking of changing subjects, Mama, what is this shit you're sending me?"

Josie heard Aunt Cathy shout, "*SHIT?* That ain't shit!"

Darla held the phone away from her ear about a foot and just shook her head. When the yelling stopped, she replaced the phone on her ear. "Okay, Mama, why do I have fifty romance novels from your favorite author?"

A squeal of delight came through the phone, and again, Darla stretched her arm out to avoid being deafened. The sounds made Josie's cat sprint from the room and hide under her bed.

"I won! I won!" Josie could hear Aunt Cathy crowing.

"You won *what?*" Darla barked towards the phone.

"I won the fifty romance novel contest!" The elated voice came tinnily through the speaker.

Josie froze, her eyes locking with Darla's. They simultaneously put their hands on their hips, cocked their heads, and said quietly, "Contest?"

"Contest, Mama?" Darla repeated, holding the phone close again.

Josie couldn't hear the answer anymore, but Darla's face ran through nineteen different emotions in two minutes of just listening to her mother. Her brow furrowed, one eyebrow cocked up, her eyes got wide, she did a facepalm to the forehead, then she began pacing the length of the living room, her foot brushing against an old, braided rug that Josie had gotten for free when an upstairs neighbor had moving out.

Finally, Darla said, "You're using our address?" and Josie got it. She just shook her head and padded her way into the kitchen, Dame Maggie Smith on pause for quite a while, she imagined, before she and Darla would get back to the Abbey. As she made herself a cup of decaf, she waited, hearing intermittent bits of the conversation.

"No, he's not naked all the time. Yes, things are working out with Josie. My job? It's going good. I don't know, she's got this doctor she might be…"

Josie slammed the green fertilizer company mug on the counter, and poured herself a vicious cup of decaf, sprinkling a little cinnamon in for the hell of it and then adding a heavy dose of milk. She heard the snap of a phone shutting, and then the slam of it against a table.

"You won't believe this one!" Darla shouted.

"Let me guess—she's using this address and your name for sweeping."

The look of genuine shock on Darla's face, as if she couldn't put together a paint-by-numbers scenario that all added up to one color, made Josie laugh.

"That's exactly what she's been doing. How'd you guess?"

"It's the most logical explanation for why we're getting all this crap."

"Don't tell me that a foam toilet paperweight from a pharmaceutical company is crap now, Josephine. It is perfectly good winnings, with a manufacturer's retail value of $13, which Mama will use to calculate out her hourly rate of $3.22 for all her hard work." Darla had taken on the supercilious tone of Cathy at her best, and it made Josie shrug and smile.

"You know, I don't care if she does this if it makes her happy," Josie said.

Darla sighed with relief, her shoulders dropping. She folded herself into a chair, her breasts reminding Josie of Laura's swell. They seemed to have gotten, in triplicate, everything that Josie had not received from the Endowment Fairy, and she wondered what it would be like to be that lush.

"I think we can expect a steady supply of this stuff. I'm glad you say that you don't mind 'cuz Mama seemed so happy to be able to now have two addresses where she could sweep from, and she said that if we get anything good that she can use to please send it back to her, otherwise it's ours to keep, and it's her way of thinking about us in the big city."

Josie held up the green mug with gusto. "To Cathy," she said. Darla scrambled to get a glass of water and the two toasted to Darla's mom and Josie's stalwart aunt.

"What kinds of contests does she enter, Darla?"

"Cash, trips, kitchen makeovers, new houses, gift cards to restaurants, jewelry, books, magazine subscriptions, although she stopped doing that when we got about two hundred of 'em. That kind of stuff."

"So, you could win any of those things?"

"I could win a year's supply of LSAT tutoring, for all I know," Darla said. "It's never anything good, it's always this crazy stuff that companies are giving away 'cuz they're tryin' to boost morale or—spread the word about their product. At one point Mama found a glitch in the software for one of these websites, and we won three hundred stuffed hot dogs."

"Three hundred *what?*"

"Stuffed hot dog plush toys," Darla said. "Mama took a bunch of 'em and shoved 'em in a pillowcase and said it was a pillow. The rest she gave to some humane society shelter for the dogs. It's what she does and it makes her happy."

"At least now we know where all this is coming from." Josie wandered back and started fishing through the box of books. "*Her Highlander's Heinie?*" She looked at Darla. "Seriously?"

Darla shrugged. "I've heard worse."

"I guess it can't be any worse than *Downton Abbey*, right?" Josie said. "Shouldn't we get back to find out what James will do next and with which nobleman?"

Darla threw her arms around Josie suddenly. The hug caught her off guard, but she liked it. No one had touched her in days. "Thank you, Josie."

"Thank *you*," she said, pulling back. "You're helping me make some sense of this crazy business we're both working in."

"Once we get this figured out, let's move on to your crazy love life."

"My love life isn't crazy, it's nonexistent."

"Why aren't you with him?" Darla said, her face suddenly serious. Those big green eyes went all innocent and sad, reminding Josie of how Darla had looked that day. How she had questioned Mrs. Humboldt about being dragged home to pack a bag, how her face had been so cherubic, and sweet, and needy.

"Because he thinks I did something unethical, and was a jerk before I had the chance to explain."

"Ooooooh. Ouch."

"Yeah, ouch." Tears filled Josie's eyes as the reality of what she said really sank in.

"You really love him, don't you?" Darla said softly. The empathy in her tone made Josie's tears spill over her lower lids and pour down her cheeks.

"I don't know what I feel for him."

"I do. It's called love. You never cry over guys."

"I cried over Davey Rockland."

"That's because he drove over your foot when he was learning how to drive his go-kart."

They laughed, Josie wiping the tears away. "Alex did the equivalent with my heart. His grandfather is one of the Alzheimer's patients in the trial I work on. Worked on." She faltered. Tendering her resignation hadn't been easy. Gian had taken it gracefully.

"And?"

"And I tried to tell him I thought his grandfather might not be receiving the drug that was helping other patients, and to get a second opinion, and he freaked on me. Went on about professional ethics and putting the research trial in jeopardy."

"Is he that kind of guy?"

"What kind?"

"The freak-out kind?"

The question stumped her. "No, actually. He's not."

"So maybe there's more going on with him than you know about."

"He made fun of me for not being a doctor."

"Ouch." Darla drank her tea. "But is that enough to give up?"

"It appears to be for him. He hasn't contacted me at all. It's been weeks."

A long sigh from Darla made the tears spring back. It was the sound of resignation, of defeat, and it echoed inside Josie's heart.

"If it's over, you need to move on."

"I know."

"If not...then you need to try one more time."

"I don't think my heart can handle being crushed again."

"You handled being run over twice by Davey." Darla's chest shook with giggles.

"That was my foot. My heart isn't quite as resilient."

"And Alex isn't Davey."

"Dear God, no. What an ass he was. How any grown woman would consider dating him..." Josie shivered. Darla's face went a strange shade of green.

Both yawned simultaneously.

Josie said, "I'm taking a nap." Sleep would give her a break from her never-ending questioning.

Her only break.

* * *

She straddled a cello, her fingers wrapped around the bow, her arm playing expertly as her nude body bent into the instrument, legs wrapped around the edges of the veneered wood, her skin melding into the stringed wonder as if she were making love to it. Hair wild and untamed, her breasts pressed into the back of the cello, she felt the music well up from her fingers, her elbow, her arm, her mind as if emanating from her core. Wet and ready for something greater than herself, her nipples slid with a friction of climax against the grain of the wood, body heated by a thick wall of muscle behind her, peppered with a sprinkling of ticklish hair. Thick thighs cupped her hips and ass, a hard, throbbing erection urgent against her cleft, his heartbeat the metronome by which she timed her skillful playing.

Hands stroked her waist, sliding up her ribcage, fingers pinching her nipples as she struggled to maintain composure, her body working from muscle memory to play the song, her core clenching and flushing in aroused agony as his hot breath tickled her shoulder, his mouth ravaged her earlobe, his hard shaft nudged her ass.

Play she did, in fury and unabashed glory, his hands settling in the valley of her heat, wetness slicking fingers that began to stroke her in time to the macrobeat, sweet love coming through each caress until the final crescendo ended the song, the cello flung across the room by rippling forearms that splintered it as it slammed into the wall, her body next, his enormity filling her, piercing her, *impaling* her with a sliding immediacy. Hands filled with her flesh as her legs gripped his hips, mouths finding each other, the hot pink nub now thrusting against his pelvis as he hammered his own beat into her.

*Alex Alex Alex* she hummed in three-four time, his cock the bow that played her strings, his hips the wood grain veneer, his neck the instrument's neck, his mouth her score. He was the conductor, the composer, the creator and her god...

And then she woke up, pelvis thrusting up into empty air, her walls twitching against flesh that wasn't there, palms aching for a hot man who was only in her dream, the sinister mistress of memory spinning with her slumber to conjure a man she had no right to touch now.

Tortured and gasping, her limbs arched and then curved inward, Josie panted into the twilight, throat tight and fingers wet with her scent. Whatever she said in broad daylight did not matter; her body betrayed her, seeking what she really needed.

*Alex.*

The tears came then, slamming into her as hard as her unsought orgasm, choking and loud, as much a release as her dreamed climax, yet not so sweet.

\* \* \*

The cat was the first clue. Josie had joined him in a ray of sunshine that poured in between the front window's curtains, and as she sat there, eyes closed, face tipped up to the sun, she took a sip of coffee and nearly choked on it. Pulling up with its front paw pads, the cat practically scaled the window until it was stretched out, lean and graceful, its nose pressed against the glass.

*What is he looking at*, she wondered, and then saw the runner rounding the park across the street. The cat's eyes tracked it, and Josie joined in. The runner's long legs, strong and muscled, wearing shorts and a tank in the cool early morning. She knew before she even set eyes on his face that it was Alex, and when he glanced over at her window, that confirmed it. She looked away quickly so their eyes wouldn't meet, not wanting him to know she was watching him, and certainly not wanting him to realize that she knew *he* was watching *her*.

She reached over and pulled the animal into her lap, stroking its fur, both of them tilting their heads to the right as Alex raced by. She craned her neck around, and at that point the cat sauntered away, its need for petting sated. Oh, how jealous Josie was. If only her needs were that simple.

Across the baseball field she saw him. He must have rounded the corner, and now he flew past at a greater distance. He ran behind the dugout fence across the large field, and then a series of multicolored metal pipes that made up parts of the children's playground; her eyes assembled the fleeting glimpses into a coherent whole. Breaking away from her trance, she padded back into the kitchen, made herself another cup of coffee, and very intentionally rooted herself at the kitchen table. She would not, absolutely would *not*, go back and gawk, trying to capture more pieces of him, as if she could hold them together and turn them into something she could touch.

Her ears perked up before she even realized that someone was near. As the realization set in, slowly she turned her head to find a strange man standing in the doorway between the kitchen and the hallway, as if a blonde surfer model had appeared out of thin air. In the seconds that her mind registered his presence, she took him in. Tall, at least as tall as Alex, with blonde, shaggy hair and eyes so bright blue they rivaled Mike's. His shoulders were broad and his chest was sculpted, the skin a little goosefleshed around his pecs, as it narrowed impossibly into curves of a six-pack that went down to a thicker thatch of hair at the waistband of impossibly painted-on boxer briefs, made of a darker, smoky blue.

Perhaps she took too long to assess the perfection of this body in front of her because it was the man, and not Josie, who cleared his throat. He dipped his head and slid his arms into a shirt, ending her reflexively lascivious appraisal before it even occurred to her that strange shirtless men surprising her in her own kitchen should maybe make her feel threatened, not intrigued. Less than a second into that thought, she figured out who he was. Another sip of coffee bought her manners, and her racing heart, a second to compose themselves.

"You must be Trevor," she said quietly, pinching her lips together to hide the smile that tried to creep out, involuntarily sultry and flirtatious. She couldn't believe this was coming out of her. Dear God, no wonder Darla had fallen for him. Josie would have had sex with him in a rest area, too, even an *Ohio* rest area. He was too young for her, she told herself. Old enough, of course, but still, she felt a little dirty thinking about him this way.

He crossed the kitchen with two steps and sat down next to her, the movement so fluid and confident that it made all sorts of parts of her perk up, not just her ears. Suddenly she didn't need the coffee to be fully awake. Long athlete's legs stretched out, nearly brushing against her calf, as he crossed his feet at the ankles and didn't seem to care that he sat before her in his underwear and a tight cotton t-shirt.

"I'm Trevor, yeah," he said, leaning forward and shaking her hand. That same hand then went and raked the top of his hair. "Man, Darla didn't tell you we were staying over?"

*We?* Josie thought. "No, uh, but it's fine, you know, hey." She held her palm up and leaned back, unconsciously shifting her shoulders back and pushing out whatever she had that passed for breasts. The guy was hypnotic; he had an instant effect on her that she found a bit dizzying. She wanted to reach out and just stroke one index finger down the ski slope of his perfect ab muscles, but held back, knowing that it would be rude.

*It would be rude, right?* she thought, the temptation so great that she cursed herself on the inside. *Down girl, down*, she almost muttered aloud.

"Oh, it's fine…uh, hey, help yourself to some coffee," she said, gesturing to the Keurig, holding herself back from jumping up.

Trevor stood, opened the cupboard above the coffee machine, and emitted a low whistle. "Have enough coffee mugs?" The cabinet looked like a Gay Pride Parade banner, every color of the rainbow represented in Darla's coffee mugs. In fact, she'd organized them in ROY G BIV color order. Darla had teased Josie about her OCD nature, but it had been more of a challenge to see whether Cathy's "winnings" really were enough to make a rainbow.

Turned out they were.

"I think we could use a few more," Josie mused.

Trevor plucked an orange mug emblazoned with a logo for some information archive service, made himself a cup of coffee, and then, when he came back to sit down, said, "You okay?" The words were clipped, no empathy in them, just a politeness that she had found ingrained in a lot of the students she had met at work.

"I'm fine," she said, giving back the qualified, neatly controlled, upper-middle-class answer. Giggling poured down the hall from the other room, and then the very sharp, unmistakable sound of a hand smacking against flesh. Trevor had the decency to blush slightly and stop making eye contact with Josie. "You don't have to be embarrassed," she said, "it's not you in there."

He frowned. "You're right, it's *not* me in there. It should be." He stood and wandered back down the hallway to Darla's bedroom, coffee mug in hand.

A long whoosh of held breath poured out of her, her body tingling, her core on fire. *You have got to be fucking kidding me*, she thought. Pinned between Alex on the outside, and Trevor Connor of all people, and probably Joe Ross, on the other side, she found herself in a vice of arousal, completely unable to touch anyone right now, except herself. Thank god for battery-operated boyfriends. She had a drawer full of them, and would probably use them later to try to exorcise this raging case of frustration. Better living through plastics. Another slap, and then Darla screamed, "Put it on a different setting, that one's too fast!"

*Note to self*, Josie thought, *add earplugs to shopping list.* Click. Someone, probably Trevor, had the decency to close the bedroom door. All Josie heard now was muffled sounds of pleasure. A level of pleasure, she assumed, that she herself would only be able to mimic with a rabbit and a few Sylvia Day novels. Even at that, it would be a poor, pathetic second to what Darla was having right now.

With a shaking hand, she made another cup of coffee, and sat down to listen to it gurgle. It sounded like the death rattle of her own sex life. A door opened, feet padded down the hall, and then a door closed. She heard the unmistakable sound of a shower starting. Her next shower would be a cold shower, dammit.

And then…chest. Blonde hair, perfect, smooth tan skin, and in strolled Trevor to open the refrigerator door, bend down, and give her a glorious view of a muscled ass hard as a marble countertop. She could think of plenty of other tasty things that could be done with that…

"Hey, Josie, whatcha doin'?" Darla walked up behind her and placed a friendly hand on her shoulder.

"Nothin'," Josie said, reaching up to wipe an imaginary bit of drool off the corner of her mouth. It turned out it wasn't so imaginary. What the hell was she doing? These were Darla's guys, it wasn't like they were in competition—she wasn't interested in them, not beyond the surface level of ogling them. The guy she really wanted was outside, running past her house. Or maybe he'd gone home by now. She wasn't sure.

Darla wore an overstretched Spongebob Squarepants shirt, and that was *it*. It barely came to the top of her thighs. Josie turned away when Darla did exactly what Trevor did, bending into the fridge to pick up a plate of fruit. Not quickly enough, though, to miss the bright red slap mark on Darla's thigh, and Josie just closed her eyes and shook her head. *They're adults, they're adults, they're adults,* she said over and over in her head, trying to will away the pictures popping through her mind. Maybe this was what Laura meant when she kept saying "TMI," but maybe it was just Josie.

The three of them sat together, plowing through the cheese and fruit that Darla and Trevor had pulled out. No one seemed to need to make small talk, which Josie didn't mind. When the coffeemaker gasped its last steamy, full-throated sound, she grabbed her cup, and walked over to the side window, staring out into the alley, simply to have something to do with herself that didn't involved eating Trevor with her eyes.

Footsteps in the hallway again, and then she turned, as if in slow motion, to find herself staring at the equivalent of a Men's *Vogue* cover model. This must be Joe Ross, and my my, was he everything that Darla had described—and more—damp and 3D right in front of her. He held a towel around his hips. *A rather small towel,* Josie noted, for you could see the indent of his muscle bending into his hip, that kind of carved look, tapering down to a bulge that made her marvel at his body as a form of art.

If it had just been the muscled dimpling of his skin against flesh, she would have been impressed. But what took the breath out of her lungs and made the air dance a little in front of her eyes, was the teasing taunting sensual combination of body, and face, and skin, and damp scent, and everything. Her eyes met his and he was startled, stepping back and clinging to the towel in his left hand, holding his only semblance of privacy.

"I'm sorry. I didn't know anyone else was here," he said, again with that cultivated politeness that no man from her hometown was capable of.

"That's okay, I'm...uh, Josie," she said, holding one hand up in a wave.

"I'm Joe," he said. He started to reach out to shake her hand with his right, open hand, and as he walked forward the towel slipped just enough for her to know that Joe dressed to the *right.*

"Oh...uh...sorry," he said, pulling back. "I think it would be better to introduce myself when I'm a little more presentable."

*Drop the towel and you'll be more than presentable,* she thought, and then froze, hoping that this was not one of those times where the words had actually come out of her mouth. No one was looking at her with an expression of horror, so it seemed safe to assume that the lascivious thought had stayed firmly in place in her mind.

Goddammit, she had expected to have her house invaded by Darla, and had known, in theory, that the two guys would at least sometimes come with the package. Darla had warned her that they didn't have their own place lined up yet for starting law school in late August, and Josie had figured that the occasional overnight would be no big deal. Now, she realized, she needed to have a giant bowl of buttered popcorn, a side of Skittles, and a big old Diet Coke for breakfast every morning, so she could properly enjoy the show. *Was that bad of her, to think that way?* Who cared; it was her apartment. This was better than Netflix.

And *waaaay* better than *Downton Abbey.*

"Why don't we go out on the porch and have our breakfast?" Darla said, walking out of the kitchen, her ass filling out her shirt in a way that Josie could never fill anything. Within what felt like seconds Darla was back, wearing a pair of shorts and a tank top, fluffing her hair and making herself a quick cup of coffee. She chose a lovely gray mug with a chimney sweep's logo on it. "C'mon, let's go out on the porch and sit and enjoy the weather."

"It's late July in Boston. There is no enjoyable weather unless you like to drink the air," Josie said.

Trevor snorted, but stood and followed Darla. As they made their way through the living room, the cat backed up into the windowsill and forced Josie's eyes to follow. Alex ran past. *Dammit!*

"Nice form," Trevor muttered.

"Thanks," Darla chirped.

"I meant that guy," he said, pointing to Alex. "He's got good form for a runner. I used to run cross country."

They settled into cheap plastic chairs Darla had trash-picked in the weeks she'd been living here. The streets of Cambridge on trash night had swiftly become Darla's version of Target. There was nothing she couldn't find when determined. Josie had to admit that the chairs were a nice touch. The neighbors used them, too, with Darla's hearty blessing. Neighbors who had ignored Josie for years were suddenly friendlier. Everyone seemed to know Darla.

Of course they did.

"Hey there!" Darla shouted, waving wildly at Alex as Josie shrank. A hand went up and waved backwards, as Alex had already passed.

"Stop it!" she hissed at Darla.

"Why? You know him?"

Joe saved her from answering that question, taking a seat between her and Darla. Dressed in loose basketball shorts, a shiny green color with white piping, the edge of his boxer briefs peeked out over the waistband, right under his navel. As he slouched, the tanned skin of his belly didn't roll or pucker. It clung to the little sculpted peaks of muscle in his six pack.

Make that *eight* pack.

She forced herself to break her gaze, knowing she'd look like a fool if caught staring at Joe. Turning her head, she saw Alex's form turn the corner to the left and pass out of sight, his powerful legs propelling him away from her.

This was killing her.

Something had to give.

\* \* \*

*Who was that on Josie's porch?* he wondered. The blonde was tall and built like a muscular swimmer, with overgrown, sun-bleached hair and the cocky confidence of a guy in his early twenties. Three or four times a week he ran on this path, knocking off four miles easily, hoping he might catch a glimpse of Josie. This was the first time it had actually happened, though, her little face peeking out from the curtains. Dotty or Crackhead had joined her—

probably Dotty. Knowing their names made him grin.

And then a young blonde woman, curvy and loud, her hair long and wild, her face animated. She touched the guy possessively. *Hers.*

Holding his breath and running were mutually exclusive, the air coming out in a great whoosh of relief. Whew. The guy wasn't with Josie. He didn't think he could handle that. Pushing his form as he ran past, he pumped his arms, legs eating the earth, running far faster than his six-to-seven-minute-mile pace. Not that he was competing with the blonde.

Of course not.

His heart raced and his calves began to ache as he made his way right past them, but he wouldn't break his new pace until he was out of sight. Whatever was going on, he wouldn't let himself look weak.

The blonde woman shouted something at him and he waved absentmindedly, then, mercifully, he hit the left turn, giving him a chance to slow way down and catch his breath. Fucking ego. Why did he care what some strange guy thought?

He didn't.

He cared what *Josie* thought.

Rounding the next corner, he knew that the bushes and playground would hide him from them until he came back up this loop. This was his third loop, which meant pushing harder than he'd expected, as each loop was two miles. Six miles wasn't that hard.

How about eight?

Eight would give him one more go-around to see what, exactly, was going on. Lungs screaming in protest, hamstrings so tight he could string a guitar with them, he continued.

Because now, he saw, there was another guy.

Sitting right next to Josie.

* * *

"You're staring at his scar, aren't you?" Darla asked Josie, who was still trying to figure out where it was safe to look.

"Uh…what?" Josie felt dazed by Joe's presence. He looked like something out of Greek mythology, sipping from a black and gold mug that said *Lipovac HVAC* on it.

"Joe's scar."

"His what?" And then she saw it, the thinnest of scars on his chest, but deep and long.

"Can you guess what that's from? Josie's a nurse," Darla explained to Joe, who nodded.

"Open-heart surgery? Infant?"

Darla's eye widened. "Good."

"Yeah," Joe said, nervous. He seemed uptight, suddenly, as if he didn't enjoy being the center of attention. Suddenly sympathetic, she imagined he was uncomfortable precisely because he was so gorgeous. Being the center of attention must be his default. Who wants to be under the microscope like that?

"Touch it!" Darla chirped.

"Touch it?" Josie wanted to touch *Alex*. Not this very … nice … young boyfriend. One of Darla's boyfriends. Darla had two and Josie had none.

"It feels so neat," Darla said, demonstrating by running her index and middle fingers down the long, bumpy line. "Can you imagine? He was just a bitty baby when it was done. Three months."

Maybe Josie did want to touch. Just a little. She reached out tentatively, her approach slow and her fingers slightly curled, like she was approaching a friendly-seeming, but unfamiliar, dog.

"Hey, here comes that runner again. Damn, he's fast," Trevor added, staring down the street. They all turned to watch Alex, whose body was slick with sweat, hair soaked, face intense and determined. His calves tightened and his tendons stood out, his body in perfect form as he ran, nearly parallel to them now. Flooded with desire and an overwhelming urge to fling herself across the street and into his arms, Josie sighed as her eyes took him in, her gaze sliding from his glutes to his sweaty chest to his face, how his calves tightened. Her breath caught and she put an arm out to steady herself; her fingers made contact with Joe's forgotten scar.

Her eyes locked with Alex's. The look lingered, his intensity riveted on her by an order of magnitude so high she couldn't imagine that mathematicians and physicists had discovered it. In Alex's eyes she saw pain, confusion, frustration, apology—and her future.

And then he slammed face-first into a *No Parking* sign.

# Chapter Thirteen

She. Was. Touching. Him.

That guy. The one next to her in the green shorts, lounging like some model from an Abercrombie ad. The kind of guy Alex had played basketball with in high school. The too-perfect rich kid who had everything spread out before him on a platter—including girls—and who walked through life as if it were water, parents treating him like the New Fucking Messiah.

That guy.

Josie's fingers were on him. Caressing his chest. Intimate and casual, like a lover. Her hands were supposed to touch Alex. Not that guy. Never that guy.

*Never.*

White rage raced through his veins as he caught her eyes, the exchange of emotion like a supernova pulse of energy. Could she feel it, too? Her face said so many things he wanted to hear. *Hello. I miss you. Can we talk? It's good to see you. I'm sorry.*

*No, Josie. I'm sorry.*

*I'm the one who screwed up.*

And then—hope. Her face broadened with the first hint of a smile, hand pulling back from the flesh bag who

344

didn't deserve her, and Alex felt grounded again. Centered. Like he'd been whiplashed emotionally back into a core of everything, pulling together the disparate pieces of himself that had slowly peeled away these past weeks.

Found.

In her eyes.

*BAM!*

His face felt it first, the smack of unexpected resistance against his head a ringing sort of annoyance, turning his eyes from Josie and rocketing him into a stellar shock. *What the fuck?* And then the pain seeped in, slow at first but roaring as his head ricocheted back, his breastbone striking something slim and hard, feet flying out from under him.

Instinct made his arms go back to catch himself, but then training overrode instinct. Surgeons needed to prize their hands above all else, so he held his hands up, still unaware of what was happening, but knowing he needed to save the hands at all costs. Pivoting in mid-air, he came down not on his back but instead on his hip, then shoulder, and finally the resounding thump of a melon hitting the ground.

*That*, he thought, *would be my head.*

A scream. His name.

Then nothing.

* * *

"Alex!" Josie cried, sprinting from the porch out into the street. *Please let him be okay. Please please please.* Those few seconds of eye contact had given her more serenity than she'd had in ages. A contract of promises in one yearning look had been initiated and she couldn't have it all fade away now. *Please please please.*

"Alex?" Darla shouted. "*The* Alex? Hey, Josie! Watch for cars!"

Trevor and Joe flashed past her, legs pushing harder, athletic prowess beating out her under-fit form. Alex was bleeding from his cheek, lying motionless, but breathing.

"Don't move him!" she screeched. "Darla, get my first-aid kit. Under the bathroom sink." *Treat him like a trauma patient,* she told herself.

Because he was.

He was so damn still, the rise and fall of his chest as he took a breath and the steady trickle of blood from his face wound both the only signs that he was alive. Legs rested on the debris-covered sidewalk; he'd fallen a few feet short of a big stretch of bottle-green glass, someone's litter from a beer binge gone wrong. Had he fallen in that...

Blood flowed from a cut right along the top of the cheekbone, tearing the soft flesh that framed his eye. Grabbing the edge of her shirt, Josie pressed hard against it, giving it pressure but avoiding moving his neck.

"What can we do?" asked Trevor, Joe standing beside him. "Anything?"

"Should we call 911?" Joe asked. "My phone's back in the apartment, but I can run and—"

"No 911," Alex moaned.

"Here!" Darla rasped, placing the frustratingly inadequate first-aid kit on the pavement. Josie needed to focus, and as she ripped through the kit, she found gauze to press against his gash and staunch the bleeding. Alex rolled from his side onto his back, groaning, changing the pressure she applied, making a small flap of skin peel back. Repositioning her hand, she made sure she pushed hard enough to stop what she now saw was a half-inch rip in the skin.

"Don't touch him," Alex whispered, eyes closed. Josie's heart did a salsa beat in her chest as her mind went into triage mode. He was moving his legs fine, knees up, now resting on his back. His hands and arms seemed safe as he rested his palms against his flat belly. The faded blue t-shirt he wore was yanked up, his bare back against the cracked pavement, and his skin glistened with sweat against the hair covering his muscled belly.

"Don't touch who?" *Was he delirious?*

"I think we should call 911," Joe declared.

"Ah, God, no." Alex struggled to sit up as Josie gingerly pulled the gauze back. The bleeding was slowing down. "No 911. I'm fine."

"Dude, you are *so* not fine," Trevor said, bending down to help Alex sit up.

"They say doctors make the worst patients," Darla announced.

Her guys looked at her, puzzled.

"You know him?" Joe asked, one eyebrow cocked.

"Josie does." Darla smirked.

"Shut the fuck up," Josie hissed. Darla's smile drained, and she pulled Trevor and Joe aside.

Alex couldn't balance in a sitting position, and his left arm stretched down in a funny way. Eyes closed, he rested with his head between his knees.

"Alex? Did you hit your head?" Waving Darla over, she gestured for her to take over with the pressure. Carefully, Josie pulled Alex's head up to make eye contact.

"Alex? Honey? Open your eyes so I can see you," she crooned, the voice natural and flowing.

Hazy and unfocused, his eye contact was poor but improved within seconds. "Josie? What happened? Did I run into a car?"

"Parking sign," Joe explained.

"Not you," Alex groaned.

"What did I do?" Joe asked, palms up.

Alex's eyes shifted from Joe to Josie. "Don't touch him," he said.

"Why are you talking about yourself in the third person? Are you the Queen of England? Bob Dole?"

"I'm not," Alex growled.

"He's talking about Joe," Darla whispered.

"Joe? What? I—" And then it hit her. The long, soulful look from Alex. His repeated loops around the park. He was checking out the situation on her porch, worried she'd moved on and was dating someone.

He was *worried*.

That meant he hadn't written her off.

"You're fast for an old guy," Trevor said, a tone of respect in his voice.

Alex winced, trying to steady himself without using his hands, but needing Trevor to support him. "Uh, thanks."

"Pain that bad?"

"No. Being called an 'old guy.' How old are *you*, anyway?" He gave Trevor a resentful, bloody side-eye.

Josie pulled the gauze back and searched for antiseptic solution. Alex gingerly moved his right arm, trying to wave her off. "You can stop. I'm fine. I'll dress it at home."

"You're not fine," she said, relief flooding her. "I got the bleeding stopped, but you need to go to an ER. It looks like you hurt your shoulder and maybe your hip."

"You called me 'honey,'" he said, smiling, then frowning, then struggling not to move his face muscles.

"I do that to all the guys who run into *No Parking* signs around here."

"I like it."

"You like hurting yourself?"

"Josie," he said softly, exhaling slowly. Was that a begging, a pleading in his voice? Or more of a reproachful tone? Was she ruining this moment—or should there even *be* a moment when he was injured and bleeding?

She would have to remember to ponder, sometime, how it was that they had moments during what were usually considered emergent situations—births, accidental traumas. No time for that speculation now—or for the possibility that the emergency at hand might, indirectly, be her fault.

Struggling to stand, Alex put his weight on his right leg, Trevor supporting him as Darla crouched, then stood, continuing pressure on the wound.

"I'm fine," he groused.

And then nearly fell as his left hip went on him. Only

Trevor's strength kept him upright.

"Let's get you over to Josie's," Trevor said in a low, authoritative voice. It made Josie's backbone straighten, and Darla's eyes flashed with surprise.

The biggest shock was that Alex acquiesced, regarding Trevor a second time, now with some respect. Hopping at first, by the time they crossed the street and made it to Josie's steps, Alex had modest control of his left leg.

"I don't think I fractured anything," he stated.

"You couldn't walk if you had," Josie answered, carrying the first-aid kit and thunking it on the porch.

"Actually, I've seen patients who could walk with hairline hip fractures," Alex replied, his voice taking on that doctor tone Josie had come to associate with rolled eyes.

Her own eyes, that is.

"Your X-ray vision powers are duly noted, doctor. If you ever leave medicine you can always go into a career as a medical intuitive. Or Superman."

"I'm *fine*."

Josie fished around in the first-aid kit and—ah, yes. There it was. A small mirror. Holding it up to his cheek, she gestured to Darla to peel back the gauze.

Alex's eyes searched the mirror. "Fuck," he rasped.

"You need medical attention," Josie insisted.

"I *am* getting medical attention," Alex said. "From you."

"But I'm not a *doctor*," she said, acid in her voice.

Alex winced again.

* * *

Pride goeth before a fall. If only his ego had been there to catch him. He'd have landed on a bloated sack of overinflated importance the size of Cleveland.

What the hell had he been thinking? Between going for a fourth lap, staring down the dark-haired dude as if he could crush his trachea with his corneas, and not paying attention to where he was going, he'd not only made a complete ass of himself, and caused moderate injuries to his face, hip, and shoulder, but he'd inadvertently reminded Josie of why she had reason to be pissed at him. And efficiently set her up to skewer and disembowel him with a barb from his own big fat stupid mouth—mere moments after she'd used a lovely little term of endearment.

That was some skill.

"Let's get you in my apartment and we can start icing your hip and shoulder. And wait for an ambulance," Josie said, nudging the blonde guy to help support Alex.

"No," he said, turning lamely toward the sidewalk that led to his house. God, this hurt. He wanted to rage and cry at the pain coursing through him. He must have fallen on his left side, because his shoulder was throbbing like a bitch and his hip was a solid chunk of pain-filled granite.

But the hands were fine.

Mission accomplished.

"Alex, you're acting like a petulant schoolboy." He froze. The words, the tone—it was like she'd channeled his mother.

Dear God.

"Then I'm a petulant schoolboy who is a board-certified physician and who can take care of himself," he said stiffly, acutely conscious of not-whining. "What's your name?" he asked blonde dude.

"Trevor."

"I'm Alex. And who's the other guy?"

"Joe."

"And you are…?" The words came out in a menacing tone. He kind of liked that.

"Darla's boyfriends."

"Boyfriend...zzz...?" Alex looked at Josie. If it wouldn't have caused searing pain, his eyebrows would be at his hairline. "You have a thing for threesomes?"

"No, my friends and relatives have a thing for threesomes," Josie retorted. Trevor looked extremely uncertain and pulled back.

"And her new job's all about—" Darla piped up.

"SHUT UP, DARLA!" Josie shouted. Darla wandered into the apartment building, muttering under her breath.

Motioning for Trevor to help him limp home, they made it about twenty feet before Josie huffed and caught up to them, carrying her first-aid kit.

"You're impossible."

"Then we're a match," he shot back.

"Seriously? C'mon, Alex. This is about your permanent health. You need to go to an ER."

"I need to get home. My first-aid kit is better—it has way more supplies."

"Size matters. Who knew," Josie cracked.

The blonde guy snorted, but stopped when Alex glared at him. "Do you have Lidocaine in there?" Alex's tone was supercilious, and he knew it, but he just wanted to get out from under the humiliation and pain. Being at home would help. He could make real decisions there, with his own kit, good lighting, and away from the ongoing misery that being so stupid was shelling out.

"Why would I?"

"I'll need it to stitch this up."

"You're going to sew your own face? Hardcore, old man," Trevor said in awe.

"Shut up," Josie and Alex said in unison.

"I know! *Shut. Up.* Who does that? Who stitches their own flesh? It's like that old movie from the 1960s— *Rambo*?" Trevor reached around Alex to shake his good hand.

"Really," Alex frowned at him. It hurt his eye. "Seriously, how old are you?"

"We meant *shut up* as in *stop talking*." Josie cleared her throat. "Darla, can you go get my keys? We need to get Alex down the street to his apartment."

"You want to fold me into your little car? Like this? Absolutely not. Just get me home." Lurching down the sidewalk with Rambo-lover his only support wasn't cutting it.

"What do you suggest? We prop you up on a skateboard and roll you home?"

"Mama actually won one for us, Josie!" Darla said excitedly, coming out of the apartment holding a glass of water for Alex. "Drink this. You need it." She turned around and rushed back inside.

"You are not putting me on a skateboard and rolling me home. That would be unsafe."

"I know!" Josie exclaimed. "You might, oh, hit a sign or something!"

Like a zombie in a cheesy film, Alex began the slow drag home, making it half a block before Josie buzzed around him again, nattering on about the ER.

"You are the worst patient!" she said, nearly bursting into tears. Something in her voice broke, though she didn't actually cry. She didn't have to. He understood emotional pain all too well.

Oh, man.

Darla came running outside, a red and black thing that loosely resembled a skateboard in her hands. "Here!"

"Darla, that's a *ripstick*," Trevor said, laughing.

"It's a skateboard!"

"No, it's not," Joe added. "It's two diamonds with wheels, connected in the center. He'd be on his ass in three seconds if he tried to roll down the block on a ripstick."

"Shit," Darla said, staring at it. "Now there are different *kinds* of skateboards? How am I supposed to know this?"

"Did your mom win you a Segway? Because that could help," Joe asked.

Josie waved them off. "You guys go back to…whatever you were doing. I'll take care of Alex." They complied,

Trevor saying something that made Darla burst into giggles.

"You will?" Alex asked, starting to pant from pain and exertion. How could he go from barreling along at a fast clip to this? Being out of breath from a snail's pace? Pain radiated through his hip and his shoulder ached. The wound on his face was crying, blood coagulating, and the throb of a new gash set in.

"If you're too stupid to get to an ER, then you leave me no choice, dumbass."

"Hey! Watch the name-calling. I'm not dumb."

"Okay, asshat."

"Much better."

*Lurch. Pause. Lurch. Pause.* He couldn't lean on her— she'd snap in two. A few parked cars gave him relief, a place to pause. Regretting the move to dismiss Trevor, he forced himself to keep going. Once he was sequestered in his own little apartment he would be able to get some mastery over this mess.

"You are the most stubborn jackass I have ever met."

"I consider that a compliment, coming from you. Where do you hide your Olympic gold medal in obstinance, Josie?"

"With my sex toys."

"So you can view it daily?"

"Hey!" she barked. "That's low."

"But true."

"Okay. True, but low. It's not my fault the only form of affection I get these days comes from molded BPA-free plastic."

"It's *my* fault?" At his driveway, he could see the end of this torture. The pain part.

"It just *is*, Alex. Like your wound. And it needs to be dealt with."

"You can't fix my gash with a sex toy."

She laughed. "I might be stubborn enough to try."

"See? You beat me there. You're the Stubborn

353

Champion."

"Right now I want to be the nurse who convinces you to get proper care." Her voice was weary, filled with sadness. She lent him a hand as he bobbled to his door.

He felt his pockets for his keys. No keys. Phone? No phone.

"I lost my—"

Trevor appeared suddenly, both in hand. "Here!" he said, breathing hard. "Darla found them on the sidewalk. Had me run them over."

Grateful, Alex took the keys, while Josie reached for the phone. Opening his door, he hobbled in, opened the apartment door, and collapsed on the couch.

Josie fished around in his fridge and came back with an ice pack and a glass of water. "Nice ice wrap," she said as she handed it to Alex, who carefully slid his arm through the wrap's hole. The wraparound shoulder ice pack had come in handy over the years with rotator cuff injuries. Boy, was he glad it had been in the freezer. The cold gave him instant relief.

"What about your ass?" Josie asked.

"What about it? Do you like it? I embedded gravel and added a few red scrapes to it just for you."

Sighing, Josie went back to the freezer and found a package of peas. "You're a regular Tim Gunn of road rash, Alex. Sit on this," she commanded.

Positioning the bag on his hip and ass, he had to admit that the cold packs made a huge difference in his comfort level. Internally, discomfort and anxiety were through the roof, because now that the crisis was over, he had to figure out what to do with Josie. Was she here out of professional courtesy? Because she really cared about him? Was there a chance to reconcile?

Or what?

Pressing the glass of his phone, Josie made a series of puzzled faces. "Aha!" she finally said.

"What are you doing?" His head throbbed, and he was

emotionally and physically wiped.

"Under 'Contacts'—Mom."

He opened his eyes and sat up. "You wouldn't!"

"I'll call her if you don't go to an ER and get care."

"You wouldn't dare." The expression on her face told him she absolutely would. "Look. I just need to clean it, apply Lidocaine, and do my own stitching." He sounded close to begging and didn't like it.

"What's her name again? Oh. That's right. Meribeth. Is it Dr. Derjian, or does she have a different last name?"

Groaning, he forced himself to stand, limping into the bathroom while clutching the frozen peas to his ass cheek. "I can't hear you!"

"But your mom can."

*Slam!* He looked at himself in the mirror. Gah! *World War Z* makeup artists couldn't have done better. If medicine didn't work out for him, he could get a job as an extra on the set of *The Walking Dead*. Road rash on his ass and one calf. The gash on his face. Probably the shoulder was just from the force of the fall, and his hip—time would tell. If it were too bad he couldn't have staggered two blocks. He was healthy. Healing would just take time.

But that gash...that would take stitches. The idea of going to any emergency room right now made his stomach heave. First off, it was July—the month when new interns come in for the beginning of their internship year. That meant he'd be handed off to some fresh-faced med student with the suture skills of Leatherface. No fucking way.

Second, being a doctor who had to be treated for running into a sign meant ridicule. Big, heaping doses of it from colleagues. Again—no way.

Pulling out his first-aid kit, he found what he needed to start cleaning the wound. And then—

*Bang bang bang.* "Alex?"

"Yes?"

"Open the door."

"No."

"Alex!" *Bang bang bang.*

"I am fine, and about to start stitching. I really don't need anyone screaming and banging in a way that might make my hands shake."

"I know damn well you can perform a splash 'n' slash C-section without shaking. So you can handle a pissed off woman telling you you're being a fool."

Damn it. She was right.

"Just...Josie, let me handle this my way." The sting of antiseptic was a welcome, if painful, diversion.

Silence. As Alex went about the process of cleaning the cut, he could see exactly how close he'd been to the eyeball. A few millimeters north and he wouldn't be able to claim there was no need for ER care.

He'd never stitched his own flesh before. Other doctors had talked about it. As he carefully looked at the wound, though, he wondered if plain old tissue adhesive would be enough. The gash was closer to the corner of his eye, and he'd have a scar regardless of whether it was glued with Dermabond or stitched.

Questioning whether he was in the right mind to do anything, Josie's insistence gave him pause. As minutes passed, he sat down on the toilet, ruminating. Sounds from the kitchen—the fridge door opening and closing, running water, the gurgle of a coffee machine—told him Josie was still out there. Why was she staying? Could he apologize and try to repair their relationship? The stress at work was fading as what felt like the Star Chamber receded into being just another case, now put to rest. Josie had been right—his grandfather's trial was broken and he was on the new medication. She'd left her job—was it because of Alex?

And then there was this threesome thing...

He stood and sighed. Time to decide. He chose the Dermabond.

And Josie.

* * *

How long was that man going to be in there? Standing in front of the bathroom door, she gave up, defeated but angry. Really angry. That gash and the way he limped—he needed to be seen. His stupid doctor ego was getting in the way, and Darla was right.

Doctors make the worst patients.

His phone was right there, where she'd left it, on the coffee table.

Time to meet Alex's mother.

A few presses on the glass and the phone rang.

"Meribeth here."

"Um, hello, Dr. ...Derjian?" Was it Derjian? Damn. Alex hadn't told her.

"Yes?"

"My name is Josie Mendham, and I—"

"Josie!" Her voice became warm and friendly instantly. "To what do I owe the pleasure?"

That was an unexpected reception. "I'm here at your son, Alex's, apartment, and—"

"You are? How delightful!"

Huh? "I wish it, um, were delightful, Dr. Derjian, because—"

"Call me Meribeth!"

"Um, Meribeth, Alex has been injured."

A beat of silence. "How, exactly, did you injure him, my dear?" Meribeth asked in a hushed voice, implying something that made Josie blush from head to toe.

"How did *I*...what... Oh, no! Not that, um, way—no! He ran into a street sign and gashed his face."

"What!" The tone of voice changed to panic. "Is he okay?"

"He's refusing to go to the ER."

"Of course he is. Stubborn boy. I'll be right there." *Click.*

*Fuuuuuuuuuuuuuuuuuuuuuuuuuuuuck*. That hadn't gone exactly as planned. Josie was strung out on the inside, but she needed to wait and make sure Dr. Mule was going to be okay. The fridge held little but milk; she refilled the ice trays. Ice would be his best friend for the next day or two.

Coffee. She needed coffee. Searching through the cabinets yielded a bag of Rao's, ground, so she made a full pot because hey—why not? Dr. Derjian was on her way.

Josie was about to meet Alex's mom.

As the coffee gurgled, she wondered what she was supposed to *do* right now. She certainly wasn't his girlfriend. They weren't even dating. Not even friends with benefits. Josie wasn't a booty call. Technically, she was an ex…something. They had been somethinging when he'd gone stupid and accused her of violating professional ethics and compromising an enormously important research trial.

And then…what, exactly, had happened? Although she'd rolled the last few weeks' events around in her head a million times, it only now occurred to her that the two most stubborn people in the world were at a standoff in Alex's apartment. He wouldn't budge. She wouldn't budge.

She'd done nothing wrong. Not one damn thing.

But if he knew that, he would have reached out. Right?

Inhaling slowly through her nose, she stretched her neck until it cracked, and she realized how tense and tight she was. Watching him on the ground, not moving, body splayed out and bleeding, had made her realize how much she missed him.

Wanted him.

Craved him.

*Needed* him.

For God's sake, she'd called him *honey*. No man had ever been called *honey* by her lips. Jackass, asshat, cracker (*that guy really was*), shithead—you name it. Honey was…it was what you said to someone you loved.

The creak of the bathroom door made her turn her

head and jump up. Alex lumbered down the hall, using the wall for support, a soggy bag of peas in his hand.

"Can you help me?" he asked. The gash was hard to see in the hallway's shadow, but as he emerged into the light and Josie walked to him, taking the half-frozen bag, she saw what he had done.

"You Dermabonded it!"

"Yes."

Peering closely, she got right in his face, professional curiosity getting the best of her. "Good job. You'll barely scar."

He folded his arms over his chest, smug now. She inhaled and the scent of man sweat and athleticism blended with antiseptic and glue. "Told you. I didn't need an ER." He sagged against the wall, clearly in pain, and Josie's sense of self was heightened, her face two inches from his, Alex's hand now resting on her hip. "But I could use some comfort care," he said in a low, suggestive voice.

Oh, how much she wanted to kiss him. Her body hummed, every inch of her skin wanting to touch every inch of his, her heart beating a pattern that only he could complete. Just as she leaned forward, pulled by a force of nature she couldn't name, someone banged on the front door.

Alex jumped and Josie pulled back, practically running to the door as Alex called out, "Who would be here now?"

As she opened the door, Josie came face to face with a familiar woman, one who had brought Ed in for the Alzheimer's trial from time to time. "So good to see you again, Josie!" Meribeth Derjian said, reaching in for a hug. Josie was suddenly very aware that she was still wearing her pajamas.

"You did!" Alex boomed. "You called my mother?" An incredulous look spread over his face as he limped closer to her.

Josie held out her palms. "Don't—I just—you were being unreasonable!" She inched backwards.

"*I* was being unreasonable?" He snorted. "And why are you moving away from me? What are you afraid of—that I'll shuffle after you faster than you can run?" He thought for a second. "Then again, I've seen you run. Maybe your instincts are right."

"Alex!" Meribeth exclaimed, rushing to him, one palm against his injured cheek before he could say a word. "Josie did the right thing calling me. But...I thought you didn't go to the ER. Did I misunderstand? You're back already? Whoever did this surgical glue thing did a great job."

If he could tighten those arms against his chest another millimeter he'd cut off his own circulation. "I did it myself."

Meribeth rolled her eyes and shot Josie a sympathetic look. "Men," they said in unison.

"Oh, no!" Alex shouted, dragging himself to the coffee pot. He pulled out a mug and declared, "You do *not* get to double team me."

"It takes two of us to get you to see reason, Alex," Meribeth answered. She gave Josie a knowing look. "Normally I have to bring one of my sisters in to help."

"Tell me about this side of him," Josie asked, smiling. Interesting. She never thought about a layer to him that required prying and intervention.

"Alex thinks he's his own island. Doesn't need help. Can handle everything life throws at him without any assistance."

Josie shrugged. "I can understand that."

"Thank you," Alex said with sarcasm. "You demonstrate your respect for my independence so strangely," he added, pointing to Meribeth as he angrily poured a mug of coffee, then struggled to get to the couch with the hot cup in hand.

"Let me get that," Josie said, taking the mug.

"See? Perfect example," Meribeth chimed in. "When he had an asthma attack during a soccer game in eleventh grade, he insisted on playing between nebulizer treatments."

"It was state championships!" Alex objected.

"When he was studying for MCAT exams for medical school, he ingested so much NoDoz he couldn't sleep for three days, and we finally had to have him hospitalized. It took about an elephant's dose of tranquilizer to get him to sleep."

"But my scores got me in!" he said as he settled into a corner spot on the couch, motioning to Josie for his mug, which she gave him.

"I thought you were Dr. Calm and Mellow. Dr. Perfect. Dr. Centered," Josie said, a dawning feeling hitting her. He was nuanced. Flawed. Imperfect. He glared at her and said nothing, but the edges of his mouth cracked into a smile.

And she liked him even more that way.

"Alex," his mother said suspiciously. "Why are you lurching about like a frog with its leg mowed off?"

"I fell."

Meribeth threw up her hands. "One- and two-word answers are your fallback, Alex." She turned to Josie. "Can you explain?"

"He saw me sitting on my porch with another guy and he ran into a *No Parking* sign."

Dead silence.

Josie winced.

*Oh, shit.*

* * *

Josie had called his mother. She'd called in his mother. No girlfriend, date, bedmate—whatever you called them— had been so brazen. He was fine. Fine! Bruised and sore with a fixed face, all he needed was for these meddling women to leave so he could drink a huge glass of water and take a nap.

Or for Josie to stay, so after that nap he could apologize and just put his arms around her and tell her everything he should have said that day he flipped on her.

Whispering, heads together, his mom and Josie kept saying "I know!" and "He does that with you, too?" Which didn't help his increasingly split mood. Frustrated that they were treating him like a child. Maybe they were right. His hamstrings ached, his hip felt like an octogenarian's, and his shoulder still hurt. Stretching his body out on the couch, he curled on his non-injured side and closed his eyes.

A soft hand on his brow. Mom. "Honey, are you okay?"

Honey. There was that word again.

"I'm fine," he huffed.

More words between his mom and Josie, and then Meribeth gave him a hug, leaning over his body and awkwardly embracing him. "You're in good hands with Josie. I have to get back to a patient, but I'll call tonight."

"Okay," he said, sleep taking over. Whatever he thought his day would look like, nearly eight miles of running, a stupid injury, and a strange back-and-forth with Josie were all enough to let his exhaustion win, and sleep prevail.

\* \* \*

"Thank you for calling me," Meribeth said. Those kind eyes and her wit made Josie like her instantly. Nonjudgmental, sharp as could be, and funny, too.

Great mother-in-law material. About as different from Marlene as two women could be.

"No problem. He needed it."

Meribeth laughed lightly. "He is a wonderful man, but Alex can be...self-contained. I assume he didn't tell you about his problems at work."

Josie frowned. "No."

"For the past month his judgment was called into question on a case at the hospital. I've never seen him so stressed out. Professional ethics are very important to Alex."

"I noticed."

"And he misapplied those in your case."

The two stood in awkward silence, until Meribeth said, "Josie, I'm about to pry."

"Thanks for the warning."

"Whatever is getting in the way of your being together, get rid of it. I've never seen him so affected by a woman before. And I'd like to get to know you better." The pressure of her hand on Josie's forearm felt good. Comfortable. Warm and caring. Like an invitation.

Josie smiled. "Me too. I just don't know…" She bit her lower lip and swallowed hard.

"You'll find your way." And with that Meribeth reached to her for a hug, the affectionate gesture so alien, so maternal that Josie felt both punched in the solar plexus and joyously appreciative all at once.

An anemic wave as Meribeth left was all Josie could muster. Padding softly over to Alex, she saw he was asleep. Admiring him like this, bruised and sweaty, she found her heart giving way. Maybe they could find their way. Maybe Josie could find her way.

Perhaps, even, Alex needed to find his way, too. Dr. Imperfect was more than enough for her.

Kissing his cheek, she went to the kitchen, poured a cup of coffee, and settled into a chair across from him. Just in case his head injury was worse than expected, she figured the safest course was to stay until he woke up.

And then—an idea.

Her phone was back at her apartment, so she used Alex's phone to call Laura.

"Hello?" Laura answered in a guarded voice.

"What should I do?" Josie hissed into the phone.

"I think you should tell him how you feel and just stop being so ridiculous," Laura answered without hesitation. "Whose phone are you on?"

"Alex's."

"Oooooh."

"No, it's not like that. I'm at his apartment. He's asleep on the couch."

"Tired him out?" You could hear the leer in Laura's voice a mile away.

"No. He was running past my house and I was touching Joe's chest and Alex got jealous and ran into a parking sign."

"What? Repeat that!"

"I can't. Hell, I don't understand it myself."

"Who is Joe?"

"One of Darla's boyfriends."

*Bzzzzzzzzzzzzz.* The doorbell rang. Who the hell could that be? Slipping past Alex, she propped the apartment door open with the deadbolt and went to the main door.

Darla.

"What are you doing here?"

"I came to check up on you. Make sure you weren't being dismembered and put in a freezer." Darla craned her neck around Josie, obviously hinting she wanted to come in. Letting her, Josie ushered her into the apartment, putting a finger to her lips, pointing to Alex.

"Laura?" she whispered into the phone. "I need to let you go."

"Only if you promise to talk to him. Openly. Honestly."

Sigh. "I promise."

"Don't do what I did with Mike and Dylan. Don't shut him out."

"He's the one who was wrong!"

"Yes, he was. But you're paying the price for you own stubbornness, Josie."

"You're right. Kiss the baby for me."

"Mwah!" Click.

Darla was gawking at the apartment. "This is newer than yours", she stage whispered, careful not to wake Alex.

"Ours. Our building." She glanced at Alex. "He okay?"

"He will be."

"Did he really sew his own eye wound shut?" Darla asked, her face a mask of revulsion.

"No. He used Dermabond."

"Dermawhat?"

"Surgical glue. Like crazy glue, sort of."

"Trevor will be disappointed," Darla joked.

"Tell Trevor to go rent a Rambo movie to get his flesh-sewing fix." A loud growl came from Josie's stomach and a lightheadedness hit her. Meeting Trevor and Joe. Alex's appearances. His injuries. Meeting his mother—all in one morning, it was just too much.

"You okay?" Darla peered at her with knowing eyes. "You're not okay."

Tears filled Josie's eyes, and she allowed them—finally—to spill over. "I'm not okay," she admitted, sitting down on a chair across from Alex, pressing her forehead against her knees.

"What's going on between you two?" Darla gave Alex the once-over, taking in his body. "He's really cute."

"I met his mom just now," Josie sobbed as quietly as she could.

"It went that bad?"

"It was *greaaaaat*," Josie cried. "She's sweet and smart and funny and I could see her as my mother-in-law." She hissed the last word in an even lower whisper, as if she were a Harry Potter character saying Voldemort's name.

"Then what's the problem?"

"I'm too fucked up for Alex," Josie wailed.

"Then go unfuckup yourself, Josie!" Darla said matter-of-factly. "No one else will do it for you."

Laughing through her tears, Josie said, "Oh, like it's so easy."

"No—it isn't. It's complicated."

Snort. "It's always complicated."

"*You're* always complicated, Josie."

That stung. "What do you mean?"

Darla's voice softened. "I know it was hard for you, growing up with your mom like that. Mama used to say she got the better end of the bargain, because while she lost a foot and her mobility, at least she kept her mind. Her sister didn't."

"Aunt Cathy said that?"

"Yes, she did." Compassion oozed out of Darla. They hardly ever talked like this, and Josie found it surreal. Eye-opening. Expanding. Not at all freakish or upsetting.

"I was always over at your place. She'd call and ask for help with you."

"And sometimes she needed it, but Josie, mostly she was trying to get you out from Aunt Marlene's wrath."

"I know." She'd known when she was eleven. She knew now, at twenty-nine. Aunt Cathy gave her a stable place to escape to, where the home was cluttered but there were regular meals, a place to do homework quietly, and Darla to curl up on the couch with and watch television. It was homey, even if it wasn't home.

"But you got to get beyond that. You're twenty-nine. How much longer are you going to drag your past around like a big old ball and chain?" Darla looked pointedly at Alex, then put her hands on her thighs and pushed herself to standing, sighing deeply, as if tired.

"And that"—she pointed at Alex—"is worth way, way more than the three or four luggage carts of baggage you've loaded yourself with."

"You make it sound like I had a choice!" Josie hissed.

"You didn't when you were a kid, but you sure as hell do now."

"This from the woman who wouldn't leave her mama until a few weeks ago?"

Darla stopped, her jaw going tense, nostrils flaring. Then she sighed, a slow relaxing that drained her anger out. "Yeah, Josie. That's right. I decided I needed to make a change and look what I got." She nodded toward the door. "And on that note, I'm going back to the apartment. Sam and Liam from the band are there and we're getting ready to go out."

"Four guys?" Josie gasped.

"No! Two's enough!" Darla shouted. Alex stirred, and Josie put a finger to her lips. Rolling her eyes, Darla slipped out quietly, leaving Josie to stew in her thoughts.

\* \* \*

Alex woke up to a dark room, the sun long gone, a small reading lamp the only source of light in the room. As he sat up, he groaned, the pain throbbing on his cheekbone and hip strong and vibrant.

"How are you?" a quiet voice asked, making him jump.

Josie leaned into the light, her legs curled under her. She was reading a book off his shelf, a piece of creative nonfiction about the history of ether.

"You scared me. I…uh…what time is it?"

She checked a phone. His phone. "Almost eight."

"I slept that long?"

"You needed it."

He winced, his face hurting and his tongue stuck to the roof of his mouth like Velcro. As if she read his mind, she unfolded herself, went to the kitchen, and came back with a huge glass of water and a bottle of ibuprofen. "You might want these."

Shaking two tablets out, he swallowed them greedily, then drank half the water. "Thank you," he said, deeply grateful. "You stayed here with me? The whole time?"

"I wanted to make sure that you didn't bang your head too hard. Just figured I'd be here until you woke up." She stood, setting the book aside. "So…"

"No! Don't leave!" he begged. "I'm…just wait."

She froze. Alex knew that the wrong words wouldn't work here, but he didn't much care anymore about being perfect. What he needed was to be real. Not talking about the stress at work, jumping to ridiculous conclusions, not calling her and apologizing were all dick moves, and he'd known it then—but it was blatantly obvious now.

"I'm sorry, Josie. Deeply sorry. And I'm even more sorry that it's taken me this long to apologize." He stood, his hip screaming, but his mobility had improved from the nap as he carefully took three steps closer to her. Running his hand through his hair, he added, "I wish I could turn back the clock."

Her eyes bored into his as she evaluated him. Trust wasn't easy for her, he knew—and he'd proven that he wasn't worthy of it. Given time, maybe, he could unprove that.

"Thank you," she said quietly.

So much unsaid hung in the air between them, like ephemeral storm clouds at sunset, unpredictable yet hovering, ready to waft off with a breeze or unleash a storm.

No one could guess which outcome was most likely.

She took a step closer. He did, too.

"I don't feel like I need to apologize," Josie said.

"You don't."

"But I do feel like I should say…something. About our somethinging."

"Our *what?*"

She brushed a stray strand of hair behind her ear, and his heart melted. "Somethinging. It's a joke between me and Laura. She asked me what you and I were doing a while ago and I said we were somethinging. I didn't have a name for it."

"Ah." They were getting somewhere. Josie wasn't walking away, or stomping off angry, or worse—indifferent.

"Alex, I've never met a man like you before." She frowned. "Or, if I have, I've driven men like you away on purpose."

"Why?"

"Because, as I told Darla today, I'm too fucked up to be with someone who is normal."

"No, you're—"

She held up a palm. He shut up. "She told me to unfuckup myself."

He laughed. It hurt. He winced. "Good advice."

"Before I can be with you, then, I need to unfuckup myself. Meeting your mother today is one example. Alex, I was so scared that day you told me you wanted me to meet her," she explained.

"Scared? Of my *mom*? Why?"

"You'd have to meet my mother to understand. You know that day you called me and we...well, we had that moment on the baseball field?"

The wide grin made his face hurt like a motherfucker, but the pain was worth it. "Yes."

"You interrupted a call from my mom. She was asking for money. Mostly for her drug and alcohol habit. She claimed it was for repairing the gutters on our house, but...she's an addict and she, well, let's just say our moms wouldn't exactly co-exist well."

"C'mon, Josie—"

She snorted. "Maybe as patient and psychologist. But that's it."

Showing him this very exposed, very fragile part of herself was a gift, he knew. Josie wouldn't do this for anyone. It made his stomach tighten and his arms ache to hold her. What he'd known was real and true and deep and broad was right before him, pouring her heart out in the only way she knew how.

And it had to be enough. He couldn't push or prod or pull.

"If I'm normal, the world is in trouble," he said quietly.

"You're more normal than me," was all she said, taking one more step closer.

*Reach for her*, his mind screamed.

So he did.

369

She accepted his embrace. Sinking his face into her hair, breathing in her goodness, he said again, "I'm so sorry. I shouldn't have doubted you. I just had this stupid case at work and I turned into a jackass."

"Asshat."

"That too. And I should have told you."

"Yes, you should," she said into his shoulder. "If I'm going to show you my belly, you have to show me yours."

Pulling back, she lifted up her shirt. "See? My soft underbelly."

He pulled his shirt up too. "There. We're even."

"Now what?" they said in unison. Alex bent down to press his forehead against hers, forgetting about the cut.

"Ow." He pulled back.

Her fingers against his cheek searched the topography of his jaw. "Give me time." On tiptoes, she kissed him lightly on the lips. It felt like a whispered promise.

"Time for what?"

"Time to unfuckup myself." And with that, she walked to his front door and slipped out like a shadow in a dream, made from nothing quite real, but no less significant.

# CHAPTER FOURTEEN

It was the green mug that caught her eye. Normally, Josie didn't go to Central Square for much, preferring to stick closer to Inman, but her days were a bit unmoored until the office space Laura had rented was remodeled and they could get the business up and running in earnest. In the meantime, she had long stretches of time, decent savings, and she'd get her first paycheck in a week or so. Hours on the phone each day and occasional trips to Mike's cabin filled her days.

Which was good, because otherwise she'd be flinging herself on Alex's lap and having sex with him under the chess tables in front of Au Bon Pain in Harvard Square.

Not that he knew she'd do that.

Here she found herself, walking to a lovely coffee shop that sold lattes she enjoyed, and made macchiato the exact way Alex liked them—

*Stop that!* she told herself. *Quit relating every. Single. Thing in your life to Alex.*

The green mug was a welcome diversion. A panhandler held it, and it looked suspiciously familiar. Huh. How weird.

As much as she wanted coffee, the local juice bar

caught her eye. Her stomach growled; she'd forgotten breakfast. How about a fresh juice? On impulse, she walked in, noting with amusement that the greenery in the vegetarian café matched the lush palm tree pattern painted on her fingernails. After ordering something yummy made from carrots, ginger, apples, and other stuff, she sat down near a bookcase covered with books patrons could read while they enjoyed their food.

She did a double take.

A string of romances—the same books, including *The Highlander's Heinie*—filled one shelf.

Wait a minute.

Wild hands flailed through the window, followed by a big pouf of yellow hair. "Hey, Josie!" Darla screamed. Quickly, Josie jumped up and ran outside, hauling her half-drunk juice with her.

"What are you doing? Following me?" Josie asked, drinking more.

"God, no. You're way too boring. I went to that clothing store where you buy clothes by the pound. Did you know they made stilettos in a men's size sixteen?"

"It's Cambridge, Darla. Of course they do."

"I got them!" She pulled out a pair of gold high heels that looked like something Gene Hackman wore in *The Birdcage*.

"Why? Is Trevor turning out to have a secret you need to share?"

"No! And even if he did, it wouldn't matter."

"Fair enough. So why buy the sandals?" A slurping sound from the bottom of her drink told her it was done.

She crinkled her nose and gave Josie a long, slow eye roll. "Because they were there, and I think they cost a couple dollars."

"Just because something's there doesn't mean you need it."

"Gold. Stilettos. Men. Can. Wear," Darla said slowly. "Besides, they cost less than that overpriced grass water you're drinking."

"Speaking of which, Darla, do you know why the exact same set of romance novels your mom won is sitting in there?" She yanked her thumb toward the juice cafe.

Darla brightened. "I asked them if they wanted them. Figured I'd spread the wealth!"

"And will you spread the wealth with those shoes?"

"Like what? Give them to a shoeless man? Of course."

"Make sure you find a matching gold belt. Only fair."

"Have you heard from Alex?"

"Way to deflect," Josie muttered. "As a matter of fact, yes. We've been texting."

"Texting? That's it?"

"We're taking it slow."

"Are you sexting?"

"No. Ewww."

"Nothing's *ewwww* about sexting, you prude," Darla argued. They began to walk slowly toward the coffee shop.

Josie snorted. "I am *so* not a prude."

"When will you two actually decide to get over yourselves and get together?"

"When I figure out how to get over myself."

The coffee shop was a long, narrow store, and the counter always was three people deep, waiting to order or hanging out to get their drink. On a whim, Josie ordered a macchiato while Darla just got a regular coffee.

"Macchiato?"

"I'm trying something new."

"I'll bet that's Alex's drink."

Josie turned away and said nothing. A guy selling a newspaper that donated money to the homeless wore a red t-shirt that was a little too familiar. The logo was—

"Darla, are you handing out t-shirts, too?" She pointed.

Darla's eyes lit up as she took her coffee from the barista. "That's Juan! He sells that *Spare Change* newspaper all the time. I gave him a bunch of Mama's winnings."

"I'm glad they're being put to good use," Josie said,

laughing softly.

Juan gave Darla a quick wave as they left. Headed home, Josie took a sip of the macchiato and screwed up her face. Too dark for her. It needed milk. The flavor was pleasant and she could appreciate the artistry of good coffee, but for her a latte meant comfort. Not just a shot of tasty caffeine. Chucking this macchiato back was a simple affair, and maybe that was the secret: a doctor on long shifts could appreciate the quality, but get it pumping through his bloodstream ASAP.

"When's the new office ready?" Darla asked.

"Sometime next week. We need to meet up with Laura in the next few days to go over everything. I can't believe you haven't met her and Mike and Dylan yet!"

"A sick baby makes the world stop," Darla said sympathetically. Jillian had come down with a light fever and a stuffy nose and Laura's world ground to a halt. Nothing serious, Laura assured her, but it meant the three new parents were up day and night, with no time for anything but Jillian.

Meanwhile, the plans for the new business cranked on. A boutique dating service that would spread through word of mouth and very careful targeted advertising, using customized software to help people find not "The One," but "The Two."

Darla and Laura loved it.

"I hope Jillian's feeling better today," was all Josie could think to say as they paused at a stop light. This part of Cambridge had a patchwork quilt of sidewalks made of bricks, some asphalted, and some concrete. Architecture was mixed, too, from boring brick buildings to 1800s gabled homes and everything in between. As they got closer to Inman Square, the streets got a little less clean, the weeds a little more overgrown on the patches of grass that poked up between pavement, and the stores were decidedly less chic.

"Me too," Darla added. "By the way, you need to find

yourself two guys real quick."

Halting, Josie gawked at her openly. "I need to what?"

"How can you work for a threesome dating service and have any credibility if you've never had a threesome, Josie?"

"How do you know I never—" Clamping her mouth shut, Josie bit off the words.

"I see," Darla said quietly. They walked for three blocks in complete silence. Great. Just great. Now Darla thought she needed a threesome to run the business. And Darla now knew about Josie's sex life. Could the day get any worse?

As they rounded the corner to their road, the distinct *beep-beep-beep* of a rather large truck backing up filled the air. Walking to their building, Josie saw it backing up right in front of the house.

Darla looked at her, brow furrowed. "You order something big?"

"No. Maybe another tenant?" The truck driver went around to the back of the truck, where they couldn't see him. By the time they reached the building, he was unloading a huge, shrink-wrapped pallet of what looked like a hundred bags of something onto the street, using a hand-cart with a hydraulic lift.

"Hey! You Darla Jennings?" he called out.

Darla froze, turning slowly, a smile on her face. "That's me!"

"Here. It's for you. Sign."

"What is it?" Josie asked, peering intently at the enormous pallet. It was half the size of her car, and looked like some sort of yard supply, like bags of mulch or potting soil.

"Cat litter," Mr. Friendly said, nodding for Darla to sign.

"*Cat litter?*" Josie gasped. "That much?"

Darla handed back the clipboard and he gave her an envelope. "Okay, then. Bye," he said, leaving the pallet on the lawn.

"Wait! No!" Josie shrieked, panicking. "You can't just leave that there!"

"Truck delivery only, lady. You want it in your house, it's another $150."

"$150!" Now it was Darla's turn to shriek. "To leave this thing on our porch?"

He put the handcart back in the truck, jumped out, closed up, and walked to the driver's seat. "Policy."

"POLICY?" Josie screamed. "You're leaving me a half-ton of cat litter in my front yard and it's POLICY?"

The roar of the engine as he took off was the only answer she got.

A tearing sound as Darla opened the envelope caught Josie's attention. Darla pulled out a letter, read for a few seconds, and then pinched the bridge of her nose. "Day-um."

"Oh God, no."

"Yep. Mama won us a lifetime supply of kitty litter."

"*Whose* lifetime? Edward Cullen's?"

"Nine lifetimes, from the looks of that pile," Darla answered, shaking her head. The shrink-wrapped monstrosity sat, crooked, on the scraggly lawn. Most of her neighbors were at work right now, but soon they'd come home, and she did not want to deal with complaints to the landlord or any of the other myriad problems that came with enough kitty litter to fill the city swimming pool across the street.

Or, at least, that was what it felt like.

"We need to move this," Josie said, starting to pace. The coffee hit her, making her a bit manic. "Let's cut open the plastic and start moving the bags."

"Josie, there is no way we can get this done without help. I can handle some of those bags, but not all. And you have the muscle mass of a decaying corpse."

"Do not!"

"You're right." Darla pinched her biceps. "Even less.

Damn, I'll bet my wrist is fatter than your thighbone, girl!"

"Now is not the time to compare," Josie said menacingly.

Darla pulled out her phone and punched some numbers, then held one finger up to Josie. "Hang on."

Josie stomped into the apartment, most certainly not willing to hang on. The view outside from the window didn't make the pallet seem any more appealing. The taste of her macchiato burned in her mouth, reminding her too much of Alex.

Alex.

Light-hearted texting and quick little comments to each other throughout the week had been cute, but Josie didn't want "cute." She despised "cute." What she wanted was more, but didn't know how to go for it. Something was stuck between her and Alex, and figuring out how to unstick it was driving her mad.

A giant pile of kitty litter didn't help. Flopping down on the floor, she spotted Crackhead, who was crouched under a small end table next to the couch. The cat's eyes gleamed in the dark, and it made a mild purring noise.

"Sure, you're happy," she said to the cat. "You have enough kitty litter to piss in for the next three centuries."

"Who are you talking to?" Darla asked, stepping in and closing the front door.

"Crackhead."

"And did he tell you you're being stupid about Alex, too?"

Josie stood and huffed off without saying a word. Storming into her bedroom, she ripped off her overly warm shirt, threw on a tank top, and stopped with her arms up as her eyes noticed something hidden under a stack of papers in the corner.

The book.

That fucking book.

*Click.* Like a telescope that shifts to focus, the movement so acute it leaves you a bit confused, Josie's brain rotated into a position of sudden, extreme clarity.

The book.

That was the key.

Snatching it up, she stared at the cover. *A Wrinkle in Time*. How could time wrinkle? Closing her eyes, she willed her breath to slow, her pulse to follow, and her mind to stay clear. A picture of Alex, smiling and accepting, was part of that sharp focus.

As silly as it seemed, her baggage really was enormous, like Darla said.

Except most of it was in her hand. Right here.

This fucking book.

Eighteen years of messy internal chaos floated away and she realized she needed to open the book, start reading, and then—

Then what?

Didn't matter. Just...*then*.

She would actually have a *then*. A future. A *more*.

As if on cue, her phone rang. Grabbing it from her pocket, she groaned when she saw the number. Mom.

"Hi, Mom."

"Hi, Josie. This a bad time?"

"Actually, yes."

Silence. Josie didn't *do* that. Always accommodating, always deferring. Marlene's voice came through with a mixture of aggression and confusion. "Well, it's a bad time for me, too." The whining was louder, though, than anything else.

"I'm sorry, Mom." Her voice was dispassionate steel. "If this is a bad time for you, too, then perhaps we can talk later." *Be officious*. Clutching the book in her hand, she held it like a talisman, as if it could ward off evil spirits. Funny how an item she'd carried around her entire life, one she'd never been able to bring herself to open and use, could be a source of comfort in this moment.

"Aren't you being a smartmouth." Josie closed her eyes slowly. That word. There it was. Marlene began the slow burn, her words punctuated with sharp drags off her cigarette, the smoldering that Josie knew all too well. "Too busy for your poor old mother, huh? Maybe that's why you didn't send the money you promised? Too busy," she spat, "playing around with Darla?"

*Say nothing*, she told herself. Just like when she was eleven. And fourteen. And seventeen. And twenty. Hunker down and weather the storm and just go on like nothing happened. It was easier that way.

Safer.

"You there?"

*No*, she wanted to say. *Nope. Not here. Gone. Long gone, hiding away where you can't hurt me, can't snap at me, can't bring strange men home and kick me out into the cold. Hidden in the abyss inside me that cracked open the day Daddy died, when you came home from the hospital six weeks later and told me I was the worst thing that happened to you. Far, far away from the you that you became, spiriting myself off to where the old you lived. Where the old you loved me.*

"I'm here."

"Whatcha got to say, then? I need my money, Josie," she wheedled. "The gutters don't fix themselves. You can pay for Darla to come out there in your fancy city, in an apartment I haven't even seen. The only time you helped me visit was when you graduated college, and that was what? Five years ago?"

"Six."

"How's that music guy from your college, anyhow? He really took a shining to me." Pause. Drag. "Might be worth moving in with you if I can see him."

"Moving. In?" The words choked out of her as if she were on the receiving end of the Heimlich maneuver, forced out of her with a resounding gag.

"You got room for Darla. Why not me?"

"No." The word came out before any filter could even try to catch it. Before her brain could process it. Before she could even gasp at the monstrous idea that Marlene would move to Cambridge and live with her. Her palm clamped over her mouth in shock. Had her mouth really done that?

Come to her own rescue?

"What?"

"*No.*" This time, it came out with deliberate force. Always evasive, using jokes and sarcasm to blunt Marlene's pleas and demands, this time she just decided it was time to face her head on. No bullshit. No dancing the two-step while juggling live fish and doing it all spinning on top of a basketball. No worrying nineteen steps ahead, like a chess player moving not chess pieces, but her own emotions, constantly putting them in danger and making calculated moves to get just enough space to breathe—

No.

*Hell* no.

She was done. Where was she supposed to have anything left over for her? For Alex? For friends and family and to build her own life? Moving six hundred miles away was supposed to give her space, but she'd made one crucial mistake in her concept of what it meant to get away: if you let the people you're trying to leave behind live in your head, you never lose them as roommates.

"No what?"

"No to everything, Mom. No, you can't move in." Her heart raced, and her peripheral vision started to fade to white. Textbook panic attack, she knew, her nurse's mind kicking in. Only it was a shame that she couldn't be objective and couldn't just see this for what it was.

Subjective and raw and all too viscerally real, she had to feel it. Not watch it.

"But Darla can—"

"That's right. Darla can. Because Darla views me as a human being. Not as some object she can manipulate to get what she wants. It's like you've seen me all these years since Dad died as some *thing* you can move around and use at will, but if I don't comply with your demands I become an enemy."

"That's not—"

"So I'm done. You know that researchers did studies years ago on how to trigger mental illness in a kid, Mom? You move the goal posts. Constantly. You make sure they never feel like they're good enough, and when you tell them how to do something and they do it that way, then you pull the rug out from under them and insist that you never said what they damn well know you said. It's a damned miracle I'm not more fucked up than I am."

"Oh, honey, you're not fucked up." Marlene's voice had turned unctuous, a fake affect that made Josie's fillings hurt. This was the voice she had used publicly when Josie hurt herself, a "doting mother" tone that made others smile in approval. The same tone she used when Josie won awards. Or impressed an adult. A far cry from real life and so painfully different from Marlene's authentic self that it could be crazymaking.

"I'm not giving you the money." Much more of this and her vision really would disappear. Her shoulders were above her ears, and a strange whooshing sound was starting to swallow the room. Was that her pulse in her ears? Would she descend into a fugue state if this went on much longer? Blacking out wasn't her idea of fun, but she wasn't sure she could stand much more of this.

*Click.*

Oh. Well. That was that.

*Holy shit. Holy shit. Holy shit.* Josie couldn't get the thought out of her mind. Never. Never had she stood up to Marlene. Never ever. Slinking around, hiding, running away—those Josie could do. Standing and facing a problem? Nope. That meant you got hurt—physically or emotionally. Being emotionally honest about feelings? Pfft—what were those? Marlene made it *aaaall* about her anyhow, so why bother? And when you made yourself vulnerable, it just gave people one more way to spear you.

Alex. Alex wasn't like that.

The book's pages were crushed in her hand, half the paperback wrinkled.

Grabbing her keys and sprinting out the door past Darla, who now sat on the porch, she reached her car and that clarity she felt earlier came back.

She knew exactly where she was going.

"Where are you going?" Darla shouted. "I got Trevor and the rest of the band coming to help with this," she said, pointing to the kitty litter. Josie stared at her, at the pile of bags, but didn't really connect with what Darla was saying. She had to get out.

Now.

"Great. I'll be back." She got in the car.

"When?"

"When I finish unfuckupping myself."

"That could take years! Where are you going?"

"To the library!" she shouted, revving the engine and pulling out of her parking spot, everything in her aligned for a single purpose, her clarity turning the abyss inside into a minimalist shelter from the storm of what was about to be unleashed.

\* \* \*

"Crackhead! Hey, Crackhead!" Darla shouted from the porch as Alex rounded the corner. Trevor, Joe, and two other guys about their age were in the front yard, moving large bags of sand from a pallet in the yard on to the porch.

"I might do 'shrooms and some pot, but I don't touch crack," a red-headed guy said drolly.

"Is that a term of endearment, Darla?" Alex called out.

She planted her hands on her hips and smiled. "I feel right at home when I'm shouting for that cat." She laughed, the sound eerily similar to Josie's cackle. "Dr. Perfect. How's your head?"

"It's better." He touched the healing wound lightly.

"What's going on here?"

"I won a lifetime's supply of kitty litter. Or, at least, my mama did."

"You only have two cats, right?" He chuckled, watching the guys haul and re-stack. "Where are you going to store it all?" He imagined Josie would have a mixed reaction, given her apartment's clean, spare look.

"You got one?" She perked up. "Trevor, give Alex a bag."

*Oof!* As if he were lifting a newborn baby, Trevor handed off a twenty-pound bag of litter. Alex's knees bent at the weight and his hip screamed.

"Thanks," he said, acting like it was no big deal. The testosterone level in the yard was up to his chin, and something primal in him made him man up. "But I don't have a cat."

"How about your mom? Your grandpa? Someone you know? Maybe take a few bags to the hospital and see if people want some?"

He set the bag down carefully. "No thanks, Darla. But it might come in handy this winter on icy walkways."

"Oooh, good selling point."

"Who are all these guys?"

"The band. You know Trevor and Joe." Both grunted a "hello." "And this is Sam, the drummer," she said, pointing to the redhead. Deep auburn hair and the kind of skin that tans, rather than burns, with greenish hazel eyes. He was the only guy wearing a shirt, something from a geeky t-shirt store, and the quick eye contact and downcast eyes were more about shyness than anything else.

"Liam's the guitar player."

"One of them!" Trevor protested.

"The best one," Liam crowed, reaching out to shake Alex's hand. Liam and Trevor could have been brothers, both possessing a natural confidence and blonde surfer-dude look, though Liam was taller, looking down at Alex as they shook hands.

"So, this is the entire band?" Josie's texts this past week had explained who Trevor and Joe were, and Darla's relationship with them, as well as the Random Acts of Crazy band. Alex hadn't heard of them, but then again, he lived in his own hospital-filled bubble.

Liam nodded. "We're all here, moving kitty litter for Trevor and Joe's puss—"

"HEY!" shouted the two guys, Joe throwing his shirt at Liam. It caught him on the side of his grinning face.

"You're here, aren't you?" Darla said, going right up to Liam and smiling. This was all good-natured, Alex could see.

"Where's Josie?" Alex asked.

Darla just stared at him. No anger, no consternation, just an open look of evaluation. He wondered how different their fathers must have been, for Darla had untamed blonde waves and ocean-green eyes, with a fuller figure, while Josie's features were dark, her body petite and slim. How interesting genetics could be. If he and Josie had a baby, it would have dark hair and dark eyes.

Even as he held Darla's look, he paused internally. The thought of having a baby, of growing a family, with Josie filled him with a sense of protection and love.

Hope, too.

Waving him toward the door, Darla said, "Let's go inside and talk. You want something to drink?" The guys were about halfway through their labor; Alex could see, now, just how much kitty litter you could pack into an entire pallet.

"You can call the local humane society, too, and donate some."

Darla clapped excitedly as she entered the kitchen. "Great idea. Lemonade?"

Alex was itching to see Josie. "No, thanks. So…is something wrong with her?"

Blinking rapidly, Darla seemed torn. "She's…not okay, but it's not that there's anything bad. It's just that Josie,

ways—but they're the wrong ways. Like, she can manipulate the hell out of a person, but she has no conscience. It's like she hit her head and turned into an asshole. That's how Mama explained it to me when I got older."

Alex's blood ran cold. "How did Josie cope?"

"She spent every bit of time she could at our house. Mama always let her. Marlene would get mad if Josie didn't keep the house clean, or work enough babysitting jobs when she was younger to give her cigarette money. When she was sixteen she got a job at the library, and Marlene took most of the paycheck. So Josie worked and stayed away from home as much as possible."

"Child services didn't intervene?"

A derisive snort. "You ever seen child services do anything good for a family? Mama said she called once, and they told her unless Josie had bruises, they wouldn't do anything."

Alex swallowed hard. "Except her bruises are on the inside."

"Yep."

"She told me once that her mother is the town barfly."

Darla pinkened, opened her mouth, then shut it tight. On second thought, she appeared to reconsider. "Barfly? Marlene's the town *whore*."

"Okay," he said as he exhaled.

"Don't judge Josie for that," she said, narrowing her eyes with an accusing look.

"Of course I wouldn't!" he objected. "Jesus, none of this has any reflection on Josie!"

"That's the part Josie needs to figure out, Alex," she whispered.

"How'd you turn out okay?" he asked.

She raised her eyebrows. "Alex, I finally moved out here after picking up a naked hitchhiker on the interstate, and then ended up in a threesome. The jury's still out on whether I turned out 'okay.'"

"I vote for a verdict of 'okay.'" They shared a smile, but Darla's faded fast.

"Plus, I didn't have a mama who brought strange men home all the time." The words came out of her mouth in a hoarse voice. "Thank God."

The implication of her words took a few seconds to sink in, and he stiffened. "None of those men ever…" Fists clenching, his insides shook with righteous anger on a young Josie's behalf.

"I don't think so. She's never talked about it. Just that her mother would scream at her to leave. Or, once, made her watch." Darla turned away as she said the words. "I think I've said too much."

He reached for her hand. "No. You haven't. And this just makes me admire Josie even more." A lump in his throat made his voice sound like wet gravel. "Anyone who can live through that and thrive as an adult is strong as steel."

Darla nodded, tears in her eyes. "She is. Except all she knows is how to be strong, Alex. To make herself safe. Josie has no idea what it feels like to be weak *and* safe."

"Where is she? It's time for me to tell her that I want her to be all those things. That I love all those things about her."

"She shot out of here earlier and said something about the library."

*Knock knock knock.* Alex looked up to find Trevor in the doorway. "Sorry to interrupt, but we're done and Sam and Liam need to take off."

"Tell them to load some up for their families to take home."

Liam popped his head in. "We don't have a cat."

Darla wiped one eye and laughed. "So what! Your neighbors have cats, right?"

"If I showed up at my parents' house with cat litter for an animal we don't own, they'd think I was tripping."

Joe appeared. "Hey, I have to get to work."

"Take some home! I know your mom has a cat!"

"My mom only uses some organic, lavender-infused stuff made from the shaved hair of reincarnated holy men turned into lambs or something like that. And it's Fair Trade. No way she'd let me come home with this." Joe sniffed.

"She realizes all the cat does is piss and shit on it, right? We're not talking about an alchemy process that turns the kitty's waste products into gold nuggets," Darla said.

Joe shrugged. "Don't argue with me—I'm not the one who buys that stuff."

"Dissecting the elimination habits of pampered pets is a fascinating topic, but I have to go. Where's the nearest library Josie goes to?" Alex paused, then smacked his forehead.

"Never mind. I know where she went."

# CHAPTER FIFTEEN

Josie hadn't been to this particular library in a few months, but it was the garden that drew her in. Underneath an ivy-covered pergola, surrounded by overgrown Rose of Sharon bushes, every flower was in full bloom, and it felt like a little womb of blossoms. What she needed most right now was a sense of wonder and a place where no one else would disturb her. The library was closed; the garden was open.

Nestling herself on a bench, she took the clutched paperback and stared at the cover. Willing herself to open it, she found page one and began the slow process of unfuckupping herself.

*It was a dark and stormy night*, the book began, and she groaned. How ridiculously silly. And then...she just became the book.

Within a short time she discovered that Meg, the main character, had a missing father. Josie's chest seized, a shocked sob stuck in it. *Oh, shit.* Had Daddy, just days before he died, given her a book about a pre-teen girl who loses her father?

Awkward, bookish Meg—like Josie. Annoying twin siblings and a curious, genius little brother—nope. Darla was the closest thing she had to a sibling, and while she'd call Darla clever, "genius" was a stretch.

An absent-minded but loving scientist mother who cooked dinner on Bunsen burners?

Hell no.

Meg's father was a scientist, too, and he'd gone missing. The town believed he'd abandoned his family, but Meg and her little brother, Charles Wallace, came to learn he'd been exploring time travel. She gasped at the concept of a tesseract—folding time to travel to new planets. The battle between good and evil sucked her in, and soon she found herself so consumed with the story that everything around her faded.

Tears ran down her face when Meg worked to pull her brother from the clutches of a giant, soul-sucking brain called IT that sought conformity and mind control at all costs (a.k.a. Evil). Meg's friend, Calvin, a popular but poor kid came to her rescue repeatedly, and the hint of a love interest tapped into a memory of a Josie who would have adored the storyline at eleven.

*Oh, Daddy,* she thought. *You were so right. I wish I'd read this. I wish I could talk to you about this.*

*I just wish.*

And then…Meg found her father. Saved him and her brother, with some help from Calvin.

If only finding fathers were so easy.

And then they were reunited with her mother, and…Meg, young Meg, had turned out to be stronger and more beautiful than she'd ever imagined.

Everyone around her saw it. Knew it, deep in their bones. Her secret weapon that allowed her to defeat IT was so simple: love.

Love conquered all.

Closing the cover, she heard the first raindrop before she saw it, for her eyes were shut. At first Josie thought it was a tear, for she was crying. Then she heard another, and another, and opened her eyes. The air had taken on a steamy quality, and in this little green sanctuary she felt cared for, loved like the furry creatures of the planet Ixchel in the book, the beings who showered Meg with unconditional love and caring. If only she'd had that.

Willing herself to stop being negative, she visualized all the people who had stepped in and shown love. Her mother (before the accident). Her dad. Aunt Cathy. Uncle Mike. Darla. Mrs. Humboldt. Teachers and professors and bosses and friends. Laura. Mike. Even Dylan.

And, of course—Alex.

So many people, when she thought it through, who had shown some caring for her. Isolated and alone all those years at home, as her mom paraded men through the house, using Josie as a servant, or kicking her out to go to Aunt Cathy's. Narrow misses; gratitude flooded her for the times she'd been perilously close to danger with some of her mother's bedmates, but had escaped unscathed. The coke powder on the coffee table, empty beer bottles ringing the house, and $5 cans of crabmeat for their cats— but no food for her.

For the past eight years since she'd escaped she had focused on all the wrongs. Where had it gotten her? Safe. Out of danger.

But alone.

Never before had she thought to focus on the people in her life who helped. Were there for her. Acted as role models or friends or just...gave her acts of kindness that sustained her soul.

Who had, collectively, helped her to reach this place of empowerment and love so that she could face an eighteen-year-old piece of baggage the size of a small paperback book.

She had done it.

Wasn't this the part where she was supposed to feel changed? Altered? Free and relieved of all the crap she'd been carrying around all these years? Instead, she felt a touch of guilt for how she'd acted with Marlene, a much larger feeling of relief for finally telling her how she felt, and an inner stillness.

Focusing on that, she closed her eyes, letting the occasional raindrop fall on her shoulders and back as she pulled her knees to her chest and just listened. Her own breathing filled her ears. Just her. That was all she needed.

Just her.

That was enough. Had always been enough.

Hot tears filled her eyes and throat, but this time through an enormous smile. For so long she'd felt unfinished. Damaged. The girl whose father died and whose mother...might as well have. The woman who came home to her after the car crash wasn't her mother. Not her real mother. Josie had fantasized that somehow there had been a mix-up at the hospital and Marlene had really died and this woman, this thing that came home and called itself "Mom" was actually a spy who had plastic surgery and was infiltrating... Peters, Ohio?

That had been the part that even her eleven-year-old mind couldn't grasp.

She laughed at her memory of it, simultaneously crying for her eleven-year-old self.

And yet...there was that stillness now inside. She could find it and be centered.

It had replaced the hole in her.

\* \* \*

Alex remembered that Josie had mentioned a little garden spot behind an area library, and he felt a sense of kismet, a larger sense of pride, as he found her, curled up on a bench under a beautiful pergola, a flowering sanctuary like something from a 19th-century novel. A light, misty rain was beginning, the kind where raindrops seem coy, and flirt with dropping, but don't quite commit. Josie had pulled her knees to her chest and appeared to be smiling as he approached her from the side and sat down next to her.

His presence seemed not to startle her, nor surprise her. It was as if his appearance were the most natural thing in the world.

"Hi," he said gently. As she tipped her face up to look at him, he saw red eyes and tears pouring down her cheeks, dotting her blouse. Or perhaps that was rain. It was hard to tell.

"Dr. Perfect," she whispered. In her hand she held a small paperback. He looked at it, then gasped.

"*A Wrinkle in Time*! Tesseracts and IT. I remember reading that in—what? Fourth grade?" He chuckled to himself. "I remember wondering if that was where my dad really was. On another planet, desperately trying to find his way back to me."

Her eyes filled with tears and he regretted his words. "I'm sorry. I wasn't thinking. I should have—"

"No. Of course you should share." Her chin shook and her voice wavered. "We should share. I've spent most of my adult life hiding from everyone and everything important, trying to pretend I didn't have a huge hole inside me, Alex. I've turned men away—nice men. Good men. I've avoided the respectful and sweet guys because I didn't think I was worth it. Crafting a life that doesn't make you vulnerable leaves you with a facsimile of one." Her voice hitched, a sob catching her. "I didn't realize that until now."

The fact that she was being vulnerable with him, opening up and talking about her inner truth made him fall a little more in love. Stretching his arm around her, he pulled her into an embrace, the feel of her body against his like their own little world.

"We're not so different," he murmured in her ear, the rain now beating steadily down on them, dewy but persistent. "I have a hard time trusting people, too. You're the first woman I've cared about enough to publicly humiliate myself in front of, well—ever."

She laughed through her tears, her body shaking against

his, the feel of her in his arms so right. His neck was damp, and now the rain came down steadily. Josie didn't seem to care, and neither did he. It transported them to a secret garden, a lush, bountiful place where they could just breathe and be.

"When you smacked into that post—"

"I was trying to be manly and run fast and powerfully to outdo the guy on the porch you were touching, Josie. I was jealous. I don't get jealous. Being jealous means being attached and I don't do that. You made me do that."

"It's my fault you smashed up your face?"

"No. I own that. It's your fault I ran by in the first place." Their eyes met and hers explored his face searching and confirming what they both seemed to feel.

"What is this, Alex?" she asked, eyes wide and intense.

"It's something."

She laughed, a small, wistful sound. "That night we were in the park, while we were making love, I started to say 'I love you.'"

"I know."

"I didn't cover it up well, did I?" Her hand brushed his wet hair away from his forehead. At the moment her fingertips touched him, he felt a wall inside crumble, a wellspring of love for her pouring out from behind it. "It's not something I generally blurt out."

"Josie, I love you, too," he said, the words so natural it was as if he were saying them for the thousandth time, something inside him expanding, taking her in and mingling their souls together to create something greater than both of them.

The rain made her hair cling to her cheekbones in thin strands, drops forming on her nose and eyelids, mingling with her tears. Those brown eyes, warm and loving, connected with his and said more now than ever before.

But her lips spoke exactly what he needed to know. "And I love you, Alex. I've never said that to any man before."

"If I have any say, you'll never say it to another man, either," he replied, pulling her closer, his lips brushing hers, her hands sliding under his arms and palms wrapping around his shoulders, their bodies unfolding to match their revealed hearts. The faded wooden bench, ivy wrapped around its feet, pressed into his back as Josie stretched to climb into his lap, straddling him, her hands on either side of his face, their mouths welcoming and exploring each other.

"Deal," she whispered against his mouth.

The heavens parted and rain poured down in large raindrops, soon soaking their shirts. Josie pulled away from the kisses and tipped her head up, smiling. Alex did the same, watching the sky pour its approval onto them, nature's baptism, as if washing clean all the awkwardness, missteps, regrets, and fears.

A wave of desire roared within, hands sliding under her wet shirt, cupping her breasts as she looked down at him, fire in her eyes, the power of her next kiss slamming into him, going straight to his core, making him hard in seconds. What had been tender yielded to something visceral and breathtaking, accessed only through love. No more questions, no more uncertainties—this was their authentic selves meeting naked and fully ready for one another, to see what passion they could unleash on a new plane of existence.

Pure love. Pure lust. Pure acceptance.

And, most of all, the full admittance that they were imperfect and could be imperfect *together*.

Josie broke the kiss, climbing off him and standing before him, chest rising and falling with deep, feverish breaths, her hand outstretched. *Take me*, it said.

And so Alex did.

\* \* \*

*I*
*Love*
*You.*

Who knew those words could be spoken so easily when meant so fully? All that she had wanted, dreamt of, imagined, and conjured now appeared before her as Alex stood up, the rain pouring down him in rivers, his hand clasping hers as she led him to a soft spot of grass under the canopied pergola. The greenery interwoven into the wood redirected the water, long streams pouring at uneven intervals. Slowly, with movement that felt timeless, she reached for him, her arms around his waist, his hands in her soaked hair, their lips bruising each other's, tongues intertwined as tremors ran through her, not from cold but from the sheer force of emotion her body contained.

She needed to unleash it.

He knew how.

Bending her down, they rested on their knees, unable to unravel from the embrace, his hands peeling off her shirt, her hands happy to do the same to him. With a rushed excitement Josie found her legs muddy, the grass a wet mattress of nature, Alex's torso the only heat she needed. Her fingers nimbly undid his pants as he reached in his back pocket for the condom.

She stopped him. "I'm on the pill."

Trust. "I didn't know that," he rasped in her ear.

"I never told you. I just…it's okay now." She took a deep sigh and confessed, "I've never made love with someone without a condom."

"Never?" His voice was so tantalizing, making her throb, wanting him in her. The rain poured down, her body soaked through, whatever clothing she had left now a second skin.

"You're the first."

"And last," he said, guiding himself and entering her, their bodies wet and slippery as he towered over her, arms on either side of her, eyes steady and burning with love for her.

"Oh, Alex," she moaned, the heat and fullness of him, the skin-on-skin contact so different. So vibrant and hot. Her insides grew and melted, shimmering and shaking as a wave built within her, something greater than all her prior climaxes combined. This one would be infused with love, a deep, flowing emotion between them that was perpetual and eternal.

"Oh," he sighed, then began to move, her legs wrapping around him. Then she remembered.

"Your hip! Your shoulder!" she called out, the rain now so loud it drowned out everything but her own pleasure and the touch of him, the push of his body into hers, the sheer wall of man over her. "Are you sure you can—"

"Josie, the day I'm too injured to do this, with you, outside in our own little garden of lust, is the day you can bury me."

Instead of laughter, a keen sense of something loving filled her. "Then I'm sad we only have seventy more years of this."

"Better enjoy every minute," he said in a low, smoky voice, water dripping off his body, drops clinging to his taut, sculpted muscles as he thrust into her, making the words disappear. The giant wave rose great within, her heart expanding with it, and Alex's body tensed just as her own froze, the exquisite joy of his heat, mouth, body grinding into hers the perfect complement to the words they'd shared.

"Oh, Alex, I—" And then she tipped over, walls tight around him, the core of her touched by his flesh, each stroke like a prayer of love, driving deep into her center, taking up residence permanently.

"Let go," he urged, his own body going taut, jaw tight and mouth crushing into hers as her calves felt his ass become granite, his hips slowed to smaller thrusts, and he let out a sound of ecstasy that matched her own cries of release, the vibration blending with the rush of rain, an ending to a perfect beginning.

With Dr. Perfect.

As her body tremored, then slowed, finally warm and glowing from the aftermath of joining so thoroughly with Alex, Josie wrinkled her nose, then wiped water off her face. Drenched. Inside and out, half naked with Alex still inside her, in a little garden behind a public library.

Reality sank in and she began to laugh. His warm eyes, covered in pelting drops, rivulets of water streaming down the planes of his face, studied her.

Thunder rumbled and two seconds later a crack from the sky made her tighten involuntarily, the shattering glass sound a little too close. "We need to get out of here," she said, memorizing this moment, their bare skin touching, bodies on the grass, mud-soaked and all-too primal.

Alex kissed the tip of her nose and pulled out, then peeled away, searching in the grass for his clothes. "I think these are yours," he said, flinging a mud-covered pair of shorts at her. The *thwack* against her chest made them both laugh.

"Here's your underwear!" she shouted above another rumble of thunder, aiming for his head. Direct hit. Both were now streaked with mud, their backs covered, faces smeared.

Their clothes were about as easy to put on as threading cooked spaghetti through a straw, but Alex and Josie managed to cover enough important parts to avoid breaking any local nudity ordinances.

"You look like you just ran a Tough Mudder," she said, pointing and laughing.

"I'd say the same of you, but you don't run."

Throwing herself into his arms, wrapping her legs around his waist, she kissed him with complete abandon and joy, the rain washing some of the mud off, until the sky crackled and Mother Nature poured what felt like buckets over them. Sliding down, she finished the kiss standing, the taste of him divine.

"We gotta go!" he bellowed, pulling her toward their cars.

"So—what's next? Where do we go from here?" she shouted. It wasn't so much an operational question, as in what to do next, but more metaphysical. Where did they go from here? What do you do when you find your true love? How do you go from being profoundly changed back to your life?

What, literally, comes next?

"How about a cup of coffee? I know this really cool diner…"

Josie groaned.

Jeddy's it was.

But no more table for one.

## THE END

# READY FOR MORE?

Thank you so much for buying and reading this book. Please lend it/share it with friends who you think will enjoy it.

Also, please write a review – reviews help new readers find my books!

**The next book in this series is *Complete Abandon*. So many readers emailed me to ask for more of Josie, Alex, Mike, Laura and Dylan that I started an entire new series – the Complete series – to keep the story going!**

**Read Complete Abandon, available now on Amazon!**

You can also read the FREE book that started the world of Laura, Josie, Mike, Dylan and Alex. Get Her First Billionaire right now and start the series!

Join my New Releases email list here: http://jkentauthor.blogspot.com/p/sign-up-for-my-new-releases-email-list.html to get the first news about all my new books.

# GRAB HER FIRST BILLIONAIRE FREE!

## COULD SHE REALLY FIND THE RIGHT GUY ON THE INTERNET?

> *"Hot, luscious piece of ass who can suck a golf ball through forty feet of garden hose seeks rippling-ab'd firefighter who has a tongue that thrums like a hummingbird and enjoys painting my toenails and eating Ben & Jerry's out of the carton while watching Mad Men."*

Laura Michaels stared at the online dating site's registration screen and frowned. That's what she really wanted to write. Here was the truth:

> *"Needy, insecure, overweight twenty-six year old Financial Analyst with three cats, a corporate job with pension and no debt seeks Mr. Impossible for way more than friendship and lots of ice cream. I'm desperate for some physical affection and oral sex with a guy who doesn't view it as some sort of favor he's granting me, and then expects to be praised like he cleaned my toilet. One night stands are better than nothing as long as you brush your teeth. So call me, maybe!"*

So when hot firefighter Dylan Stanwyck responds and asks her out, it's just too good to be true. When she searches him online and learns he offers himself up for date nights in bachelor charity auctions, she wonders if she's on the right planet.

Because what could a guy like that see in a fat girl like her?

## OR WOULD HE NOT BE WHO HE SEEMED?

Trawling through the online dating profiles isn't Dylan's idea of fun, but it's been more than eighteen months since their lover, Jill, died, and Dylan and his unconventional partner, ski instructor Mike Pine, need to find a new love. While their threesome situation is more complicated than a contract from *Fifty Shades of Grey*, at least one aspect is simple: Laura Michaels, the cute, soft blond from the online dating site, seems like a good fit for at least a first date. Soft curves, gorgeous hair, eyes that light him up from the computer alone, and a profile that makes her seem smart and interesting – he has no problems asking her out.

The problem is letting her in.

Dylan and his not-quite partner have more secrets than their unconventional romantic relationships, and this latest snafu is a mixed blessing, for both became billionaires overnight after the third in their threesome, Jill, died. With her estate finally settled and Dylan and Mike the recipient of an annual income that gives them enough to buy entire towns in the Midwest, the two were left reeling. Months after the lawyer explained their new-found fortune, Dylan still works his regular shifts at the station while Mike remains on the slopes as a ski instructor, but with a caveat; now he owns the entire resort.

But if they tell Laura everything, they risk losing a chance at a new bond.

Two problems may have one lush, ample solution as Laura meets her first billionaire on her date with Dylan, but with a stunning twist at the end...

**Get *Her First Billionaire* FREE now on Amazon!**

**If you want the whole series in one, single boxed set, grab *New York Times* bestselling series *Her Billionaires: Boxed Set* for a discounted price. 450+ pages of heat and fun!**

# OTHER BOOKS BY JULIA KENT

Suggested Reading Order

Her First Billionaire – FREE
Her Second Billionaire
Her Two Billionaires
Her Two Billionaires and a Baby
Her Billionaires: Boxed Set
(Parts 1-4 in one bundle, 458 pages!)

It's Complicated

Complete Abandon (A Her Billionaires novella)
Complete Harmony (A Her Billionaires novella #2)
Complete Bliss (A Her Billionaires novella #3)

Random Acts of Crazy
Random Acts of Trust
Random Acts of Fantasy
Random Acts of Hope

Maliciously Obedient
Suspiciously Obedient
Deliciously Obedient (the trilogy is done!)

Shopping for a Billionaire 1 -- FREE
Shopping for a Billionaire 2
Shopping for a Billionaire 3
Shopping for a Billionaire 4
Christmas Shopping for a Billionaire

# ABOUT THE AUTHOR

Text **JKentBooks** to **77948** and get a text message on release dates.

*New York Times* and *USA Today* Bestselling Author Julia Kent turned to writing contemporary romance after deciding that life is too short not to have fun. She writes romantic comedy with an edge, and new adult books that push contemporary boundaries. From billionaires to BBWs to rock stars, Julia finds a sensual, goofy joy in every book she writes, but unlike Trevor from *Random Acts of Crazy*, she has never kissed a chicken.

She loves to hear from her readers by email at
JKentAuthor@gmail.com,
on Twitter @jkentauthor
and on Facebook at
https://www.facebook.com/jkentauthor
Visit her blog at http://JKentAuthor.blogspot.com